Praise for Mary Hughes'
Bite My Fire

"Bite My Fire is a truly irresistible read I didn't want to end. Ms. Hughes made me laugh, made me blush, and swept me away for hours upon hours of enjoyment with this fabulous tale."

~ *Joyfully Reviewed*

"...I couldn't put this story down...Elena is awesome...Bo [is d]istracting, mysterious, and oh so hot!...I cannot wait for the next story!"

~ *Fallen Angel Reviews*

"...Mary Hughes has created a very unique and fun book to read...a book that will make you giggle and pant at the same time..."

~ *Whipped Cream Erotic Romance Reviews*

"...a fast-paced tale filled with intriguing characters, a colorful locale, snappy dialogue and plenty of sizzling hot sex..."

~ *Mystical Nymph for Literary Nymphs*

"...I loved this hilarious paranormal story that in turns had me laughing out-loud or fanning myself..."

~ *The Romance Studio*

Look for these titles by

Mary Hughes

Now Available:

Biting Love Novels

Bite My Fire

Biting Nixie

The Bite of Silence

Biting Me Softly

Bite My Fire

A Biting Love Novel

Mary Hughes

A Samhain Publishing, Ltd. publication.

Samhain Publishing, Ltd.
577 Mulberry Street, Suite 1520
Macon, GA 31201
www.samhainpublishing.com

Bite My Fire

Print ISBN: 978-1-60504-780-5
Digital ISBN: 978-1-60504-680-8

Cover by Natalie Winters

First Samhain Publishing, Ltd. electronic publication: October 2009
First Samhain Publishing, Ltd. print publication: August 2010

Dedication

To my incredible kids. I'm so glad I get to be your mother.

To Deborah Nemeth, editor most excellent. As with Santa, I have no true concept of how hard she works, I'm only wonderstruck and grateful for the goodies in the stocking Christmas morning.

To my husband Gregg, my first reader and evil plotting buddy. I know it's going to be good when you cackle.

Especially to you, the exceptionally good-looking, smart, and talented Reader. You make all the gestational pain worthwhile.

Acknowledgements

Thanks go to the dedicated professionals who shared their expertise with me. Any errors are my own.

Chapter One

Officially the murder was SCH-1, but I called it the Case of the Punctured Prick.

The first homicide ever in Meiers Corners was my cherry-breaking case as a police detective. Okay, probationary detective. Okay, third shift probationary detective. But a girl's gotta start somewhere, right?

I was at the station reading *Midwest Police Monthly* when the phone rang. A glance at the line showed dispatch. Something going down—like assault with a Super Soaker.

The senior detective on graveyard was supposed to take it, but Blatzky was in the can, fourth time that night. He was six months from retiring, but I think he actually checked out a year or two back.

So I took the call. "Hey, Alice. What red-hot crime do we have in Meiers Corners tonight? Shopping cart stolen? Mrs. Gruen jaywalking in her sleep again?"

"Something better, Elena." Alice Schmidt was our nightshift dispatcher, also six months from retiring. She'd been six months from retiring since I started as a beat cop. At least eighty years old, she was from the generation that worked until you dropped. She was convinced the day she actually retired, she'd keel over. "Where's Blatzky?"

"He's in the john again, poor guy," I said. "Diarrhea."

Alice snorted. "Too many beers. Or doing a little 'solo investigation', if you know what I mean."

"Alice!"

"Your luck, though. Body's on Fifth and Main."

"*Body*?" My heart started to pound. All my life I dreamed of being a detective, lusted after it. The only thing I hungered more for was a good lay, but that was another story.

Three weeks ago, I'd made it to the detective's desk. Staying here was another matter.

"Body, where?" My feet hit the floor and I grabbed my notebook, jotted date and time. *18 August. 2:16 a.m. Early Tuesday morning.*

"Nieman's Bar. At first Ruffles thought the vic had just passed out. Bar time and all."

"Ruffles is the witness?" I scribbled the name.

"Naw. New kid on foot patrol, just switched to third shift. He found the stiff. Poor schmuck took an early retirement option. The stiff, not Ruffles."

I wanted this case so bad my teeth hurt. A potential *murder.* Instant ticket to success for whoever solved it.

But I was junior detective on shift. Junior probationary. Regs clearly stated senior personnel got first dibs so I stuffed my ambition back in the bag. "I'll get Blatzky."

"Naw, hon. Don't bother. He's just riding his paycheck 'til retirement. He won't want to work."

"Still..." I raised my voice. The second floor gent's was a converted closet, so I didn't have to raise it much. "Blatzky! Officer Ruffles found a body in Nieman's parking lot. You want it?"

There was a groan from the bathroom. "Six months. Just a hundred eighty-two days to go, was that so much to ask? No, I don't want no goddamn bodies!"

I punched a silent *yes* but kept my voice cop cool when I said, "Okay, Alice, I'll take the case."

Take it, solve it, and earn the Chief of Police's blessing.

My eyes slid toward the forbidding portrait of Chief John Dirkson behind me. *Blessing,* of course, was the operative term. It would take at least a blessing, and probably a miracle, to get that coveted permanent shield.

Bad enough I was going for a traditionally male job. Worse, this was Meiers Corners, more conservative than Queen Victoria. Worst, Dirkson—with his handlebar mustache and woolly sideburns straight out of the nineteenth century—was the very definition of ultra-conservative WASP.

And here I was, a twenty-six-year-old Irish-Latina female.

Normally I wouldn't have worried. I didn't submit to prejudice, I fought it. Not to mention I worked hard and played by all the rules.

But my future was in the hands of a hidebound Victorian throwback. Chief's blessing, right. Maybe I should light a few votive candles under the picture, just in case. And recite the Prayer of Saint Dirkson, counting on my Grandma Sanchez's red bead rosary.

Hey, I was Lutheran, but it couldn't hurt, could it?

I shook myself. What was I thinking? Method and order would solve this case—Dad taught me that.

So. Rule one, secure the crime scene. "Alice. You said Officer Ruffles reported the body. Did he secure the area?"

"Yes, but I'm not sure how. It's the middle of Nieman's east parking lot."

"Well, I'll find out when I survey the scene." That was rule two.

Rule three was collect evidence. I'd do some of that on scene too, but best to bring in our CSI. "Did you call Charlie?"

"I'll tag him after this," Alice said.

"Anyone ID the vic yet?"

"Napoleon Schrimpf. You know, Napoleon's Gym."

"'Where Shrimps Conquer the World'?"

"That's the one. Five-foot-five King of Compensation." Alice snorted. "He didn't conquer the world, but he did try to conquer every female he met."

Rule four was uncover means, motive and opportunity. Here was a possible motive. "You think one of those supposedly conquered women might have conquered back?"

"Dunno. I do think Schrimpf plowed one love furrow too many."

Ugh. Still, I made a note. "Any sign of foul play?"

"No marks, no blood. From Officer Ruffles's report, the most suspicious thing was the stupid grin on Schrimpf's face."

Probably not murder, then. My pulse slowed. I tucked the notebook into my pocket. "Sounds like a waste of time. Still, I'd better take a look."

I checked my Springfield XD (not an S&W or Glock, but let's not get into *that* discussion) and backup piece and hiked over. Nieman's Bar was five blocks from the cop shop and four blocks from the heart of Meiers Corners.

Well, four blocks from downtown. Since our town pumped beer as blood, I guess Nieman's *was* the heart.

I sweated through my T-shirt as I hoofed it. Our dog days of August were more like hot-dog days. Two thirty in the morning and the temperature was still well over eighty. I wiped my brow and kept up a brisk trot. This case was my bullet-train ticket to Detectiveville. Nothing going to slow me down.

At the scene I did a quick check-in with Alice. In a bigger city, that would have been so HQ could keep tabs on us. Alice just liked knowing where we were.

The crime scene was cordoned off with several miles of yellow tape. A gangly, potbellied young man in a rumpled uniform marched in front. Literally, high stepping like a Lipizzaner and spinning around with a cross-legged twirl that nearly threw him off his feet.

Daffy Duck guards the crime scene. It didn't help the image that his dark cap had a yellow beak. I guessed this was Officer Ruffles.

As I approached, he fumbled out his gun. "Halt!" He held the gun turned sideways, parallel to the ground. Stylish, if you were a TV punk.

"Whoa, Daffy. Point that thing somewhere else." I flashed my badge. "Detective O'Rourke."

"Ohhh." Ruffles straightened and put the gun away. "A *girl.*" I opened my mouth but he sailed on. "Not that I'm bigoted. I know it takes even more balls to make it as a girl cop. Well, balls isn't the right term. But what would it be? Pussy? That already means not-balls. Not that I'm biased. I could say pussy. Pussy clanks when she walks. That works."

His mouth was shadowed by a thin, feathery mustache. While he talked I watched it flap. "Excuse me, Officer...Ruffles?"

He nearly brained himself saluting me. "Officer Dirk Ruffles at your service, miss. Or ma'am. Or..."

"Detective will do." I glanced at the crime-scene tape. Ruffles had wrapped everything in sight like a cheery yellow mummy. "You secure the area, officer?"

"Yes, ma'am. Detective Ma'am." His voice was a muddy rasp, Cartman with lung cancer. Hard to listen to, but impossible to ignore. "I'm training to be a detective. My uncle says I'll be a great detective. Well, not great exactly. 'Tolerable' was the word he used, but that's *almost* great. My uncle..."

"Good for you, Ruffles. Tell me how you found the body." I started to hack through the tape. It stuck to me like cobwebs.

"First on scene, ma'am. Detective Ma'am. Got the call at two-oh-four. Nieman's is shutting down by then. Couple of drunks coming out of the bar stumbled over him. The vic, that is. I interviewed them. The drunks, that is. I asked the hard questions. You'd have been proud of me, Detective Ma'am. My uncle says I'll be a detective in no time. He says..."

As I endured Ruffles's rasp, I fought tape. I managed to wrench open a hole big enough for my five-nine and slid one leg through. When I ducked to get the rest of me in, my shoulder-length curls swung against tape and stuck. Pulling the other leg through, I turned to try to wrest the hair loose. My hips swiped tape and my butt stuck.

"... and Schrimpf met her in the bar. So one drunk says to the other, 'Fella walked into the bar.' And the other says, 'He hit his face!'" Ruffles guffawed. "Hit his face when he walked *into* the bar. Get it?"

"Yeah, I get it." I yanked tape off my jeans, tore it from my hair. Tore off a bunch of hair, but with my mop, who'd notice? "Next time, Ruffles? Use less tape."

He stared blankly at me. "On the bar, ma'am?"

Apparently Ruffles's gun was aimed, the trigger pulled, but he had forgotten to load. I found a barrette in my pocket, clipped back my mass of hair. "Officer. You said Schrimpf met *her* in the bar. Who?"

"Actually the first drunk said that." Ruffles flipped out his notebook. "No, wait, it was the second drunk. The second drunk said that."

"The correct term is *witness.*" I had to fight not to grind my teeth. "What, exactly, did the second *witness* say?"

"The second drunk witness said, *ahem.*" Ruffles jutted out his skinny chest, held the notebook up like Charlie Heston with a set of stone tablets. "'Schrimpf met her in the bar'." He looked brightly at me like an eager puppy who's peed on the paper—only it turns out to be your English homework.

A deep, cleansing breath kept me from giving him a yellow tape enema. Barely. The boy didn't have a clue. "Thanks, Officer."

I turned my attention to the body lying next to a bright yellow sports car. Oops, Ruffles had mummified that too. Underneath the tape was a black Audi, probably the vic's.

The ME would log the detail, but I estimated the corpse's vitals with a trained eye. Five feet, five inches tall. Weight one-sixty, mostly upper-body muscle. Brown eyes open to the night. Face relaxed, except the mouth. Alice was right about the snarky smile.

Moving down, the victim wore a white sleeveless tee, not quite a wife-beater. And not out of place, considering the heat of the August night. But I'd have expected Schrimpf to wear a manly black. Maybe white to emphasize his tan?

Except, looking closer, the body *wasn't* tan. In fact, its skin was as pale as mine, sheet white in the moon's glow. It made it easy to see there was no visible blood on skin or clothes. But Charlie's evidence techs had better equipment and chemicals. The lab would not only test for blood, but vacuum for bits of hair, skin and other clues to the killer's identity.

That was, if there *was* a killer, and it wasn't just a post-bartime heart attack. I logged pale skin and lack of blood and moved on.

Schrimpf's jeans were the expected black. They were rumpled around his feet, the silver caps of his cockroach killers just peeking out. His hips were exposed.

I do mean *exposed.* Schrimpf went commando.

Behind me Ruffles had started another monolog on his uncle. Or it might have been Hamlet's soliloquy, I didn't know and couldn't tell you.

Because I was staring at the Schrimpfster's pecker. Shriveled, slightly crusted, barely poking up from of a sack of loose skin.

And, just at the base, were two dark holes.

☙❧

Next step was interview the witnesses. Unfortunately, Ruffles had released them. I could have tried phoning but it was nearly three a.m. and they were probably already tucked in their beds. I decided to let them snore off any alcohol and catch them fresh that evening.

But I had to do *something,* so I canvassed the neighborhood. I knocked on the doors of Randy's Candies in the west, Bob's Formalwear in the east, Kangaroo Comics in the south and Good

Shepherd rectory in the north.

All closed.

Frustrated, I scanned the area around the rectory. Nieman's was flanked by nothing but asphalt and dark shops. I wanted to solve this case *now*, but I didn't want to waste time humping from one end of town to the other, futilely knocking. So I took a quick sampling with my cop sense.

I called it my "cop sense", a sort of Spidey-tingling that was combination warning and awareness. Nothing mystical about it. I didn't believe in the paranormal (enjoyed reading it but didn't believe) so I knew it was probably just a heightened perception from paying attention to my surroundings.

But it had saved my ass a couple times. Saved other asses too. And it was *never* wrong.

I was sweating outside the rectory at Good Shepherd's. Ruffles was a block over, marching away. Except for Ruffles and me, nobody alive was in the area. I'd swear to it.

But my neck prickled. A presence—something—

Some*one* behind me.

Chapter Two

I spun. Went for my gun. "Hold it right there...!"

My voice died in my throat. My XD pressed against the most amazing abs I'd ever seen. Washboard, eight-pack...whatever, licking those abs would be like tongue-surfing warm ocean waves.

A black tee stretched in all the right places over a torso ripped enough to star in *300*. Bronzed cannon arms, dusted with blond hair, crossed over a battleship chest.

Very male. And *very* big. Viking big. With him, even my five-nine felt petite. I choked on a whimper as my eyes continued helplessly up.

Strong, corded neck. And his face...sweet Suzy's Cream Cheesecakes. Warrior big and warrior *gorgeous*. Cheekbones cut from granite, arching blond brows, carved jaw. Thick wavy blond hair. Eyes the brilliant blue of the Mediterranean in summer. A fiercely beautiful face, the kind that jolts you in the gut.

Or that wrenches you in the cunt. Especially if it's been a while since you got a good lay (five years, three months and three days, but who's counting? Don't blame me, I've *tried*. The great god of FUBAR seems to have it in for me, at least as far as consummation goes).

But big, bad and yummy here was a stranger. Worse, he was wandering near a murder scene. Alone. By the Big Book of Police Rules, that made him a suspect. I firmed my grip on my gun. "Where'd you come from?"

Viking Guy's eyes chilled to ice blue. "None of your business."

He spoke in a dark rumble and radiated intensity. Ultra-alpha. I tamped down frissons of arousa...annoyance. One-handed, I whipped out my badge. "This says otherwise."

He barely glanced at it. "A cop?"

"A *detective*. Tell me what you're doing here. *Now*." I underlined the word with a tiny push of my gun.

"If you must know, I was patrolling. For my neighborhood watch. Please don't shoot me—Detective." He raised his hands and stepped back, though honestly, he didn't seem all that worried.

But he was cooperating. Slowly I holstered my gun. "Word of advice, buster. Don't sneak up on people like that. It might get you killed."

He arched one blond brow, all arrogance. "Like the little man in the parking lot?"

"What?" My hand snapped back to my holster. "How'd you know about that?"

"The yellow tape does rather stand out." The guy's voice had smoothed down. When he wasn't channeling Christian Bale his voice was dark silk, stroking my flesh like black satin sheets and lazy summer loving.

Shit, *suspect*. Not bedroom material.

Except thinking of that golden body, that satin voice *in bed*...I inched my hand from holster to jeans, surreptitiously adjusting the crotch.

The guy's eyes followed. His lips started curving.

Part of me was annoyed, but part was struck dumb at what the curve did to his lips. Like a gently swelling sea, that half-smile could lap my shores anytime.

Fuck, I was getting horny over a suspect. I *had* to get laid. I yanked out my notebook. "I'll need your name and address. Then you and I are heading to the station for a chat."

"Ah. That might be a little difficult. I patrol until dawn."

That's exactly how he said it. Not "until five" or "third shift", but "until dawn". I gave him my best cop glare. "Let's start with your name. We'll see about dawn."

He shrugged—I goggled. He was a big guy with massive shoulders, and that delicious, sinuous motion showed me he was all muscle. Acres of luscious, corded muscle.

When he plucked the notebook from my hand, it was a good thing, because the pages were starting to rattle.

Some blond men look pale and effeminate. There was nothing girly about the large dark hands engulfing my notebook. Handing him the pencil, my fingers brushed palms hard as iron.

Great galloping Krispy Kremes. Touching him was as exciting as palming my gun. My thighs were fast slicking up, and it wasn't sweat.

I clamped my eyes shut in frustration and mortification. Years of unconsummated sexual foreplay were finally taking their toll. Apparently I wanted to jump the bones of anything wearing boxers and a blush, murder suspect or not.

There was some scribbling, then the notebook and pencil were pressed into my hands. I took a deep breath, cooling my unwanted arousal. "Thanks for your cooperation. Now, if you'll just come with me to the station..." I opened my eyes.

He was gone.

"What the hell?" I tore out my flashlight and panned the area, staring indignantly at empty streets and blank buildings.

Where the heck was he? Viking guy wasn't a small self-effacing dude who could disappear easily. Just to make sure, I touched my Spidey-sense. Nobody and nothing.

How could he have gotten off my radar so quickly? He must have run like the wind. I flicked off the light, then flicked it back on at another thought. But no, he'd written a name and address in my notebook. The handwriting was bold and oddly runic.

Bo Strongwell. Address on Seventh and Lincoln. Looked familiar...oh, shit.

It was the address of my sister's apartment.

I marched up the river toward Lincoln, fueled by a prick of anger and a Viking-sized stabby sword of worry. Even at its largest, my entire family had fit on one five-by-eight photo. Dad, wife Brita, me, sister Gretchen, brother-in-law Steve, their daughter Stella.

Half were dead now.

My sister and niece were my only living relatives. Six months ago, after her husband Steve was killed, Gretchen moved to Seventh and Lincoln and became almost a recluse. She never invited me to her new digs, so I knew next to nothing about the apartment building where she lived. Since Steve had been her soul mate, I thought she was hurting bad and didn't push. Now I wondered if I should have.

My cell rang. Stifling a curse, I flipped it out. "O'Rourke."

"Elena, it's Alice. Robbery in progress, the AllRighty-AllNighty convenience store. I need you to check it out."

"Can't Keck do it?" Graveyard shift was two detectives, one car and one foot patrol. Or I guess with Ruffles, quack patrol. Keck drove our car.

"He's on a domestic disturbance."

"Blatzky?"

"Still in the can."

"Shit."

"Good one," Alice laughed. "Shit, shitter. Maybe you're finally loosening up a bit."

"I didn't mean... Oh, never mind." A fricking robbery. Why me? I had a murder and a vanished suspect who lived at my sister's address. But who else was there to handle the robbery? Not to mention it was my job. My sister had lived in that apartment the last six months without incident, and this time of night she'd be locked up safe and tight. I hoped. "Okay, Alice. I'm on it."

The AllRighty-AllNighty was a converted corner gas station on Ninth and Eisenhower. From my townhouse it was a two-minute walk, forty-nine seconds if I was jonesing for a pint of chocolate chip cookie dough. I checked my gun and backup piece and broke into a trot.

The store's empty two-car lot was lit bright as day. Peering through the big plate-glass window, I saw the Great Pyramid of Cheops.

Oops, just a tower of MGD six-packs. But the Great Beeramid was between me and the checkout. I edged over to see the robbery still in progress.

Trembling behind the register was owner Kurt Weiss. Wiry and blond, he resembled a poodle in pants. He was shaking so hard that if he really were a poodle, he'd have peed the floor.

Threatening him was a hundred thirty pounds of ripped jeans, hooded sweatshirt and bad attitude. Magnifying the attitude about a thousand times was the bulge poking in Hoodie-man's sweatshirt pocket.

The distinctly gun-like bulge.

My heart broke out thudding. The perp was possibly armed and dangerous, so I didn't crash in, Miranda Rights blazing. Not with the innocent poodle...civilian in the line of fire. Best to get the robber out of the store before I took him down.

But the downy-faced, gangly robber looked about fifteen. My heart kicked up a notch. Newbs were highly unpredictable. I needed to get inside in case the kid got violent.

I drew my XD, muzzle grounded, and tiptoed toward the door. Silently I slid onto the old-fashioned pressure mat.

The automatic door whooshed open with a *shht*, a duet with my startled *shit*. Of all the idiotic moves. The kid *must* have heard. I held my breath, ears straining.

And winced. The Volka Polka radio station blasted my eardrums at open-road volume. Yeah, this was Meiers Corners—more German than bock beer and schnitzel. The mayor yearly petitioned the president (Reagan through Obama) to change the official national anthem to the "Beer Barrel Polka". Both our radio stations were All Polka, All the Time.

The automatic door was barely audible over the omnipresent oompa. Neither Kurt nor the kid paid any attention as I slipped in behind the beer display.

A short stack of bills lay on the counter. Kurt's mouth was moving. I pricked my ears. The "Clarinet Polka" clog-danced happily over my cochlea. Concentrating, I filtered through reedy deedles to pick out Kurt's words.

"That's all the cash I got, kid. Really." His voice was high and tight, but that was normal. He yipped like a poodle too.

The kid pressed forward in his pocket. "How 'bout you look again."

"Please! Monday nights are slow. Just take the money and go."

"No way, asshole. Look again." The kid pressed harder in his pocket. "Or else!"

Things might get messy. I grabbed my gun with both hands, flexed my fingers. Focused. My focus was so tight, the sudden electronic *tweedle-tweedle* drilled straight through my skull.

Damn! What peckerhead's cell was ringing? I was gonna slap that phone onto a mixer, stuff it up said peckerhead's ass and hit purée. I was gonna...why was my hip buzzing?

The "oh-no" second from hell hit me. *I* was the peckerhead. I dove for my pocket. Robbery in progress, and my cell phone was ringing. Two idiot moves in two minutes. This *never* happened to the *CSI: Miami* guys. Where was my head that I hadn't powered off before going in? Big murder, sure. Escaped suspect living at my sister's apartment, yeah. But *still.* I flipped the phone open to jab off the power.

Heard a small "Elena? It's Gretchen."

Speak of the devil. My sister. Just bend me over and spank me with a waffle iron. This didn't even happen on *Reno 911.*

Popping the phone to my ear, I whispered, "Gretch, now's not a good time."

"Don't you dare hang up." Gretchen's tone was strained, but as a six-month widow, she probably needed to get laid too. "You *promised.*"

"Gretch—"

"You said you'd babysit for me. No matter when."

There was a robbery going on. There was a robbery and my sister was asking me to babysit. This couldn't even happen to Barney Fife. "We'll talk about this later."

"You *promised.* It's just a couple hours."

Kurt was digging under the counter for cash, stirring great clouds of dust. The punk shifted nervously from foot to foot, almost like *he* was going to pee. Why me? What demon of stupidity had I pissed off? Normally our biggest crime problem was amateur hookers.

"Elena, you promised. Any time." Her tone changed, softened. Became my baby sister. "What if I say please? Pretty please with puke on top?"

Oh, for Pete's sake. Worked on me every time. Still. "Okay," I whispered. "Sure."

"You'll do it?"

"Yes." I needed to talk to her anyway, not to mention corner Mr. Bo-Suspect-Strongwell. What better way than with an invitation?

"Great! Six tonight." She hung up.

"Wha—?" Why *tonight,* of all nights? I checked my mental calendar. August eighteenth. Nope, hadn't imagined it.

Tonight was Gretchen's wedding anniversary.

Hoist the red flags. If I weren't working...but I was. I punched off my phone, shoved it into my pocket.

Another peek showed Kurt pulling the cash drawer and upending it on the counter. Dimes, nickels and quarters plinked and rolled.

The kid fell to his knees, scooped up coins. When he got back up he clinked. "Fifty bucks and five forty-three in change. That's piddling pathetic." He pointed to a carton of cigarettes behind the counter. "If you can't come up with the cash, gimme that."

Kurt gasped. "You want merchandise? I can't do that!"

"What are you yapping about? This is a fricking robbery!" The kid poked the thing in his pocket. I really hoped it wasn't a gun. "C'mon, asshole. Hand over the butts."

I had to derail this, pronto, but without rushing the kid into doing something stupid. I cast through my mental Golden Book of Police Procedure, came up empty.

Until a non-regulation idea leaped to mind. Not regs, but I was desperate. I holstered my gun, hoped like hell Kurt's nerves hadn't affected his brains. I pulled my driver's license from my wallet. Popping my head around the beer display, I waved. When I had Kurt's attention I flashed my license.

Kurt blinked at me. Slowly, he turned to the kid. "I can't sell cigarettes to a *minor.*"

Praise the Great Donut. He got it.

"I'm not a minor!"

"I believe you," Kurt said, "but I have to follow the rules. No cigarettes. Unless you've got some form of ID?"

"Uh...yeah." The punk groped around in his sweatshirt. "Yeah, of course I have ID. Just let me dig it out."

I nearly snorted. A law-abiding crook. Only in Meiers Corners.

He fumbled out a nylon bifold. "Here."

"Albert Zeit." Kurt's voice was loud enough to carry over the still-noodling clarinet. "Nine-oh-one West Grant. Yeah, okay. You're eighteen. Here's the cigarettes."

"About damn time." The kid swept up cash and carton and swaggered out the door, jingling like all eight of Santa's reindeer. I made for the door after him.

"Bad Girl Sex Tricks" caught my eye. Hey, all *right.* Kurt had stocked my favorite magazine, *Sass-Cgal.* I edged closer. "Five Naughty Positions Sure to Wow Him."

Ooh. That article looked mighty interesting. I reached for it, only to snap back. *I had a job to do.* Sucking up my celibacy, I hit the pressure mat and slid outside.

The oompa slid out with me. Before I was halfway, the kid spun. Yanked his hand out of his sweatshirt.

Pulled a gun.

Time slowed, telescoped. In a year-long second, I went for my own firearm.

Before I could reach it, a blast of wind came out of nowhere. Roaring and whirling, it caught my ponytail hard enough to pop the barrette. My hair flew into my eyes.

I was totally blinded.

My hair *attacked* me. Driven by the wind, my wild spirals became a writhing, carnivorously curly mass. My hair put me in a wrist lock and forced me to my knees. My own fucking hair.

The wind roared louder, lashed like hot breath on the back of my neck. I thrashed to see. Vague shapes fought before me. I caught the impression of the kid—

And another male, warrior hard. My whipping hair seemed to form a body strong and lithe as a racing clipper. Huge muscles pumped like steel cannonballs.

My pussy did a slow, wet smile.

Fuck. Just whap me with a billy club. In the middle of a robbery gone bad, and I was getting horny over the wind. I *really* needed to get laid.

I pawed through my tresses. They stuck like slimy seaweed. An eternity passed before I finally fought clear.

The wind was gone, the night eerily still. The kid lay on the sidewalk in front of me in fetal position. His wrists were tangled in his shoelaces.

A squirt gun lay next to him. A damned squirt gun.

The kid wasn't moving. I fell on my knees beside him to check his pulse. He started wriggling. "Don't! Don't hurt me."

I patted his forearm to reassure him, pulled my hand back. His wrists hadn't just gotten tangled in his shoelaces.

His fingers were tied to his shoes.

Bemused, I contacted dispatch. The domestic disturbance must have been resolved because Alice sent Keck. Then I got to work on the laces. It took me ten minutes to free the kid. A wind that tied Scout knots? Huh.

When the patrol car rolled to the curb I ducked Zeit in and recited his name—and home address. Yeah, I sent the kid home. Robbery is a felony, sure. But this was Meiers Corners.

We had the ultimate discipline. Pissed-off parents.

ଓଃ

It was now almost five a.m. I could have chased down Gretchen or tried to interview more suspects. But first shift came on at six and I shared my desk. If I wanted to start my paperwork, I had to do it before Lieutenant Roet claimed my space.

Hoofing it toward the cop shop, my Spidey-sense kicked in. Not threatening, exactly. But letting me know I wasn't alone.

I slowed. The tingling had an odd overtone, something like danger, but not quite. Hand to gun, I stopped. "Who's there?"

The darkness swirled. When it resolved to the large, lithe body of murder suspect Bo Strongwell, I was more than a little disturbed. If he wasn't dangerous, I didn't know who was. I glared. "What're you doing here?"

Big blond and menacing glared back. "I was about to ask the same thing. I leave you alone for ten seconds and you get balled up in an armed robbery."

"The kid wasn't armed...damn." I hadn't meant to give away info. I planted fists on hips. "Hey, buster. *I'm* the cop."

Amusement touched his lips. "Not just cop. *Detective.*"

So he remembered what I said when we first met. So what? It didn't mean we were destined for each other or anything. "Yeah. Glad you remember it. Now, you're here, why?"

"As I told you, I'm on patrol."

"Right, until 'dawn'. Where'd you run off to, before?"

He gave me a slightly pitying look. "Patrol means 'walking around', Detective."

"I know what patrol—never mind. Listen, buster. You're coming with me to the station."

"Certainly, I'll walk with you." He held out his hand, indicating I should precede him. The perfect gentleman. In an invincible, muscle-y sort of way.

I jutted my own hand out, smiled like Freddy Krueger. I was *not* having a murder suspect at my back. He shrugged and sauntered off. I followed, and got an eyeful.

Strongwell wore a pair of faded jeans that had been worn until they were maybe a molecule thick. And what they revealed...holy donut, the man had thighs like tree trunks and an ass like a stallion's.

Zero fat on his waist, back flaring into shoulders broad as a boulevard. His tight black tee showed off arms the size of Moscow. Lots of sleek, perfect skin mounding over muscles like small Volkswagens. The man could have made a fortune selling anabolics. "Do you wrestle?" I blurted without thinking.

He turned his head slightly, one brow raised. "Are you offering?"

"What? No." Although wrestling with Mr. Mounds-o'-Muscle here, grabbing and bumping and writhing... "No, I was just, well, making conversation." Embarrassment propelled me up alongside him.

"Certainly. Then in the interests of making conversation, tell me about your case." He ambled along next to me, hands in pockets, an expression of mild curiosity on his face.

Hey, someone interested in my work. Nobody had asked me about it since Dad, so I opened my mouth to spew...and caught myself just in the nick. "I'm not able to divulge anything at this time."

"How professional of you, Detective. Am I a suspect?"

My face heated. His lips curved, which made him so handsome my heart flipped. When his blue eyes joined in with a twinkle, my stomach melted and slid into my pudendum with a hot splat.

His lip-curve became knowing. "You can cross me off your list. I was on the other side of town from sunset until about quarter after two."

Which, unless a dead body was lying smack in the middle Nieman's parking lot for the entire evening and no one saw it, alibied Mr. Bo Strongwell for the time of the murder. Probably. "Anyone see you?"

"Several people, Detective. A couple in Settler's Square, and three or four at the Bed and Breakfast Smorgasbord, including Otto."

"I'll check with them. In the meantime, I have some questions for you."

"Unfortunately, I still have to patrol. Perhaps another time. Here we are." He gestured behind me.

It was the oldest trick in the book. I'd stopped falling for misdirection about the same time I gave up my teething ring.

But for some reason I was compelled to look. And in the instant I was distracted, Bo Strongwell disappeared into the night.

Chapter Three

I was typing up my notes when the desk phone rang. Our phones were the same black Bakelite they'd been for thirty years, so no caller ID. But they had those little light-up cubes, so I knew it was the direct line for my desk. Since I'd only been detective for three weeks, I doubted it was for me. "Detectives' unit, O'Rourke speaking."

A harsh alto rapped out, "Hold for the mayor."

I shuddered. Even if she hadn't said "mayor" I'd have recognized that bark. Mayor Meier's secretary Heidi placed all calls for him (he was technically challenged, to put it kindly). Heidi looked exactly like the title character from the book with her blonde braids and blue eyes. Well, except for her spike-heeled hip boots. And her penchant for all things black leather. Oh yeah, and her heavy hand with the stud gun.

A click was followed by a booming, jovial, "Elena, *meine* dear young *Freundin,* who I have since diapers known! So good to speak to you, *ja*?"

Shoot me with a Mauser. "Mayor Meier, so good to, ah, listen to you. *Ja.* Um, aren't you at work a little early?"

"When I am hearing about the terrible death of our good citizen, Napoleon Schrimpf, I must immediately in be coming. This is just what we do not need." He pronounced it "goot" and "yoost vat ve do not need". Mayor Meier was the prototypical jolly German. Think Santa in lederhosen.

Still, he was the mayor. Time to do my official cop thing. "Yes, Mayor. It's terrible. But the department is more than up to the task of solving the crime and bringing the perpetrator to justice."

"*Ja, ja,* I am sure." In the background, I heard a strange stinging sound. I couldn't quite identify it under the mayor's rolling tenor. "But I have heard this disturbing news just while at the Mayors of Urban Centers United Society conference I was."

Sometimes the mayor's *Deutsche*glish was hard to follow. "You heard while you were at a conference at three in the morning?"

"*Ja,* well, the meeting had moved to the Boom-Boom room at the hotel and a lovely young lady named Tawny was doing the dancing on the lap of the mayor of—"

"Good! Um, so what is it you want from me, Mayor?"

"This is a horrible crime." The mayor paused and I heard a distinct *crack*. Like a snapped bungee, or a... "The other M.U.C.U.S. members gave for me a terrible ribbing. I can no longer my head hold up."

...Or a whip.

"Now I am much disturbed, *ja*?"

Heidi. Black leather. Whip. Much disturbed, *ja*-fuckin'-*ja*.

"You must solve this crime right away, *liebchen*." Hiss-*snap*! "Or our tourism will go kaput."

Oh, if only my hearing would go *kaput*. "I understand, Mayor Meier."

"*Nein*, I do not think you do. The pressure of the other mayors, it is beyond tolerance. *Und*—" he lowered his voice until I could barely hear him, "—*meine* good Heidi is not happy, you understand?"

Oh yeah. That I understood way too well. "I'll do my best, Mayor."

"*Ja*, I know. But just to sweeten the pot, I will a good word for you for the full detective with the Chief of Police in geputtin'."

I tried to untangle that. "A good word", "Chief" and "full detective" I understood. But was "geputtin" a real word? "Well, thanks, Mayor..."

"*Ach, ja*." He chuckled. "Our own little Elena O'Rourke—who I have known since diapers you were wearing! I know you will not fail me."

As he hung up, I heard the whip cracking. For the mayor's "goot verd", I'd *try* to solve the case. But to avoid Heidi's displeasure—I'd make *sure* of it.

ꕥ

Six a.m. came. After I turned over my desk to Lieutenant Roet I punched my sister's speed dial. Four rings clicked over into voice mail. I hung up and hit it again. And again.

"H'lo?"

"Gretchen, it's Elena. Are you okay?"

"Elena?" There was the rustle of movement, muted, like bedclothes. Then her voice came again, clearer. "Do you *know* what time it is?"

"You're the one who called me at four a.m. Aren't you up yet?"

"No. Or at least, I *wasn't*." She sounded a little peeved. "Can this wait?"

"I wanted to make sure you're okay."

There was a slight pause. "Why wouldn't I be?"

"I don't want to alarm you, but there's a murder suspect living in your building."

"A *what*?"

I winced. Smooth move, O'Rourke. "It's probably nothing. But if you come across this guy you should be careful. Especially with Stella."

"I see. Who is this suspect?"

"Big, blond, rugged good-looks. Says his name is Bo Strongwell."

"Bo *Strongwell*?" Her tone was utterly flabbergasted. "*Bo* Strongwell?"

"You know him?" In either emphasis.

"Know him?" she echoed.

"Is there a reason you're repeating everything I say?"

"I'm repeating everything...?"

"Gretchen!"

"Yes. I mean, no." That snapped her out of it. "I'm just surprised. I've seen him around, sure. He seems like such a nice guy."

"That's what they say about all the killers. Look, it's probably nothing. But be careful, okay? I'll be there tonight and I'll do some digging then. Six, right?"

"Or a little earlier. We're going dancing at the Alpine Retreat and Bar, and I want to be sure to have enough time before you go to work."

"Which reminds me. Why are you *dating* on your wedding anniversary?"

"Me?" she squeaked. Another pause, long enough to be suspicious. "Well, because I could only—" dead spot, "—this time."

"I'm sorry?"

"Because only—" dead spot, "—this time."

"Gretchen, I couldn't hear you. Could you—"

"Sorry, Elena, I have another call coming in. I'll see you tonight, okay?"

"But Gretch—" I was speaking to an empty line.

The wonders of technology stank sometimes. Well. Gretchen was all right for now. And I'd warned her. I would see her tonight and grill her then.

But I'd worry in the meantime.

ᘓ᠅ᘐ

I was a little gritty-eyed from a difficult night but I decided to try interviewing a few suspects before going home. While I didn't have a lot of information yet, a killer was usually someone the victim knew (according to *Murder Investigation for Dummies*). Someone at home or work.

Napoleon Schrimpf's home was on Eleventh and Walnut. I'd tried calling his wife from the office, and now I called again. No answer. Wanting to get notifying her over with, I headed south.

The sun got hotter as it rose. Phew, I'd be glad when this heat wave broke. By the time I reached the Schrimpf home my tee was soaked.

Knocking on Schrimpf's carved wood door produced no results. I walked the perimeter, but the big house was closed up tighter than Strongwell's ass...no, not going there. I trudged back through the rising thermals, not thinking about Viking-strong bodies and blaming my wet jeans on the evil daystar.

Napoleon's Gym was next on my list. The sun beat on my dark hair the whole way. When I finally got to the gym I was pathetically grateful for the air conditioning. I think if I'd stayed outside any longer I'd have burst into flames.

At the gym I interviewed five employees. But the sun must have fried my brain because I couldn't pick out one liar. And that disturbed me.

See, similar to my cop sense I had a truth radar. Before you point out that Schrimpf's employees might have been telling the truth, let me say *everyone* lies. Yeah, as a cop I was born cynical. But *this* was from experience.

The wonky truth radar might have been because I'd been on the job eleven hours straight. But I should have been stronger than that. Tougher.

I wasn't totally stupid however. I needed a clear head to solve this case. Obviously I needed sleep. I packed up my ego and went home.

 ଓଃ

That evening I went to see my sister, who'd picked her wedding anniversary for her first date as a widow.

I craned my neck to scope out the four-story cream-brick apartment. Housing on the northeast side was mostly old. What wasn't small and homey was run down and tired.

Not this building. It boasted beveled glass, gleaming yellow metal, beautifully varnished wood and a Steel Security system, very discreet and very pricey. Very un-north side. Cop sense twitching, I checked my gun (thumb safety on, chamber empty), then rang the buzzer. The door opened.

I hit a time vortex.

Standing in the doorway was a hundred forty haughty pounds of honest-to-goodness *butler*. Black coat, striped vest, silver hair, the whole enchilada.

"Uh, I must have the wrong place." I backed out of the entryway.

The little guy made an elegant gesture toward the inside. I guessed it was Butlerish for "come in". I reversed, inched toward the threshold. The sweet, cool air enticed me all the way.

Jeeves closed the door behind me. "Whom do you seek, miss?"

Whom. Butler Guy really said *whom.* He made it into a two-syllable word, *who-um.* Cue the *Twilight Zone* music—who didn't use *who*?

"I'm here to see my sister. Gretchen Johnson." Speaking of *Twilight Zone,* if this was an apartment lobby, I was Rod Serling. No mailboxes, no buzzers, no discarded trash or cigarette butts. Just lots of polished wood that might have been mahogany. A floor of freaking *marble.* Ultra-efficient central air. Not a lobby, a foyer. A real, live foy-*yay.*

Butler Guy raised one silver eyebrow. "Your sister, miss?"

That, unfortunately, I was used to. Gretch and I didn't look like sisters. Heck, we didn't even look like the same species. Technically, Gretchen was my half-sister. Same father, *way* different mothers (one an international fashion model, the other a German nanny—guess who got the *normal* mom?) Gretch and I were as alike as peas in a pod, if one were a fairy princess pea and the other a big brunette basketball. Albeit a model-slim basketball with good bones, good skin and an awesome rifle-range score.

"Yeah. I'm Elena O'Rourke. But..." But this couldn't be where *my* sister lived. We weren't poor, but working certainly wasn't optional. I stared at the floor. Marble? Nah. It had to be vinyl. Just looked like marble—shit. Was that a *crystal* chandelier?

Jeeves's face cleared. "Oh, yes, Ms. O'Rourke. Mrs. Johnson is expecting you. This way."

It was the right place after all. I should have been relieved, but wasn't. I followed Butler Guy up a sweeping staircase with a thick Oriental runner (did they even stock runners at Walmart?) wondering if Rod and I did share some DNA. Because what would my sister be doing in such a place? Unless...and if you're thinking what I was thinking, you get ten bucks. Which is about the cost of a Meiers Corners blowjob.

But my own sister, a hooker? With a five-year-old daughter? No way. No way Gretchen would... Damn, was that a Ming vase on the landing?

"Elena!" Arms out, my petite blonde sister trotted toward me across carpeting that couldn't be silk. Gretchen was pretty, loving and blessed with tons of energy. Think captain of the high school cheerleading squad, only sweet. "Thank you for coming! Stella is so excited."

My concerns melted at Gretchen's sunny face. I love my sister. I'd do anything for her, brave anything to keep her safe. "Your first date in forever, Gretch. How could I not come?"

I enveloped her in a hug, careful not to crack a rib. Besides our difference of forty-some pounds, I'm a black belt. Even most men don't have my muscle.

Or my cop instincts. My Spidey-sense kicked in. Danger. Behind me.

My gun was out and pressed into Bo Strongwell's rippling abs before recognition made me groan.

As if Strongwell could care less that I'd almost shot him (again), his fiercely beautiful lips curved slightly. For just a second our eyes met, and some primitive recognition lanced between us, immobilizing me.

Either that or the heat flash-fried my brain. While I stood, eyes eating up the chocolaty goodness of Mr. Mounds (-o'-Muscle) Bar, Gretchen *slipped between him and the gun.* "Elena, wait." Her breastbone hit the barrel.

I jerked the XD sideways. "Don't do that!" I said, the same instant Strongwell barked, "Gretchen, no!"

Instantly my sister was behind him and he was glaring at me with eyes gone the color of the frozen Arctic Ocean. Like it was *my* fault.

My sister squeaked. "Mas...sir. Please don't hurt her. This is my sister, sir. Elena." She peeped from behind the guy's bulk. "Elena, this is Bo Strongwell. He's the, ah, building supervisor."

Sweet cream-filled Berettas. A glorified janitor. Dangerous, right. I holstered my gun. "Didn't I tell you not to sneak up on people like that, Strongwell?"

Gretchen's face went white, but it wasn't like I'd thrown up on the Japanese Prime Minister, or anything. I'd just reamed out a grunt who, no matter how gorgeous, richly deserved it. You don't sneak up on a cop.

Strongwell didn't get upset, though. His eyes thawed to a rich sapphire. Those sexy lips started curving again. "I will heed your advice in the future, Detective."

It was all I could do not to nibble that warm, ruby curl. Fuck. The wind, and now a suspect housing flunky. I *had* to get laid. "See that you do. Gretchen? Stella's waiting."

"Yes. All right." Gretchen slunk past the Viking, stopped. Gave an odd little jerk of her head. Like a signal or salute of some kind. Her eyes darted to me and she blushed.

Sudden date and now this. She was *so* getting grilled. Hey, solving mysteries was my job—with my sister, it was my *duty*. In my defense, I waited until we got to her apartment before confronting her. "Why are you dating on your wedding anniversary, Gretch? And what's that guy to you? And why didn't you mention Strongwell was your building super when I talked to you this morning?"

"It didn't seem important." Gretchen wouldn't look at me, busy opening the door. "I appreciate you babysitting. Stella's got a new Bratz. You'll probably be playing dolls until her bedtime."

My dear younger sister was avoiding the subject. I hadn't stood for it when she was sixteen and sneaking nooky in the back seat of our dad's old Escort wagon (with Steve, who she later married, but *still*) and I didn't intend to stand for it now. I opened my mouth to press her for answers.

And was ambushed by forty pounds of PJs and baby shampoo.

Luckily, I had good reflexes. I caught my niece and swung her in a full circle, her legs kicking behind her with glee. "Hey there, Starshine."

"Aunt Lena! Aunt Lena!" Stella's bright blonde curls bounced as I set her on her feet. "I got a new doll, wanna come see?"

Aunting came before grilling. I put my questions on hold. "Kiss your mom first, Starshine, and wish her luck on her date."

The five-year-old gave her mother a big smack. "Mommy and Daddy have a date," she sang.

I eyeballed Gretchen over Stella's head. You can't explain everything to a child, but Date Number One as her new daddy?

Gretch sent me an eye-shrug. "Be good for Auntie Lena, now." She gave Stella a quick kiss and let herself out.

I stared at the shut door, trying to settle my worries. Realizing they weren't going to settle (she was my kid sister, after all), I turned to Stella. "All right, Starshine. We've got some serious playing to do."

The hour until Stella's bedtime passed quickly. Stella liked playing with me. My dolls had car chases and investigated crimes. Don't tell Gretchen.

But it cranked Stella up a little. It took a snack and three stories to get her to bed. And she wasn't down long.

I was watching a rerun of *Buffy* and leafing through an article titled "Not With the Sexy Guy You Love? Love the One You're With" when a door slammed. The toilet flushed, and flushed again. The door opened. Little feet ran along the hallway, and another door slammed.

I dropped the article (*which* sexy guy was moot when I didn't have *any*) and hoisted myself up. An unnerving running-water sound led me into the bathroom.

The toilet had overflowed. Water pooled on the floor, soaking my sister's braided rug. The bowl looked clear, and the water had gone down some, so I tried an experimental flush. It only proved there was more water to slop over.

Grumbling, I dug into the cabinet under the sink, found the plunger and plunged. It worked—if what I wanted to do was rinse the already soaking-wet rug.

A little blonde head popped around the door. "Is it broken, Aunt Lena?"

"Looks that way, Starshine."

"Does that mean Pookie is drowned dead, Aunt Lena?"

"Pookie?" I had a sudden, horrific clue as to what might be stopping up the toilet. A hamster or gerbil. Poor Pookie. Now just another shoebox in the O'Rourke family pet cemetery.

"Pookie's my teddy," Stella said.

I breathed a huge sigh of relief. "Don't worry, Starshine. Teddies have built-in scuba. Pookie will be okay once we get him out."

"How do we get him out, Aunt Lena? Do you do plumbing? Daddy always swears when he does plumbing."

I didn't bother to correct present-tense Daddy. Maybe Date Number One had already auditioned on the casting couch. Maybe that's why Gretch was calling him "Daddy".

"I don't do plumbing, Starshine. I'll call in a professional." I went to the contact list by the phone and found what I wanted right at the top. "Go back to bed, Stella."

"But Aunt Lena, Pookie'll be scared."

I tried to think like a five-year-old. "Pookie'll be embarrassed to be caught in the toilet."

She giggled. "Silly Pookie." After I promised to bring her the teddy bear when he was rescued, she trotted off to her room.

Then I picked up the phone, and dialed Bo Strongwell, Viking building manager.

Chapter Four

A simple clog, but I didn't hesitate calling. Bo was a suspect, he'd avoided my questioning, and this was a perfect opportunity to corner him. Besides, what work did a building super do? Deposit rent checks, change light bulbs? The building wasn't big, maybe sixteen units. And, despite the gorgeous outside, pretty basic. Gretchen's apartment had two small bedrooms and a single bath. A tiny kitchen, and my sister loved to cook.

And not one single window in the whole apartment.

Apparently you can suffer brain damage from snorting too much fingerprint powder. I saw that and didn't think anything more of it.

Bo answered on the first ring. "What's wrong?" he barked.

Well, no need to *snarl* at me. Especially when his black satin voice was so much better. My nipples tightened at the memory of black satin and I gritted my teeth. Annoyed at both his tone and my stupid nipples, I snapped back. "The toilet's wrong. Blocked."

"Detective O'Rourke? Is this an emergency?" His voice smoothed down.

"Hello? Five-year-old and no toilet? Hell yes, it's an emergency."

"I see. And you're calling me because...?"

"Because you're the building super and it's your job? Wait. Don't tell me you have to go *patrol*."

"Sunset's not until seven forty-nine." There was a smile in his voice. "I'll be right there, Detective."

"Right there" was ten seconds flat. I opened the door to Bo (and his four-foot wrench), wondering where his apartment was. Even next door would have been a fast run.

And he had that huge tool to carry.

Following him to the bathroom, I decided to practice my professional observation skills. Six-foot four, weight two-twenty. Heavily muscled. He glided like an athlete—or a hunter. His butt was so tight I could've bounced bullets off it.

O-kaaay, maybe that wasn't so professional.

Bo attacked the clogged toilet, handling his big wrench like a sword or an axe. It made me think of horned helmets and furs and sweating male torsos. As he worked, his biceps clenched and flexed. My body clenched and flexed in rhythm.

I ground my teeth. What, did I now have a thing for sex and toilets? True, in college, Poindexter "Baldy" Beine and I stayed late to do a chemistry lab and ended up making out in the attached bathroom. That was one of my first brushes with Murpheous Interruptus. I was sitting on the throne with Poindexter's head between my thighs when his unknown-to-me steady girlfriend found us and tossed mercury fulminate in his hair. It was only my quick action, shoving his head into the bowl, that saved "Baldy" from worse than burning off his hair (hey, the water was fresh).

But I must have been more scarred by my aborted sexual encounters than I thought. My body's ready-to-eat reaction couldn't have been because of Bo. I was not instantly, wildly attracted to a janitor/suspect.

"Pookie's a bit bedraggled." Bo held the small toy up by one ear. I wondered how he'd gotten it, since the toilet drained directly into a pipe in the floor and he hadn't taken the throne out.

I was immediately distracted by the water pouring from the stuffed bear, running over Bo's strong hand, down his powerful arm. Wetting his T-shirt until I could see the outline of a taut nipple. Molding the tee to the rope of muscle flaring along his side.

"It's nothing that..." My voice came out husky. I cleared my throat with a quick swallow. Hopefully Bo couldn't see *my* nipples poking their heads up to take a peek. "Nothing a few rounds in the dryer won't fix."

His eyes flashed down my front and that almost-smile flirted across his lips. Damn. Stupid perky tits. I was *so* getting a padded bra next paycheck.

I plucked the bear from his fingers and practically ran to the utility closet. I couldn't hear Bo following, but I could feel him, a sexy satin shadow running over my skin.

Sexy satin shadow? What was I thinking? I was not attracted to Bo Strongwell. I was only extremely, excruciatingly horny. But not because of Mr. Muscle-y Maintenance Man. Because I hadn't gotten properly laid in five years, three months and three days.

I stuck the bear in the dryer. Said the first combative thing I could think of. "Pretty cheap apartment, with no windows." Hell, he was standing right behind me, radiating ultra-intense sexual heat. I had to say *something*. And preferably something to counter that very wrong idea I'd given him, all husky-voiced and stiff-nippled. So I challenged him, so what? As Vince Lombardi said, a good defense is a thump on the head. Or something like that. At least I didn't shoot him.

A single warm finger grazed my cheek. Electricity shocked my skin. Jagged down my throat, exploding in my gut. A single touch, but it generated a whole storm system in my body.

All that from one touch, what would sex with him be like? my body wondered, and my mind smacked myself.

"It makes the apartment safe from intruders," Bo said.

I stared into his blue eyes, now the color of tropical waters. Safe from intruders? Oh yeah, no windows. But what about the intruders already inside? I backed away, barely suppressing the urge to go for my clutch piece. "Uh, sure. Well, thanks for rescuing Pookie."

He gave me another devastating half-smile. "My pleasure, Detective. I must go now, but feel free to call me any time."

And then, before I could go into complete melt-down, he took his killer smile and dark stroking voice and glided out the way he'd come.

I slumped onto the couch. What the hell had just happened? Was I so hard up that anything wearing pants and fogging a mirror would do? Well, anything fogging a mirror with gracefully curved lips. Anything wearing pants molded to a bullet-bouncing ass. Anything with thick blond hair and shoulders to block out the sun... I snatched up my magazine and tried to read. "Five Friction-Filled Moves to Wrap Him Up Tight"...ow.

Gretchen came home just before nine. She looked happy and sated. I barely noticed, racing off to work.

Well, I also barely noticed because I was struggling to put graceful lips and Viking bodies out of my head. Like pink elephants, they only recalled every instant of the encounter. Bo's body. Bo's flank, taut under his wet tee. Bo's abs, rippling under my gun.

Gretchen, peeking from behind his warrior mass.

I was nearly at the station when my brain woke up with a bang. Gretch had put herself between my gun and the building manager. *Had risked her life.*

And that odd little jerk, that nod.

Why had my sister *bowed* to the maintenance man?

ଔଓ

At the police station, I brewed strong, hot coffee and sat down with a cup to think. I needed to interview the witnesses, but I needed to organize my thoughts more. My brain was whirling, I got that. I was excited, because of the case. But that didn't explain the eager buzzing in my vulva, like not only my brain expected big things.

It also didn't explain why I read *Sass-Cgal* instead of my usual *Midwest Police Monthly* while I drank my joe. And why, when I saw the sample for Hulk It Perfume (Guaranteed to Turn Him into a Raging Testosterone Monster), I tore it open and swabbed it all over my body.

Two cups of coffee later I managed to put away *Sass-Cgal* (Blatzky yelling about the pervasive stench of Hulk It as he fled the office might have helped) in favor of the ME's prelim.

The report was succinct. *Two puncture wounds to the scrotum, three-point-five mm diameter* (which I translated to size four knitting needles). *Victim bled out.*

Poor sucker. Stabbed viciously in the balls. Gored genitals, bad enough. But slowly seeping blood until you lost consciousness...wait.

If the victim bled out, *where was the blood*?

I checked my notebook. No blood soaked into Schrimpf's clothes. None pooled on the pavement or spattered the car, confirmed by the crime-scene photos. I pulled out a magnifying glass to check. No bloody footprints or drips or even drag marks nearby.

Winds that tied Scout knots, apartments with butlers and now this. It was almost...unnatural.

Unless the vic bled out elsewhere. If he was moved to the parking lot *after* he was drained, that would explain it.

Sure. Nothing unnatural about it. Schrimpf was somewhere else—when he was stabbed in the balls by some rabid prostitute (who knitted).

Oh yeah. That made so much more sense.

I wished there were someone I could talk to about this. Someone smart, with my sense of justice. Like my dad. When Dad was still alive, I'd call him a couple times a week with questions. Do I take sociology, should I buy a car. Stuff I could have answered on my own, but Dad's opinion was always so reassuring. I wished now I hadn't wasted my questions.

Of course, I could have bounced ideas off Blatzky—if he hadn't skedaddled because of the Hulk It.

So I fell back on tried and true. Analyze evidence, interview witnesses and suspects. Dig up information on everything and everybody. Even a weird case was still a case, and by-the-book hadn't failed me yet.

Statistically, the prime suspect was Napoleon Schrimpf's wife of four years. I had tried to contact her yesterday. Suspect, sure. But more importantly, someone had to inform her she was now a widow. I dialed (the phones were that old) the number. When the line cut in on the second ring I braced myself for the difficult duty.

"Schrimpf residence, Martinez speaking."

"Josephine Schrimpf, please." (Napoleon and Josephine. Honest, that was her legal name.)

"I am sorry, Mrs. Schrimpf is out of town." The woman had a slight accent reminiscent of my Grandma Sanchez.

I identified myself. "I need to speak with Josephine as soon as possible."

"Is this about Mr. Schrimpf's death?"

Gossip travels fast in Meiers Corners. Bad if you're trying to keep a secret, but in this case I wouldn't have to break the awful news. "I'm afraid I can't discuss it with anyone but Josephine. Can you tell me where she is, when she'll return?"

"Mrs. Schrimpf is at a convention in Las Vegas. She booked a return flight the minute she heard about the death. I expect her back late tomorrow evening."

"Is there a number where I can reach her in the meantime?"

"I'm sorry, I am just the maid. Mrs. Schrimpf did not leave anything with me."

I got a vague buzzing at that. I'd have said Martinez was lying, but couldn't tell over the phone. I made an appointment to see the widow the next evening, thanked the maid and hung up.

Next I did a little digging on Schrimpf—and Bo. Neither had criminal records. Schrimpf paid his taxes and bills on time. Strongwell paid ahead. Both were remarkably clean.

The only thing that popped were a couple domestic disturbances called in on the Schrimpfs. But when the officer investigated, both Josephine and Napoleon said nothing was wrong. Either they were liars or their neighbor was channeling Gladys Kravitz.

By this time it was ten thirty. Time to tap the witnesses at Nieman's Bar. So to speak.

Nieman's was a typical neighborhood tavern. Bartender, mirror, peanuts, amnesia supplies—all the amenities. A bar ran the length of the room. Tables lined the far wall, but Nieman's didn't have waitresses. Customers ordered for themselves. Serious drinkers sat at the bar, where they wouldn't have to stumble to get their next drink.

Tonight's crowd was mostly old regulars, and I do mean old. Tuesday was Ladies' Night elsewhere in the universe, but at Nieman's, it was Seniors' Night. Not one person was under sixty.

They tried to look young. The lighting should have helped, being just this side of blackout. But hip and trendy to these folk meant chunky gold necklaces and polyester.

If these people had freshness stamps they would've read "Best used by last century".

A few of the more daring women snapped themselves into vintage spandex. One old grandma's saggy bod was bound by two ultra-wide rubber bands (skirt and tube-top). Her scrawny legs and arms were bare. She looked like a skinny Michelin Man. Granny knocked back a shot of something, chased it with beer.

I put down my two bucks and ordered a cola with lime. While I waited, I scanned the bar for the wits. Maybe if I was lucky, I'd find out more about Schrimpf's hookers. The holes in the vic's balls suggested a crime of passion. Wife, or mistress.

Unless Schrimpf had pissed off a carpenter with a nail gun.

But the stabbed scrotum was why I didn't favor Viking Bo Strongwell for the murder. Why bayonet Schrimpf's balls if you could just step on him and squish him?

I found the witnesses at the far end of the bar. Putting on my regulation cop face and manners, I strode over and flashed my badge/ID case at the smaller of the two guys. "Are you Dieter Donner?" I pronounced it Dye-ter, but I should've known better.

"That's *Dee*-tehr, cutie." Donner was a small, shaggy man with bright blue eyes and teeth too big for his face, like a horse's mouth slapped on a collie. "What's a cutie like you doin' in a place like this?" His words were slurred.

"Original. And that's Detective Cutie to you." I turned. "You, sir?" Donner's partner was a large distinguished-looking man, bald but for a skirt of hair hula-ing around his ears. Surrey with the fringe on top, 'cause if Donner was the horse, this guy was the stately old carriage.

The carriage stood and bowed, offering me his seat. "Franz Blitz at your service, Detective Cutie."

Donner and Blitz. Thunder and Lightning. Honest to Pete, would I make this up?

Blitz continued, "May my compatriot and I buy you a drink?"

"Thanks, I already ordered something." The bartender slid my cola down to me as I sat between them. "I just have a few questions."

A cheer erupted from behind me. Donner hiccupped. "In a minute. Brunhilde Butt is dancing."

I turned, only to be blinded by the sight of the grandma tottering on top of the bar, *pulling down her tube top.* She yanked it all the way to her navel before her nipples were exposed.

"Aw." I winced. "That's just wrong."

"Take it off! Take it off!" Rhythmic pounding started on the bar.

Donner cheered. "She's goin' all the way!"

It was like a car wreck—I had to look. Grandma yanked up her skirt. I prayed for a layer or two before the ship hit the iceberg, but...ye gods! I had no idea they made orthopedic thigh-highs. And I really didn't want to see if granny's rug matched her sparse silver curtains.

The old woman did an experimental strut or two on the bar. A bump-and-grind was followed by a wince of pain. But the way her hips moved made me think she'd had it at one time, and in spades.

It wasn't her imagination slowing her down, it was the arthritis.

Unfortunately the arthritis also tripped her up. Strutting along, Granny hit a puddle of beer, slipped. Her size six loafers flew up into the air, peanuts scattering like shot. She bounced off a fat drunk like he was an airbag and pitched onto the floor.

"I'm okay!" She sprang to her feet. The spry move was followed by another wince. I thought it was the arthritis until Granny picked a swizzle stick from between her thighs. Ew.

"Show's over." Donner held up a finger for another beer. "You got some questions, cutie?"

"Detective Cutie," Blitz corrected.

"Yes." I wondered if I got hazard pay for this. "About the body you found last night."

"Napoleon Schrimpf," Donner said.

"Worth ten thousand a month," Blitz said.

"Spent half of it on greedy women," Donner started.

"And the other half on hookers," Blitz finished.

"We're his accountants," Donner said modestly.

Sitting between them, my head bounced like a demented ping-pong ball. "You." I pointed at Blitz. "Just you talk. What greedy women?"

"Wives. Schrimpf had to buy a bigger house just to store all their clothes and shoes."

"I see. And the hookers?"

"Lana," Blitz said.

"And Lena," Donner added.

My head swung.

"And Loni and Lori," Blitz said.

My head swung back

"And Luci." Donner.

I was getting dizzy. "Enough—!"

"Don't forget Drusilla," Blitz said.

I blinked. "Drusilla?"

"Drusilla," they said together. "Schrimpf's favorite."

I hit Main Street, looking for streetwalkers.

Technically, not all of Meiers Corners' hookers walked the street. Some worked Nieman's parking lot, and one or two even had a flop.

But Main was where most went, especially the younger ones. Blowing guys in cars, maybe hoping for a ride out of Dodge in lieu of cash since ten bucks a blow was definitely sub-standard wages. (There was actually some talk about unionizing. A couple gals even picketed for a few days. But they never could decide whether to go Teamster or AFL-CIO.)

On my second circuit my cop sense buzzed. I spun, hand on gun. Sure enough, a gang of five bore down on me. I tensed for a fight.

"Officer O'Rourke!" A mass of short skirts and skimpy halters tottered toward me on skyscraper sandals. Meiers Corners' part-time hookers. "Yoo-hoo!" The lead prostitute waved at me. "Donner and Blitz said you wanted to talk to us so we came right away."

My father's Irish saints preserve us. Weren't hookers supposed to be hard, dissolute and disillusioned? Since when were they peppy and helpful?

Oh, yeah, since this was Meiers Corners. The five surrounded me in various states of happy jiggle. "I'm Lana," the lead hooker said. "This is Lena, Loni, Lori and Luci."

Breathlessly, Luci said, "You want to know about Nappy Schrimpf?"

My head turned to her.

"We can tell you all about him," Lena said. My head turned again.

"Mostly all about him." Loni quivered in excitement. My head followed.

"Well, at least a little something about him," Lori chimed in.

My head...yeah. I was getting dizzy *again*. "Ladies, please." If Donner and Blitz were split five ways, they'd make the L-gang. "Did you know Schrimpf or not?"

"He wasn't much for talking," Lana said. I think it was Lana.

"He liked blows," Loni said. Or it might have been Lori.

"But that's about it," Luci said. Pretty sure it was Luci.

Scarier thought. Maybe Donner and Blitz had split in emulation of these five. "Nothing else? You sure?"

"His favorite was Drusilla." Lena said this, but all five faces beamed.

"We want to be just like her." Lori. Or maybe Lana.

"She's full time, you know." Luci. Loni. Fuck.

"Yeah, I've heard," I said. Maybe I should have just given up and called them all Lanalenaloniloriluci. "Do you suppose this Drusilla knows anything about Schrimpf's death? Anything useful, that is?"

"She should," one of them said. At this point I'd rather have shot myself than caring who.

Until she added, "Dru was with him right before he died."

I now had four possibilities. Well, unless it was a random killing, but Schrimpf's pierced pouch argued against that. With the intimate nature of the wounds, the widow was most likely. Josephine was out of town, alibied. But alibis could be broken.

Second most likely was some other "conquered" female. Lana and the rest of the "L" gang—or the Schrimpfster's favorite, Drusilla.

The third possibility was a disgruntled employee or vendor.

Fourth was Mr. Mystery, Bo Strongwell. But he only had one hit on the MMO Top Three, Opportunity. In fact, nothing obvious connected him to Schrimpf. Well, other than proximity. And the fact that he set my teeth on edge. And set other parts tingling. I hushed my nipples. Alibied, too, for what it was worth. I still had to confirm that. So he was fourth, but a distant fourth. Although for my peace of mind I wished he were distant-er. My pussy objected loudly. I told it to shut up too.

I spent half an hour canvassing for Drusilla without success. So I returned to the station and hit the employees again. I hadn't done so well on the first go-around, probably because I'd been bushed.

Fresh now, I started phoning. It was late, almost midnight. But I was up, right?

I spoke with a dozen people. The conversations were short, but I got *tons* of new information. I couldn't believe it. *Great* stuff. I made notes of *everything*. The best involved sex and Twinkies.

I had no idea people could swear that inventively.

Unfortunately, I didn't learn a lot about the case. I needed an inside scoop, preferably one that worked the same wacko hours I did.

Like my best friend, Nixie Schmeling.

At five-foot nothing and a hundred pounds, I could have lifted Nixie with one hand. But she'd'a kicked my ass if I did. Nixie's diminutive size and blonde curls camouflaged a screaming Amazon princess. She was a tattooed punk musician with a permanent hard-on for anyone cramping her style. In some ways I envied her. She was more out of place in Meiers Corners than I was, but it never kept her from being anything less than herself. She was purely, plainly, through-to-the-core Nixie.

Nixie didn't work directly for Schrimpf. She studied Taekwondo at Mr. Miyagi's. (Miyagi Park, but a body double for Pat Morita. Blame the Bluebird of Coincidence.) She also taught satellite classes for Miyagi, saving to move out of her parents' house. Conveniently, the satellite was Schrimpf's Gym. And as a musician in the bar band *Guns and Polkas*, Nixie would be awake and available.

When I got to the Schmeling bungalow I didn't ring the doorbell. Hey, I didn't want to wake Mrs. Schmeling and earn one of her lectures. That woman *invented* guilt. Instead, I stole to the back of the house and found a clod of dirt. Before my parents moved us to Chicago my sophomore year, Nixie and I had done our share of sneaking out. I wound up and launched the clod at her second-story window, was rewarded with a soft clunk. Ha. Still had it.

A face popped into the window. I waved. The face disappeared, and a moment later the back door opened. A tiny doll of a woman popped out, curvy in skinny jeans and a Noisebot T-shirt that read Make Awkward Sexual Advances, Not War.

She trotted down the stairs. "'Sup, Badge-Bitch. We gonna go get hammered?"

Nixie was twenty-five, but her vocabulary was straight out of *Superbad*. Fortunately she was a lot smarter than she talked.

"When I get my permanent shield we're going to fry our brains sunny-side up. But tonight I was hoping for a consult on a case.

Caffeine Café? I'm buying."

"Sweet. Let me go put on some clothes."

"What do you call what you're wearing?"

She glanced at herself, grimaced. "I call this 'Concession to the Maternal Sensibilities'. It'll just take a sec to get normal." She disappeared back into the house. When she trotted back out she wore a threadbare Garfield hoodie with the sleeves ripped out, a belly-baring tankini, a black sequin skirt and a pair of Candie's boots. "I hope they've got some of those Seven Deadly Chocolates scones. Those things are wicked hardcore."

We started off, our pace matched despite our height difference. I said, "So how's your folks?"

"Puritanical and lovin' it. 'Course, they call it 'stability'. How's Gretch?"

I didn't want to go into it. "She's fine."

"Can you make 'fine' sound any more like 'deathly ill'?"

Never try to lie out loud to a musician. They hear things the rest of us don't even know exist. It'd be spooky if it weren't so annoying. "All right, if you must know. She's acting funny. I'm afraid it has to do with her new apartment manager, who's a suspect in my case."

"Um-hmm. He's a hottie too, I take it?"

"Well, yes. But how did you know?"

"When you said 'acting funny' it sounded worried. But 'apartment manager' didn't sound worried. It sounded breathy. As in 'I can't catch my breath, because my lungs and all my internal organs hit my pussy and exploded'."

My cheeks warmed. "Um, maybe. But his being handsome is one reason I'm worried. I mean, Gretch is a new widow. Vulnerable, especially to hunky guys."

"I thought you wanted her to get out. Date."

"Not guys with sex on the brain. Nice guys, like Steve."

"News flash. Even nice guys have sex on the brain." She gave me an appraising look. "*Gals* too."

I didn't have to be a musician to hear that her emphasis on gals meant *me*. "I don't have sex on the brain."

"Sure you do. You've gone without it for how long now? Three years?"

"Five. It's three months. And, ah, four days. If I were counting."

"Which clearly you aren't. How many hours?"

"Six." I mumbled it.

"Not jonesing at all. Seconds?"

"Forty—fuck. Just drop it."

"Forty-fuck? Hmm. Clearly not obsessing. Not feening one little bit about sex. Not desperate-horny at all, especially not about Mr. Hottie

Apartment Manager. Milliseconds?"

"Enough already!" I gave her my patented cop glare, guaranteed to send a perp into stuttering shivers. Then I remembered that this was Nixie, who could spear even Vice Principal Schleck with her finely honed Attitude. Not even the cop glare would pierce her armor. There was better ammunition. "I heard they had carrot cake at the Café today."

That sidetracked her immediately. "Ooh! Inch-thick frosting?"

"Yup. Cream cheese." Nixie is small so she has to eat frequently. She tends to forget that, but the rest of us don't. She gets crabby when she's not fed.

At the Caffeine Café (our local twenty-four/seven brew and chew) we ordered scones (they were out of carrot cake, dammit) and caramel mochas. We hustled our loot to our accustomed back table, me with my back to the wall, her next to me. She was nibbling scone as she sat. "So spew. What's so important?"

"I fielded a possible murder case last night. Napoleon Schrimpf."

"Murdered how?"

"Blood loss. From a couple of puncture wounds. To the, ah, scrotum."

"The King of Compensation, sucked dry. Ain't that a karmic slap to the shortie vampire."

"Vampire?"

"A cheap-ass bloodsucker. Schrimpf pays...well, *paid* as little as possible while squeezing out every last drop of value. Employees, vendors, you name it. Vampire, ha. He could have been a lawyer."

"Could he have pissed off somebody at his gym enough for murder? Or a vendor?"

"Could have. But didn't." Nixie chowed half her scone, washed it down with mocha. Tiny body, roaring metabolism. "He hired them young, was pretty easy with scheduling and gave great recommendations. Works pretty well with the minimum-wage folk. Mr. Miyagi had some pithy things to say before he sent me there, but Miyagi would never kill him. Well, not by poking holes in his balls, at any rate. Miyagi'd be more likely to kick the Schrimpfster's 'nads through his ears."

"Um, right. And the other vendors? Did you hear anything there?"

"I'm onsite three days a week, so yeah, I heard some things. Schrimpf squeezed money pretty hard. But the vendors put up with it because—get this—he paid on time."

"Bottom line?"

"I can't see anybody at the gym doing Schrimpf. The words are there, but the music is wrong, know what I mean?"

"It doesn't pop for you." I sighed, reminding myself that ninety percent of the job was paperwork and the other half was legwork.

Proving or disproving alibis, exhausting leads whether they pointed to dead ends or not. There were a lot of threads. But only one would be right.

Chapter Five

Waving goodbye to Nixie, I caught a whiff of myself. Despite the Hulk It perfume (surely not because of it), I stank to high heaven. This heat was taking quite a toll on my wardrobe. I headed toward my apartment to change. My route took me past the defunct Roller-Blayd Company.

Lit by a single street light, the boarded-up building looked desolate. My trot slowed, uneasy. A cloud passed over the moon. A chill flitted down my back.

Instinct whipped me around, gun out.

"*Bleh*! Don't shoot! It's just me, Dracula."

My XD pointed at a slender man in white makeup wearing a plastic cape and a set of fangs faker than a porn star's boobs. Dracula, right. "Bleh, yourself." I stowed my gun. "Halloween's not for another two months, buster."

He shrugged, sending sinuous ripples through the cape. Well, as sinuous as a trash-can liner could get. "I want to get laid more than once a year." He was doing a bad Bela Lugosi, *vant* and *lehd*. The fangs gave his words a slight lisp.

"You get laid in that outfit?" I crossed my arms under my breasts and shot him an eyeful of skepticism.

Creepula's gaze followed my arms. "You'd be surprised. Very, very—" *velly, velly*, "—surprised." A smile drifted onto his face.

What was he looking at? Irritated, I glanced down... Stupid perky nipples. "Not much surprises me, Mr....? Er, Mr....?"

He glided closer, bang into my personal space. "*Bleh*. As I said. Dracula." The abandoned warehouse loomed behind him, utterly dead. His gaze pierced me, a bright, unholy red.

Brown. Bright brown, *not* red. I stiffened my spine. "Sure. Dracula, first name 'The'. Look, buddy, why don't you move along? Nothing here to interest an innocent civilian."

"I am anything but innocent." Dracula took another step forward, his red mouth curling in a sensual smile. His shoes kissed mine.

"Indeed, I am the opposite of innocent. I am wicked. I am *Vampyre*." His corny accent made it vahm-peer.

But the moonlight gave his fake fangs a disturbingly real glint. I had to force myself to meet his eyes. They gleamed like rubies, intense, unblinking. I started to feel odd. Hot and unsteady.

Dracula bent toward me. His fanged mouth opened.

"Sorry to interrupt." The dark satin voice sounded anything but.

I sprang back, cheeks burning. Bo Strongwell glided up, his face more chiseled, his body bigger, his aura more dangerous than I remembered.

Dracula squeaked and faded into the night.

Bo's head snapped around to follow. His whole body tensed, as if poised for pursuit, a deadly hunter intent on his prey. It was a strange image for a glorified janitor, but it stuck.

And that peeved me. "Strongwell. What are you doing here?"

Bo's head swung back to me. He relaxed slightly, crossed heavy arms over muscled chest. "What am *I* doing here? What are *you* doing here?"

"I asked you first." Juvenile, but he got under my skin.

"So you did. Care to discuss it while we walk?" Without waiting for an answer, Bo hooked my arm and started off.

Toward the cop shop, not home. I opened my mouth to object.

"What is that scent?" His elegant nostrils flared. His head dropped toward me and he inhaled. "Ahh. You."

I flushed. "It's hot out. And police work is stressful. And—"

"It's delicious." He licked his lips, a subtle caressing with his tongue.

"Ah, sure." Flustered, I traipsed alongside him. "Oh, hey. That must be the perfume I'm trying out."

"No. It's you." His eyes closed and he took a deep breath. His thick fringe of dusty lashes were soft against the carved granite of his cheeks. "Mmm. Absolutely delightful."

"Really?" Pleasure washed away my embarrassment. I didn't think he was smelling anything but perfume, but maybe I didn't have to go home and change. Without thinking, I put a hand over his. His skin was intriguingly warm and smooth, roughened near the edges by small golden hairs. A shudder of excitement hit me, as if he wore a thin glove of sheer energy.

I pulled my hand back. Whoa. That was weird. Gingerly, I touched him again.

A buzz jolted me, streaking from fingers to chest. My nipples tightened and tingled. My heart rate jacked, my eyes popped wide. Surprised, I glanced at him, to see if he felt it too.

"Exquisite." His nostrils flared as he drew another deep breath.

His lips pursed like he was tasting something really good. He had the most beautifully shaped mouth, the color of good red wine.

Janitor and suspect, yes. But a damn good-looking janitor-suspect.

Suddenly, his brows cinched into a frown. His eyes snapped open and the energy clicked off.

My brain clicked on. We stood in front of the Blood Center. I was on duty. Bo was a *suspect.* I tugged away. "Don't think you can get off so easy, Strongwell. I asked you a question. What are you doing wandering around an abandoned warehouse?" An empty building, the perfect place for illegal, immoral activities. Murder. Mayhem. Illicit sex.

Although looking at him, at his size and strength, maybe not murder. At least not with wimpy little knitting needles. Illicit sex, though...lots and lots of illicit...damn. "You'd better have a good reason. Other than *patrolling.*"

He almost smiled. "What can I say? I live my job. Let's move away from here."

"What's the matter? Blood Center give you the willies?"

His smile broadened. "You're clever, aren't you?"

Even that half-smile made me want to gobble his delectable lips. I tore my eyes away, lit on Dolly Barton's beauty salon (and MC gossip center), which reminded me I had a haircut appointment. Which distracted me enough to blurt, "I live my job too." Which embarrassed the crap out of me. Again. What, was I trying to pump him or befriend him?

"You have a very pretty blush, Detective." His expression soft, he grazed a fingertip over my cheek.

I felt Bo's gentle touch like a tattoo machine driving permanent lust under my skin. I swatted his hand away, but feebly, like a girl. "*Working.*"

"Can't we work and enjoy ourselves at the same time?" He murmured it, lips barely moving.

Holy Donut, that ruby mouth was fascinat—damn. "No. We can't." Or at least I obviously couldn't. I marched down the street, crossed Lincoln with only the barest of look-both-ways-before.

Bo caught me outside the Fudgy Delight, cuffing my wrist. I wasn't a small woman but his hand made my arm look almost delicate. I stared down at where we were joined, skin to skin...another jolt of sensation rippled through me.

Dammit, I was *on duty.* Never before had I had such trouble maintaining a proper distance. Frankly, it scared me. "Let go!" I tugged. Pulling against iron would have been more productive. I got exactly nowhere. The man was strong as a horse.

But I was smarter. I jerked up and back, right against the break between thumb and forefinger where his grip would be weakest. I put my whole body behind it.

It worked beautifully. I yanked free.

And sailed smack into the door behind me. Old and weak, the lock gave. The door burst open. I tumbled in.

The Fudgy Delight had been a dance hall in the forties. It had a small stage, room for a couple dozen tables and a recessed dance floor. I tumbled through the door straight down a short flight of stairs into the dance pit, ended up sprawled on the lacquered wooden-slat floor. Around me, stripes of moonlight picked out café-style tables, some in the dance pit, more on the level circling it.

Bo was instantly on his knees beside me. And I do mean instantly. I was still sliding when I saw him reaching for me.

"Elena. I'm so sorry, I couldn't stop you...are you all right?" His fingers ran over my limbs, head and neck, checking for injury. "Any tingling, burning? Loss of feeling?" His tone was actually worried.

Nobody worried about me. They worried about Gretchen or Nixie, but not me. As a child, I was the big girl who took care of herself. Later I was the cop who took care of herself—and everyone around her. Bo's concern was nice.

"I'm fine." More than fine. His skimming woke every body part he touched, incited tingling need. Burning, yes, but not the nerve-damaged kind.

"Thank goodness." He pulled me into his arms, burying me momentarily against his massive chest.

It was like being slammed into a wall. Sweet chocolate Glocks, Mounds-o'-Muscle here was actually harder than he looked. I drew in a surprised breath, choked on it. A masculine scent, steamy and spicy, nearly dropped me unconscious. As it was I started trembling. "Uh, Strongwell?"

"Damn it, Elena, you're shaking. You're *not* okay." He held me away from him. Zeroed in on my eyes, which must have said exactly why I was shaking.

I licked my lips. His gaze dropped precipitously to follow, his pupils dilating big as dimes. He yanked me in. Hot lips descended.

Bo kissed me.

His mouth, warm and firm, pressed against mine. Circled masterfully. A tongue licked the seam of my lips with bold expertise.

My trembling increased. My hands fell onto his cotton-covered chest. It was like palming velvet-covered boulders. My lips parted slightly in amazement.

His tongue flicked at the opening. Little sparklers lit where he licked, small crackles of sensation, tiny zaps that made my lips swell and throb. He kissed me, silky soft, licking little shivers at the corners and edges of my mouth until I wanted to scream.

I grabbed Bo's head, pent-up lust twisting my fingers into his thick hair. I vaulted onto my knees. My knees and shins rapped hard wood but hunger overwhelmed any pain.

I kissed him back.

His kiss changed, his head angling, his jaw working. No deeper, but harder. Taking command, not giving me the option to stop, even if I wanted to.

Which I most certainly did *not.*

Suspect, yeah. Janitor, yeah. And maybe he was doing my sister, though I hoped not.

But Nixie was right, I was desperate. The last time I was intimate with a guy was at a police convention in a conference room that was supposed to be empty. Except we forgot daylight savings time. Just when the guy settled down to a workout at the Y, forty people walked in. Too bad, because his jump rope was extra long and thick. That frustrating little scene, with variations, had been going on for the last five-plus years.

So I was a bit, um, eager.

I tried to tell Bo that with my open mouth, my thrusting tongue. That he didn't have to go slow. That he didn't have to be a gentleman. That he didn't have to arouse me because I was already pitched at frantic.

That my head had already catapulted to rumpled sheets and writhing damp bodies and please-oh-please filling my empty ache.

He heard. His powerful arms cinched me close. A low rumble of approval lapped at my ears. His tongue thrust into my mouth, deep, stabbing like a flaming sword. I was not small but his tongue *filled* me. I tasted timber ships and roaring fires. Sea spray and raids and rich plunder. He drove deep again. And again.

I grabbed his ears and tried to crawl into his mouth.

His fingers tightened in my hair. His other hand thrust into my waistband, tugged the shirt hem out. Strong fingers rasped directly onto my skin. His hand was big enough to span my entire back. I shivered.

His hot palm caressed me, burning friction. His fingers were fire, licking down my spine. Flames lapped the delicate hairs over my back cleft. The night was humid, but that made steam roar out of my ears.

I arched into him, my breasts rubbing the powerful swell of his chest. My nipples tightened, pleading mutely. Need fired deep inside. My panties dampened.

Abruptly he broke the kiss and raised his head. His eyes were closed, his nostrils flared. "Fuck, Elena...that scent...*your* scent."

Thank you, Hulk It.

"And your *taste.*" Bo bent, nuzzled my ear, his breath tickling the lobe. "Mmm. I want to taste all of you, Elena. Every succulent inch." He bore me to the hardwood floor, held me there with the weight of his

Viking body. His hips pressed into mine.

A huge bulge prodded my belly. I gasped. *Was that a cock or did he have a Viking warship in his pants?*

A rush of desire hit me between the legs. My knees, still throbbing from the floor, parted. One thickly muscled thigh thrust between mine, pressed intimately. Rhythmically. Suddenly my knees weren't the only thing throbbing.

His palms planted on either side of my head, he stared down at me, deeply, as if reading my thoughts. And maybe he could because slowly his mouth curved in a sexy, knowing smile. "We have time, Elena. Let's do this right." His eyelids lowered, heavy with desire. Exquisitely deliberate, he bent his head toward me.

Hot, slick lips met mine. I opened, eager for the fiery thrust of his tongue. But he slid his mouth over mine, superbly unhurried, tasting me thoroughly, drinking in my panting breath. Licking and nibbling and tonguing until I was going crazy.

Years of unfinished foreplay sharpened every smell, every sound, every sensation. My nostrils filled with the rich, dark scent of male. My ears rang with Bo's deep sighs and my own frustrated groans. My body rocked with frissons of desire.

I circled his strong neck with my arms, wrapped my cop-long, cop-strong legs around his waist and rubbed against him in bold, needy strokes. He shifted to nibble my ear. I tightened my legs and rubbed harder, until I was practically grinding his monster erection with my pubic bone. "Enough of slow, dammit!"

At last, he growled. Deep, bone-buzzing, heart pounding. His mouth left my ear to trail wet fire down my neck. One hand slipped under my shirt, found my breast. Palm and fingers cupped and kneaded while a thumb rasped my nipple erect. "Do you like that?"

I trembled under him. "Wonderful. More."

"More?" His tongue glided over the side of my neck. Sharp nips followed. "Yeah, I'll give you more."

His hands ran fire over my breasts, his mouth sucked pleasure along my neck. His hips ground slowly, inexorably into my vulva.

The heat of his body, the thrilling pressure, poured liquid excitement into my belly. I rocked harder against him, close to...something. Something big compared to even my vibrator. Way beyond frustrated foreplay. "*More.*"

Bo's hips jerked. His cock swelled until it burned the entire length of my vulva. "Lord, Elena. Do you want to kill me?" He muttered it against my neck, breath hot, sharp teeth scraping skin.

So close. I wriggled under him. Perspiration dotted my skin. "More, now!"

He growled. Released his full weight against me. I only thought I was under pressure before. He smashed me into the hardwood floor.

Crushed my breasts and hips with his overpowering male strength. And I loved it.

I grabbed his head and pressed him closer. "That feels so good." My heart was pounding. My whole body was throbbing. His tongue swiped long strokes over my throat. Sharp. Hot. Shocking.

"Damn. The smell. The sound... Elena, are you ready?"

I was panting so hard my breath caught in my throat. "*Ungh.*" Please, do it. Whatever *it* was. I writhed under him, seeking...seeking...

"You want it?" His teeth, needle sharp, pressed into the skin.

Pricks of desire lit my neck. My throat was swollen with need. I forced the words through. "*Yes.* Finish this before I implode."

He let out a soul-deep sigh and his teeth stabbed into my throat.

Pleasure knifed me hard. Lanced from neck to groin. My pussy clenched and released like a metal spring. *Sproing.* I came, so violently I could smell it. Could feel it drenching my panties.

Hot liquid trickled down my neck. Bo's tongue rasped over me, licking ardently. "You taste like heaven, Elena. I've never...not in all my life..." He groaned, so deep it might have been coming from his toes.

I floated in a cloud of bliss. And here I thought my sexual frustration was from lack of penetration. Who needed intercourse when they could climax from... I came to and realized Bo had *bitten* me. I scrambled out from under him, swayed unsteadily to my feet.

He rose instantly, with a muscular ease that mocked me. "Elena—"

"You *bit* me!"

I wound up and punched him good.

Bo's rock-hard abs barely dented, but he gave a quite satisfactory huff. He stepped back, eyes shuttering. He touched his belly but said nothing.

"What the hell was that for?" I clapped a hand over my neck where he had bitten me. "Look, I don't do kinky stuff like..." I felt—nothing. No blood, no wound. Just smooth, whole skin. "You'd better not do that with my sister." I felt a lot less sure of myself.

His eyes glowed eerily in the moonlight. "I don't." His mouth barely moved, and his voice was half growl. His fingers were clenched at his side.

"Well, good." I cut an involuntary look at his pants. The zipper was raised in mountainous relief against his hips. Oh heavenly days, what would that have felt like inside me?

Would have being the operative terms. 'Cause *I* wasn't going to find out. The best orgasm in years, and I'd gone and punched the man who'd given it to me.

Way to go, Elena. First guy in five to float his armada on your sea, and you sink his battleship. Well, looking at Bo's zipper, maybe not sink. In fact, he looked impressively unsinkable. Like he'd sail long and hard... Fuck. *I* wasn't going to get the chance.

My sister, maybe. *Widows have needs too,* a little voice whispered. *Shut up,* I whispered back. "Gretchen has had enough shit in her life, Strongwell. So if I ever hear of you trying that biting stuff with her—"

Quite suddenly Bo relaxed. His lips curved slightly. "Jealous?"

I gasped. "Over an apartment manager? Hardly!"

"Good." He still looked smug. "I'd hate to think a little kiss and love-nip scrambled my dear detective's brain."

"Little...*little*..." I had climaxed from that "little" kiss. And he'd gotten the Washington Monument in his pants, so it wasn't like it was one-sided.

I spun away. "Just stay away from my sister."

Silence. I turned back, but he was already gone.

Chapter Six

I slammed out of the Fudgy Delight. The broken door popped immediately open. I tromped back, bashed at the thing 'til it latched. Then I tramped down the street, hands thrust in pockets, sweating bullets. For which I was *glad*. The wretched summer heat matched my wretched, wet mood.

Damn strong, lusty men, anyway. Getting you all hot and riled, then lamming. That frustrated coupling at the police convention had by no means been the only big one that got away.

First time was senior year with Pieter Schmidt.

Like a sore tooth, I poked myself with memory. I'd been making out with Pieter in the back seat of his VW in our driveway. Dad and Brita weren't home. Gretchen was. She thought Pieter and I were burglars and got scared.

Other people's scared sisters would have run and hid, or called the cops.

Gretch turned the garden hose on us, full blast. Which wouldn't have been so bad except the VW's wiring was shot. The water shorted out every single electrical system on the car.

Wipers flipped, headlights flashed. The horn blared loud enough to wake the deaf.

Pieter nearly ripped off the door trying to escape. As he ran away, the whole neighborhood was mooned by his naked ass. I remember thinking Pieter had a nice butt.

Strongwell's butt would make Pieter's slink away in shame.

No. Not thinking about butts, especially not suspects' butts. I jammed my hands further into my pockets. Lights flashed red and bloody across my jeans. Surprised, I looked up. I had just passed Nieman's Bar.

My jaw clenched. I'd let my emotions drive me off-course. Resolutely, I headed back up Fifth.

Nieman's neon sign cast eerie red shadows on the walk. Shee-it. Freaky lighting. Murder scene nearby. I could be starring in a horror flick. Next there would be chittering violins.

I paused. Listened. Nothing. I kicked at a street post, welcomed the pain juddering through my toes. Obviously I had to put away my *Bedside Vampire Collection.* The clang reverberated on the sweltering night air, sounding almost like...a moan.

A low *male* moan. Followed immediately by a high feminine scream. I kicked into a run. Another scream sounded, *right on top of me.* I ground to a halt. Slapping hand to holster I scanned the streets. Candy store west. Alley and parking lot east. All dark, lifeless.

The movie heroine breathlessly surveys the area. The camera slowly pans front. The audience shrieks, "Look behind, look behind!"

But the idiot heroine never looks. The monster *leaps* out of nowhere to kill her.

I whirled. Nothing. Should have consulted my internal radar instead of my nerves. I released a sheepish breath.

The scream came again. Something scuttled in the shadowed alley. I sprinted toward it.

Only to be met by a swirl of darkness and stopped cold by a hard hand planted between my breasts.

"Detective. We can't keep meeting like this."

I looked up, and up. Thick blond hair, raw masculine planes. A body to stun a truck. One that had, only minutes before, stunned *me.* Bo Strongwell.

"What the hell are *you* doing here?" I couldn't believe it. If this really were a movie, it'd be *The Maintenance Man from the Black Lagoon.* Or with Bo's muscles, maybe *Blue Lagoon.* "Let me pass, Strongwell." I struggled to get by him.

"I thought you were returning to the station." He caught me by the waist. "It's dangerous to be out alone at night."

"I'm a *cop.* And I heard a scream."

I was no lightweight, but Bo simply lifted me off my feet.

I know fifty ways of subduing a suspect. Not one of them floated into my beleaguered brain at that moment. "Let go!" I destroyed any dignity I had by starting to flail.

"Get away from her," said a smoky baritone from the alley. I didn't recognize the voice. "The lady said no."

"*Bleh*! I just wanted a quickie. Don't hurt me, please," a second voice whimpered. "I wasn't doing anything wrong. Why should she not even give me a quickie? Please, *bleh*!"

That voice I knew. The loony vampire wannabe. "Count Crackula!"

"Crackula?" the baritone laughed. "Nailed him in one, didn't she?"

I stopped flailing long enough to home in on the voice. A well-built blond man emerged from the alley. Good grief, another Viking. He dragged Count Creepula by the fake vamp's cape strings. Fakeula dangled like a puppet from his hand.

Viking Two was almost as tall and almost as Krispy-Kreme handsome as Bo. He wore a leather vest over a sleeveless black tee. Dark blue jeans clung to muscled legs, fell over well-worn boots. His hair tumbled in ash-blond waves to the tops of his leather-clad shoulders. A diamond studded one ear, and rings decorated his fingers like brass knuckles. I expected tattoos but didn't see any.

Bo set me on my feet. Pointed at Viking Two. "Elena, this is Thorvald. He's my, um, assistant."

"A building manager needs an assistant?" What did this Thorvald guy do, stamp the rent checks before Bo deposited them?

"Strongwell?" Fakeula squeaked. "Oh, shit, no." He started struggling twice as hard.

"Stop that." Thor shook the smaller man until he looked like a Bobble-head.

"Don't hurt him, Thor." A very shapely shadow emerged from behind Viking Two. "He didn't get anywhere."

Out sauntered the most gorgeous female I'd ever seen. Glossy black hair rippled from a widows peak to the small of her back. Her red sequined gown swept the pavement seductively as she walked. The gown molded slim hips and exposed a depressingly huge, absurdly high bosom.

She walked with a grace that could knock out a bachelor at forty paces. Porn on a pair of stiletto heels. I'm not gay, but looking at her I could see why some women were.

"Hello, Bo," the woman said. Purred, actually. She had a voice like a vibrator set on "orgasm".

I dragged my eyes from Melinda Melons to slash Bo with a suspicious glare. If *I'd* been ogling Titzilla, Mr. Crotch-Rocket was probably eyeing her up like his favorite cold beer.

Surprisingly, Bo's baby blues were on me. They even crinkled a little at the corners, like he knew what I'd been thinking. Like he thought I was jealous.

I was emphatically *not* jealous. I cleared my throat, made a sound suspiciously like a harrumph. "I heard a scream."

"Oh, I'm afraid that was me," Elvira-on-steroids said. "I get a little enthusiastic with my clients." She waved one languid hand at...well, he might have been Studula a few minutes ago but he was Slackula now.

Except she was *lying.* Fakeula hadn't gotten anywhere with her. She'd said no and Thorvald had backed her up. I'd overheard them. But to my disgust, my internal lie meter stayed flat.

A flirty little tune tinkled on the night air. Calypso of some sort, coming from Fakeula's pocket. The small man flushed, shot a glance at Bo. Looking for permission to answer his phone? What was it with these people? Did they think Strongwell was King For a Day?

Bo nodded. Flakeula pulled out the phone, opened it. "*Bleh*?"

Which I guessed was fake vampire for "Hello".

Freakula's flush darkened to a dull red. "Yes, that was me." He turned away, lowered his voice. "But, master, I didn't mean to... Well, yes. It was what you asked for. To make trouble for him, but..." I could barely make out the words, must have gotten some of them wrong because they made no sense.

But one thing suddenly did. DD-lady. A hooker. Stunning. *Favorite.*

Who she must be hit me, and I grinned. "Nice to meet you—Drusilla. How'd you like to come to the police station with me?"

଴

"Yes, I was with Nappy Schrimpf Tuesday morning. I left him very...happy."

Happy Nappy. Now there was a Dr. Seuss book that could never be published.

Five forty-five a.m. Drusilla sat across a thick, scarred table from me in the police department conference room. With its tiled floor and institutional feel, it doubled as the interrogation room.

Actually, the lamp made the space triple-purpose. Different wattage for interrogation, conference, and lunch. We couldn't afford three rooms. We could afford the three-way bulb.

I sat under the lamp's highest setting, feeling every line of fatigue on my face. So far it had been a difficult, disappointing night.

My biggest disappointment? A hundred fifty watts didn't reveal a single wrinkle on Drusilla's perfect face, even after three hours of grilling. No fair that someone with bazooka boobs got sledgehammer-me-between-the-eyes features. At the very least she should have had split ends.

Life, I recalled, is rarely fair. I compensated best I could, with my snarliest cop glare. "So you're telling me Napoleon Schrimpf was fine when you left him?"

"Righter than rain. Sprawled in the driver's seat of his Audi, smoking one of those big cigars he likes. Nappy always did like a big smoke after the big slurp."

That was an image I could do without. "And you don't know anything about the puncture marks we found?" A TV detective would have sprung that information on her. Lured her into a trap. "Ah-ha! I didn't tell you he died of *puncture* wounds." But a TV detective didn't have Dolly Barton's Gossip Network to contend with. Half the city already knew as much or more than I did.

"Puncture marks?" Drusilla's mile-long lashes swept upward. I really hoped they were fake. But when she blinked, the curving sweep told me they were not only real, but un-mascara-ed. *So* not fair. She blinked again. "I have no idea how he got puncture marks, Detective O'Rourke."

I put aside envy to concentrate. Lying, or not?

For the life of me, I couldn't tell. Not a ping on my internal meter. I squared my shoulders. Gonna have to do this the hard way. "You were the last person to see Napoleon Schrimpf alive."

"Probably." She shrugged, a graceful lifting of one semi-bare shoulder. "We finished at one forty-five. According to Dolly, he was dead by two a.m. Not even Nappy could find another blow in that time."

I jumped on that. The time, not the blow. "One forty-five? Not one forty-six or one forty-seven? Or even ten to two? How do you know so exactly?"

Drusilla pulled a compact out of her purse, considered her reflection. "I am a professional, Detective O'Rourke. How can I make money if I don't keep to schedule?" She patted powder on her nose.

I considered it. If she was telling the truth, somewhere between one forty-five and two a.m. Schrimpf had left the parking lot, bled to death and then—what? Walked back?

Not likely. But I couldn't prove or disprove it. I needed to find the actual site of the murder. If her timetable was accurate, it was somewhere in a seven-minute radius. Otherwise, I'd have a new number-one suspect.

"All right, Drusilla, you can go." Turning to a fresh page in my notebook, I tossed it to the table in front of her. "But I'll need your full name, address and phone number, in case I have further questions."

Her eyes slid away from the mirror, and her cheeks colored. "Certainly, Detective O'Rourke." She looked everywhere but me or the notebook. "Bo had business cards made up for me. They're in my coat. If you'll just wait here...?"

I blinked. WTF? Her uneasiness was telling. Her cards—especially who made them—were a shock. Their location was a lie. Who wore a coat in this heat?

She was trying to pull something, and I wasn't going to let her get away with it. I opened my mouth to stop her.

In that blink, Drusilla was gone.

I leaped to my feet. Angry that *another* suspect had gotten away, sure, that was it. I certainly wasn't boiling mad that *Bo* had *business cards* made for her. Certainly didn't care... Fuck. When? Why?

I was going to find out. I dashed after her.

And ran into a gangly, rumpled blue chest.

"Detective Ma'am! What a surprise!" A blue cap with bright yellow bill peered at me. Duck in a uniform.

"Yeah, uh, Officer...Ruffles, wasn't it? I'm kind of in a hurry, so if you'll just move..." I slid to the side.

He slid with me. Or actually, sort of clumped. "Isn't this amazing? I was just saying to myself, Detective O'Rourke is on third shift. *I'm* on third shift. I wonder if I'll see her here some day? Of course I just started third shift. I was on first shift, but I switched so I could watch Oprah. Now I'm on third shift and can watch Oprah and you're on third shift and I wondered if I'd see you, and here you are."

The boy had the lung capacity of a whale. He finally took a breath and I jumped in quick. "Brilliant deduction, Officer. Now, if you'll excuse me—"

"How is the case going, Detective Ma'am? The murder of Napoleon Schrimpf?" He practically quacked in excitement.

Ruffles had been first on the scene. I probably owed him something. It wouldn't take long to fill him in. And in a three-mile-radius city, where could Drusilla really hide? Besides, Ruffles was blocking me like a Bulls guard. "I just talked with the last person to see Schrimpf alive. I have other suspects, but—"

"How exciting! Your own murder case. Better almost than watching Oprah. I love Oprah. She's so smart. And so are you. I bet you have lots of cases, don't you Detective Ma'am? But this murder is the biggie. My uncle said that can make or break a career. By solving a murder case. Well, I suppose that would make a detective's career. Not solving it would break it. But I know you'll solve this one."

"Thanks for your confidence. Now if you'll excuse me, I have to be going." I edged around him, toward the door.

Dirk Ruffles followed, close enough to be a second skin, talking all the way. "I'd love to see how it's done. A murder investigation, that is. I bet if we worked together, you could teach me a lot."

"Maybe. But really, Officer Ruffles. I'm going, er, someplace. Someplace I need to go by *myself*. Alone."

"Sure! I'll come with you!" He grinned brightly at me.

I grinned back. My grin floated in the air a full five seconds after I whirled and clipped as fast as humanly possible to the ladies' john. Cowardly, I know. But I was desperate.

Dirk Ruffles loped along behind me, jabbering the whole way. He kept talking even when I opened the restroom door.

"Officer? Uh, I have to go...in here."

"Sure. Go right ahead. My uncle says I'll be a detective some day and you're really smart so I'm sure you could teach me..."

I ducked into the ladies' room.

And shrieked when the door opened behind me.

"...could teach me a lot. So where are we going first? Should I take my gun? It's locked in my uncle's safe right now but if I explain what it's for—"

"Ruffles!" I grabbed him and wrestled him bodily out the door. We were the same height and I probably had more muscle and more training, but it took every bit of it to get him out of that restroom. Not because of his strength. Think of trying to flick off a booger. You'll get very close to the sensation of getting Dirkenstein out of the ladies' bathroom.

I muscled him out, drove the door shut, and held it. His muffled voice continued on the other side. "...I'll have to get the bullets too. My uncle keeps those in the lockbox at his bank..."

Frantically, I glanced around the room. I'd used the first-floor john a hundred times but had never really seen it. Three stalls, vanity, sink and mirror. Two papers taped to the mirror. One was a wanted poster, unsolved TP-ing of the mayor's house. The other—hey, Blatzky still had those three Golden Retriever puppies for sale...dammit, focus. Single light fixture. A wooden doorstop in the corner.

And a window. Thank heavens.

I jammed the doorstop under the door. Fled to the window and jerked it open. The door creaked behind me. I threw a panicked look over my shoulder.

The door cracked open. Dirk Ruffles's voice floated through, clearer. His fingers wrapped around the edge. The door opened wider. *He was coming.* Like a horror movie. Like winter. Dirkenstein was coming. The doorstop slipped—a leg came through.

Freaked, I wedged through the window. Scrambled out. My pants snagged on the latch. I was *caught.* A frenzy of wriggling did *nothing.*

"Detective Ma'am?" The muddy rasp followed me like a curse. "Where are you...?"

My pocket finally ripped. It flapped in the wind as I ran away.

As I fled, er, beat a strategic retreat, my cell phone rang. I swore, snapped it out. Unknown number.

Pacing the sidewalk, I worked to get my breathing under control. When I wasn't in danger of hurking all over the phone, I flipped it open. "O'Rourke."

There was a dead space. Then, "Elena O'Rourke." The voice was hollow and faint, like an old guy with his head in a tin can.

Pause, echoey, and asking for me by name even though I'd identified myself. Telemarketer. Should have put my cell on the National Do Not Call list. "Whatever you're selling, buddy, I don't want any."

"I am not selling anything, Elena O'Rourke. I am giving you information."

"Right. What's this information going to cost me?"

"This is free advice, Elena O'Rourke. Watch Strongwell."

Speak of the devil. "That's the third time you've used my name, pal, but you haven't spilled yours."

"Watch him closely, Elena O'Rourke. If you wish to solve your murder case."

"Look, who is this?"

"Who I am does not matter. Only that you keep careful watch on Strongwell, Elena O'Rourke. Or else."

"I don't take anonymous threats too kindly, buddy."

There was a sound like a growl. "I am—" and I didn't quite catch the first name but it sounded like Lorne, "—Ruthven. Watch Strongwell, Elena O'Rourke. You will discover your killer."

"Listen, Ruthven. Are you saying Bo is the mur—damn." The call had ended.

But there it was, of course. A lead. A hot steer that said Bo was the murderer.

And in my gut...I didn't buy it.

Dammit all. My strength as a cop was following the rules. The rules said smoke meant fire. Ruthven had practically accused Strongwell of the murder. I myself had found Strongwell nearby, just after the murder.

So why did my cop sense say *no*?

I kicked a street post. Left leg, this time, so I banged a different set of toes. The pain helped me concentrate.

Of *course* I didn't believe Ruthven. Why should I? I didn't know squat about him. He could be a cheat or a thief. He could be the murderer himself, for all I knew.

So I hit speed-dial for dispatch. "Alice. I need a trace. A phone call to my cell, just now."

"On it." Keys clicked rapidly. "While I've got you on the line. Do you have plans for your day off? Not work. Fun plans?"

Fun. I'd met Alice my second day on the job, when she invited me over for tea. We'd had a nice conversation about police procedure. The next time I came she served the tea with a couple jiggers of brandy and by the time I left we were the bestest of best friends. Since then it was like she'd made me her special loosen-up-Elena project. She was always after me to go bowling, or out for drinks, or to join her at the nude beach (since Alice looks like the old *Night Court* bailiff, that's an image). "Probably watch some tube. Have you got the number yet?"

"Almost. *CSI*?"

"Naturally." And *Angel*, although I kept that secret. "The number?"

"Yes. I've got it. I'm looking up the name." More key clacking. "Why don't we go see a movie instead? You need to loosen up more." (See what I mean?) "You're so like your father. He was always working too."

"You knew my father?"

"Sure. The law enforcement community here's pretty small. I knew both Patrick and Brita. I could tell you stories...damn."

"What?"

"I've got the name."

I shoved the phone under my chin, yanked out notebook and pencil. "Shoot."

"CIC Mutual. An insurance company in the Loop. They do my homeowner's."

I nearly dropped the phone. "Downtown Chicago?"

"That's right. What's going on, Elena?"

"I'm not sure. Thanks, Alice." I shut the phone and slid it into my pocket.

Ruthven was legit. But why would an insurance guy from Chicago be interested in a murder in small-town Meiers Corners? Not just interested, but curious enough to get the cell phone number of the lead detective on the case? Did CIC carry Schrimpf's life insurance? Or maybe they covered his gym?

Maybe I should consider Ruthven's tip seriously. It wasn't like I had a lot of other hard leads. But my instinct, honed by experience, guided by intelligence said Bo wasn't the killer.

It did say Ruthven was an ass.

Of course, my cop sense also said Bo was dangerous. But I was sure he didn't do the murder...almost.

Business cards, though. That was another story.

Chapter Seven

"Open up!" I pounded on the door of Bo's apartment building. It smelled like cedar, its handle and hinges gleamed like gold. The rising sun sparkled and refracted through the glass like it was crystal. That door practically screamed money.

I didn't care. He'd made her *cards*. "Strongwell! I want to talk to you!"

The door swung open. A shocked face capped by silver hair greeted me. I'd forgotten about the butler. "Ms. O'Rourke?"

I didn't like scaring him. But I muscled past anyway. "Where's Strongwell?"

"The master is downstairs." Butler Guy sounded scandalized that I would even ask.

"The master, huh? You've been watching too much BBC, Jeeves."

"The name is Butler, miss."

"And what do you do for a living? *Buttle*?" Tim Curry was such a hoot in the old movie *Clue*. A sexy hoot, if there is such a thing. "Well, Butler, I want to talk to Strongwell. Don't bother seeing me down. I'll find my way." I started toward the stairs.

"Miss! You can't!"

"Yeah? Give me one good reason." I searched around the staircase I'd used to visit my sister. It went up. There was no obvious way down.

"Miss, please don't." Jeeves was close to panicking.

"Where's the damn stairs?"

"Right in front of you, Detective." Bo Strongwell glided down the front staircase with the muscular grace of a wild animal. His dark satin voice slid over my angry nerve endings like fingers tweaking an engorged nipple.

I glared. Shit! What was it about this guy that sent me into vibrator land? "Jeeves said you were *down*stairs."

"I was. I had to check on a problem." He left me hanging as to whether he'd gone down to check the problem, lived down and had gone *up* to check the problem, or was downstairs and had come up here because...hey, *I* was the problem.

My cheeks heated. "I have some questions for you, buster." The "buster" got a gasp out of Jeeves.

"I'm sure you do." Bo didn't lose an ounce of smooth. "But I'm rather busy at the moment." He rested his hand gracefully on the round end of the banister. "I don't suppose..."

"No. Don't suppose. Talk. Drusilla—"

"Detective, much as I'd like to—"

I raised my voice to override him. "She told me a very interesting fact. That you and she—"

"Detective O'Rourke, please. It would be better if you'd come back later." Bo's hand clenched on the newel post.

"It would be better if you answer *now*." I stalked toward him, jaw set, mega cop face on. "And it's either talk here—alone—or I'll pull you down to the station. Your choice."

Another gasp came from Jeeves. A glance showed him fluttering behind me like a striped-vested butterfly. "Detective O'Rourke, please! Master Bo is not to be threatened like that."

Bo's hand came off the post, waved a resigned stop. "Don't upset yourself, Mr. Butler. The detective is most determined. We'll use the parlor."

"But sir..."

"Thank you, Mr. Butler. That will be all."

The silver head bowed stiffly and Butler left. What was it with these people? Calling a building super "master" and kowtowing like he was some sort of royalty?

"This way, Detective." With a sigh, Bo glided around the corner, opened a door. "So. How goes the investigation?"

"I'm asking the questions." I followed him into a room—and dropped my molars on the floor. One by one, *plink-plink*, like "Endearing Young Charms" onto a Bugs Bunny xylophone.

I had imagined the building jammed with small units like my sister's. Residential cubicles. Bo led me into something that was definitely not a cubicle, too striking even to be merely a "room". It was—a chamber. A frilly blue-and-ivory chamber loaded with stuffed sofas, plush chairs, glossy end tables and crowned by a redbrick fireplace with marble mantle.

A *parlor.*

"This is just creepy." I gaped from the doorway. Nobody had rooms like this any more. They died in the eighteen hundreds. Archeologists dug up their bones.

"It's meant to be inviting," Bo said dryly. "For company."

"If you were born in the Renaissance."

"Not my time." He led me to what was too small for a sofa, too big for a chair.

Following, I got a lungful of hot, exotic male. Reminded myself of *cards*. "Right." I sat. "Drusilla."

"Can I get you some refreshment first? Wine, perhaps? I have a nice Pinot Noir." Bo moved restlessly to a walnut cabinet in the far corner. Opened a small carved door to display a wine rack full of bottles.

"At six thirty in the morning?"

He glanced at me. "For you, it's the end of the evening. Your shift's over."

"I'm still working. So thanks, but no."

"Coffee, then." Shutting the cabinet, he pushed a button next to a speaker on the wall. "Coffee, please, Mr. Butler."

"Right away, sir," came through the grill. I rolled my eyes.

Moments later Butler bustled in with a silver tray. He set it on the polished little end table next to me and clicked paper-thin china cups onto gold-trimmed saucers, then poured rich, steaming coffee from a slender silver pot.

During this production, Bo floated gracefully toward the window. He pulled aside heavy Damask draperies to peer out. After Butler left, Bo said, "Bright morning."

"Yeah, and the weather's fine. Would you stop playing nomad and sit? You avoiding me, or something?"

He let the curtain drop. His shoulders tensed, then, with a roll, I saw him consciously relax.

When he turned, his expression was carefully neutral. But his nostrils were flared and his eyes were that vivid violet. "Of course Detective. I live but to serve." He sauntered over and sat.

Right. Next. To. Me.

"Erk," I said.

He picked up my coffee. "So. You have some questions." As he handed me my cup his thigh pressed intimately along mine.

Questions? Yeah, like could he please dial down the body heat? And like, what the hell kind of cologne he was wearing, Raging Hormones No. Five? "Who *exactly* is Drusilla?" I managed. Before I could stop myself I added, "And what's she to you?"

Bo shrugged, a gesture curiously as graceful as the Happy Nappy Hooker. "Besides living in the same city? Nothing."

"I don't believe that. You know her. She knew you."

"Not because I'm a customer." His amusement was clear. "I know a number of people in the city, Detective. And I have many connections."

"I'm sure you do." I drank coffee. My eyelids peeled back. Was this coffee or black hole in a cup? It took a couple of held breaths to step my heart rate down from hummingbird. "Like Dracula?"

Bo picked up his own cup, took a cautious sip. "He isn't really Dracula, of course."

How big a chump did he think I was? My mouth opened to spout something flip—when my brain kicked in. Bo Strongwell, even if he was a grunt, had proved himself a particularly *sharp* grunt. Cape man was not Dracula. I knew that. He knew that. I knew he knew I knew... Skip it. Anyway, why state the obvious?

To see if I believed it? Or to make certain I didn't? "Are you sure? He had the fangs."

"I'm sure. I've met the real one."

Dracula was a fictional character. I waited for a ping on my internal lie meter. Even kidding would register as a small lie. A teasing lie, a fib.

Nothing.

I drank more coffee to cover my confusion. Nearly went into cardiac arrest. Put the cup down on the silver tray, wincing when it rattled. A couple more deep breaths helped the caffeine overdose, but the scent of powerful male sent me reeling.

So I held my breath and waited for my system to settle down. For my lie meter to kick in.

Still nothing.

Well, damn. My lie detector has been a constant my whole life. It had never failed me. I could read anyone.

Now no ping, *nada*. I was going to demand a refund. Twenty-six years of trouble-free operation, then bang! Two different people blank on the meter in the last two days. Bo and Dru.

Beauty and the Bo. I wondered if they were connected.

I wondered if there was a warranty. Knowing my luck, it was twenty-five years.

At that point I had to breathe or pass out. I sucked in air. Crisp, male-laden, tongue lolling—ye gods. I swallowed hard. Maybe I was asking the wrong questions. Something simple, that was it. Kidding, fibbing, way too complex. I had to ask him something straight and personal, Magic-Eight-Ball easy. Name, that was good. I was curious anyway. "What's Bo short for? Beauregard?"

He smiled. My toes curled. His smile broadened. "It's just Bo, Detective. Not short for anything."

I waited, breathing as shallowly as possible. But aside from the toe-curling...no reaction. No ping, either lying or not. Not even a "maybe—ask again later".

What did it mean?

"You're the detective. Why don't you look it up?"

I blinked. Had he just answered my *mental* question?

No, impossible. I must have said it out loud. No one could read minds. Especially not a grunt, no matter how sharp.

Then he added, "Or maybe you can...ask again later."

Freaky. If he wasn't reading my mind, he already knew me so well he could guess my thoughts. Either made me really uncomfortable, though for different reasons. I jumped to my feet. "Thanks for the coffee. But, um, gotta go."

Bo's eyes darkened. "Sit down, Detective."

"Um, why?"

"Because I want to kiss you again."

"I don't think—"

"Then *don't* think." He snared my wrist, yanked.

My knees buckled. I sat. He cupped my face with one hand. Big and strong, it cradled me from chin to temple. His lips descended until they were a breath from mine.

Apparently the Hulk It was still working its magic. And now that we were on a soft couch, not a hard wooden floor...I caught at his hand. "No biting." I meant it to sound sharp. It came out breathy.

"No?" Bo's teeth closed gently on my lower lip. Teased. "I got the impression you liked it."

"I hammered your gut. You call that liking it?"

"You pulled your punch, Detective." Bo's lips feathered along my cheek. "And my abdominal muscles are quite strong."

"Yeah." I slapped my other hand over my mouth. Wiped off drool.

"I barely felt it." He kissed along my jaw. "The reaction I meant was your big shudder, not your little tap."

I muffled a groan. "You think I climaxed from a bite? You've got one swelled head, buster."

He took my hand put it on his zipper. "*Two*, actually." Mr. Monster was swimming in Loch Ness.

My groan unmuffled. "Look, Strongwell. I'm *working*."

"Consider this a coffee break." He nibbled down my neck.

I swatted at him. "Would you stop with the neck thing? What is this, Dracula II? The Apartment Manager of Dracula?"

Bo found the top button on my shirt. Opened it and licked my collarbone. The man had a tongue like a cat, all warm and rough. "Do you want it to be?"

"No." My fingers twined in his thick hair. Probably gave him the wrong impression, like I was greedy for him to bite me or something. So I tried to explain. "I don't like knives and I don't like needles and..." Something floated across my brain. Something related to the case.

"Do you like this?" Bo opened another button and cupped my breasts, plumping them up into the opening. Kissed the tops, hot little butterflies dancing over my skin.

Any sane thought flitted away. "I...I don't know." A few kisses and I was panting. If I'd been thinking, I'd've been thoroughly demoralized. I was so far from thinking I actually leaned into him, encouraging him.

His thumbs flicked my nipples through the bra. Electricity zapped what few synapses still functioned. I gasped. "Fuck."

"I agree." Male satisfaction filled his voice. His tongue worked the tops of my breasts between kisses. "Damn, Elena. You taste so good." The sharp edge of teeth skated over my skin.

"Stop with the biting!" I whacked his cheek but my hand had gone weak, crumbling against his chiseled bone like an oatmeal cookie.

It didn't help that my five-year underfed pussy was jumping up and down yelling *if she doesn't want it, bite* me!

The teeth were replaced by a tongue. A warm, clever tongue, dipping into my bra and finding all my most sensitive places. Cleavage, tops, sides. Bo breathed on my skin and it *sang.*

"Stop it." I panted. "Bo—"

"I like that, Detective. I like hearing you say my name." He slipped a hand into the cup of my bra, palmed the nipple. His caress sent sparks through my breast. "Say my name again. I want to hear you *moan* it."

He peeled back the bra and latched onto my nipple with his hot mouth. Suckled. The sparks hit the step-up and fried me into cinders.

"*Bo.*" To my dismay, I moaned.

"You smell so good, Elena. Great Freyja, you taste even better." He bared the other breast, swept his tongue over the peak until it hardened like rock candy. His fingers were hot pincers working my other nipple. "So sweetly responsive. You're so excited. I can hear your heart pounding."

He opened his mouth. His hot breath inflamed me. His teeth scraped my sensitive skin.

I shuddered. My fingers wound in his hair.

Which meant when he bit me, I nearly ripped him bald.

"Nuts!" I tore him from my breast. He got a couple licks in before I pushed him away as far as I could. On the couchlet, it was all of six inches. "What the hell do you think you're doing? I said no biting."

Bo wouldn't look at me. He stared at my breasts, his mouth working, his fingers gouging grooves into the back of the couch.

His intense stare unnerved me. I suddenly remembered double-D Drusilla and covered my Thank-Goodness-It-Fits Near-Bs with my hands.

"Don't," Bo growled.

"Don't what?"

"Don't be ashamed. Your breasts are beautiful."

"How the hell...?" How did he know what I was thinking?

And did he really think my boobs were beautiful?

It was stupid, it was insane, and it was just what I needed to regain my balance. I nudged my tits back into their cuppy homes. "Then why bite a hole in them? There's no creamy filling, I can assure you."

At that, Bo finally looked up at me. His eyes softened to a warm blue and they crinkled at the corners. "Matter of taste."

"Yeah, well, I don't want you tasting—" I looked down.

No bite mark. Not even a bruise.

I'd *felt* teeth. I'd felt the knife-edge tang that meant punctured flesh. Was I going crazy?

I must have been, because even after all that, when he slipped his fingers into my hair and kissed me lightly on the lips, I let him.

"You're right," Bo murmured against my mouth. "I apologize. I got carried away. You do that to me." He nudged my thigh with his leg. The motor started all over again.

I held back a groan, only to have it slip out when he circled his palm over my nipple. He kissed lightly down my neck. I moaned. His teeth nibbled...and we were right back where we started!

I leaped up from the couchlet, wondering if it was coated with Spanish Fly. It *couldn't* be me. "What the heck is this piece of furniture, anyway?

Bo's perfect lips curved. "A love seat."

Figured.

ଔଌ

Seven a.m. I paused with a forkful of Denver omelet halfway to my mouth. As casually as I could, I asked, "So what's with you and your building super?"

Gretchen and I were at the Caffeine Café. They had "Breakfast All Day" but we O'Rourke girls were contrary. We were eating it—gasp!—in the morning.

Before Steve died, Gretch and I had a weekly get-together here. After, she hadn't wanted to meet. I was giving her space, so I shrugged it off.

Now, if she was dating, she was eating, dammit.

A look of surprise brushed her face. "Me and Bo Stron...nothing. Nothing at all's going on. Hey, did I tell you Carla Donner called from New York the other day? Out of the blue. You remember Carla. She was one of my best friends in grade school."

I could read a lie on almost any face in the universe. With my sister, I could *smell* it.

Or maybe that was just my hash browns. I dug into them, fried golden and crispy. "C'mon, Gretchen, it's me. Big sis. You don't have to be coy. Strongwell's good looking." Great looking, actually, especially his big, muscular...everything. "And a widow's got *needs*, after all."

"Just what do you mean by that?"

"Well, nothing. Except you know what you're missing."

Gretchen stabbed omelet. "Oh, for heaven's sake. Elena, just because I turned that garden hose on you in high school is no reason to be catty. Besides, Pieter Schmidt wasn't right for you."

"That didn't come out right. I just want you to know you don't have to lie to me about Strongwell." I poked at my hash browns. "Although I don't think he's right for you, either. But it'd be perfectly natural if you were doing him."

"Doing...?" Gretchen dropped her fork. "Elena, I'm *not* sleeping with Bo."

"Why not? Is he married?"

Oddly enough, that seemed to shock her even more. "No, of course not."

Thank goodness for that. I'd hate to have been interested in...for my *sister* to have been interested in a married guy. "Gay?"

"For heaven's sake, Elena. He's not married, gay or anything but perfectly, absolutely normal." She picked up butter knife and toast, slapped about an inch of butter on.

Her tone was indignant, but underneath I could hear something off. She was lying. But about what? Married or gay? Or—not absolutely normal?

I didn't think Bo was married. My nipples didn't think he was gay. Which meant Bo was...not normal?

"What's going on, Gretch? With him, with you? You're acting strange, you know." A beat, and I hit her with, "Who exactly is Strongwell that you *bow* to him?"

Her knife hand fell slowly to the table. Surprise, denial and dismay crossed her face. And finally *busted.*

"What's going on? Well." Gretchen started playing with her toast, breaking it into tiny bits. "Things have been hard for me since Steve died."

"I know. But you have to talk to me, Gretch. Please." I watched more toast-mangling. "Pretty please with pus on it?" When even that didn't get a smile, I put down my fork. "C'mon, Gretch. I'm your sister. You can trust me."

Impulsively I took her hands. Released them, wiped butter from my fingers and took them again. "I only want to help."

"Do you? Really?" Her eyes rose, strangely pleading. "Then drop your case."

"My *case*?"

"The murder. Please, Elena. You said you want to help. That

would help."

"Gretch, I can't. And even if I could... Why are you protecting Strongwell? Do you care about him?"

She blanched white. "Of course not, Elena. He means absolutely nothing to me."

My lie meter pegged.

Chapter Eight

That morning I had my six-week trim at Dolly Barton's Curl Up and Dye.

Dolly's had been part of Meiers Corners forever. The salon was part of what made the Corners unique. Part of why, though our little city had been swallowed long ago by the great whale of Chicago, we hadn't been digested. Like Jonah. Or old chewing gum. Um, yeah.

Corners people found everything they needed in the Corners. We had our own art museum, lumber yard, newspaper and truck line. Our own local blood center, part of the Hemoglobin Society. We even had our own symphony orchestra, consisting of three violins, a flute and a tuba.

But mostly we were our own city because Meiers Corners had the greatest communications system known to man—Dolly Barton.

To say Dolly was the town gossip was like saying the Bush and Clinton families had minor political aspirations. Dolly knew *every*thing that went on, sometimes even before it happened. The *Corners Times* editor got most of his news tips from Dolly during his weekly eyebrow trim.

Dolly herself was a seventy-year-old platinum-blonde dynamo. She was four foot eight, forty-two D and looked exactly like the country singer except older and shorter. Like a Dolly Parton Mini-Me. She wore pink fifties diner-style uniforms and chewed a wad of gum as big as your head.

A tinkling bell announced my arrival. "Hey sugar," Dolly greeted me. She called everyone sugar. "I'll be right with you. Just have a seat." She rattled a can of hair spray. Holding one hand flat over her current customer's face, she sprayed a typhoon with the other. I recognized Mrs. Schmidt of the PTA under the lacquered helmet of hair.

I settled in the waiting area. The chairs were covered in hide of dead nauga. *Pink*. I picked up a magazine announcing Dewey had won the presidency. Well, not really, but you get the picture.

"All righty, sugar. You're up." Dolly swept hair while Mrs. Smith counted out singles.

I set the magazine down and made my way over. The only article that caught my interest was "How to Get More Sex on Those Busy Weekdays". I had to get "some" sex before I could get "more". Although, thinking of Bo, the man who probably had sex tattooed on his ultra-tight buttocks—

Dolly clicked scissors. "What are we doing today?"

I cleared my throat. "Just a trim, Dolly. Hey, have you ever heard of Hulk It Perfume?"

"Sure. Five hundred an ounce. I don't carry it, but I can order some."

"Five hundred? *Dollars*?" I might have gasped it.

"Need some oxygen, sugar?"

"Uh, no." Damn. I had liked bringing out Bo's testosterone monster. Well, except for the biting. I thought maybe...but not at five hundred dollars an ounce. Not for a glorified janitor.

"Sit." Dolly pointed to the chair in front of the shampoo sink. As I sat she swirled a cape around my neck. "Heard you fielded the Schrimpf case."

Even for Dolly, that was fast. "I only caught it yesterday morning. How did you find out?"

Dolly slapped shampoo on my head and worked it in like she was mixing bread. "Police Chief Dirkson was here for a mustache wax. He's counting on you to solve it quick-like."

"Oh goody. No pressure."

"Don't you worry, sugar." She snapped gum. "If anyone can solve it, you can. Those O'Rourke genes. Though it's pretty big stuff, a murder."

"Especially when the chief wants it solved yesterday," I muttered.

"*Big*." She laughed. "Isn't that a hoot? If anyone *wasn't* big, it was Napoleon Schrimpf. Neither above or below, if you get my drift."

"Uh, Dolly..."

"They say size don't matter. But it sure does, sugar. It matters a lot. I know from experience." She hauled me up from the basin, wrapped a towel around my head. "Now that Schrimpf, he was as small as a ten-cent vibrator."

My face heated. "Dolly, I don't think we should be talking about his peni—"

"I mean head size, sugar." She winked. "C'mon over here." She towed me to the main chair. Unwrapping the towel, she flicked it into a pink laundry hamper. "Now I see a lot of heads. A lot. And I know what I'm saying."

"That, uh, size matters."

"You betcha. They say it's how much the brain wrinkles. But I know heads. Take yours for example." She circled my skull with her hands. The scissors stuck up from her fingers like metal feathers. In the mirror I looked like some weird sort of primitive warrior.

Dolly cracked gum. "This is a good head. Healthy hair, nice rock-solid skull. And big."

I wasn't sure if that was a compliment or not.

"This is the head of a smart, honest person."

"Um, thanks."

"Napoleon Schrimpf? That was the skull of a money-grubbing cheapskate."

I was beginning to get her drift. "He didn't tip?"

"Not a red cent." Dolly pulled up sections of my hair, clipped them out of the way. "He was a small man, sugar. Inside and out. That's why he had so many hookers. To make up for the size of his pecker."

"Dolly!" I knew the words, but it was embarrassing to discuss with a woman who'd cut and styled my mom, my step-mom and both my grandmas. "Let's not gossip."

"Not gossip. Fact. He came in here for a weekly shave. And it wasn't his chin, if you know what I mean."

I remembered Schrimpf's naked genitals. Now that I thought about it, he had been hairless—"Dolly!"

"This is a full service salon, sugar." She put a saucy emphasis on *full.*

Okay. I was a cop. I could handle this. "All right, then. If you shaved Schrimpf, ah, personally, maybe you can answer a question for me. Did he have any unusual...body piercing? You know, like maybe a ring...or something...through his..." Damn. I could swear like a college freshman but for some reason talking genitalia was dirty. I swallowed, forced myself not to be a pansy. "Scrotum?"

She popped gum. "Napoleon Schrimpf? Nope. Not that I didn't suggest it. We're a full—"

"—full service salon," I finished for her, shuddering slightly. I wanted to know everything, but I didn't want to know *everything.* "So last time you saw him, he didn't have any...punctures? In his sac?"

"Punctures? Plural?" Dolly stopped cutting.

"Yeah, two. Why, you know something?" I caught her eyes in the mirror. Wide, pupils shut down to pinpricks. "What? What is it?"

"Nothing." Dolly stepped behind me, my mass of curls hiding her face. "Absolutely *nothing.* Did you hear about Bonnie Titus? Drove her husband's new Porsche into Lake Michigan. How he affords to keep that woman in cars and still get four-hundred-dollar haircuts in Chicago—"

Dolly had been chatting amiably. Gossiping, her life-blood. And she'd snapped it off like a tourniquet. "Dolly? Is something wrong?

Schrimpf—"

Dolly snatched up the hair dryer. Turned it on to its loudest setting—which happened to be *fry*.

Talking over it was difficult. Hearing was impossible. I made one more attempt while I paid but she refused to say a word.

And she handed back my tip. When I got home, I saw why.

A frazzled halo floated around my face. My hair looked like Doc Brown, Einstein and Beakman all rolled into one.

I sighed. Then I fetched a bucket and filled it with ten bottles of conditioner. Before I stuck my head in I gathered a stack of magazines. This was going to take a while.

ঔ

That night I was up and out the door at seven, eager to solve the case. I headed straight for the cop shop, anticipating the medical examiner's full report would be on my desk.

The report was on my desk, all right. Under Detective Gruen's loafers. He was yakking on the phone.

Since it was Gruen's phone *and* desk until nine, I couldn't justify knocking his size tens off. So I wasted some time rearranging stuff around them. I moved three sets of framed pictures, Lieutenant Roet's wife and eight children, me and my family, and Gruen's mother and their six Great Danes. I stole some peanuts from the ever-present box of Cracker Jacks Gruen used as a paperweight. Munched as I dusted under the calming desk fountain Roet had installed after the birth of kid number five. I putzed around for a good fifteen minutes, but Gruen never noticed me.

So I chanced gently tugging the report out from under his heels. He must have had concrete in the soles. Those feet weren't moving without a semi.

Gruen chuckled. "Wanna meet when I get off, Lana?

Lana? Gruen was talking to one of Meiers Corners' high-flying Ls? I lost it. I shoved at his dogs, hard.

He glared at me, barked, "Get out of here, woman! This isn't your damned desk until nine." His tone abruptly changed, became sweet and beguiling. "No, sweetheart, not you. I'm talking to O'Rourke."

But his feet never moved.

I said, "Look, I just want the ME's report."

"Not 'til nine! And if you don't stop hovering, I'll put in for overtime."

I left, frustrated. Tramping the sidewalk, I kicked random street posts, which hurt my toes. I'd have rather kicked weeds or garbage, but there weren't any because this was Meiers Corners. Cleanliness wasn't a pastime, it was a neurosis.

I trundled by Nieman's Bar, questioned a few regulars, but didn't catch anything new except a bra in the face. Come to think of it, that wasn't even new—Granny Butt's lingerie was manufactured in the forties, probably by Boeing alongside their B-17s. Then I tried walking Main but hooker row was strangely deserted. Or maybe not so strangely. Not only was it sweltering, it was early on a weekday. Most of Meiers Corners' ho's were part time.

All that activity only took me until eight. The widow Schrimpf wouldn't be home until after ten and my desk wouldn't be free for another hour. There was nothing for me to do except work up a sweat.

My tee was already damp despite a shower and antiperspirant slapped on with a trowel. I thought about going home to change, remembered what happened the last time I started home, and decided to go check on my sister. Just to see if she was all right. Really.

As I crossed Jefferson I heard a *foosh* of water that sounded like a gigantic toilet overflowing. Remembering Pookie, I broke into a run. Lincoln hove into view, and with it, a geyser.

Not a real geyser. An open yellow fire hydrant gushed water all over the street and over a passel of shrieking, giggling kids.

Smack dab in the middle of the kids was Bo Strongwell, wearing nothing but cut-off jeans and acres of sleek, wet skin.

Bo was tossing children into the spray, splashing them, picking them up and whirling them through the stream of water. His muscles gleamed under the street light, big honed steel cables, working easily. Massive pecs spread across his chest like eagle wings. His shoulders, broad enough to support a skyscraper, were plenty broad to support the couple of kids he tossed on top of them.

He turned, large hands anchoring the laughing children on his shoulders, face split in a huge grin, and saw me.

The grin leveled out to that sensuous curve. "Detective. What are you doing here?" His belly worked as he spoke, clenching and releasing in a way that made my own stomach clench in tandem.

"Hunting up witnesses. Suspects."

"Am I a witness or suspect?"

"You're suspicious," I admitted. "But in this case, I was in the neighborhood and thought I'd check on Gretchen and Stella."

"They just went in." He slid the children gently off his shoulders. They joined the other kids running around the open hydrant.

I tossed a hand at the gushing water. "What's this?"

"Didn't you hear? It's because of the heat. A lot of the older housing isn't properly air conditioned. The city's opening hydrants all over the north side of town. Heat relief."

"Your building's got air."

"True. But I thought someone should be out with the kids." He shrugged, his massive shoulders two delicious scoops of ice cream I wanted to lick.

I gritted my teeth. Sure, I needed to get laid, but I didn't have to say buh-bye to my dignity because of it. "At night?"

"There are kids' programs at the library and schools during the day."

"Oh. Well, I just came by to check on Gretch. I guess if she's okay, I should head back to the station."

"You're more than welcome to join us, Detective." His lips curved invitingly.

I thought about it. It *was* hot. Might be kind of fun to splash a little. Play in the spray with big semi-naked Viking guy, getting wet...ooh, wet...my shirt sticking, my nipples rising... I felt the prickling fullness that signaled my nipply fantasy was becoming fact. *Adios,* dignity. Or at least until I got that padded bra. "Can't. I'm on duty. And my gun isn't quite waterproof."

"Ah, Detective. Always so punctilious."

I put fists to hips. "Have I been insulted?"

That got a laugh out of him. "I just meant I admire your sense of duty."

"Oh. Okay then. And, um, it's nice of you to watch the kids."

"Why, thank you, Detective."

Since I knew where Bo was, I felt safe enough to head back to my apartment. Punctiliously *not* thinking of naked, wet Vikings. There, I stared at my dresser drawers, wondering when a dozen panties and two dozen T-shirts had thinned to a couple of each. Pulling out a skimpy thong and a snow-white tee, I hoped this wasn't an omen of things to come.

I should learn to smack myself when I think things like that.

When I returned to the cop shop, Detective Gruen wasn't in the office. Captain Titus was.

Ernest Titus was shift captain and my direct boss. He was a chunky forty-something with a head round as a jack-o'-lantern. He was losing his hair and tried to cover the bald spot with orange hair-in-a-can, but that only made it worse.

The captain's name was written Titus but we all pronounced it Tight-ass (though not to his face). Titus insisted the name was "Tit Us", but I wasn't sure that was any better.

Ernest Titus went to school with my father. As a fifth grader Tight-ass beat up my dad and stole his lunch money. In ninth grade, my father broke Titey's arm in return. Dad got suspended for it but Tight-ass never beat him up again. Whenever Titus saw me, he always started rubbing his arm.

"It's been two days," he said, pacing and chafing his Armani. Oh, yeah. He also thought he was going to be Chief of Police some day, and tried to dress the part. Would have worked better if he hadn't paired the Armani with a bright green shirt and neon pink tie. They clashed horribly with his hair. "Two days, and no arrests. That doesn't look good on the department's record."

I put on my official face and manners. "I've got several leads, Captain."

"*Leads*?" Titus's voice got high when he was stressed, like a cat being gutted. "You call a hooker and a couple of drunks *leads*?"

Now probably wasn't the time to mention the apartment manager who suspiciously was in the neighborhood at the time of the murder. And who suspiciously showed up wherever I was. (Although sometimes I showed up where Bo was. Which was also suspicious, though I wasn't sure how.) "The ME's full report just landed on my desk, sir. The widow gets back tonight. I'll interview her. And—"

"And we need this case solved!" The chafing increased. If his sleeve were a foreskin, he'd have already climaxed twice. "Bah! You're a rookie detective, in over your head."

"I'm *not* a rookie *cop*," I said, stung.

"Our department's reputation is at stake. The mayor's already phoned three times."

"He phoned me too, Captain."

"Did he threaten to turn *you* over to his stiletto-shod secretary?" Titus shuddered. "This can't go on. I'm giving you a partner."

"Blatzky's not available." As in "in the can".

Titus bared teeth in a truly scary jagged-pumpkin smile. "Not Blatzky. I want someone young. Energetic. Enthusiastic."

And I *wasn't*? Twenty-six—the new sixty-five? "I don't need a partner, sir."

"Well, you're getting one. Or you're off the case." He stalked out.

I stared after Tight-ass. *Off the case*? The ME's full report lay before me, but it stayed closed. Lieutenant Roet's serenity fountain burbled at the edge of my awareness. Blatzky came out of the bathroom, grabbed a couple issues of *Midwest Police Monthly* off my desk and went back in.

I reached for the phone. Stopped myself. Dad wasn't around any more.

Mechanically, I started cleaning my gun. Wednesday wasn't my usual night but I needed something to take my mind off...young. Energetic. Enthusiastic.

Finally I turned to the ME's file. Schrimpf died at approximately two a.m. of blood loss. There was no sign of a struggle, no bruises, no debris under the fingernails. There were some cracked ribs, like someone'd tried CPR, but they were post-mortem.

Nothing to explain the loss of blood, except the puncture marks.

Saliva residue (dried spit to you and me) was found on the vic's testicles. DNA testing indicated two separate people but no matches were found in the national database, meaning we couldn't identify whose spit it was. One was probably from Drusilla the BJ Queen (*there* was a fast-food-chain name) but I'd have to establish probable cause to get a sample to prove it. Or trick her out of it somehow.

I flipped a page. And stared. I guess there were some surprises after all.

No foreign particles were in the puncture wounds. No fiber, no dirt and no metal or paint particles.

The murder weapon was something short, slim and sharp. I *had* imagined a wife with knitting needles, or an under-tipped paperboy and a couple of rusty nails. Gotta watch it with those paperboys.

But whatever caused the holes in the base of Schrimpf's penis, no foreign particles meant they weren't nails or metal knitting needles. Plastic needles maybe, but those were usually dull and bendy. Not what I'd use to pop skin.

I flipped another page. And was shocked.

The body was almost *completely* drained of blood. Less than a pint left.

Why was that shocking, you may ask. After all, death was from loss of blood. Like a car running out of gas, right?

Except a car engine can run on a nearly empty tank. You can't do that with people.

The average person has five to six quarts of blood. Ten to twelve pints. Lose one pint, no problem. It's your standard blood donation. Two pints, you start getting woozy.

If you lose more than two pints...shock. Shock, from only one quart out of five.

Lose two to three quarts—only *half* the body's blood supply—it's *death.*

I got up to pace, thinking furiously. Behind me, Lieutenant Roet's fountain gurgled, underscoring my thoughts. Over nine pints of blood, gone. Schrimpf's heart would have stopped long before his blood ran out.

Which meant one of two things, if that fifteen-minute window was right. Either the wounds were gaping holes that ran blood without the heart pumping or—

Or something sucked it out.

I double-checked the ME's report. Schrimpf was not a hemophiliac. And the punctures were only half an inch deep. Small, about the size of a nail or brad. Too small and shallow for the vic to bleed out.

I don't know what made me think fangs.

Okay, I do know. Count Jack-offula and Vamprucilla.

And Bo and his orgasmic biting.

I was definitely going insane. Even if such creatures existed, those three didn't qualify. I had proof. Double-D-Drusilla had used a mirror, for heaven's sake. When she was powdering her nose in the interview. And I'd seen Bo this morning. Bright sunny day, no coffin, the whole nine yards.

Though he'd been behind a heavy curtain. And sometimes he moved like a ghost.

Nuts. I slammed the ME's report shut and stalked out. This was a *case*, not a horror story. I was a *detective*. Methodical, logical. By the book. A cop, grounded in reality. I believed it was real if I could *bite* it.

Well, maybe not the best way to put it.

Point was, I was a detective and I had a job to do. A widow to interview. I got resolutely to my feet and left the office.

As I tromped out of the cop shop, I half-expected Bo to show up. He didn't. Someone else did, unfortunately.

"Detective Ma'am! Imagine meeting you here." Officer Dirk Ruffles dashed up the stairs, carrying a donut and waving a paper cup of coffee. Dark liquid sloshed out of the cup, splashing several people. Clueless, Dirk raced toward me.

Sweet Bavarian cream-filled donuts. And me wearing white, the cosmic "kick me" color. I held up my hands. Dirk skidded to a halt.

His coffee didn't. A Rorschach test landed on my clean shirt. Great. As I squeegeed off the worst of it, I said, "It's not so surprising, Officer. After all, this is the police station. And we're both police. Now if you'll excuse me, I have work to do." I headed out.

If I thought that would end the conversation, I was wrong. He followed. "We're both police...you're so smart! I bet that's why you're a detective."

My lie meter stayed flat. Dirk wasn't being sarcastic. It made me sad for some reason.

"But guess what? It's not Officer any more." Like the bolt-necked monster, Dirkenstein lumbered on. "My uncle was absolutely right. My uncle is an important man, did I tell you that? He had drinks with the President of the United States once. And—you're not going to believe this—he actually shook hands with *Oprah Winfrey*. There was supposed to be a picture, but somehow the rewind kicked in before it was supposed to, and all the film rewound in ten seconds flat and ripped off the spindle and exploded the camera. I tried to fix it, but plastic pieces shot everywhere, and of course the film was ruined—"

"You got a promotion?" I remembered the yellow crime scene mummy and felt sorry for whoever had to deal with the kid now.

He thumped his chest. Just like a gorilla, honest. "I did. I'm a detective, just like you. In fact, I'm your new partner!"

ભ્રૂ

Reeling from my heart attack, I barely made it to Widow Schrimpf's. Unfortunately Ruffles made it easily, gabbing about his uncle, his goldfish and his third grade teacher's affection for meatballs (and, oh yes, Oprah) without stopping once.

Young, energetic and enthusiastic in spades. But Captain Titus had omitted "brain-damaged".

"Really, Ruffles. I'd rather do this alone," I said for the infinity-plus-one time.

"Sure thing, Detective Ma'am. You and me alone."

I mounted the stoop. Polite hints just didn't work with this guy. I tried again. "I mean I can handle this from here."

"We sure can!" Dirk mounted the stoop behind me.

"No, I mean you can go back to the station."

"And I will, right after we interview the widow."

I was being buried alive by a horrible Dirkslide. "Officer...Detective Ruffles. I appreciate the help, but—"

"Glad to be of service, ma'am. Thrifty, brave and loyal, that's me. Like a Scout."

Like a Scout, or a Saint Bernard? "Just wait here." I resisted the urge to add, "Stay, boy."

"But Captain Titus wanted me in on the ground floor. To charge with the first wave. To be first out of the gate, to run with the leaders, to—"

"Yeah, okay, I get the drift. Look, Ruffles. I've been a detective longer than you." For all of three weeks, but still. "Let me do the talking, hmm?"

"But Detective Ma'am. We could do good cop, bad cop. I'd be the bad cop. Not that you couldn't handle it. After all, a girl can be every bit as good as a guy, or bad as a guy in this case, except in a different way. Softer, and not as strong, and well, really not as bright—"

That was too much. "All girls? Even—Oprah?"

His muddy eyes blinked in surprise. "Oprah's not a girl, Detective. She's a goddess."

"Look, Ruffles, I'm senior cop. I'll do the talking." I hitched mental suspenders and raised my hand to knock. The door was a lot like Strongwell's. Carved wood, gleaming yellow hardware and beveled windows.

But the yellow metal was brass and the windows were glass. Not gold and crystal. How could a maintenance man own a better door than one of the city's richest men?

I wasn't thinking straight. Well, with Dirkenstein's yammering, who could? Bo Strongwell wouldn't *own* his apartment building. As I put on my regulation cop face and manners I made a mental note to find out who did.

I knocked. A voice came from inside. "I'll get it, Martinez." The door opened to reveal Lady Godiva.

Chapter Nine

Josephine Schrimpf was *naked.* Absolutely starkers. Only her long blonde hair, rippling over each breast and fluffing out strategically at the apex of her thighs, kept me from slapping her with a five-hundred-dollar citation for public nudity.

She stared past me at Ruffles, radiating a sexual heat so strong I had to take a step back. Ruby lips, plump as pillows, glistened. Exotic hazel eyes were outlined black as an Egyptian whore, appraising Dirk as if fitting him with goat hooves and pan pipes.

It was only after I picked up Dirk's jaw from the sidewalk that I realized Lady Godiva wasn't really naked. She wore a peach string bikini under all that hair. An ultra-tiny.

Or maybe just strategically placed band-aids. "Mrs. Schrimpf?" I said.

She noticed me for the first time. "Yes?"

I presented my badge. "I'm Detective Elena O'Rourke, ma'am. May I come in?"

Next to me, Dirk said, "*Ahem.*" Really. I swear on my Grandmother Sanchez's cheese-and-onion enchilada recipe. My eyes rolled. "And Detective Dirk Ruffles. We have a few questions for you about your husband, Mrs. Schrimpf."

"Oh." Widow Schrimpf waved us in with a casual hand. If she was grieving, it didn't show. "Can I get either of you a drink?"

"I'll have a martini," Dirk said. "Just a hint of vermouth. With an olive. And—"

"*Water,* please. For both of us." Where'd this kid learn law enforcement, James Bond Tech?

"Martinez," Mrs. Schrimpf called. "Two waters at poolside, please. And another Old Fashioned."

Poolside. Very rich and chic. At least Strongwell didn't own a pool. I hoped.

The in-ground pool was the obligatory Hollywood kidney shape, for lying around, not swimming in. Mrs. Schrimpf settled languidly into a lounge chair and gave a blasé wave toward two others. She must have used that lounge a lot. The skin showing on her (i.e. most of it) was evenly tan, a deep brown licked golden by the flickering tiki lights.

Which was fine now, at twenty-something. When she was fifty, she'd be spotted and leathery from UV damage.

All right, that was catty. But I was discouraged from the captain's chewing and Drusilla's disappearing and Dirk's...Dirking. And it seemed everyone I met lately was either heart-poundingly handsome or rocket-salute beautiful.

Maybe they all read some article I hadn't. "Six Secrets to a Gorgeous New You...Unless You're Elena O'Rourke, Then Forget It."

Ruffles clumped over to the chair next to Mrs. Schrimpf and dumped himself in, and I felt cheered. Not *quite* everyone was perfect. I pulled out my notebook, angled it to catch the flickering light. "Mrs. Schrimpf. You were out of town the night your husband died?"

"Yes. Attending a fitness convention in Las Vegas. I help Nappy with the business." A maid shuttled out with the drinks. Josephine took hers without a glance, drank off half. "I was Nappy's lead aerobics instructor. Until we became partners."

Smiling at the maid, I took my water from the tray. A sunny orange slice was deep-sea diving amid a coral reef of ice blue and green cubes. Good grief, didn't rich people even do plain water? This was almost too pretty to drink.

So I used it to rinse the coffee out of my shirt. It took most of the glass, and by the time I was done cloth was plastered to my entire front, every asset outlined. My nipples stood out like two little pebbles. Dirk didn't even notice, riveted to Mount Widow. I did *not* care.

"It isn't called aerobics any more, of course." Josephine laughed, slightly brittle. "It's called power walk."

"Or step class," Dirk said. "If you want trendy."

That earned a smile from the widow. "Or even cardio kickboxing. But in my day we called it aerobics."

I looked closer at her. Fine lines decorated her face, and her neck was ever-so-slightly crepey. A discreet scar ran along her hairline. Widow Schrimpf was not the youthful goddess I first thought her. "You were with your husband how long, Mrs. Schrimpf?"

"Five wonderful years." Her voice broke at the end. Finally, a sign of grief. My internal lie meter pointed to genuine.

Dirk patted her hand. "You two must have been very happy." I wanted to poke him. Who was doing the interview here?

She sniffed, slewed him a grateful look. "They were the best five years of my life."

I consulted my notes. "I have that you were married *four* years ago."

"Oh, we couldn't *marry* until Nappy divorced Cora."

"Well obviously." Dirk patted her hand again. She smiled into his eyes.

Was this an interview or old friends week? "All right, Mrs. Schrimpf. Who exactly is Cora?"

"Nappy's previous wife. Had a face like a dog. In her divorce suit, Cora asked for an absurd amount of money. A huge alimony *plus* child support."

Dirk sat forward, expression all sympathy, if a little muddy. "How old were the children?"

"What children? Cora had five poodles!"

"No," Dirk said.

"Yes!" Josephine said.

"The Magic Eight Ball says 'Maybe'," I muttered. Which reminded me of when I asked Bo about his name, and found he was so clever (or so attuned to me) he might have been reading my mind.

Fortunately, these two weren't Bo. They paid no attention. "Of course, with Cora's face, maybe those dogs really *were* her children." Josephine laughed. Dirk joined her, a sort of snort-wheeze sound. I rolled my eyes and waited.

While I waited, my brain ran this new info through the hamster wheel. Maybe ex-wife Cora Schrimpf killed Schrimpf for revenge. I added Cora to my notebook.

When the widow finally wound down, she rearranged herself on the lounge. "Naturally, Cora didn't get a cent. Nappy had made her sign a prenup." Josephine took her time rearranging, displaying most every asset she had. She was rail-slim, but her boobs stood out like basketballs.

Dirkenstein's snort-wheeze faded into a pant. He had caught sight of the Rocks of Gibraltar. All these men and their blubbering around big boobs was getting irritating.

Until I remembered that Bo liked my Near-B's. Maybe I didn't have to resort to "Relationship Deflating? Pump Up the Cleavage!" I said, "You weren't your husband's first wife, Mrs. Schrimpf?"

"Oh, heavens, no. I'm seven. Lucky number."

Seven wives? Talk about compensation. And some men only bought sports cars.

And talk about possibilities. I now had six more suspects.

Then I realized how "lucky" number-seven Josephine was. Schrimpf was fifty-five years old. Seven wives in about thirty-five years meant each Missus lasted an average of five years.

"Lucky" Josephine was coming to the end of her tenure. And I bet Number Six wasn't the only one to sign a prenup. If Schrimpf hadn't died, Lady Godiva here would be naked in more ways than one.

"Do you happen to know the names of any other ex-wives, Mrs. Schrimpf?" I sat, pencil poised over notebook. No doubt she would know at least a couple, and possibly be eager to implicate them.

"Of course. Cora, who lasted all of a year. Before her was Carla, the sixteen-year-old. Then there was Candy and Connie and Cathy. They were all models for *Playme Boy* magazine. And his first wife, Cindy, was the porn star. Apparently she worked with Ron Jeremy."

Whoa. That was worse than the L-girls. What was it with Schrimpf? And did his Rolodex only have two letters? "Thanks. Know any of their current locations?"

"Well, let me think." Maybe her brains were connected to her boobs, because to "think" she crossed arms under her breasts, plumping them even bigger. Dirk's eyes bugged out and I think his little mustache caught on fire. "Cindy, Cathy and Connie went into business in Florida, selling hot dogs. They wear really tiny bikinis and skate around. They call their business Go-go Wieners. Apparently they're doing very well for themselves."

"Uh, yeah. Mrs. Schrimpf, that's a little more info than I—"

"Nappy loaned them the money to start up. I get Christmas cards from them every year. They seem really happy. I thought, if Nappy ever divorced me, I might join them."

"Right." There went three suspects. "And the others?"

"Candy and Cora breed poodles in California. Nappy sent Candy to school, you know. To be a vet."

"Great." I made two more hash marks. Apparently Schrimpf was a tightwad—except with heart's desires. "And the other one?"

"Carla Donner? She's on Broad—"

"Did you say Donner?"

"Yes. Dieter Donner's daughter." She laughed, her chest heaving like a tsunami. "Try saying that five times fast."

Dirk obligingly started. "Dieter Donner's daughter, Dieter Donner's daughter..."

But I had made the connection. Not just to my witness, but to my sister. Whose grade-school friend was Carla Donner.

ઉଓ

I managed to get rid of my Dirkenshadow by telling him I was going home to change. I didn't lie, really. I only had one tiny little stop to make first.

The gold on this door was not brass, nor the crystal glass. Expensive, but I banged on it anyway. If Bo Strongwell or whoever owned it could afford it, he could afford to replace it.

Almost immediately the door opened to Jeeves Butler. I stalked past him into the foyer. The chilly air hit the last bit of damp on my shirt. My nipples woke up, saw Strongwell wasn't around, and deflated with a mutter. Stupid nipples.

"Detective! This is a private residence." Butler Guy flitted after me like a silver moth. "And Master Bo is not at home."

"Cool your jets, Jeeves. I'm here to see Gretchen."

His wings flapped once before settling down. Butler smoothed a hand over his silver pate. "Oh...well, in that case, my apologies. I'll get Mrs. Johnson." He paused. "On second thought, it's almost midnight. Miss Stella will be in bed, and maybe Mrs. Johnson as well. Perhaps you would come back tomorrow?"

"I won't take long. Don't bother escorting me. I remember the way."

"But Detective O'Rourke—"

I bounded up the staircase, two at a time. Despite the butler's assurances, I expected Bo to pop out at any second. He didn't. But I was *not* disappointed.

Making it unmolested to Gretchen's door (*unfortunately,* my pussy murmured. *Shut up,* I murmured back), I raised my hand to knock. Heard—running. Some scuffling.

And a high-pitched giggle, followed by a distinctly male laugh.

My mind flew to Bo. Not that he was on my mind, I just remembered how my sister acted toward him... All right, he was definitely on my mind. And other portions of my anatomy. *Me, me! Down here!* To shut her up, I yanked on my pants so hard I gave myself a wedgie.

Butler Guy was wrong. Bo was here, with Gretchen.

I shrugged it off with a jerk. Big deal. So Gretchen was entertaining Bo. Six-month widow (with needs) entertaining a man so virile he kept the Rocky Mountains in his jeans. So what?

So *what*? I wanted to run away and hide. I wanted to shriek and kick down the door. I wanted—

More running. More giggling, a *child's*. Stella's? What was she doing up so late?

But if Stella was with Gretchen and Bo, it couldn't be too pornographic, could it? I knocked. There was instant silence. I leaned in. Heard some whispering.

Stella's voice piped, "Who is it?"

"Auntie Lena, Starshine. I'm here to see your mommy. Can I come in?"

The door cracked open and small blue eyes peeped through. "Mommy's not home."

"She's not?" I tried to keep the shock out of my voice. Gretchen would *never* leave a five-year-old alone. After the attack that killed her husband, she'd only gotten more protective.

Except, duh, Elena. Stella wasn't home *alone*. Bo was with her.

Well, Mr. Laugh could be Date Number One. But though I fervently wished otherwise, Bo was more likely. Gretchen wouldn't leave Stella with a man she'd only known a short time.

Unless Gretch had known Date Number One *longer* than a short time, but that meant she'd met him before her husband died which meant...bad things. I couldn't believe she'd betray her high school sweetheart. So that meant...I was getting all balled up.

I stopped thinking in favor of doing. I eased into the apartment. Glanced around. "Felt" around with my cop sense. Except for Stella, the place was empty.

"Starshine. Your mommy didn't leave you home alone, did she?"

"Oh, no. Daddy's here."

That did it. The whole "Daddy" thing was just wrong. Steve was dead. What did Gretchen think she was doing, leaving a child alone with an imaginary "daddy"? What was she doing, telling Stella that in the first place?

Gretch was acting so strangely. All her life she'd been Ms. Abby Solutely Normal. Mrs. American Dream. She married her high school sweetheart, was a stay-at-home mom. She and Steve even had the cute family bungalow inherited from Steve's grandmother.

Then *bang*. Twenty-four hours after the attack that killed her husband, Gretchen sold the bungalow. She moved without a backward glance.

That was enough to worry me. But what buried the big-sister meter was that it hadn't stopped there. Gretchen started making other irrational, *unnormal* decisions. The mugging had messed Steve up pretty bad but she ordered an open-casket viewing. Fortunately Stark and Moss had done a great job piecing him back together. He looked good as new—better, even.

Then, for no good reason, she'd ordered Steve's coffin closed.

At the time I thought she'd get over it. Maybe Dad would have known better. Because instead of getting over it, she got worse. These days Gretchen refused to go outside after dark. Not for any reason at any time. Not to shop. Not for work. Certainly not to date. Well, not until *her wedding anniversary*.

Daddy's here. It was the thirteenth round in a magazine that held twelve. Maybe I should have minded my own business. But I *had* to know who Mr. Laugh was.

So I searched the apartment.

Trust sure, respect yeah. All that didn't matter jack when it was my baby sister. So shoot me.

There wasn't much apartment to search. Maybe five places a grown man could fit in or under. Only two that could hide a Viking like Bo. I found—nothing. Nobody. Whoever Mr. Laugh was, he had apparently evaporated into thin air. Or he was unnaturally good at hiding.

Damn. There was that unnatural thing again.

The front door slammed. "I'm home." My sister, sounding breathless. "I got pasta for dinner, and a nice Shiraz. Do you suppose..." She stuttered to a halt when she saw me. "Elena."

"Gretchen." I glared at her. "You wanna tell me what's going on?"

She paled. "Stella, honey. Go to bed now, sweetie."

"I wanna play with you and Daddy and Aunt Lena."

Gretchen winced. "Auntie Lena and I are just going to have boring adult talk. But when that's done, how about I read you a story?" Apparently that was a good bribe because Stella immediately scampered off to her room.

Gretchen led me to the kitchen, pushing roughly through its tiny saloon doors. She started to pull boxes and bottles from plastic bags. Put them away without a word.

"Dinner at midnight, Gretch? And what happened to Stella's bedtime?" I sat at the kitchen table and waited for my sister to say something. Anything.

She silently stowed groceries, stacking cans of sauce in the pantry, lining up cartons of yogurt in the fridge, as if each item were a carefully placed brick in her levee of normal.

Her emotional dam might be solid, but mine cracked. "*When,* Gretch? Steve's *dead.* When are you going to tell Stella?"

Gretchen's hand, setting crackers on a shelf, faltered. "Elena, you don't understand. It's not that simple."

"You're right, I don't understand. So explain it to me."

Gretch didn't turn. "It's because of the attack."

"Everything is, these days."

She shot a glare over her shoulder. "Do you want to understand or criticize?"

I held up a hand. "Sorry. Go on."

"The attack—" Gretchen heaved a breath. "There were two of them. Strong, and fast. I sheltered Stella from most of it. But she...heard them. Heard them rip Steve...to shreds."

I had seen the remains. A rabid wolverine would have left more. It was one of the excuses Gretchen had for a closed coffin. Sensible, except Steve looked fine at the viewing.

"Stella was traumatized." Gretchen stuffed away a few more boxes. "Hell, I was traumatized. I did everything I could to make us feel safe again." She turned to me, eyes burning. "I'll *do* anything to keep us safe. *Anything.* If it takes Stella's father living with us to make her feel safe...even if it's only the memory of him..." She dropped the empty bag into the recycling bin. "Whatever it takes."

"That's not what I mean and you know it." I pulled a bag of cans over to the pantry. "I don't mean lying to Stella about her dad being dead. I mean you passing off your date, your *lover*—" slammed cans emphasized my words, "—as Stella's *father*."

"My...lover?" Gretchen's face went white. "I don't know what you're talking about. Say, I told you Carla Donner called me, right? From New York. She's finally on Broadway."

Did I remember Carla? It was why I'd come. Right now I could care less. I opened my mouth but Gretchen sailed on.

"Only took her three years, but it's expensive living there, waiting to be discovered. Napoleon Schrimpf gave her the money that made it possible. What a coincidence, huh?"

Another suspect gone, but it no longer mattered. I felt my sister's evasion like a punch to the gut. "Gretchen, I heard a laugh. A *male* laugh." I smashed my empty bag into a ball, rammed it into the bin. Before I could stop myself, I added, "Was it Bo?"

"Don't be silly." Gretchen's color returned to normal. "He's out on patrol. Elena, I don't want to argue." She picked up a bag of frozen food. "I have some good news. A lead on a job. You've been badgering me to get out of the house."

"Gretch, don't. No more avoidance."

"The Blood Center's hiring." She tugged open the freezer. "Did you know they've been picked as the new Midwest regional distribution center for the Hemoglobin Society? I guess the old one in Springfield burned down. Imagine, thousands of units will pass through."

She was babbling. I slapped the freezer shut. Willed her to look at me. "I need to know. Who was the man you left Stella with? *Alone*?"

That, at last, got through. She stiffened, then whirled to face me, color high. "Implying I'm a bad mother? If Stella wants to think of him as her daddy, then that man was her daddy!"

"Fine." I walked away. Spun. "Why does an apartment building have a butler?"

I wanted to knock her off balance. Gretchen simply jerked a cupboard open and dragged out a pot. "You must have misheard. He's not *a* butler. His *name* is Butler. Mr. Butler."

"*Mr.* Butler, I see." I let my sarcastic tone tell her I wasn't buying it.

"You've changed, Elena. You used to be at least a little trusting." She stared at me as if I'd sprouted fangs. "Now it seems you're always on the job."

Implying *I* was a bad sister. It stung. "That's not true."

"If you say so." Her sarcastic tone matched mine. "Mr. Butler's in One-A. He answers the door as part of building security, so people don't just get buzzed in. Did you come to ask me that? You could have picked up a phone."

My bullshit meter was pinging off the scale. My sister was lying to me. Big, obnoxious, toxic lies. The last time she'd done that, she was sixteen and covering for her lover Steve. What—or who—was she hiding now? "Where's Bo?"

"I told you. On patrol." She stuck the pot under the tap, jerked it on.

That rang true, which surprised me. "Right. For his neighborhood watch."

"Is that so hard to believe?" Gretchen turned and smiled, not nice. "Or do you just not believe *me*?"

"I'm doing this as your sister, Gretch. For your own good."

"Sure. Your obsession with Bo is obviously *not* the issue." She slammed the tap closed. "Don't start harping on Bo, Elena. He works harder than you can imagine." She dragged the pot to the stove.

Obsession...! "Works hard, right. Building super, incredibly hard work. Collecting rent once a month, plunging the occasional toilet."

"He does *far* more than that."

"Yeah? Like what?"

"Like...like...stuff." Gretchen turned a stiff back on me and stood, quivering.

"Sure. Like seducing my little sister so she *lies* for him. Massive hard work."

She spun to me. "You have no idea what you're talking about. Don't harass Bo, Elena. He's overburdened as it is."

"Overburdened. Yeah." I leaned against the wall. Bo, overburdened? Maybe as in needing a back brace for his cock. But with actual work? I didn't think so. "Sure."

"He is!" Gretchen stalked to the pantry, pulled out a bag of spaghetti. "You should know. You get the exact same way when you're overworked. All crabby, then banging at it twice as hard."

"I do not."

"Do too. Both of you have too much responsibility. But *you* have a whole department to help. Bo has just Thor and Stev—just Thor to help." She tossed the bag on the counter, marched to the stove.

But I'd caught it. "Thor and *who*?"

"No one." My sister twisted the burner dial so hard she almost broke it. "Do you have any more questions? Because if you're done with the interrogation, I have some supper to make. And a story to read my daughter."

"I'm done. For now." I left. The set of her jaw told me I could get answers out of her, but only if I broke bones. I wouldn't do that unless the secrets hurt her worse.

Anyway, there was only one more question, and I didn't have to ask it. I could find the basement stairs on my own.

Chapter Ten

Moving silently through the cool, empty foyer, I kept alert for Mr.-my-ass Butler. Any minute, the silver head would pop around the corner. Any minute I'd hear a ringing "Detective!" as I eased open a door and saw—

Wow. Kitchen with a capital Itch. Vast tile floor, gleaming stainless countertops, institutional-sized refrigerators and freezers. Oddly, the grandeur was frosted with homey touches. Crayon art was pinned to the refrigerator with photo magnets. Hand-knit dishrags hung from the sweeping faucets. A cookie jar sat on a butcher block island.

Bo's "apartment" building was getting weirder by the minute. I slid through the empty kitchen toward the back door, hoping it led to the basement stairs. Hoping I could clear up at least *one* mystery.

The last time I was here, the butler let slip that the master was *downstairs*. Jeeves obviously didn't want me down there. Naturally, that meant I wanted to see it. Bad.

Grasping the black metal knob, I opened the door. To my left was a walk-in pantry the size of China. To my right was the backyard, as vast as the Russian steppes.

Straight ahead were a set of bare wooden stairs leading down. Bingo.

I put one hand on my weapon and crept down, skimming my other hand over a rough wood handrail. Step by step I went, feeling blindly for each with a toe. *Creak.* I sucked in a breath, held it. Counted sixty slowly before I started down again.

An eternity later I got to the bottom of the stairs. And at the bottom was—

A perfectly ordinary basement.

Cinder block walls. Concrete floor. To the left were four washers and four dryers lit by a small shop light. The rest of the basement was dark.

I let out a disappointed breath. So normal. Wandering a bit, I tried to figure out what had panicked Jeeves so. Maybe Bo had been downstairs doing his *laundry*. Jeeves hadn't wanted me to know Viking-manager was doing something so domestic and unmanly.

But what had I expected? Dungeons? Buried bodies?

Coffins?

Disgusted with myself, I crossed back to the stairs. My sister's behavior, this apartment-cum-manor house, Bo himself—it all argued there was a mystery. I hated an unsolved mystery.

But nothing was out of place or odd, certainly nothing dark and dangerous. I trotted up the steps but hesitated at the top. Something was bothering me. I had seen something.

Slowly, I came back down. No. I hadn't seen *some*thing—I had seen *nothing*. Half the basement was dark. But the furthest corner was not quite the same dark as the rest.

It was a door.

I crept toward it, hand on gun. Like a bad Christmas ballet, Visions of Coffins danced in my head. I stretched out a tentative hand. The door, metal painted gray, was cool and enigmatic under my fingers. No window. I couldn't see what was on the other side.

Whatever—whoever—was there, we would both be surprised.

I eased the door open.

No one jumped me. But that might only mean they were waiting further on.

Beyond the door, the dark was completely solid. Even straining my eyes, I couldn't see a thing. But I smelled...earth.

Rain-fresh, newly tilled soil. Coffins? Or mass burial?

Sucking in a fortifying breath, I stepped into the gloom. The door swung shut behind me with a clang.

I jumped. Tore out my XD. Dammit, I was trapped. The dark hung on me like a heavy black wool blanket. My eyes were fish-wide. I was trapped and I couldn't see. I couldn't hear anything over the pounding of my own heart. I tried to spin but my legs weren't working, mired in the nightmare darkness.

My gun hand trembled.

That snapped me out of it. I'd trained long and hard with that weapon. I was acting like a kid, not a cop. I had questions, I wanted answers. The fact that this was a private residence and I had no warrant was not an issue. I wasn't gathering evidence for court, just worried about my sister and niece. Digging in my pockets, I found my flashlight and switched it on. It revealed a rather ordinary-looking hallway. The floor was concrete.

A concrete floor. Why had I smelled earth?

Eight doors notched the hallway. I tried the first door on the right. It was locked. The next door was also locked.

Carefully I twisted the third knob. It turned.

I cracked the door, shone the light through the opening. Walls, pictures, a dresser...it was a bedroom. A perfectly normal bedroom, with a chest of drawers and a bookshelf filled with books.

The only even slightly unusual thing was the bed. The four-poster was huge to the point of absurdity. Its blue comforter look more like the Norwegian Sea than a bedspread.

I wondered if this was where Bo sailed his Viking longboat. And what nymphs played with him in this bouncy sea.

Phooey. Gretch was right. I was obsessed. I was obsessed with a big gorgeous man I knew nothing about—who I wanted to know nothing about! I pulled the door shut with a decisive click and stomped back up the hall.

Only to stop. Where was that earthy smell coming from?

I returned to the Norwegian Sea room. Sniffed. Went two steps to the door on the other side of the hall. The scent was stronger here. I tried the knob. It turned silently. I eased the door open and shined my light cautiously in. The beam hit pay dirt.

Literally. Dirt. The source of the smell. Fresh-turned earth, amazingly sweet.

But why? Indoor farming? I felt around for a light switch, found nothing. The ceiling showed no light fixtures of any sort. Without light, what could grow—mushrooms?

I flashed the beam around the room. It took me a moment to realize what I was looking at.

The room was the size of a cozy den. Like a den it had bookshelves and DVD racks. An entertainment center on a raised metal platform held a huge HDTV and a kick-ass sound system.

But no couches or chairs.

And the floor was nothing but carefully raked soil.

Maybe I was dreaming. Normal basement, normal bedrooms...and this. Why? Were any of the other rooms like it? And what did Bo Grunt Manager have to do with this?

Rather than a mystery solved, it was a mystery deepened.

ઉ૪

Within moments of hitting fresh air, I felt like a fool. I tramped west on Lincoln, heading for Nieman's Bar with some idea of double-checking the parking lot for blood. It wasn't the long way around it seemed (Meiers Corners' streets were laid out like a checkerboard—any way that didn't involve air and wings was the long way around) but that wouldn't have mattered. I was mad.

I was mad at Captain Titus for assigning me a partner simply because I hadn't solved the case in twenty-four hours. I was mad at the case, for not being *solved* in twenty-four hours. I was mad at Dolly

Barton, for having spoiled any chance of a trap that would let me solve the case in twenty-four hours. I was mad at Kiefer Sutherland, for solving all his cases in twenty-four hours. I was mad at Dirk, just on general principles.

Of course, I was really maddest at me.

My escapade in Bo's basement embarrassed me. However I justified it, it was not by-the-book behavior. Dad would have been appalled. I was worried about my sister, yes. Scared for her and her small daughter. But breaking into and entering a man's den...and bedroom... I almost didn't recognize myself.

Was Gretchen right? Had I changed? Had fear for her overcome my personality as well as my better sense? Had something about Bo so unhinged me (well, besides his überhot kisses...and his suckling my nipples...and oh, yeah, those big hands down my...*ngh*) so unhinged me that I fell off that line of rules and regs that defined Elena O'Rourke?

Automatically I pulled out my phone, hit speed dial two. Dad.

"'Sup, Badge-Bitch?" Nixie.

I groaned. I'd reprogrammed dial-two six months ago, when the phone company had finally reused the number and I'd woken Annie Roet (and her new baby triplets) the third straight night. The screaming had been deafening. And the kids were noisy too. "Sorry, Nixie. Wrong number."

"Calling your dad again, huh. What about?"

"Oh, something stupid I did. I'll never break the rules again. No matter what."

"Yeah, I'm so onboard with that. Rules and authority *über alles*, woot."

I snorted. "*You* can get away with acting different. I *am* different."

"Uh-huh."

"I *am*. I'm a too-tall Irish-Latina cop who looks like a beauty queen and has the sexual luck of a spayed cat. Rules and regs are the only things that keep me balanced."

"And I'm a too-short punk rock musician who goes a little nuts around Christmas because they butcher the same five songs in so many new yet unoriginal ways. Elena, did you ever wonder why rules are such a BFD to you?"

Big effing deal, I translated. "Well, I always thought it was because I'm a cop."

"And why are you a cop?"

"I don't know. Justice seems to be in my blood. Like my dad."

"Exactamundo, *mi amiga*. Like your dad. Do you have any idea how awesome that is? To be so like someone, they can understand you with only a few words—or none at all?"

I shuddered a breath. "God, I miss him."

"I hear you. That kind of connection, it's rare. That's why you're so snarky. You're lonely, you want to fit in."

"And rules make me fit."

"Well, *I* think that's *baka*. But in your world, rules equal normal. Follow the rules, hey-presto! You're normal."

"You're saying it's only an illusion."

"True dat. A symptom of you being lonely. If you had another partner like your dad, you wouldn't be such a rules-slave. You wouldn't have to be."

ଓଃଚ

My cop sense started tingling at the corner of Fifth and Lincoln. Someone behind me, but several yards away. Hand to holster I turned. Movement flickered farther up the street. Dolly Barton's or the Blood Center.

Tiptoeing toward Dolly's, I took another reading of my cop sense. Not exactly dangerous, but not totally innocent, either. Not at two thirty in the morning. Could be Strongwell. I didn't relax my guard.

A slight figure flitted through the shadows in front of the Blood Center. I edged closer. The figure was slim, moving with a flutter and crinkle peppered with *blehs*. Oh, joy. Count Ickula. He was popping around, trying to peer in the windows.

"They don't take donations until morning," I said.

The fake Count Dracula startled badly. He tottered, wheeled a few times and nearly landed on his keister before catching himself. "I do not wish to donate," he said with as much dignity as a man in a kid's costume and bad Lugosi could muster. "I want to make a withdrawal."

"Withdrawal? This is a blood *center*, not a blood *bank*. What are you really doing here, Drac? And what the hell is your real name?"

"I have told you my real name. Dracula."

"Right. Name and address, buddy. *Legal* name." I flipped open my notebook to a fresh page, shoved it and a pencil under his nose.

He took it and scribbled. "Why are you so suspicious of me, Detective O'Rourke? I am not your nemesis." He cast me a sly look from under his brows. "Strongwell, though, is another matter."

Not again. After Tin-Can Ruthven, that poked my suspicions twice as hard.

Of course, suspicion was my middle name. Elena O'Suspicion Rourke. "Just what do you mean by that?"

He passed back my notebook. "I have only heard rumors, you understand. A spree of similar killings in Meiers Corners in the past. Strongwell's...involvement."

Bo's name in conjunction with a killing spree jarred me. I glanced at the page, saw Drac had written a name and an address, and pocketed it.

"Really. What kind of killing?" I meant to trap him. Conveniently, I had forgotten about DNN (Dolly's News Network).

"Exsanguination, Detective O'Rourke. Murder by blood loss."

"Big word for such a little guy." I used sarcasm to cover the second jolt. Bo and past blood-draining deaths? But even if I accepted that Strongwell was tied to a bunch of deaths... "This is the city's first murder. That's public record."

"Not according to my source. Perhaps the death of Napoleon Schrimpf was the first *recorded* murder. But paperwork does not always record the whole truth, hmm?" Fakeula's smile was smug.

"Are you suggesting there was a *cover-up*? In stick-up-the-ass-honest Meiers Corners?"

"I can only tell you what my source told me."

"And that source would be...?"

"Confidential." The smug smile grew.

"Natch. I'm going to check this out, Drac."

"Yes, Detective O'Rourke. I'm counting on it." The smile broke into a grin, street light glinting off surprisingly white teeth.

"Oh, right. I just bet you are. Did your oh-so-confidential source happen to say how Strongwell was involved in these earlier 'murders'?" I let my sarcasm carry.

He pouted. "You do not believe me."

"Let's just say you're pretty quick with the accusations, but not much on details. Well, if that's all you've got..." I turned and made like I was leaving.

"Strongwell betrayed him," Drac bleated.

"Strongwell betrayed *him*." I turned slowly back. "Betrayed who?"

Fakeula blushed. I guessed he hadn't meant to give that away. "My informant. He was charged with the safety of Meiers Corners."

"This informant isn't much use without a name."

"Deep, um, something." The harder Drac's brain worked, the lighter the Lugosi. "Deep...deep...oh yeah! Deep Blow Job."

My eyebrows winged into my hairline. "Deep Blow Job. Uh-huh. Sure you don't mean Deep *Throat*, Drac?"

"Deep Throat, Deep Blow Job, it is the same thing, is it not?" The accent was back with added irritation.

"You never heard of Watergate?" I sighed at his blank look. "Okay, your informant was on the MC police force when these killings happened. Then what?"

"Not the police force. A more grass-roots sort of organization."

The neighborhood watch thing again. That irritated me. How could Meiers Corners have an organized neighborhood watch without the police knowing? Without me knowing?

On the plus side, though, it meant Bo Strongwell had been telling the truth, at least about that.

"Deep Blow Job...er, Throat was in charge of the organization. Yes." Fakeula nodded vigorously. "Strongwell had just joined. But Strongwell was eager, wanted more responsibility. More authority. So when news of the first murder came, Strongwell petitioned Deep Throat to be in charge of investigating it."

"Wait. I thought you said Strongwell was the killer."

"Worse, Detective O'Rourke." Fakeula eyes kindled with relish to an almost unholy red. "When he discovered the killer's identity, instead of stopping him, Strongwell urged the killer to commit *more* murders."

Shock rendered me momentarily speechless. That didn't sound like Bo at all. That he could kill, well, probably. But Viking-guy seemed like a man to do it with his own hands. "Why? What would he gain?"

"Gain?" Fakeula blinked, eyes fading to brown. "Gain. Well, power, I guess. Yes, power to step into a leadership position—with a Chicago crime organization!"

"Wow. Strongwell's a leader in Chicago crime." I nodded. Yellow flags were going up all over the place. First, Fakeula's explanation was way too pat. Second, if Bo was that rich, what was he doing living in Meiers Corners? This wasn't Lake Geneva or Glencoe.

But most of all, I just didn't believe it. Bo Strongwell, Mr. Dusk-to-Dawn Patrolgod, a criminal? And not just a criminal, but a sleazy behind-the-scenes mastermind?

The problem was, I didn't know if that was my cop sense talking or my need for Bo to be a good guy. Because if I reacted so strongly to a bad guy, what did that make me? "Explains the fancy digs. Doesn't explain why he's still in little Meiers Corners instead of the big city."

"Who *cares*?" Creepula's irritation was back, tenfold. "The point is, Strongwell betrayed Deep Throat's trust." The sly look returned. "He'll betray you too."

"Yeah, well..." My cop radar pinged. Incoming. *Fast.* I whirled.

Tall, yummy and Scandinavian loomed over us. Unfortunately this Viking had long hair, an earring and yards of black leather. Bo's assistant manager. I cast back in my mind for a name. Thorvald.

Viking Two planted fists on admittedly delectable hips and glared at Dracula. "Causing trouble?"

Fakeula squeaked, backed away. "No sir, not me. Just leaving, actually."

"Then scram."

Fakeula spun, ran off.

I took off after him but he was too fast. "Wait! Dammit." His skinny ass disappeared around the corner. I whirled on Thorvald. "I was *questioning* that man."

Viking Two cocked an eyebrow at me. "It sounded more like he was telling you lies. Bo Strongwell is no traitor."

"You're biased. Being Bo's partner and all." Even though I privately agreed with Thorvald, my job was to listen to testimonies and compare them to the facts. And if there had been other blood killings, what Fakeula said lined up unfortunately quite well.

Thorvald stiffened. "What did you say?"

"Just that, as Bo's partner, you've got to support him."

He shook his head. The ash blond waves brushed his leather shoulders with a kind of shushing sound. "I'm his assistant. Not his partner."

"And the difference is...?"

"A big one. At least to Bo. Look, I was listening before I interrupted. I don't know the details, but something like that might have happened—only in the reverse."

How had Thorvald been near me for that long without my cop radar kicking in? Unless he was listening two blocks away, he should have at least blipped. "Something Fakeula said had a grain of truth?"

"Yes. Bo trusted a guy to take care of a job for him, but the guy shafted him instead. Since then Bo's been a little touchy when it comes to partners."

Partners. I thought briefly of Captain Titus and young, energetic, enthusiastic and cerebrally unburdened. "Yeah, I get that. But that's not Bo's call, is it? Isn't it up to whoever owns the apartment? Or runs the neighborhood watch?"

Thorvald stared at me blankly for a moment. "I thought you were Gretchen Johnson's sister."

"I am. We don't look anything alike, but—"

"And you don't know? How did you meet Bo, then, if not through her?"

"I don't know what?"

He shook his blond head. "Anything, it seems. Look, I just wanted to make sure Crackula wasn't causing any trouble for you. And to straighten out his cockeyed story. I'll see you around."

"But—"

Thorvald was gone. Poof. Almost like... I blinked at the empty air where he'd been. No. Couldn't be.

I could not have just seen a man disappear in a cloud of dust.

Chapter Eleven

I resumed my tromping toward Nieman's Bar, less belligerent this time. More doubtful. Things were not adding up.

Or rather, things were adding up in ways I didn't like. Bo Strongwell was either betrayer or betrayed. He was accused of murder by people I didn't trust but might have to believe. He was defended by people I trusted but didn't believe.

Too many fingers were pointing at him. It made me uncomfortable. Strangely, it was something of a relief to be uncomfortable for something other than because he was big, muscled and tongue-dropping handsome.

On the way to Nieman's I phoned Gretchen. I wanted to make sure she was okay, and to warn her she was living with a man who might be not just a murderer but a mass murderer.

She told me in no uncertain terms what she thought of my suspicions. They included several anatomically correct but impossible acts. (Well, maybe only highly improbable if Strongwell were involved... Damn.)

Arriving at the bar parking lot, I got down on my hands and knees. The crime scene team had gone over the asphalt with chemicals and more, but I wanted to see for myself. Nope, not even a trace of blood.

Dusting hands on jeans, I resumed walking. What did it mean? How could Napoleon Schrimpf be almost completely drained of blood without any showing up at the scene?

Well, there were several *hows*. The big question was *why*?

Before returning to the cop shop, I decided to stop by Otto's Bed and Breakfast Smorgasbord to check Bo's alibi. Otto was outside, sweeping his porch. Our conversation was short. Or at least my side was.

"Hey, Otto."

"Shame on you, Elena!" Otto stuck the butt of his broom into the porch, leaned heavily on it. He was a stereotypical innkeeper, round in the middle and pointy at both ends, like a kid's top. He probably swept so much to balance himself.

He shook a finger at me. "Bo Strongwell is no murderer. He was here the terrible night of Napoleon Schrimpf's death. Patrolling for the watch, making the streets safe for honest businessmen and their guests. How could you not believe him?"

"I didn't—"

"Bo Strongwell, a murderer." Otto *tsked*, loudly. "Shame on you for even thinking of such a thing, Elena."

"But—"

"What, you will not take the word of an honest businessman? Fine. Guiseppe Zweibach and his wife were here that night celebrating their fiftieth wedding anniversary. Bo Strongwell brought them a nice Liebfraumilch to toast to another fifty. Ask them. Or are you so mistrustful you do not even believe pensioners in their golden years?"

"I didn't say I didn't trust—"

"I should hope not. Well, that's all. Say hello to the good Alice for me."

So I had to downgrade Bo's position on the suspect list.

When I reached the cop shop, I did a quick reconnoiter outside for any ominous Dirksasters. Seeing a clear field I hit the stairs for the detective office.

In the office I checked the files for Fakeula's "murders". As I remembered, the worst recorded spree was a gang of thieves who'd knocked over Randy's Candies while KinderTagen (local daycare) was on a field trip there. Yeah, stealing candy from babies. Nothing even close to possible mass murder.

While I was hunting, I heard a grunt behind me, smelled wafting beer-cheese breath. Blatzky had, amazingly, emerged from the Can's Festival.

"*Midwest Police Monthly* come yet?" He reached over my shoulder and pawed through my stack. "Hey, *Sass-Cgal*. 'Interviewing for the Missionary Position'. All right!"

I slapped his mitt. "I bought it. Mine."

"I'm senior on shift. Mine." He snatched it, skedaddled for the john.

From whence I'd never see it again. I spun, half-rose from my chair, grabbed a corner of the magazine and launched myself backward.

The magazine came back but Blatzky came with it. We sailed into the desk. Stacks of paper and magazines went flying. Picture frames hit the floor like bullets, pencils scattered like shot.

Blatzky held on like a terrier. I tugged and twisted. He tried to stomp on my instep. I dodged, which threw me off-balance. I grabbed for the desk and missed. He scrabbled for footing and missed. We went down.

The *Sass-Cgal* spurted from our hands, landed splat in the mess of paper on the floor. I landed on Blatzky's fifth vest button, aka his gut.

His breath exploded in a cloud of Milbenkäse. "Shit, O'Rourke!" He gasped a few times like a fish, then bellered, "Get off, you weigh a ton!"

"Do not." I scrambled off, slightly miffed. Weigh a ton? Strongwell didn't think so.

Smack me. My ego stamped valid by a murder suspect. Embarrassment made me jump to my feet.

Blatzky rolled his head to take in the mess. "Why are all these files out, anyway?"

I offered him a hand up. "Someone said there were murders here before Schrimpf."

"Murders? Nah." Blatzky took my hand, nearly pulled me back to the floor levering his bulk against me. "Some suspicious deaths, though."

"When? I didn't find anything."

He snorted. "That's because these files don't go back to the twenties."

"The twent...you mean the *nineteen* twenties? Flappers and the cat's pajamas?"

"Yeah." With a grunt, Blatzky bent over to pick up a stack of papers. "My first partner was this old guy, Heinrich. His first case. Never solved it, and I think it ate on him. He was always yakking about it."

"Details?" I picked up pencils and pictures.

"A body was found on Main, drained of blood."

Drained of blood.

"A week went by, then more bodies showed up, all over the city. Maybe half a dozen. A month this went on, then suddenly stopped. Never found out what was killing them, or who. Never found out why they stopped."

"That's weird."

"Weird, yeah." Blatzky dropped papers on my desk. "Heinrich went a little crazy over it, you ask me. Mumbling about monsters, creatures of the night, if you can believe it."

"What, like Dracula?" I laughed heartily, to show I certainly did not believe such nonsense.

"Yeah. If you wanna see the case files, they're in the basement. That is, if you can brave the man-eating dustbunnies."

"Later, if I need to. I'm female, so I guess I'd be safe."

"Oh. Yeah. I keep forgetting that. You're a cop first." Blatzky snatched my *Sass-Cgal* and scuttled for the john.

My mind churning, I didn't even try to stop him. Fakeula had told the truth, again. There were killings, and they did involve exsanguination. But in the nineteen twenties? That was almost a century ago. It was impossible for Bo Strongwell to be involved. Even if he were a lot older than he looked, in nineteen-twenty he wouldn't have been more than a pinprick in his grandpa's condom stash.

Except...what if Bo really were some sort of ageless creature? Like Dorian Gray or a vampi...no. No effing way. There were pecans, there were cashews and then there was just plain nuts.

I needed to confront Fakeula with this information. See how he tried to explain the date discrepancy. I pulled my notebook to get his real name and address.

Stared. Vlad Dracula, Fifth and Grant.

Which was the fucking Roller-Blayd factory. I cleared my desk and hit the street.

I'd stomped about a block when a shadow slid up beside me. Between one breath and the next, my gun was out.

Bo's big hand covered the muzzle. His thumb plugged the end.

Immediately I jerked it up. "Don't *do* that." What, did he think he was Wile E. Coyote? I shoved the XD into its holster. (A mini slide. At one time I'd used an inside holster but the advent of superlow jeans put the kibosh on that. Oh, and though a lot of detectives carried concealed, I never bothered. I mean, this was Meiers Corners. The whole town already knew I carried a gun. Dolly even knew how many bullets I had on me at any point in time.)

Bo smiled. The streetlight sparkled on his teeth, caught out a dimple. Oh, damn. It wasn't enough that his face was straight out of *Yummy Desserts Illustrated*. He had to have a killer *dimple* too.

"What are you doing here, Strongwell? Don't you have a real job?" I started walking, a bit more normally now.

"This is my job. Or at least, part of it. You knew that."

"Yeah, neighborhood watch. You and your assistant Viking. Don't see how it pays the bills, though." I wondered for a moment what Bo's thick blond mane would look like, as long as Thorvald's. Thor's hair, Bo's face...surprisingly, it was easy to imagine Bo in battle braids and a horned helmet.

He flashed the dimple. Reading my mind? Shaking off the image, I hoofed west, toward the abandoned warehouse. Bo sauntered along next to me.

I remembered Thor's story about Bo's betrayal at a partner's hands and decided to test the waters. "Where is your *partner*, anyway?"

Bo's stride caught. "Thor isn't my *partner*." His voice went flat.

Bingo. "Assistant, then. He was on the streets earlier. Neighborhood watching."

He smoothed out. "Thor's at the apartment."

"Stamping rent checks and whatnot, huh?" I tucked my hands into my pockets. "And you're here because...?"

"I was patrolling and saw you. Things are a little anxious around town since Schrimpf's death. I thought you might want some company."

That rang true. The pre-dawn morning was dark and overcast. Sidewalks were empty, deserted. I had to admit, his company *was* nice. Not that Meiers Corners was generally a dangerous place. But unless Napoleon Schrimpf sat on some plastic fangs and jacked off with a misplaced breast-pump, *someone* had killed him.

"So, Detective. Anything new on the case?"

My suspicions sprang online, but more out of habit than anything else. I mean, what could I tell him that Dolly probably hadn't already related? And he seemed genuinely interested, which was nice.

Still, I made him work for it. "You have a reason for asking?" I raised one eyebrow.

He shot a brow back, conscious imitation. "Just making conversation."

"Uh-huh." I jammed my hands further in my pockets and tried not to be either amused or annoyed. In truth, I kind of enjoyed our sparring. "I can say I've heard some rumors."

"About your case?"

"Maybe. A historical precedence." We sauntered east, side by side. His pace matched mine, effortlessly. It was...companionable. "Know anything about exsanguination?"

"Blood loss? A bit." He smiled slightly, like it was an in-joke. "Rather desolate downtown these days, isn't it?"

"Avoiding the question?"

"Not at all. You're referring to the Killer Vampire of the nineteen twenties, aren't you? Dark out too. Dawn is six-oh-eight this morning. Less than half an hour away, but you'd never know it."

"Patrolling from dusk to dawn. What, instead of a time clock, you have to punch a sundial?" But he was right. Not only was the sky overcast, windows were unlit. Signs were dark. Even the streetlights were yellow and dim. Despite myself, I shivered. Tried to keep up the banter, but it wasn't so easy. "You're what, thirty? And you heard about this decades-ago killer how?"

"My grandfather told me, I think. It's an urban legend. Sort of a Meiers Corners Hook Hand."

"I see." My cop sense started tingling. Trying not to be obvious about it, I scanned the area. We were on Fourth and Adams. Buildings pressed tightly together here, mostly dry-as-dust offices. A bank, accountant's office and lawyer's office were cut by narrow, unlit walkways.

The buildings were as dry as their occupants. Brittle brick, darkened by age, slightly uneven, with shadowy gaps. Like hillbilly teeth. It was spooky.

So when a dark figure rose from the gloom behind us, I stiffened. It passed under one of the dim yellow lights and glowed all white, like a ghost. My hackles rose.

The ghost waved. "Hey, Elena."

I relaxed. "Dorie, hi. How's business?" Dorie Baecker was head baker at the Pie Delight. She looked the part, a sort of Pillsbury Doughboy with bangs.

"Great. Gotta rise and shine," she quipped, just before she was yanked out of sight.

"What the...?" For a split second, I didn't get it. She'd disappeared soundlessly between two buildings about twenty feet away. Like a mugging, but Meiers Corners didn't *have* muggings.

Next to me, Bo kicked into a run. He was at the walkway before I could blink. Automatically, I pursued.

A skeletal man leaped from the gap, tackling Bo. Bo rocked but didn't go down. He punched the man in the face, snapping his skull back.

"Police," I yelled. "Stop!"

A scream cut me off. A second gaunt man had Dorie by the neck. His head bent toward her throat.

"You," I said. "Let her go, now."

The man ignored me, his mouth opening like he was going to take a big bite.

Bo had his hands full with the first guy. This one had ignored my warnings. Unless I acted, fast, Dorie was going to get an impromptu tracheotomy. But I couldn't shoot because she was in the way. So I put my head down and charged.

I barreled into them, popping Dorie loose. She fell back against the brick of the law office, gasping. I cut her a quick glance to make sure she was okay.

In that split second, horny yellow fingernails dug into my shoulder and dragged me into the gap. Unnaturally strong hands threw me to the pavement. Wiry weight fell on top of me. Even with my trained reflexes, I couldn't stop him. He had my wrists manacled above my head before I registered I was down.

Dorie squeaked and ran away. Her footsteps rang, retreating rapidly.

I had more immediate concerns. Unholy stench filled my nostrils. Stringy hair fell into my face, blinding me. Red eyes glowed from the depths.

I fought using all the tricks in the book. Wrist-twist, hip pop. My attacker avoided or countered my maneuvers with absurd ease. A mouth opened above me. Saliva splashed onto my face.

Long fangs reached for my throat.

Doubling my struggles did *nothing.* The fangs descended and I was utterly helpless to stop them.

And still I fought, uselessly.

A roar exploded in the mouth of the gap. Closing in fast. Shockwaves of sound caromed off brick. I couldn't tell if it was friend or foe—or even man or beast.

But whatever it was, it was very big, very loud and *very* angry. I redoubled my struggles.

I heard a tearing sound. Hot, viscous fluid deluged me, drenched my shirt. My nostrils filled with a sharp, coppery odor. I flinched as the stuff soaked through to my skin.

Long fingers fastened around my attacker's neck. Bo's, dark and strong. He lifted and flung the guy like a sack of potatoes. The sight of Bo—broad shoulders twisted as he threw, muscles pumped to mountains—burned into my brain.

I rolled to one shaky elbow. The slashed remains of the second attacker lay at the entrance. The body was headless. Guts streamed from its open belly and the cave of its chest was empty. The heart had been dug out. My eyes raised to Bo.

He stood with his impossibly broad back to me, head bowed. I opened my mouth. "What..." It came out a croak. I tried again. "What happened?"

Bo took a deep, shuddering breath. Blew it out and straightened. Inhaled deeply and deliberately. Exhaled, and finally turned. His lips were pressed into a thin line and his eyes were unnaturally bright.

"Let's get out of here." He grabbed my arm, jerked me to my feet and dragged me away.

"The fuck!" I dug in my heels. Bo simply picked me up and carted me rapidly down the street. I struggled, uselessly. "That's a crime scene! I need to report it, get it cordoned off, start the paperwork—"

He plopped me on my feet in front of a big blue mailbox. Looked deep, and I mean *deep,* into my eyes. "You didn't see anything. There was no attack. No crime."

Whoa. He was into serious denial. I didn't know what had just happened either, but I knew it *happened.* I plucked blood-soaked cloth from my ribs and held it out. My white tee was now dark red. Damn, first coffee and now this. No more white. "No attack? What's this shit all over my shirt? Heinz Fifty-Seven?"

Bo's eyes blanked. Then he breathed in a bushel of air, released it on a hard puff. "You're the most stubborn, strong-minded female I have *ever* had the misfortune to meet."

Of all of that, I only heard "misfortune". "*Me*? Don't make it like I forced myself on you! You're the one who keeps dropping in on *me*."

Bo released my shoulders to plant fists on hips. "Oh? Like when you called me to rescue a stuffed bear from your sister's toilet? Or when you stomped into my home, demanding to see me?"

My gut imploded like I'd been punched. "The first was your *job*. And the second was mine."

"And at the fudge store? Was that your job too? Shuddering and moaning and rubbing your wet little crotch against me?"

"Shut up!" I screamed.

And kissed him.

Well, it worked for the heroes, why not us girls too?

My hands dug deep into his hair, yanked his head down. I mashed my lips into his. He spluttered in protest. I speared my tongue between his lips. With a groan, he opened. His mouth tasted strangely metallic, like he'd been chewing on a gum wrapper. I didn't care, thrusting into his heat, touching everything I could reach, lips, teeth, tongue, even a swipe to the roof of the mouth. Like I could devour him.

I was vaguely aware of the slowly waking row houses around us, of papers hitting stoops in the distance. But I didn't care. Maybe there was something to that violence-and-sex thing. Because though I'd started it to shut him up, though we were outdoors with only the waning night for privacy, five years, three months and five days was suddenly not going to be one more *second.*

I launched myself up, wrapping my arms around his neck, twining my legs around his hips. He caught me under the butt to settle me against his rapidly lengthening erection. He ground it against me, fingers biting into my glutes in his urgency. That hot shaft felt so wonderful even through four layers of clothing. It would feel amazing skin to skin.

Apparently Bo was just as eager. Four layers thinned to two when he parked my butt on top of the mailbox, and a zip was followed by a scalding nudge.

I hadn't passed third base for...well, yeah. Long enough to make me a little crazy. I fused my body to Bo's. Bit his lip. His erection jumped. I bit and licked his chiseled jaw, on my way to his ear. Tongued the lobe, then sucked it. It was so tasty in its soft nest of hair. I wondered what else would be tasty in a soft nest.

Bo groaned, rubbed himself against me. My bones clanked metal as his cock stuttered over the thick seam of my jeans. Oh, for a short, short skirt. And nothing else.

I teased his ear with my tongue. "Why do you make me so hot? You're like guns and chocolate and beer all rolled into one."

He laughed between groans. "Yeah? Well I feel like a perpetual redwood around you." He shoved a hand down my jeans, encountered my wet slit. "Aw, damn, Elena."

I shifted my hips so he could slide deeper. A single hot finger invaded me. I stifled a scream. My legs automatically scissored, squeezing him, practically cutting him in two. He gasped. Didn't stop the finger. It slid deeper, withdrew to kiss the edges of my inner lips. When I was about to scream anyway, it slid forward, touching heaven.

Bo wiggled that clever finger until I jangled like a bell. I practically chewed off his earlobe. I clung to him so hard I'm surprised I didn't pull his head off.

The slap of rolled-up newspapers grew nearer. I clung and chewed and rocked frantically against Bo's strong body. Through it all he kept vibrating. I was teetering on the edge of climax, my whole body abuzz. Especially my breasts. My whole chest purred in pleasure, so loudly I could almost *hear* it—

Wait.

I could hear it, actually. Or I heard something rumbling between us. A deep rhythmic *rrrr*, like a lion's purr.

Uh-oh. A squirrel-sized cat had scratched me once, and I still had the scars. The beast matching this lion-sized purr would have claws like switchblades. I launched out of Bo's arms, steadying myself against the mailbox. "What the hell?" I cast around me. *Where was it*?

My roving eyes lit on Bo. The sight of him distracted me really fast from monster cats. He stood statue-still, blond head back, eyes squeezed shut, pants pushed down just under his—omigod.

It was as big as my forearm. A table leg. Made my Big Mama vibrator look like Pokey Jr.

And I wasn't talking about his belt buckle.

Bo's eyes slit open. They glittered in the streetlight, blue darkened almost to purple. "You have incredibly bad timing." His voice was rough.

"*I* have bad timing?" I nearly shrieked it in my frustration. *He* wasn't the one who was about to see light at the end of a five-year tunnel—only to be *luminis interruptus* by a freaking *cat*. Speaking of which... I checked my front. Blood, but drying, not mine. No claw marks. Must have only sounded like a crazed animal was right on top of me. "I heard a cat." Now that I wasn't in imminent danger of being scratched to death, I felt a little sheepish.

"A cat." Bo's face went perfectly blank.

"Uh, yeah. Growling. Or maybe, uh, purring."

"A purring cat." Bo's eyes quieted. So, unfortunately, did Mr. Forearm. "Are you allergic to cats? Or perhaps purrs?"

"No, no. I like cats. Dogs too." My face was very warm. "My place is too small for a pet, though."

"I see." He put away his toys and zipped up. The overcast sky was lightening behind him.

Damn. I had blown it. My shot at heaven—or at least a chance of some serious fun. Now the countdown would continue. I had to fight not to grind my teeth into dental powder.

And double damn. Considering Bo's frustrated face, I might not get another chance. But I bet Mr. Viking Battleship could. He could get plenty of other chances. Hell, with an erector set like that, he could probably stage his very own lottery.

Jail me and throw away the key. I *knew* I should have followed "Ten Pointers to Ful-*fill*-ment". Oh please, St. Dirkson, could it get any worse?

At that moment the paperboy came around the corner. The first rays of gray-tinged sun filtered over the rooftops, hitting his cheeky grin.

Bo winced. "Elena, I've got to go."

Toss the key and say hi to Bend-over Bubba. I prayed to St. Dirkson and got St. Murphy instead. "But—"

Before the word was out of my mouth, he'd poofed.

Chapter Twelve

Dark clouds gathered as I trudged back to the scene of the attack. I remembered it being around Fourth and Adams but somehow Bo and I had gotten all the way to Eisenhower. Near my apartment, I thought with uncharacteristic bitterness. He could have taken me home to bed, if he'd wanted to. Obviously he hadn't. I stuck my hands deep in my pocket and pushed the thought away. I had work to do.

By the time I got to ground zero, the sun barely showed through small breaks in the heavy clouds. It was already uncomfortably hot, the humid air sluggish. I turned into the walkway.

Nothing was there.

I frowned, looked again. Had the bodies been dragged away? I knelt, studied the pavement. Two black scorches marred the concrete.

I blinked. But the scene didn't change. No bodies, no blood. Just black marks, streaked with dust and ash.

Well. I'd heard of spontaneous human combustion, but this was ridiculous. I snapped on gloves, poked my finger into the charred mass. Something crumbled. I leaned closer, saw little blackened shards, like bits of bone.

Char marks. Red-eyed attackers. And Bo had bitten me. Connections were snapping on in my brain, scary connections. Like maybe Bo knew what had happened in this walkway after all. Like maybe *he* was responsible for that empty chest cavity.

Fuck. As my friend Nixie would say, this was *baka.* It was insane to think these streaks were the remains of vampi…no. There had to be a perfectly logical explanation. A not-nuts explanation. A cop explanation.

I pulled out a baggy and pinched up a sample of the charred stuff. Charles Samuel Ignatek was going to earn his money analyzing this.

ᴄᴕ

At home, I tried to sleep. My old room air conditioner couldn't have cooled a hamster cage. Pitting it against the August heat made it sputter, cough and finally die.

Hot, damp, I dreamed of Bo licking me like an ice-cream cone and woke up with the sheet wadded between my legs. After straightening the bedclothes I lay back down but tossed and turned in the oppressive heat and humidity. Slept not at all.

The heavy rain clouds finally broke around two, and with them, the heat spell—but the cool weather didn't help my personal heat spell. Counting sheep backfired because I ended up counting fantasy licks. Finally I fell into a light doze.

At six p.m. I woke. Too early, but I got up anyway. Over two days had passed since the murder. I had to solve this case, and soon.

Grabbing pencil, notebook and a big cup of joe, I plopped down in my living room. I'd push some order into my life by organizing the case.

I slashed a grid onto the page, listed my suspects in the first column. Headed the other three means, motive and opportunity.

Josephine Schrimpf. She had motive. No opportunity, supposedly being out of town at the time. I made a note to check her alibi. And search her house for means. She might refuse my request to look, but that would tell me something too. I phoned her, made an appointment to meet at ten p.m.

With strong motive, Josephine Schrimpf was my top suspect. But not the only one...my eyelids drooped.

I blinked. Poured another cup of coffee. Got up with it and took a turn around the couch.

Drusilla. She was the last person to see Schrimpf alive. She had the best opportunity. And she had been acting decidedly strange.

But why kill a paying customer? I sank back onto my sofa. No motive. I didn't know if she had the means. I would need to find her, quiz her again.

Who else? Though less likely, one of the bar patrons might be involved. I would need to interview Donner and Blitz again, find out who was at Nieman's that night.

My head jerked up. I shook it. Huh, nearly fell asleep. I drank more joe and considered whether the killer might be someone connected with the gym. But Nixie was pretty savvy. If there were rumblings, she would have heard them. I put that on the bottom of the list.

Of course, it was always possible Schrimpf was a random killing. In the wrong place at the wrong time. But with no sign of a struggle, and Schrimpf wounded in a rather...personal place, I thought it more likely the killer was someone Schrimpf knew.

There was another possibility. I couldn't quite remember who, but I knew there was someone else...my head jerked up again. Damn. I'd been pushing pretty hard but I was stronger than this. I *had* to be. Not only was the badge riding on it, but my pride.

The widow, Drusilla, somebody at the bar, an employee or vendor. I had my suspects, my MMOs. Now I just needed to find evidence to prove which was right.

I nearly jumped out of my chair when my phone started beeping. I flipped it out, saw the reminder for my ten o'clock with Josephine Schrimpf. Damn, it was already nine thirty. I bolted for the shower. I'd have to go straight to the widow's.

The hot water cleared the cobwebs from my head. I washed quickly, but something made me grab my scented shower gel. Not thoughts of Bo. I dressed in thong and low-slung jeans with an *S* for sexy stamped on the butt (also not for Bo). Then I hunted through my nearly empty drawers until I found a scoop-neck navy lace knit top that barely covered my breasts (not for Bo—for Dirk and his coffee attacks).

My cell rang while I was going through my final checks. I recognized the caller ID. "Hey, Alice." XD loaded, thumb safety on. Check. Clutch piece, check. Pockets loaded with everything from gloves to pencil. Check. Good to go.

"Hey, Elena. Want to go bowling? Alba Gruen called in sick."

"I'd love to, but I'm working." Suiting words to action, I hit the street, barely noticing the wash of bright stars.

"Play hooky. C'mon, you only live once."

The cooler weather let me head for the Schrimpf home with a fast, determined stride. The clear air hit my nose in a sweet rush. I finally felt fully awake. "Alice, I have a case to solve. A permanent badge to earn. Justice to serve. Remember, if I don't solve the case, a murderer walks free."

She *tsked.* "You sound so much like your father. Such a burning need for justice. You're a lot like him, you know. A fighter for justice."

"Fighter for justice? That sounds like some sort of crusader. I'm just a detective, doing my job. Careful, plodding, by-the-book."

Alice laughed. "Proves my point. That is so Patrick. By-the-Book O'Rourke, we used to call him. Such a wonderful public defender. Well-respected."

I waited for traffic on Seventh before crossing. "Well-respected, but not very well paid."

"None of us are, kiddo. You were always trying to be like him. I remember that little briefcase Brita got you. You put on one of his ties and carried that case around like it was grafted on."

"You knew Brita too."

"We got to be good friends. I have to say, she wasn't happy leaving Meiers Corners."

"No. She wasn't." One of the reasons I thought of her as Brita instead of Mom. "Dad had to go. His talent was wasted here, defending shoplifters and jaywalkers. He got bigger cases in Chicago." No traffic on Sixth. I trotted across.

"More money too."

For some reason, that stung. "He was still a lawyer of integrity."

"Integrity? Is that why he moved to Chicago? Got them fancy digs on Lake Shore Drive, instead of commuting?"

"Come on, Alice. You know the place was part of the job. He needed it to entertain, to lure in the big clients."

Alice huffed a sigh. "All right, I admit I only heard Brita's side of it. She felt like a fish out of water after he joined that firm. The parties, the jet-set lifestyle wore on her."

Another sting, worse because I knew it was true. I hit Fifth, almost turned south, but that would take me past the lonely, spooky Roller-Blayd factory where loony Count Wannabe hung out. I decided I'd skip it.

"It wore on both of them. Alice, I'm sorry about your bowling, but I have to go."

"Elena, wait. Don't hang up." She paused. "Look, kiddo. I apologize for upsetting you."

"*De nada*. It's okay." I glanced down Fifth. On the other hand, was I man or mouse? Or in my case, woman or...um, wombat. I turned south. Drac still owed me a proper name and addy.

"Elena, I'm sorry. I guess I'm still angry over it. If Patrick had listened to her, they might be alive today. Hell, if he'd just followed his own feelings for once, instead of going by that stupid book—"

"What do you mean?"

"Elena—" Alice never searched for words, but she did then. "Brita called me that night. The night they...crashed. Four years ago. She called because she and Patrick fought."

"No way. Dad and Brita never fought. They loved each other." Jumbled feelings pushed me back into motion, faster now. I made for Roosevelt at a trot.

"I'm telling you, that day they fought. Over a stupid party, of all things. It was the last in a month of holiday shindigs. Brita was sick and tired of the posing and posturing, and didn't want to go. Your father said it was part of the job. He didn't want to go either but declared they had to whether they wanted to or not.

"Dad insisted on doing things properly. Nothing wrong with that."

"Elena, it was a party. They were both tired, wrung out. And a little out of their element. It wouldn't have hurt them to miss one party. All that drinking...well."

I spun east and hit Roosevelt at practically at a gallop. Like a gaggle of Dirks was after me. Or would that be a gabble of Dirks?

Then I realized I was unconsciously running toward Nixie's. My friend, a haven of safety.

Not while I was on the job. Patrick wasn't the only By-the-Book O'Rourke, dammit. Resolutely, I turned south again. "You're not implying Dad was irresponsible, are you?"

Alice laughed, not a happy sound. "Your father? He was more reliable than death and taxes. But reliable didn't stop that snowstorm. Didn't stop that truck. Didn't stop the alcohol from throwing fuel on the flames."

"Dad would *never* drink and drive. They got a ride home from the senior partner that night. In the company limo. Dad knew his limits."

It was a verbal slap, but Alice only said, "I heard one of the seatbelts was pulled out. Like someone had started to buckle up, but stopped."

And there it was, of course. My dad always wore a seatbelt. Not wearing one was a spanking offense in our family. If Dad and Brita had been wearing their seatbelts that night...I might not be alone now.

The Roller-Blayd factory loomed ahead, desolate, dead. Seeing it so empty hurt for some reason. I walked faster. "That truck hit them pretty hard. The seatbelt might have been dislodged in the crash. The belts were tucked into the seat cracks. Dad probably didn't even know they were there. He—"

"Your gut tells you differently, Elena. Your father was a wolf in the courtroom. But socially? He hated to make waves or stick out in any way. I think that's one of the reasons he followed the rules, so he didn't make waves. No matter what it cost him. Or Brita. He did it to be normal."

Oh God. To be normal. Nixie was right. That's why I did it. "You think the partner talked him out of it. Scolded him, or belittled him. 'Oh, we're too rich to die'."

"Doesn't that make sense?"

"Nothing about that night makes sense!" I ran from the warehouse, not even bothering to check for traffic. "All I know is, if Dad had followed the rules and worn his damned seatbelt, he would have been okay."

"*Or* if had he *followed his heart* and stayed home. Patrick and Brita would also be alive if he hadn't played by anybody's rules but his own."

I ground to a stop, sagging against a street sign. Dad wouldn't have died in that stupid, meaningless way—if he had followed his heart. His heart, instead of the rules.

Maybe I should—

No. I had decided never again, just this morning. I kicked the post, resumed my trek. "Rules have a purpose, Alice. They make life better, safer. Make us fit together." Made the abnormal normal. Gave deviants purpose and path. "You should know. We're both police. We defend law and order."

"Honey, I just don't want to see you end up like your dad."

"My dad was honest and brave. It would be an honor to end up just like him. And Alice—he would have wanted this case solved. He would have wanted *me* to solve it."

"Maybe." A pause. "But Brita would have wanted you to go bowling."

"*Goodbye*, Alice." I hit disconnect. *This* was why she made me her project. I wasn't sure if I was warmed by the idea or pissed, but one thing I did know. By the book was the answer. For this case. And especially for me.

Punching up voicemail, I listened to a message that had come in while I was talking—or arguing—with Alice. "Hello? Hello, Detective Ma'am? Hello? Where are you?" I recognized Ruffles on the first syllable. "I waited at the station so I could join you but you weren't there and Detective Blatzky said you weren't coming in but I knew you wouldn't leave without me unless this is some sort of test of my detective abilities to see if I can find you—"

The message went on for another five minutes. Good thing I *hadn't* answered. By the time I got back to Alice, she might really have died of old age.

As I hiked toward the widow's, slower now, I pulled out my notebook. The widow, Drusilla, the bar. Employee or vendor. But I was missing a name. That annoyed me. The most important investigation of my career. Who the hell—

"Hello, Detective."

Oh yeah. Strongwell.

While I did *not* believe Fakeula's accusations (really, how reliable was a guy who called himself Dracula?), there were niggling questions. Why had my sister warned me off the case? What did her warning have to do with Bo?

Why was he so damned sexy? Why did I feel like a volcano about to erupt around him?

No, no, not those questions. What was it with that odd basement of his? Why did my lie meter not work with him? And most interest...irritating of all, "Why do you keep showing up where I—" I whipped around.

My bark vaporized into a pant. Bo's tight sleeveless tee showed off his mammoth biceps. Worn jeans limned his bitable butt. He looked like a muscular Mount Everest just waiting to be climbed and conquered.

Celibacy was apparently eating away my brains.

His eyes closed and he took a deep breath. "Mmm. That scent..." His eyes flew open, a startling violet.

"What?" Couldn't be me. Hulk It was way out of my salary range.

He stalked closer. "I try to stay away. But you're too much for me."

"I am?" I had to steel myself not to back away. I kept forgetting that, up close, Bo was *big.* Tall, imposing, yes. But physically, that chest could have fit two men with muscle to spare. A warrior's arm band circling one of those thick biceps could have belted my waist. "Er, too much cop?"

"Too much woman. What a pretty top, Detective."

Too much *woman*? Wow. No one had ever said that about me before.

Bo traced my lace neckline with one finger, grazing my skin. "You have the softest, sweetest breasts."

No one had said that, either. Unless he was buttering me up...ooh, butter. Slipping and sliding, in and out... I batted his hand away. "Hey, buster. That's sexual harassment."

"And such lovely pants." The hand came right back, splaying across my rump, branding me. "You have a delectable ass, Detective."

"Stop it, Strongwell. That's totally inappropriate." I tried to put a sharp warning into my voice. Not only did I have questions, starting with disappearing blood and ending with dirt-floor rumpus rooms, but we were on the fashionable East Side of Meiers Corners, for pity's sake. Right in the middle of a nest of upper-class residential busybodies. It reminded me uncomfortably of this morning's indiscretion. Carried away by lust, then *rejected.* "Stop. This is way too public."

But as he kneaded my glutes, my eyes fluttered closed and I leaned eagerly into his six-four. That (and my little whimper) *might* have undermined my "stop".

"Stop what, Detective? This?" Bo pulled me close. His erection strained hot against my belly. "Or perhaps this?" His fingers delved down the back of my jeans.

Half my brain cells dribbled out my ear. He cupped my buttock, skin to skin, caressed firmly. The rest of my brain jumped out to find them.

I groaned. "Stop...both..." My mouth said stop but my hips angled back and up, trying to slide my pussy under his firm grip.

"Or maybe you mean *this.*" One big hot finger slid in, then a *second.* I shuddered. My pelvis started rocking into his fingers.

"No, stop...hell." Why couldn't my head and hormones agree? Or one of them just kill me and take over? "*All* of it. You're a suspect. I'm a civil serv...civil ssss...shit!"

Bo had yanked my pants and thong to my ankles. On his knees, he splayed hands between my thighs and *spread.* His mouth landed on my pussy. His breath was *scorching.*

"Madonna's metal mammaries! Stop it, Strongwell. We're in *public.*" I leaped away, horrified. Dolly Barton's gossip network would slaughter me, Captain Tight-ass would crucify me. Goodbye badge, hello part-time janitor using my own hair as a mop.

My jeans-hobbled ankles threw my balance. My leap turned into a series of frantic hops. Windmilling, I went down.

Bo rose smoothly to his feet and caught me, one-handed. He yanked me in, hand splaying across my naked butt. My entire butt. Either the man had huge hands or *Sass-Cgal's* "Tight 'n Tiny Tush in Three Minutes a Day" really worked.

"I want you, Elena." His voice was all animal growl. "And you want me. I can smell how ready you are."

"I'm not ready to get fired! What if someone sees?"

"Easily taken care of." He lifted me off my feet, effortlessly carried me into the deep night shadows of a towering tree, and pressed me against its dark trunk.

My naked butt hit bark. Rough, living wood scratched skin made hypersensitive by his touch. Warm summer air played softly over my damp and throbbing lips. Stars above, I wanted this man. Needed him.

Bo dropped to his knees and took up right where he'd left off. Thrusting my thighs apart, he invaded.

His mouth landed right on the sweet spot. He kissed me deeply, intimately. Wetly, with a swirl and a suck that nearly sent me through my skull.

"Stop it!" My fingers dug into his thick blond hair. To push his head away, but his tongue flicked my little red light-switch. I *pulled* instead, practically grinding into his face. My slick wet lips slid against his granite jaw. Stubble added to the blazing friction.

He sucked me in rhythm to my grinding hips. My body clenched against the sweet buildup. "Dammit, Bo, you can't make me come in the middle of someone's yard!"

"No one can see us here, you know." His assault changed from sucking to lapping. "Mmm. You taste wonderful, Elena. Woman-sweet."

A house light flipped on down the street. It didn't touch us in our dark shadows. "Woman sweet?" I writhed under his expert onslaught. "I'm a cop, not a woman."

"You didn't let me finish." He lapped harder. "Sweet, yet strong. Piquant."

"Pee-kent? What the hell is that?" My breath rasped as my body began to gather.

"A tangy contradiction. Endlessly fascinating. You tremble when you're close to climaxing. You're so strong, yet you tremble."

"And what about you, Mr. Pee-kent?" I rolled myself faster against his burning wet tongue. "You're a janitor throwing around thousand-dollar words. A murder suspect patrolling like a cop." I groaned. "More. Give me more."

"Bossy thing, aren't you?" Two hard fingers slid into me, filled me. "I like that." He began thrusting.

I gasped. "I'm so close…harder. Faster."

"My pleasure." His tongue worked my clit harder while his fingers shot in and out. I pumped against him in counterpoint.

"So close…*more.*"

He sucked. The hot tugging sent a shocking thrill through me. My fingers tightened painfully in his hair. He gave a grunt, muffled, his mouth full of me.

I braced my shoulders against the tree, jacked my pelvis into him so hard I nearly pushed him off his knees. It drove his fingers in to the hilt. I ground myself into them with a choked cry. "Oh, more, *please.*"

His mouth left me. A breeze cooled where he'd been. "Elena."

I stood there, throbbing helplessly, his sudden stop pulling my gaze to his face. His eyes glowed like blue moons from between my thighs. Staring intently at me, he slowly, deliberately opened his mouth—and rested the points of two very long eyeteeth on my mons.

I gasped. Jerked away.

He grabbed my thighs, slammed me back against the tree trunk. His hands locked me in place, jailing me with his hard male strength.

When I was immobilized, he bit down.

Live wires drove into my mound. Streaks of lightning hit deep in my pelvis. Exploded back, arcing through belly and breasts. I throttled a scream as a climax's onset sheared through me.

Licking my clit like a thirsty animal, Bo shifted. Thrust a hot finger home.

The orgasm hit me hard, rammed my body like a truck. A two-ton load of ecstasy. It slammed into me again and again. Rolled over me until I was flatter than butter on August blacktop.

And then he thrust a second finger and bit harder, and I climaxed again.

Bo lapped up my orgasms like pudding. "Elena…oh, Elena you taste *wonderful.*"

Yeah, well, I felt wonderful. I came down slowly, pulsing with aftershock. The earthquake climaxes washed me clean. Made me limp and sated as a…as a really limp and sated thing. I tried to say it but it came out more like, "Yuh waffle winful."

"Come home with me." Bo's voice rumbled against my thighs. His words pulsed with that mysterious catlike vibration, that deep purr. Except there was no cat.

The only thing against my legs was Bo.

My brain cells climbed back in. Only Bo. So Bo was purring. Bo was—a cat?

I didn't freak (which alone should have worried me) but I did try to disengage. He pressed kisses to my naked belly. "Bo." My voice was a croak. I cleared my throat, tried again. "Strongwell. Let me go."

The kisses stopped. The purr, if that's what it was, died. His mouth was slightly open, and he was panting. Very slowly, his gaze lifted.

His eyes were practically incandescent. The intense desire I saw there shocked me. Unrelieved desire, made stunningly visceral by the heavy erection pulsing against my knees. Which reminded me that I'd gotten orgasm with a capital *O*, but he'd gotten squat. I felt like the worst kind of tease, regardless of purr-related issues.

"Um, Bo...I have to go to work. But, uh, maybe we can make a date for later." The lacy curtain of a nearby mansion was just dropping back into place. Too dark for anyone to have seen anything, but I winced. "Somewhere a little more private."

Bo's eyes clamped shut. "A date." His voice held a world of pain.

"Well...maybe we can do more than lick. After work."

"Oh? Even though I'm a *suspect*?"

"You're not very high on the list," I mumbled, flushing.

His eyes opened directly on mine. His gaze was that piercing, mind-reading one. He rose. "I suppose. My apartment?"

He didn't sound happy, but he wasn't rejecting me. I let my breath out. "Yeah. Great."

"Until later, then." Bo glided away.

Five years, three months and five days. My vigil was near an end, at last. I stood there, watching that tight ass, until the darkness swallowed him. Then I started swearing.

I had totally forgotten to question him.

Chapter Thirteen

Unfortunately, I had that ten o'clock appointment with the widow. So I couldn't run after Strongwell and grill him like I wanted to (with oil on a bearskin in front of a very large fireplace). So after pulling up my jeans, I resumed my determined stride toward the Schrimpfs' residence. *Not* noticing the row after row of stares from behind fancy curtains. Much. They couldn't have seen anything. Nothing terribly lewd, at any rate.

I clung to that. 'Cause our police captain wasn't called Tight-ass for nothing.

My cop sense tingled, alerting me to the approaching rumble of a powerful engine. I turned. A black Town Car crept past me. I watched myself slide along its mirrored windows, my image stretching and scrunching like I was in some creepy funhouse. But Town Cars were the Meiers Corners fleet vehicles, so I wasn't too worried.

Until right behind me, big, black and mobbish did a U-ey.

Well. Maybe they were only lost. Still not worried—much—I started forward again.

The Town Car shadowed behind me.

O-*kay*. Worried now. Definitely worried. I scanned for some sort of cover. Pink plastic flamingos, too thin. Garden trolls, too squat. (This was the rich section of town, but money didn't always mean taste.) The only thing vaguely Elena-shaped was a largemouth-bass mailbox. I ducked behind it.

"Who's there?" I called to the vehicle. "Show yourself." Automatically I put my hand over my gun.

The Town Car slid menacingly to the curb right in front of where I hid. The rear passenger door popped open.

And banged smack into the mailbox. The sick crunch of metal announced a thousand-dollar repair, minimum.

Gangly Dirk Ruffles sprang out with more enthusiasm than sense. Gone was the rumpled blue uniform, replaced by a rumpled blue suit. He had paired it with a yellow fedora. No longer a duck in uniform, now he was a duck in a suit and tie.

"Hello, Detective Ma'am! I phoned but you didn't answer. But I found you. Am I a good detective, or what? Are we going to interview a suspect? Is it the widow? Do you think she'll offer us drinks again? Do you think I can have a martini this time, shaken not stirred? I told my uncle about Mrs. Schrimpf's martinis, even though I didn't taste one. I always have a martini when I watch cable, though, so I know what they taste like. Well, at least what Barnacle Bill's Martini Mix tastes like. I had a martini after I got off work while I watched reruns of Oprah on cable and my uncle..."

Why Officer—now Detective—Ruffles was using fleet transport I didn't know. But as he prattled on about martinis and his uncle and what he saw on cable my eye started twitching and I didn't *care.* In self-defense, I ran away.

Dirkenstein lumbered along behind, yakking the whole time. The Town Car followed. The faster I ran the faster he lumbered. And yammered. It sapped the strength from my legs, my body—my will to live. In desperation I turned. Held up one hand and braced myself. "Detective Ruffles!"

He lumbered into my hand, which stopped him but not the yammering. "Yes, Detective Ma'am? By the way, I like it when you call me Detective Ruffles. Sounds so official, doesn't it? *Detective* Ruff..."

Like a heavy, muddy river, the best I could do was divert the flood. "How would you like a *solo* investigation?"

"Me?" His feathery little mustache sucked in with his surprised breath. A single frown line wrinkled his forehead. "*Me*?"

"Captain Titus wants this case wrapped up as fast as possible. It will double our effectiveness if you go awa—er, take half the work." I was almost ashamed. Would it be so hard to let him come along? Just for one shift. Eight hours, dogged by Dirkenstein. Besieged by nonstop blather for four hundred eighty minutes, or five hundred forty counting lunch.

Yeah. It was either find him a job or bang myself repeatedly in the head with a lead pipe. "The captain needs you, Ruffles. I need you."

"Oh, yes, Detective Ma'am. I'm your man."

"Good. Here's what I want you to do." I kept my sentences short and simple. "Before Schrimpf died, he lost a lot of blood. But no blood was at the scene. That means Schrimpf bled out *someplace else.*"

"Yes, ma'am. Someplace else!"

I closed my eyes so Dirk couldn't see me roll them. He was so painfully enthusiastic. Like a kitten climbing your leg to be petted, even when you were wearing shorts. "Draw a ten-minute circle around Nieman's Bar, Detective Ruffles. Search that circle—and find that blood."

"Yes, ma'am!" Dirkenstein saluted, hitting himself sharply in the forehead. I looked closer at his frown line—or was that a *dent*? Dirk galloped back to the Town Car. He popped into the rear seat, popped back out, saluted me again, and popped back in. The door slammed, not quite flush because of the crumpled edge. The Town Car rocketed away.

Heaving a sigh of relief, I turned onto Widow Schrimpf's front walk.

I had to solve this case soon. Josephine Schrimpf was my top suspect and I was here to break her alibi. My future as a detective rested on it. I donned my cop manners and rapped on the door.

When I was in grade school we used to amuse ourselves with line drawings. I would draw a vertical line. Then I'd stick two triangles point-first into it, one on either side. A man with a bow tie stuck in an elevator.

Two parallel lines with four circles (two on each side) was a bear climbing a tree.

The Widow Schrimpf's door opened. I couldn't decide if I was seeing tits stuck in an elevator, or tits climbing a rope.

She stepped back and waved a glass of amber liquid toward the inside of the house. "Detective O'Rourke, right on time. Do come in. Can I get you a drink?"

No maid? It occurred to me if Sappy Nappy was as horny as everyone said, the *maid* might have as much motive to kill him as the *missus*. Maybe more. "Where is Martinez? Does she have the night off?"

"I just sent her home, actually. I'm going out of town. Why pay her if I'm gone?"

"You're *leaving*?" Anyone with a TV knew you weren't supposed to leave town if you were a crime suspect. By trying to duck out, Josephine Schrimpf was practically shouting her guilt. "I'm sorry, Mrs. Schrimpf. I'm afraid I'll have to ask you to put off your trip."

"But why?" Josephine blinked long-lashed eyes at me. "I'm so overwhelmed arranging Nappy's funeral. Surely I deserve a break? The house is so empty without him." She squeezed out a tear.

I gave her my best cop glare.

Josephine shrugged, as if to say, "A girl's gotta try." Briskly she continued, "It's only for a few days, to New York. They have the best shopping. And I just heard about a place called the Model-T Escort Club. The men have car names, like Mr. Thunderbird and Lexus DeVille. I'm just dying to take an SUV for a test drive, if you know what I mean." She winked.

Ri-ight. "The investigation isn't closed yet, ma'am. I need you to stay in town."

"That's silly. It's been three days. Surely you've solved the case by *now*."

Oh, for a bullet to chew on. "This isn't a crime show, ma'am. We don't solve cases in an hour."

"How disappointing." Josephine sipped her drink. "So did you come all the way over here just to tell me I can't leave?"

"No. Mrs. Schrimpf, I want to search the premises."

She nodded. "All right."

I blinked in surprise. She couldn't mean *all right.* "I want to search, ma'am, but I don't have a warrant."

"No problem. Search away. The faster you finish, the faster I can go to New York."

I wasn't expecting that. First, no one ever cooperated with the cops in *Midwest Police Monthly*. And second, I hated to admit it, but I didn't like her. I didn't like how she treated her servant and I didn't like that she didn't seem to mourn her dead husband at all. And I was jealous to death of her thirty-six Cs. I'd thought she'd fight me. I *hoped* she'd fight me. I was looking forward to slapping her down. "No, you don't understand. I want to search your *house.* Top to bottom."

"Well, I didn't think you wanted to search my underwear drawer, Detective O'Rourke." She smiled slyly. "Or maybe you do? Nice thong, by the way."

I glanced back, saw I'd yanked thong above jeans after Bo's handiwork (and oh, boy, was he handy...shit). I blushed and doggedly tried one last time. "Mrs. Schrimpf. I want to look for damning evidence."

"Yes, Detective. Look away. I hope you find something. Plant evidence, if you want to. I mean, we're talking about riding Mr. Mustang here. Upstairs first, or down?"

I gave up. "Basement? Or, um, root cellar?"

The Schrimpf abode was meticulously clean. Martinez, if she was the housekeeper, earned her buck ninety-five. Four immaculate bedrooms, five squeaky-clean bathrooms, a totally innocuous basement and two spotless offices later I was about to give up.

"One more bedroom." Josephine pointed at the last door.

This had been a total waste of time. And with everyone pushing for the case to be solved yesterday, time was one thing I didn't have. I didn't want to look.

But it was my job. By-the-book thoroughness (and the specter of Tight-ass) made me grab the knob and twist. The door opened to mega-equipment. Benches. Pulleys. Straps. At first I thought I was seeing a home gym.

Except...the straps were shiny and link-shaped. And there were no weights.

I blinked. The pulleys and straps were *chains.* The benches were equipped with cuffs. A pair of shackles hung from the ceiling. "What...what's this?" My voice was a little gaspy.

The goofiest smile appeared on the widow's face. "Nappy's Happy

Room."

"I...see." I blinked again, but both the dungeon motif (bad) and the goofy smile (far, far worse) were still there. Yeesh. Apparently I had led a rather sheltered life.

But I was a cop. A *detective.* Information was my job, dammit. I pulled myself together, entered the room. "So what made Nappy happy, Mrs. Schrimpf?"

Josephine floated in behind me, caressed a hand along the bench. "We would have a couple drinks. Then I'd put Nappy in here and feed him a couple more. He liked to get a little sloppy, if you know what I mean."

Yeah, I got that. I'd have to get totally soused before I'd let anyone tie me to a rack to do unspeakable things...unless he had big hands and battleaxe shoulders and a killer dimple...eek.

Josephine fondled a cuff. "I'd turn out all the lights and change into my costume. Then I'd light a single candle, and—do him."

"*Do* him?" My voice cracked.

"*You* know." She pursed her lips and did a silent whistle.

Not getting her drift, I shook my head.

"Swallow the sword, Detective O'Rourke. Chew the meat. Play the skin flute."

Good grief. Where did people come up with these things? The images made me want to burn out my retinas with mace. "Blow job?"

"Right." Josephine smiled and drank off her liquor. "It was Nappy's favorite form of sex."

"I...see." I'd read an article on blow jobs, in *Great Housekeeper,* of all places. "How to Vacuum-Suck His Upholstery 'Til He Screams." I had *not* picked it up with Bo in mind.

"This is the costume." Widow Schrimpf went to a clothes rack and pulled out a long, flowing black dress. She handed it to me while she dug around for some other things.

Deep V-neck. Tight skirt and wasp waist. Tags of fabric fluttered at the wrists and the flippy little hem.

"Here's the rest." Josephine plopped a black wig on her head and stuck some dentures in her mouth.

Dentures with fangs.

She reminded me eerily of Drusilla. "Mrs. Schrimpf. When you, uh, blew Napoleon...did he ever ask you to do more? More than blowing and, um, licking?"

"Of course." The widow chomped her dentures and grinned saucily. "Got us into trouble more than once. Just Sunday night, in fact. Nappy screamed a little too loud. The neighbor called the cops. Can you believe it?" She chomped the fangs again. "'Course, I might have nipped just a teensy bit too hard."

Well, this certainly explained why Nappy was shaved. So

Josephine didn't get a big mouthful of hair when she...and Drusilla...

Things came together with a bang.

଼

"Drusilla! I know you're here, you fanged little whore. Show yourself!"

I stalked the black asphalt parking lot outside Nieman's Bar. I'd been stalking for the past half hour, and getting more and more frustrated. "Where are you?"

"There's no need to get foul, Detective O'Rourke." Drusilla glided from the shadows, a dress like liquid gold flowing over her voluptuous figure. She held a PDA and was clicking something off. "And I prefer 'lady of the evening' to 'whore'."

She would. I stalked up to her. In her four-inch spiked heels I looked her square in the eye. "Did Napoleon Schrimpf ever ask you to put in fake fangs and bite him?"

She smiled pertly. "Which question do you want answered first, detective? Did I put in fake fangs, or did I bite him?"

"Whichever gets me a yes."

"Yes, he asked me to bite him. Nappy enjoyed playing vampire. But the sex *is* superior." She raised both sleek eyebrows suggestively.

"Spare me. Did you bite him the night he died?"

She toyed with one long black lock. "I may have."

"And did he bleed to death out of his scrotum or did you suck him dry?"

"Really, detective. How vulgar." Drusilla tossed the lock behind her shoulder. A single hair was left on her dress, black stark against the gold. She peeled it off and dropped it. It floated to the pavement. "Nappy enjoyed a little bite. A little sip. But never more than that."

"So you're saying you didn't kill him? Even by accident?" I stared at her, hard. "C'mon, Drusilla. It'll go easier for you if you cooperate."

Drusilla's gaze hardened in return. "I am cooperating, Detective O'Rourke. And for your information, when I bite—I don't leave holes."

The intense will suddenly revealed in those long-lashed eyes almost unnerved me.

Almost. But who had the gun here? "Fine. Another question, then. Did Happy Nappy make noises about you being number eight?" Josephine's tenure was coming to an end. Had learning about Dru pushed the widow into murder?

Dru relaxed back into insouciance. "Number eight? Oh, you mean wives. Of course he did. But—" She tapped her PDA. "I'm not the marrying kind."

"Schrimpf was rich. You could have bought a lot of men, married to him."

Drusilla shrugged, a graceful rise and fall of one shoulder. "Wouldn't have done me any good. Nappy made all his wives sign those annoying little prenuptial agreements. Besides..." She winked. "I'd rather the men pay *me*."

"I bet you would." Unfortunately, that made sense. But Josephine wouldn't necessarily know that. And even a thirty-six C was trumped by a pair of DDs.

"You know, Detective O'Rourke, I think something like this would have happened sooner or later anyway."

"Something like what?"

"Nappy. His little predilections. Booze and violent sex. At least he died happy."

Testosterone plus alcohol. The chemical equation for idiot-chloride. "All right, Drusilla, we're done for now." If I was to believe her, Drusilla had no motive. Means, yes. Opportunity, hell yes. But not a single reason to kill Napoleon Schrimpf. "This time, though, you're not leaving before I get your full name and home address."

Her lips ripened into a full smile. "I don't have a household, Detective O'Rourke. But the last name is Strongwell. And if you need to talk with me, I'm here every night."

She melted away into the darkness, leaving me gaping.

And leaving that single black hair.

Chapter Fourteen

"You're married to *Drusilla*? Why the hell didn't you tell me!" I stomped into the marble-floored foyer so hard even my soft soles rang satisfactorily. I had tons of questions for Strongwell, but right now this was top of the list. He was a suspect connected to another suspect, and he hadn't said squat—bad enough. But how the hell had I had orgasmed with a married man?

Bo's reply was mild. "I'm not married to Drusilla, Detective. Nor anyone else." He turned from me as if he'd answered the only question that really mattered. "Come upstairs."

I followed him up the sweeping front staircase. The smooth silk muffled my angry steps, much less satisfying. "Then why the fuck is her name Drusilla Strong...oh. Is she your sister?"

"Not in the way you're thinking. Dru lived in my apartment building at one time. We became like a family to her. When she left to go out on her own, she kept the name."

"A family?" I added without thinking, "Is that the reason for the communal kitchen?"

"You *have* been efficient, Detective. Here we are."

He opened the door to the fourth floor. A corridor lined with thick Berber carpet stretched the length of the building. On the left were two doors, probably a pair of apartments. Four doors on the right were evenly spaced.

I stared. "How many people live here?"

Bo's lip did the amused curl-thing. "There are twelve units. Currently we have twenty-four adults, eight children and two old ones—that is, retirees."

Adults, children and *old ones*. Oh, excuse me, retirees. I must have been getting used to all the oddness because I simply asked, "Four units to a floor?"

"Four on the second and third floors. Two each on the first floor and here."

"And those four doors on the right? Pretty small apartments, crammed in like that."

"Those aren't apartments, they're bedrooms. This is mine." He opened one. "Like to see?"

I sucked in a breath. *Bo's bedroom.* Bo was showing me his bedroom. As in, his room with a *bed.*

Not daring to breathe, I peered in. Small for an apartment, but as a bedroom...*Bo's* room with a *bed...*

It was spectacular.

A massive four-poster dominated the room. Heavy oak, piled high with pillows, even bigger than the trampoline downstairs. A soft russet-and-indigo quilt spread across it like a warm summer sky. Lamps glowed on either side.

I released my breath and braved entry. Past the bed was an *en suite* bathroom in deep green and old gold. I peeked in. Emerald marble shot with gold topped a waist-high oak cabinet. Mediterranean tile floor, heated, unless I missed my guess. The shower mimicked an Amazon waterfall. Toilet—*and* bidet.

"If you've got all this, why the rooms in the basement?" The words were out of my mouth before I remembered what they revealed. That I had snooped in Bo's building. And had found his freaky root-cellar-cum-den.

"Don't panic, Detective. I knew you'd been downstairs. I smelled you when I returned this morning." Bo loosely grasped my shoulders and turned me for a gentle kiss. The warm play of his lips made me reel.

That must be some sniffer. "Working." I pulled away. "You didn't answer my question."

He smiled at me. His dimple caused collateral damage. "You're working? All right. How goes the investigation?" He pulled me in again for a deeper, harder kiss. My brain nearly short-circuited.

Two could play at that game. I tugged his shirt up, slid my hands under to pet those amazing abs. Short little hairs tickled my fingers. Yummy. "The investigation goes fine. So why the basement? It's not to grow mushrooms."

"No, it's not. Any new suspects?" Bo nipped my lips, soothed them with the silk of his tongue. Shoot me with a Glock, the man could kiss. Heat curled in my belly.

"Nobody new." Drusilla wasn't new, her ranking had just changed. I leaned in, kissed him back, touching my tongue to the chiseled edge of his upper lip. His lovely stomach clenched under my fingertips.

He growled, low in his throat. "Do that again."

So I did. Tracing his lower lip with my tongue, I prompted, "Basement?"

His stomach was still rippling under my fingers. "Some are guest rooms." His arms banded around me. "I have a bedroom there, but it's to sleep."

"The den?" I slid my tongue between his lips.

He gave a soft groan and pulled me tighter. "Where I relax. Before you ask why, the smell and feel of the soil soothe me." Mouth gliding tantalizingly over mine, he edged me toward the bed.

"Uh-huh." Answering a question before I asked, always suspicious. If he weren't such a great kisser, I'd cuff him. To the four-poster. Spread eagle. Or maybe *because* he was such a great kisser... Focus. Questioning suspect. Handcuffed, naked suspect... I groaned.

"I love those sounds you make, Detective." He nuzzled my neck. "Those sexy little moans in the back of your throat." His breath heated my skin.

"Working," I gasped. Yet my eyes closed, my head tilted to give him better access. I barely choked out, "What's this room for?"

"This is where I make love."

Make love. Bright heat exploded in my belly at that. "Not...me. Not now. I'm...on duty."

"You. Here. *Now.*" Bo took my mouth in a kiss so hungry and wanton, I knew he'd been holding back before. "I'm going to gobble you up, Detective. I can't wait another second. I'm going to kiss you and lick you and taste you, all of you. I'll make you come. Then I'll mount you and fuck you until you're screaming. And after we're both sated I'm going to do it again."

I had two choices. I could either continue to ask questions...or I could finally get some.

His tongue thrust into my mouth. He tasted of passion and need. Of hot, demanding male. My body quivered in immediate response.

Okay. Maybe an early lunch break wouldn't hurt. I rubbed myself against him. "Know what, Strongwell? We're wearing too many clothes."

He growled. "Way too many."

After practically tearing me out of mine, he tossed me naked onto the bed. I leaned up on one elbow, eager to see him strip.

But my eyes must have been affected by those five years, three months and five days. There he was, standing next to the bed, his gaze burning over my entire body like I was a yummy dessert. And then he sort of—wavered. Still Bo-shaped, but transparent. Gauzy. I could even see the paisley pattern on the wallpaper behind. And then he thinned almost to a cloud of mist.

His clothes crumpled to the floor.

I blinked. The illusion of mist was gone, and there he was. Viking-big, Viking strong.

And totally, gloriously nude. And I thought, *who the hell cares how he did it.*

He climbed on top of me, big and masculine. Naked flesh seared naked flesh. He was deliciously heavy covering me. His mouth was on my neck.

I arched. "No biting."

He nibbled down my collarbone. "Not even one teeny love-nip?"

"Not even a scrape of pearly whites."

"No?" He closed his incisors gently on one nipple and tugged.

"*Argh!*" I came off the bed, smashing my breast into his face.

Bo barely moved. "Was that a good *argh* or a bad *argh*?" He licked across to the other breast.

"Bad argh." I ended on a squeak when he latched onto the other nipple and sucked. "Argh," I said. "Argh, *argh*."

"Bad argh?" Bo's hand slid between us as he sucked.

"Very bad—*argh!*"

He found my clitoris with his fingers, took a good long stroke. I screamed. He chuckled, damn him.

Somehow I found strength to pull out from under his captivating pleasure. "All right, enough." I put both palms against his shoulders and pushed.

I got the satisfaction of seeing confusion cross his features.

"What's wrong, Detective?" He sat back on his haunches. Muscles in his thighs and butt bunched deliciously.

"Lie down, buster. You already did me earlier. Your turn." All those articles, I had to try *some* of them. Like "Ten Reasons Licking His Popsicle Will Make Him All Yours". Because I wanted this gorgeous male to be mine, all mine.

A slow, sexy smile drifted onto his face. "Why, Detective. How democratic of you." He stretched out on the bed, folding heavily muscled arms behind his head.

I took his thick erection in one hand. It was hot velvet under my fingers. "You're not completely off the hook, buster." I cranked my hips up by his shoulders, so he could use his lovely strong hands on me. "You still have to do some work."

My words were muffled as I opened my mouth over the velvety head of his penis. He was seeping salt. A lick and a swirl gave my lips the lubrication they needed ("How to Blow 'Til He Explodes", steps one and two).

He still hadn't touched me. Thinking he needed encouragement, I threw one leg over his neck, straddling his head. "Come on, big boy. Get your hands busy down there."

I fisted the base of his cock for balance, then clamped my mouth around him. He smelled and tasted squeaky clean. Eagerly I took my first big plunge.

And nearly asphyxiated myself when he latched onto my pussy and suckled.

Sweet exploding stars. I was shocked, but it felt so *good.* I stayed where I was, that monster cock embedded in my throat, and purred my happiness.

My throat muscles worked him. Bo groaned. I pulled back slightly to tickle the eye of his cock with my tongue and he groaned again, deep in his chest, a rumble I could almost feel.

It wasn't me purring. I *didn't* want to know what was making that lion's purr. Or who. Even weird wasn't going to stand in the way of this—*this* being a building pressure in my body that went beyond bathrooms and quickies in the street.

Turned loose in private, Bo was a maestro. He rubbed and sucked, pressed a finger to my clit and vibrated until my blood *boiled.* Just as I was about to burst he backed off, licking gently.

Then he started over again with the rubbing and sucking.

"Hey, I was nearly there."

"I know." There was a wealth of male knowledge and satisfaction in his voice. "I want this to last."

Frustrated, I rubbed myself. "What if I can't wait?"

He swatted my hand away. "I'm not giving you a choice. It's my turn, remember?" He breathed on my pussy until I thought I'd scream.

He began kissing my sensitive labia, gently, sweetly. Gifted me with light licks. He pushed me toward the edge slowly, deliberately, finally lapping until I parted.

"Bo, please!" I pushed myself into him, desperate to satisfy my growing ache.

"Not yet, Elena. I'm enjoying myself." His teeth nipped my swollen outer lips. Bit and tugged gently. I wiggled in torment.

Two could play that game, dammit.

I kissed his sac, licked and nibbled. Played suck-the-popsicle with his shaft, enjoying the slick, smooth feel. At the top I took the head between my teeth, bit down lightly.

He arched hard. Started lapping at my clitoris, running his tongue up and down the nose. Licking eagerly.

Yeah. *Got* him. I started to come—and he backed off.

Only to begin *over*, kissing and licking.

I groaned in frustration. The purr (his purr?) rumbled deeply in my ears. "Fuck," I muttered, sucking his cock back into my mouth. Glad one of us was enjoying himself.

Bo, in that slow, maddening way, drove me to the edge—again. This time as he lapped me near climax he thrust a single finger into me. Drove it in wetly, over and over. Slow. Deep.

My hips rocked wantonly, trying to speed up the rhythm he set. I pressed myself harder against him as my arousal climbed. Mouthed his cock faster.

But he thrust and sucked rhythmically. Patiently. Always that same slow, inexorable grinding and thrusting, driving me insane.

I was dripping wet and ready to come. I'd been ready for hours it seemed, primed but kept on that sharp knife-edge by a master.

He began sucking in counterpoint to his finger-thrusts. His hot mouth pulled on my bud with slowly increasing pressure. His finger drove into me, a bit deeper, a notch harder. I went higher yet.

And then, suddenly, he changed rhythm, thrusting and sucking together.

I shot scary-high. I lifted my mouth from his erection, panting. The Grand Canyon of orgasms loomed before me. I was hanging out the open door of a jet plane, about to plummet from the stratosphere. Facing a climax as hard as hitting earth at terminal velocity.

Splat. Death by orgasm.

Suddenly I didn't want to fall.

That's when Bo grabbed my hips with both hands, sat up, and *devoured* me.

My feet were in the air, my butt raised higher than my head. Blood rushed to my brain. And a man was eating me alive.

I screamed. Death by orgasm, unless I incinerated first. Bo's mouth was driving me into a raging inferno.

Biting back another scream, I seized the root of his huge erection in two fists. *Damned* if I was dying alone. Opening my mouth wide, I rammed his penis down my throat. He growled his pleasure. I pistoned on that gorgeous cock 'til it practically smoked.

The damned thing actually grew bigger.

Rumbling filled my ears. Sharp nails pricked my butt. I ignored it all, slave to sensation. My tongue, rasping over his smooth, hard erection. Bo's lips, silk on my wet vulva. His tongue, hot, rough, licking. A satin finger, running along my inner crease. Smooth and cool, rubbing deep while Bo licked me with the skill of a gourmand.

Not a finger. Too sleek, too cool. Sliding along the crease as his hot tongue flicked my clit. More like a candle...or a knitting needle—

Electric needles, the crack of lightning. An overpowering climax. Bo had his mouth down there. Just as he did now.

"Don't—!" Hot, sharp (omigod *fangs?*) speared my pussy.

I detonated. Climaxed so hard I felt like I was imploding. So hard it terrified me. So hard I tried to stop, panicked by the colossal plunge.

Bo seized my wiggling hips. His tongue worked me, stroking the climax bigger and stronger and harder. I writhed in extreme pleasure for what might have been eternity.

He bit again. I shattered completely. Blew into a thousand pieces. A hoarse cry ripped from my throat. Never...oh, stars, I'd never... I felt absolutely, exquisitely destroyed.

His licking changed, bringing me down. Soothing me. Caressing me, loving me gently.

After that Uzi orgasm, I melted into a boneless, mindless blob. I was utterly relaxed, at peace. Maybe the orgasm really had killed me, and I was in heaven. Yeah. This was where good girls went. And bad girls. Mmm.

When I opened my eyes I lay face-down on Bo's body. My cheek was cushioned by his muscular thigh. Yummy. The heaven theory gained favor in my mind.

Then I saw he was still semi-hard.

I scrambled to face him. Well, more like oozed, but hey. "Didn't you...?"

"I did." Bo raised himself on his elbows. His eyes were glowing slits. "There's more."

Glancing over my shoulder I saw him expanding up his ripply belly. *Yeah. There sure is.*

I managed to crawl into place and get one leg over his hips, though I was still more oozing than scrambling. *He* thought that was funny, by the curve of his lips.

Too bad. Because *this* was it. The conclusion to the season-five cliffhanger of *Elena's Abstinence*. I grabbed Bo's erection in one fist and positioned myself. Straddled that gorgeous, tall sea monster and put the head into my vestibule.

I was one stroke away from coming home. I looked at us where we joined. It looked like heaven. It felt like heaven. It sounded like—

It sounded like my cell phone.

Chapter Fifteen

"Fuck!" I stumbled off the bed. I was going to find my gun. Find my gun, find my phone, and *shoot* it.

I wasted ten seconds turning around in circles, trying to find my jeans.

"Here, Detective." On his stomach, Bo leaned off the bed, plucked the phone from my pants and held it out to me. Amazing abs. As strong as they looked.

I snatched the phone, swearing some more. What was wrong with me that I couldn't catch a break? Murphyous Interruptus stalked me even here. Then I saw the number and groaned. *Dirkenous* Interruptus.

But I was a responsible police officer. I followed all the rules. I flipped the phone open. "*What*?" Yeah, responsible officer, but damned frustrated responsible officer.

"Detective Ma'am? Is something wrong?"

Two seconds away from filling a five-year black hole... No, nothing *wrong*. "I'm fine, Ruffles. Why did you call? You find something?"

"Yes, ma'am. Or, no, ma'am. Or—"

"Just spit it out. Report."

"There's no blood, Detective Ma'am. I looked in a ten-minute circle, like you said, but nothing. Should I go farther away?"

About to say yes, my brain kicked in. "Schrimpf couldn't have wandered far after Drusilla left him." Not if he was as sated as I was after Bo...well. "A few blocks at most. Are you *sure* there was no blood?"

Although if there *was* blood, even Dirkenstein couldn't have missed it. Nine pints was a *lot*. Two pints in a quart, four quarts in a gallon...picture a gallon of spilled red milk. Major gaggage.

"I didn't see any, Detective Ma'am. Nobody else saw any, either. I went door-to-door."

Which meant...well, what did it mean? Had someone siphoned off all the blood?

Or had someone sucked it out?

Someone...like Bo? I couldn't see him being the type to chomp balls. Pussies, yes. I ran a finger over my labia, surreptitiously checking them. Wet, but not bloody. Was I *imagining* it?

I glanced at him. He lay on his back, hands folded behind his head. A small smile was on his face and a *large* one on his pecker. He didn't look guilty. He looked smug. Or, considering my beyond-Asgard orgasm, maybe it was simple pride. Ooh, there was a theory that needed testing.

Smack me with a nightstick. I had a murder to solve. The murderer might even be Mr. Bitey here. Yet all I wanted to do was pound his gorgeous warrior body into the mattress.

I was so fucked.

"Detective Ma'am? Are you there?"

"Yes, Dirk." I checked Bo's bedside clock. Just before one a.m. "I need you to go back to the scene. Check inside all buildings and garages in the immediate vicinity."

"Immediate vicinity, yes, ma'am." A pause. "Um, that means within ten minutes of the bar, right? Is that walking or driving? With a speed limit of twenty-five m.p.h. that would be about four miles except there'd have to be time for parking and killing so maybe only a couple miles and—"

"Dirk! Focus."

"Yes, ma'am. Ow!"

There was some muffled swearing. Ruffles must have saluted—and actually brained himself this time. I didn't know whether to laugh or cry. "Oh, and good work so far, Detective Ruffles."

"Yes, Detective Ma'am. Thank you, Detective Ma'am. Ow!"

The salute again, no doubt. Thank goodness Dirkenstein didn't know karate. He'd have chopped his head open.

As I closed the phone, I let it play in my mind. Missing blood. Mysterious biting boyfriend. Dirt floor dens and separate bedrooms for sleeping and...oh, yeah, making love.

"What was that all about?" Bo, all ultra-casual sexy on the bed.

It reminded me of where we were before the electronic leash rang. Well. I could try to interrogate the suspect.

Or I could get back to getting some.

I wanted—no, I *needed* the completion that intercourse would give me. Not just because I'd been waiting five-plus years. No, not just because the last time I was in a bedroom with a sexy guy his cat had mistaken hairy balls for jingly balls and had done an impromptu vasectomy.

But I needed this, I realized, for the simple human connection. With Bo.

Okay, "human" might not have been the right term.

I needed to put down the O'Rourke Rule Book for an hour. To try being spontaneous, being *normal*, just this once.

So I smiled at Bo. "Do you really care what that was?" My voice emerged as a sultry purr. I crawled onto the bed.

Bo smiled back and reached for me. Oh, yeah. This being myself felt absolutely awesome.

My cell phone rang again.

"Dammit!" I leaped off the bed and snatched it up. I was going to shoot it and launch it out the fourth-floor window. Then I caught the number, and swore. "It's Tight-ass. I have to take this."

Bo sighed from the bed, so deep and wistful I nearly tossed the phone out anyway. My voice was clipped with frustration when I answered. "O'Rourke."

Titus was equally short. "Detective. Headquarters. Ten minutes. Got that?"

"But...I'm on lunch break. Sir."

"I don't care if you're on your deathbed!" His voice scaled up an octave. "Unless you want to be *Officer* O'Rourke and back on the street, you'll get your ass here." He slammed the receiver down.

I stared at my phone. Slowly closed it, wishing for once I wasn't so damned responsible. Rules and regs had always been my salvation. Right now they were downright sadistic. "I have to go."

"I gathered as much." Bo came off the bed in one graceful motion. He started hunting for my clothes, scattered to the four walls of the room as if he hadn't taken them off me, but exploded them off.

In contrast, his own lay in a neat pile next to the bed. I lifted his shirt. It revealed his pants. I lifted the pants. Underneath were his socks—still tucked in the shoes. I handed everything to him, remembering that weird way he'd seem to mist. Maybe it was possible to teleport out of clothes. A truly zipless fuck.

If it weren't so weird, it would have been totally sexy.

As I slipped my thong and jeans on, I watched him closely. He put his pants on one leg at a time, perfectly normal. Of course, even normal looked sexy on Bo. And the way he shrugged into his shirt, muscles working smoothly...*uh.* I adjusted my jeans. "I'm sorry. I'm really disappointed."

One corner of his mouth lifted. "I guess I'll have to work harder next time."

Harder? As in, I'd have a *bigger* orgasm? Would I even survive? "No!" I flushed. "I didn't mean...I meant I'm disappointed I have to go."

"I know that, Detective." Bo glided over and touched me gently on the cheek. "I'm disappointed too." Holding my chin in thumb and forefinger, he pressed a soft kiss onto my lips. "Later? After you get off work?"

Five years, three months and nearly six days. It would have to do.

ଔଓ

Captain Titus was hopping mad when I got to the station. His round face was as red as his hair. Well, orange. All the shift personnel had vanished, except for Blatzky, and even he only snuck in to nab a donut before retreating to the men's room.

I slid behind my desk. It was a shield between us, although I would have preferred bulletproof armor. Tight-ass paced the floor like a caged tiger. A pumpkiny, scrotty sort of tiger, but still scary.

"You're taking way too long, O'Rourke." If his red face hadn't said *riled*, his voice, headed into the ionosphere, would have clued me in. Or the frantic pumping of his Armani. "Almost a whole week since this gruesome murder occurred and still nothing. Our department's reputation is in shambles. I'm removing you from the case!"

Shit. This was my punishment for ignoring the rules. Think fast, O'Rourke, and talk faster. "Captain Titus, I object. It's only been three nights since Mr. Schrimpf died. Besides, who else would take it?"

"Blatzky," he began.

"Sir, you know Detective Blatzky is swamped." By beer and the toilet, but hey.

"Dillon on first shift—"

"Captain. With all due respect, the murder happened at night. Most of the witnesses are night people. A third-shift detective is best."

Titus rubbed his semi-orange pate. "That's true. I don't want to lose control...I mean lose the case. It *is* a third-shift matter." His voice lowered as he calmed.

"Absolutely, sir. And I'm the best third-shift detective available to head the case." Actually, the *only* third-shift detective available to head the case. Blatzky was still in the men's room, and Ruffles...was Ruffles.

Tight-ass grabbed a donut. Parked one butt cheek on a nearby desk and chomped. "All right, O'Rourke. You'll keep it for now. But tell me what you've got. And I want to know *everything*."

I spieled off the basics—leaving out the whole biting/sucking thing. I mean, I wanted to convince him I was responsible and sane. Vampires-in-Meiers-Corners wasn't anywhere near the rational starting line.

Tight-ass nodded. "Keep an eye on that widow, Detective O'Rourke. She sounds like a suspicious character to me."

"But what about the blood, captain? Or rather the lack of it? Don't you think that's important?"

"Lack of blood? That's not a clue," he scoffed. "*Blood* is a clue. But *no* blood? Shows your inexperience."

Flames rose in my cheeks. "I'm sorry, sir."

Tight-ass smiled, a creepy jigsaw in his pumpkin head. "That's all right, Elena, my dear." Hearing my name in that smarmy, over-familiar tone tossed ten chips into the creepy pot.

Then he patted me heavily on the shoulder. "Keep me apprized of the case. Everything that happens." He started rubbing. "I want to know everything you do, everything you find." He rubbed lower. Brushed the tops of my breasts. "Even the blood. I'll help you through this, rookie." The hand circled down to my nipple.

Make that just plain *creep*. I jumped out of my chair. "Gee thanks. Sir." I spoke through gritted teeth. "I'll be sure to keep you in the loop. Captain."

His eyes narrowed. "See that you do. Detective." He chomped the last piece of donut, and walked away.

଼ജ

Bo was expecting me after my shift was over but neither of us knew how quick my meeting with Tight-ass would be. So I headed back to the apartment, to finish what we started. True, we'd be starting from a dead stop, but Bo's motor was top of the line. Zero to sixty in three seconds. I figured it'd be a piece of cake to get back in the race.

And it was still my lunch hour, right?

When I got to the apartment, though, Bo was nowhere to be found.

My sister found me instead. She grabbed me by the shoulder and hustled me into her apartment. "You took Dru in for questioning!"

In the morass of job anxiety, guilt and sheer horniness that made up my current psyche, sisterly charity was hard to find. "Drusilla? You call her Dru? Gretchen O'Rourke Johnson, how the hell do you know a *hooker*?"

Gretch scowled and jerked a nod at little Stella sitting on the couch. I clapped a hand over my foul mouth. Fortunately Stella was engrossed in smearing yellow fingers on butcher paper. She was singing "A Hundred Bottles of Root Beer" and didn't hear us.

Then I realized it was nearly two in the morning. "What the hel—heck is Stella doing still up?"

"She was having trouble sleeping." Gretchen dragged me into her tiny kitchen.

"But—"

"No, Elena. This isn't about Stella." Gretch confronted me, hands on hips, back rigid. "I'm talking to *you* about *Dru*. Leave her alone."

"What?" I blinked my disbelief. "Why do you care?"

"Dru used to live here. Before Ste—" Gretch's cheeks flushed. "Before Stella and I came. In fact, she moved out just to make room for us."

"This was Drusilla's apartment?" I wondered about Gretch's flush.

Had the Double-D bimbo akimbo "entertained" here? Left a used Rough Rider for Gretch to find? "And your good friend Dru gave it up for you?"

"Um...sort of." Her eyes flashed sideways.

Gretchen was lying, but I couldn't place how. I took a stab in the dark. "She had one of the basement rooms?"

My sister's eyes widened so far they nearly fell out of her skull. "How do you know about the basement rooms?"

If information were the cards in a game of sheepshead, I had two trump. The basement rooms was one. The rest of my hand was fail, but Gretch didn't know that.

I played the other trump. "The basement is where Bo *sleeps*." My throat tightened. Slept, as opposed to where he *made love*.

Other things tightened on that.

My sister's face went white. "Elena...no one can know. I don't know how you found out, but you can't tell anyone."

"Oh? And why not?"

"Elena, please! It's our *lives*. Stella's and Steve's and mine."

"Steve's dead," I said automatically, and thereby lost the pot.

Gretchen's color came back, tipped over into red as her expression hardened. "You don't *really* know, do you?"

I planted fists on hips, mirroring her. "I know enough. I know you've been acting crazy since the attack that killed Steve."

She turned away with a shrug. "So I'm scared, so what? It's not unusual after an attack as brutal as that."

"Not just scared. You act like monsters are after you."

She spun back, eyes flaring. "Because there are monstrous people out there!"

"Oh, for the love of—not monst*rous*, Gretch. You're acting like they're *real* monsters." I barely choked my anger back. My fear. My sister was desperately in need of help yet she was *blocking* me—no, more. She was *lying* to me. Her own flesh and blood, and for what? For the sake of a sexy apartment manager and a hooker? "And why the hell do you bow to a maintenance man like he's some sort of royalty?"

Gretchen blanched. "I feel safe here, and I'm grateful, that's all."

"Right. Grateful enough to sleep with Strongwell six months after you buried your husband? Grateful enough to pass him off as 'Daddy' to your daughter?"

"*What*?" She braced one hand on the counter.

"Come on, Gretch, talk to me. Pretty please with pus? It's eating you, this lying about Strongwell. I *know* it can't be good for you—or Stella."

"Leave my daughter out of it. You know *nothing*." Gretchen slapped the counter to underline her words. "*You* think the world can be conquered if only you're smart enough. Strong enough." She grabbed my arms. Her fingers bit painfully into me, and fear iced her eyes. "But there are things out there, Elena, awful things. Inhuman things."

I twisted free from her punishing grip. "*Inhuman*? Why does it have to be monsters, Gretch? What's gotten you so spooked you're lying to your own sister?"

"Oh, let's not fight, Elena." An angry tear ran down Gretchen's cheek. She swiped it away and started rummaging in a high cabinet. Very carefully, she took down a pink-and-gold china teapot. Two matching cups and saucers joined the pot on the counter.

The pretty little set had been her mother's. Many a scraped knee and bruised heart had been comforted by Brita's tea set. Gretchen waved to the small kitchen table. "Sit. I'll make us some tea."

She turned from me and busied herself with kettle and cups, humming as if the last few minutes hadn't happened at all.

"Gretch..." I sank into a chair, at a loss for words. The avoidance, the sheer denial was not my sister. "How did this happen? Why are you so scared? Did Bo do this to you?"

She turned from the counter, delicate cup in one hand, her face a study in shock. "Master Bo has been nothing but...supportive and...and kind..."

"*Master*? Do you hear yourself? He's a fucking building supervisor, not a king."

She slammed her other hand, balled into a fist, on the counter. "Don't you talk about him that way, Elena, don't you dare. Stella and I owe him our lives. Bo Strongwell is the most generous, the most noble...he's worth two of any of us. Even you, Elena. Don't you dare badmouth him."

I stared at her, stunned. My sister, the only person I cared about, was deserting me for a fucking maintenance man. This was worse than being alone.

Dad would have known what to do, but I had no idea how to handle her. I never felt his loss more. "You've gone off the deep end, Gretch. Ever since you came to live here...it's got to be Bo's fault." I stood. "If you won't listen, I'll just confront *him*."

She only laughed at that, waving the tea cup recklessly. "You don't mean that. He's far more powerful than you can imagine, Elena. Bigger and stronger and faster. You're *nothing* in comparison."

I patted my gun. "Is he stronger and faster that this? I'm sick of the lies, Gretchen. I'm marching right down to that mysterious dirt-floor den and I'm going to have the *truth*—if I have to shoot Strongwell to do it."

"Don't you dare go near him!" Gretchen screamed, throwing her cup into the wall. It shattered instantly.

There was sudden, awful silence in the kitchen, punctuated only by Stella's piping voice. Sixty-seven bottles of root beer remained.

A small sound escaped Gretchen's mouth, like a sob. "Oh, no...what have I done? My cup, my beautiful cup." She knelt, swept the tiny shards together in her hands. As I wavered to my feet she jerked, as if she had cut herself. But she didn't stop. Didn't stop sweeping the tiny sharp bits of ceramic into her bare hands. Tears dripped down her cheeks.

My retort died in my throat. I knelt next to her, gathered her in my arms. "There, there, honey." I caressed her head. "It's okay. I'll make it okay."

That's when I smelled metal. Copper...or iron.

I held her away from me. "Gretchen. Let me see your hands."

She wouldn't meet my eyes. Her fingers were clasped tightly against her stomach. I put my palm over them, used the calm, soothing tone I'd perfected babysitting her. "Gretchen, come on. Let me see. Let Big Sis see. Pretty please with puke?"

It still worked. Slowly, Gretch opened her hands.

The first thing I saw was the red gloss. A thin sheen, covering her palms like strawberry jam.

Blood.

Ceramic shards glittered in the blood. Welling from numerous tiny cuts, it began dripping through her fingers onto the floor.

"Your poor hands." I raised her to her feet and led her to the sink, turning on the water to rinse her cuts.

A loud bang made me whirl. The kitchenette's saloon doors blew open. A man filled the doorway, chest heaving.

"What the fuck did you do to my wife?" Steve Johnson yelled.

Chapter Sixteen

An hour later I trudged along the night-shadowed sidewalk, hands in my jeans pockets. What the hell did I do now? I still felt like I'd been sideswiped by a truck.

My cell phone rang. Caller ID showed the cop shop.

Who now, I thought, fearing Dirkenstein, or worse, Tight-ass. "O'Rourke."

"Hi, Elena. It's Charlie."

Our CSI, Charles Samuel Ignatek. Yeah, I know. And physically, he could have been William Petersen's twin. Meiers Corners was ground zero for weird. We had a lawyer named Denny Crane and a Taekwondo instructor called Miyagi. Charlie's initials and his Gil Grissom face was sitch normal for us.

"Interesting sample you sent me, Elena. Where did you say you found it?"

The small baggy of charred dust was from the alley where Bo and I had been attacked. "I didn't say. But it was on the paperwork with the sample."

"There was nothing with the sample. No ID, no forms, nothing."

Not good. Even one slip could lose me the detective race. "I swear I didn't forget—"

Ignatek chuckled. He had a nice, masculine chuckle. "I know you didn't. You're precise and careful with evidence. Which makes the absence of the paperwork quite intriguing, yes?"

I wondered what he was driving at. Hopefully nothing freaky. I'd had enough freakiness in the past few to file a Schedule C as my own circus sideshow. "But you got the sample. You were able to analyze it?"

"Oh, yes."

Analyzable, therefore *not* supernatural. My tension eased. "What is it?"

Instead of answering, he asked, "Does it have anything to do with your current case?"

"Nothing that I know of." Anxiety notched back up. I didn't get what was with all the questions. Was Ignatek pumping me for Titus?

"Can you at least tell me where it came from? How long ago you got it?"

"In town. Not long ago," I hedged. "Why?"

"Because I recovered amplifiable DNA, Elena."

I remembered the muggers' unnatural strength. The red eyes. The flashing teeth. "What kind of DNA? Animal?" Animal—or *monster*?

"Human DNA."

"Human? You're absolutely sure?" The instant it was out of my mouth I could have smacked myself. Of course he was sure.

But there was a strange hesitation before Charlie answered. "Well, that's why I asked where it came from. I sent the sample through CODIS. And got a match."

"That's good, right?"

"Usually. In this case, Elena, I'm not sure."

"Why? Does the DNA match the spit from Schrimpf's balls? Is it our murderer?"

"No, unfortunately. It's for one John Smith, age thirty-six."

"Smith?" I swore. "How many thousands of people does that name match in the US alone?"

"With the DNA? Exactly one."

I stopped walking. "But...well, then, what's the problem?"

"It's only a very small one, Elena. John Smith had AIDS. He died a year ago."

"Died?" To say that was a problem was an understatement. A long-dead man had attacked me yesterday. Impossible.

But a lot of impossible had been slopping over the reality dam lately. After thanking Ignatek (and promising I'd forward any information as soon as I had it) I flipped the phone shut. Stuck my hands in my pockets and thought hard.

How could this have happened? The evidence wasn't contaminated. I had collected it myself, and Ignatek was thorough and exacting. A prank, maybe? John Smith's cremated remains, smeared in the alley? But for what purpose?

One thing I knew for sure. There had to be a natural, logical explanation. The dead did not come back to life.

Despite what I'd learned at Gretchen's just an hour ago.

"What the fuck did you do to my wife?" Steve Johnson had yelled.

"I'm okay, I'm okay." Gretchen had held up her hands, two bloody-red stop signs. "I did it to myself, Steve. Calm down."

He took a deep breath, turned his head away. "Sorry. I'm sorry, honey. I just...the blood scared me."

I caught Gretchen's wrists, gently brought her hands back under the running water. It scared me too. Everything about this scared me. My sister's secrets, my going after them out of loyalty and love, my only alienating her more because of it...and my brother-in-law, surprisingly active for being six months dead.

I urged Gretchen into a chair, found a clean dish towel and wrapped her hands before escaping to the bathroom for bandages and disinfectant. At that point if I could have left her to bandage her own hands, I might have. But I sucked up my sanity and returned.

While I dressed Gretchen's hands, Steve paced in the background. Keeping my voice low, I said, "What's going on here, Gretch?"

"I'm sorry I didn't tell you, Elena. But I wasn't quite sure what to say."

"The truth would be good."

"Yes." She paused. "Steve, honey, why don't you get the kettle?" And then her eyes started tracking. Like she was thinking.

This was going to be a whopper.

She smiled directly at me, blue eyes wide and guileless. "It's really quite simple. We *thought* Steve was dead. But he wasn't. And while we weren't looking, well, he woke up and wandered off."

"Just climbed out of the casket, huh? Wasn't he embalmed?"

"Oh. No, we, um, couldn't afford it."

"I see. And you didn't say anything at the time because...?"

She hesitated. "Well, amnesia."

"Amnesia."

Steve set three cups on the table. He opened tea bags, dropped one in each. "Temporary amnesia."

"Yes, that was it." Gretchen nodded. "He had temporary amnesia. We didn't know where he was or even that he was alive. At first we thought someone had stolen the body. So nobody said anything."

Steve poured hot water into cups. "I regained my memory just a few days ago."

"I would have told you sooner, Elena," Gretchen said. "But you're busy with your case and all."

Steve went into excruciating detail about how sometimes you *thought* people were dead but they were really just low-respiration coma victims. That was what happened to him. With the temporary coma causing the temporary amnesia. All perfectly logical.

And a lie. I was gut-sure they were both spilling enough toxic falsehoods to start their own global climate change. Couldn't prove it with Steve, though. My internal truthometer was blank, just like with Drusilla.

Just like with Bo.

The mysteries were piling up. Lie meter on the blink. Steve returning from the dead. Dirt-floor basement rooms. People running around looking like refugees from *Dark Shadows*.

There was no obvious connection with Schrimpf and his punctured prick. But I *felt* that if I could figure out even one of these damned mysteries, the whole thing would unravel. I think my gut knew what was wrong.

But my head still denied it. I mean, come *on*. Miracles and magic might abound, but the only ones you heard about were the ones witnessed by loonies. And I *couldn't* lose my sanity.

At least, not before I got my permanent detective's shield.

I opened my mouth to grill them both, to wring the truth from him, from her. To tear them apart and finally get to the bottom of this.

Then Steve smiled at Gretchen. And she smiled back.

Oh, God. They looked so happy. I couldn't do it.

When Dad and Brita died, grief and desolation hit me hard because I went through it alone. That was when I moved back to the Corners, hungry for some sense of family, of security. I never wanted Gretch to have that experience. I ached for her when Steve died, and was there for her as much as I could be. Which was unfortunately never enough.

So if Steve's return made her feel safe and loved, I guess I had to suck it up and be happy for her.

But if he hurt her, I'd shoot him.

So I'd give their story...and Steve...a chance. Not exactly regulations, but it wasn't up to me to be Gretchen's conscience. Only her big sister.

ଔ

I looked up, saw the familiar doors of the cop shop. I might have mislaid my mind, but at least my feet weren't lost. I mounted the steps. My hand hit the door. I stopped.

Captain Titus. Great Donut, preserve me. He'd want a report. What could I tell him, that long-dead men had attacked me? That my brother-in-law had risen from the grave? Considering how Tight-ass reacted when I mentioned the lack of blood at the scene, he would be less than impressed.

But I had to say *something*. Maybe, like the ME, I'd state only provable facts. Tight-ass might come to the same insane conclusions, but I couldn't help that.

Just the facts, ma'am. Unfortunately, that didn't give me a whole lot to talk about. I was doomed.

Hand on doorknob, I waited. For a miracle, maybe. Or lightning. Bolts of electricity would hurt less than Tight-ass's screech. Maybe I was waiting for my cell phone, which always rang at the most absurd moments. For once I *wanted* to be interrupted. Where was it when I really needed it?

Tweedle-tweedle. I pulled the phone out, stared at it. Since when did things go *right*? Had I fed a hungry stranger who was a leprechaun in disguise? Had giving Steve a chance before I shot him rebalanced my karma? If Lutherans even believed in karma. I snapped the phone open. "O'Rourke."

"Detective Ma'am! It's Detective Dirk, calling to report still no blood, and to get my next assignment. Do you like that? The Detective Dirk, I mean, not the no blood. I thought it was more friendly for doing community outreach, at a school, say. Detective Ruffles is so stuffy, and if we're trying to reach kids, we have to be hip and trendy. The name has a ring to it, doesn't it? De*tec*tive *Dirk*. D.D. Same initials, like all the best old-time movie stars. Doris Day, Lily Langtry, Roy Rogers."

"Katherine Hepburn." I massaged my temples, one-handed. Which was worse, death by Tight-ass or drowning in a flood of Dirk? Although it was ridiculously reassuring that my karmic scales were still off-kilter.

"Lois Lane, Fred Flint—"

"Ruffles! Look, you did a great job with the blood."

"Thank you, Detective Ma'am. I've learned so much from you. Almost as much as I learn from Oprah. And my uncle said—"

"—so I have another task for you. Top priority. This might make or break the case."

That shut him up. Almost. "Really?"

"Josephine Schrimpf was out of town the night of the murder. Or she *says* she was. I need you to run that down for me."

"Run it down? Like road kill? And a car?"

"Uh, no. I mean find proof. Evidence that Josephine went to that convention. Plane tickets, hotel reservations, phone calls."

"Something that shows she wasn't in Meiers Corners the night her husband died?" Dirk caught on at last. "What if I can't? Captain Titus thinks Mrs. Schrimpf did it, you know. Although I like her, because she knows how to mix a martini, I think, and—"

"When were you talking to Titus?"

"Huh? Oh. When he field-promoted me. And then when he assigned me as your partner. Oh, and he called me today and met me for lunch. I had tuna salad on rye. Ice tea to drink—with a twist of lemon. The lemon had seeds so I scooped them out with my spoon and some of the juice got on the tablecloth but lemon juice takes *out* stains so I didn't worry—"

"Er, yes. Good luck, Detective Dirk." I flipped the phone shut.

Only to have it ring again. Hooray, another delay. I snapped it open.

"O'Rourke!"

I sucked in a breath at the jet-engine voice. Buddha on a unicycle, karmic balance had gone dark side. "Captain Titus. What can I do for you?"

"I've been delayed by an, um, meeting. But I'll want your report first thing when I get to the station. Five thirty this morning, got that?"

"Yes, sir." I clapped the phone shut, amazed. Merry Christmas, Tiny Tim! No more shooting people first and asking questions later for me.

Of course, my vivisection was only postponed. But I now had time to get every single solid fact I could. I trotted into the building, new resolving adding spring to my steps. And when I cozied up to my computer, Dirkson's painted eyes watched over my shoulder with interest.

I started with the prime suspect, Drusilla. The Happy Nappy Hooker had risen to number one on my chart when I discovered Schrimpf's idea of foreplay was fang-play. And I was glad. Not because I was jealous or anything. Just because she shared a name with Strongwell, who was a good kisser...all right, *great*...and licker...I wasn't jealous. Really.

A few mouse clicks got me her DMV record. A feminine five six to my five nine, she was thirty pounds lighter than me and younger by seven hundred and thirty days.

Handcuff me and shove a Taser up my ass. She was younger, prettier and had bigger coconut surprises than me. *And* she'd lived with Bo. I reminded myself forcefully that I *wasn't jealous*. Not threatened in the least.

Right.

I moved on to her other records. Social security, tax returns were all in order. (Well, except she listed her profession as "wind musician". I shuddered to think what kind of instrument she was actually blowing.) No rap sheet, which surprised me. Even some of our part-timers had been nailed for solicitation.

Drusilla had gone to Our Savior's Prep, *the* private school in Meiers Corners. Her school file noted she was an orphan from Chicago, guardian Bo Strongwell. I stifled a snort. Guardian. Like he'd been that much older.

I caught sight of the tuition and whistled. He *was* that much richer. Apparently being a grunt paid well these days.

While in school and for several years after, Dru lived at Bo's. She moved out six months ago, consistent with Gretch's story. Address unknown. Considering Drusilla's occupation, that wasn't as odd as it might have been.

What *was* odd was her name. Driver's license, social security number, tax returns—all the records were in the name of Drusilla *Strongwell.*

She couldn't have been born that way. I looked for a legal change of name. *Nada.* And without some idea of what her name had been, I couldn't search for a birth certificate.

Dead-end for now. I let it chug in my subconscious and did some digging on my other mysteries.

First up—the meaning of the name "Bo".

Not because he was on my mind or anything. I punched in my search criteria, was directed to a baby name site. I was just looking because...because...aw, hell, I couldn't even come up with a good excuse. I was thinking about him all the time. His sea-blue eyes. His battleship chest, his bronzed cannon arms. His riptide abs, his dragon-prow coc...there it was.

Bo. Old Norse, meaning—a householder.

Well, wasn't that a disappointment?

Wait, *disappointment*? Was I expecting something like Blood Drinker or the Fanged One? Good grief, I had to stop reading Anne Rice and watching horror flicks. Well, unless they brought back *Buffy*. Or if there was a *Kindred: The Embraced* marathon over Labor Day.

I went on to the next question. Looking up John Smith in the death records.

The name was so generic it would have been impossible to find. But Ignatek had the social security number. Using that, I got the state and county—Jefferson, Wisconsin. Doing the death certificate search, I found two John Smiths deceased during that time. Only one was thirty-six.

I got lucky then. John Smith's parents were named on the certificate, Quincy and Abigail. A Quincy and Abigail Smith lived in Maidstone, Jefferson County. Smith was common enough, but how many Quincy and Abigails were there? I picked up the phone. It was quarter to four in the morning, but I could leave a message.

To my surprise, a querulous tenor answered. "What do you want? Make it snappy!"

Or maybe it was a crabby alto. I couldn't tell. Age roughened the voice until I wasn't sure if it was male or female. But it was definitely peevish. "I'm sorry to be calling so early. But may I speak to Mr. or Mrs. Smith, please?"

"Something wrong with your hearing? I'm *Mrs.* Smith. You'd better not be selling something, missy. Well? Speak up! What do you want?"

I couldn't get word one in until she took a breath. Annoying, but not in Dirk's league. "I'm sorry to bother you, Mrs. Smith. I'm Detective Elena O'Rourke with the Meiers Corners police in Illinois. I'd like to ask you a few questions about your son John."

"Ungrateful boy. I wanted grandchildren. But no. John had to be gay. Can't you even adopt, I asked? And John *would* have adopted—except for that partner of his. 'We're too young for children'," she mimicked in a high voice. "The partner, not John. John was a dutiful son before he met *Hubert*. I wish John had stayed together with that nice Donald. *Donald* would have adopted."

"Uh, yes, Mrs. Smith. I understand John died of AIDS."

"No, young lady. He *died* of a trip to San Francisco."

"I'm sorry?"

"Hubert went to San Francisco for a convention. John *could* have stayed home. But no. He went along. A honeymoon, that Hubert called it. Quincy and I would have paid for a honeymoon if it had been Donald. *Donald* would have wanted children, but not *Hubert*."

John died on the trip? But Ignatek said AIDS. "I don't understand, Mrs. Smith. Was there a plane crash?"

"There was a *rally*. 'Take Back the Night'. A feminist rally, do you believe it? Not even a gay pride parade. Donald would have done Gay Pride. But not *Hubert...*"

The more she talked, the more confused I became. Maybe Mrs. Smith *could* give Dirkenstein a run for his money. "John was trampled by the crowd?"

"No, no, keep up! John was attacked by a *gang*. Knifed to death in a dark alley." Her voice broke. "My poor boy." Then she snarled, "At least that Hubert died too."

"John was knifed?" I wondered what that had to do with AIDS.

"Stabbed. Viciously. John almost bled to death, detective. He was rushed to the hospital. But he was so weak...he got an infection."

And died. No immune system. She was making sense at last. I was so relieved that I nearly missed it.

The attack. Stabbed. Nearly bled to death.

Then died, yet showed up here a year later.

No. Impossible. "Mrs. Smith. By any chance, did John have an identical twin?"

"You been reading too many horror stories, missy. No."

I thanked her and called the San Francisco police.

After identifying myself and explaining what I was looking for, I was put on hold. While I waited, I typed "Johnson, Steven" into my death records search engine.

A deep, sexy voice came on. "Officer Mancuso." He growled with almost the same erotic timbre as Bo.

In fact, despite the lick-fest in Bo's bedroom I shivered and my pussy clenched. Ouch. Shift couldn't end fast enough. I obviously desperately needed to get *laid*.

Carefully controlling my voice, I identified myself. "I have a question about an attack there a year ago, Officer Mancuso. One of the victims was John Smith from Wisconsin. You were the officer on patrol?"

"Smith...Smith..." I heard some key clicks. "Ah, yes. My partner and I interrupted the...attack."

Maybe I was primed for it, but the hesitation was strange. "Was there something unusual about the...attack, officer?" I mimicked his hesitation.

Another pause. "Not really, detective."

My lie meter didn't work well over the phone. I had only my basic intuition, but that was pinging off the charts. Why was a fellow cop lying to me? "I understand John Smith and his partner were stabbed. Can you tell me what kind of weapon was used?"

The pause this time was definitely darker. "Where did you say you were from, Detective O'Rourke?"

I shivered, and it wasn't excitement. If there hadn't been half a continent between us I would have had my gun out. "Meiers Corners, Officer Mancuso. Please answer the question. What kind of weapon was used?"

"Stiletto. Excuse me, detective, I have another call coming in." He hung up.

I slammed the phone down. Dammit! Just when I was getting somewhere...the death certificate search had a hit. I stared.

Steve was alive, but his death certificate had *not* been annulled.

Why? Why was a living man still legally dead? And I didn't believe that "we've only known for a few days" crap.

I tapped a few more keys, trying to find something that would give me a clue. There were no amendments. It didn't make sense. Unless Steve and Gretchen were trying to scam the insurance company?

It didn't sound like my sister, but I checked. Steve had a single policy, for two thousand dollars. That wouldn't have even covered the funeral. They wouldn't have risked jail for a couple grand. Especially not with Stella.

Could it be that he really was still...? No, it couldn't. Though I loved to read about it, I refused to believe in a world where dead men walked and turned to ash with the help of a well-placed stake.

Not without hard proof, at any rate.

The phone rang, my direct line. "O'Rourke."

"Detective O'Rourke. I have information for you pertaining to the murder."

The voice was a light baritone with an Eastern European flavor. Slavic, or Romanian. I wished, not for the first time, that the cop shop had caller ID.

"Your name, sir?"

"My name does not matter. The new body does. It has been drained of blood."

Bloodless body? I was *very* interested. But... "It's against police department rules to accept anonymous tips. Your name, please."

"The body is in Nieman's parking lot. I know you'll do the right thing, Detective O'Rourke."

He hung up.

I immediately contacted Alice, but she couldn't get a trace. So. Either follow department rules and forget about it, or...hell. Dead body? Killed just like Napoleon Schrimpf? Yeah, good luck putting that out of my head.

It was probably a fake report, piggybacked on a lurid murder. But I couldn't let it lay. Besides, walking might clear my mind about Mancuso and John Smith. I checked my gun and backup piece, prepping to go.

My spine tingled. My head snapped up.

Bo sauntered into the room, twinkling his dimple at me. "Hello, Detective."

Chapter Seventeen

My spine was joined by a tingly trio chorus. We were happy to see him, my breasts and pussy and I.

Still…"I'm working."

"Coffee break?" The erotic note in his voice reminded me of the last break I'd taken with him.

"Yes...no. I can't. I have legwork to do." I rose and brushed by him.

"Legwork is my specialty," he purred as I strode by.

My stride hitched. "Shit, Bo. Don't do that."

"Do what?" He flicked eyes along my legs and licked his lips.

My stride hitched again. I tugged my jeans, adjusting the crotch. The man gave me a permanent squishy.

With cop determination and rigid self-discipline, I made it...outside, Bo following. I hit Adams Street headed west. "What are you doing here, anyway?"

"After you left I went out on patrol. My patrol took me here." He sauntered easily next to me, his hands in his pockets. It tightened his jeans across the front. He was bulging against his zipper.

"Doesn't he ever rest?" Blushing, I pointed at Mr. Not-So-Little Viking.

"Not around you, Elena." Bo's voice dipped into black satin.

My stride lurched as my panties stuck big time. "Fuck."

"Mmm. Yes. That's what I'd like to do with you."

I glared. "I'm *working* now. Save it for end of shift." Though I snarled it at him, the warning was for both of us.

He put a large, warm arm around my shoulders. "Think of this as foreplay." His whisper tickled my earlobe.

Foreplay my ass. This was *eight*play, at least. "Why here? Shouldn't you be walking around your *neighborhood* for your neighborhood watch?" His presence was making it impossible to think. Maybe if he were patrolling over on the northeast side of town my brain would work again. Ten light-years from where my pussy was screaming would be better, but I'd take ten blocks.

I needed my brain with me. I needed to keep alert. The tip might be valid. Murderers often returned to the scene of the crime (*Elementary Deduction*, chapter two). Besides, I needed to reflect on what Mrs. Smith had told me. On what Officer Mancuso had told me—and not told me. I needed my head on straight, and it was hard with Bo and his curving lips and Viking Horn of Plenty so close. If only Bo and his distracting lips (and other body parts) hadn't shown up. If only Bo hadn't arrived *just* as I was about to get somewhere—

Damn. Bo appeared shortly after I'd gotten off the phone with *Mancuso*. Mancuso, who'd had another call coming in.

Or was it a call to make? A call to Bo, telling him to come distract me from the dead John Smith—and real answers?

"Enjoying our walk, Detective?" Bo's voice broke into my thoughts. Deliberately?

I had to focus. Despite Mr. Bo-dacious distracting me. Schrimpf. Puncture wounds. Mr. Seriously Built Bo-dy. Mr. Drive-Me Bo-nkers. No, no, focus. Red-eyed attackers and charred remains of dead men. Mr. Bo-*de*licious.

Focus.

Mancuso had admitted that John Smith had been killed by stilettos. Long, thin knives. Like knitting needles, or nails, or...just say it Elena...*fangs*.

At the very least it was suspicious. And at the very worst? If I'd really stepped into the *Twilight Zone* (both Rod's and Stephenie Meyer's), I was dealing with evil creatures of the night. And how'd I make an arrest then?

Still, as Sherlock Holmes said, "When you have eliminated the impossible, whatever remains, however improbable, must be the truth." So. Say John Smith was really a vampire. Say Schrimpf was killed by a murderous vampire.

DNA evidence still said Smith wasn't the killer. But Bo might be. Damn, I'd swapped spit with him half a dozen times and hadn't bagged any of it for evidence.

"What's going on in that beautiful head of yours, Elena?" Bo's arm tightened around my shoulders.

Beautiful? Bo thought I was...shit. Focus. Say the killer was a vampire, or at least a wannabe. A second body would tell. I needed facts. Impossible bite-hole evidence was still evidence. Checking out the anonymous tip jumped from interesting to vital. I hit West Fifth, struck south.

Bo's hand struck south too. One finger traced lazy curlicues down my collarbone, over my breast, around my nipple.

"Stop that." Talk about diversions. "We're in public."

"No one's around." Bo caught my nipple and pinched.

I jumped. Seized his wrist, but it didn't even slow him. "It's Friday morning. People are up early. Someone might *come*."

"Hopefully you." He pinched and plucked.

I twisted his wrist, trying to capture him in a hold. "Jig's up, Strongwell. I know you're just trying to distract me."

He turned out of my hold and somehow got both brawny arms around me instead. Kissed me softly. "Is it working?"

I gasped. At his audacity, and at the hot feel of his warrior's body flush against mine. I thought about running but as long as there weren't any trees or mailboxes for him to back me against, or doors to fall in, I *should* be okay. "I know you're connected somehow. To Drusilla. To Mancuso." I pulled out my big guns. "*To Steve's uncanceled death certificate.*"

"I have no idea what you mean, Detective." With easy strength Bo pushed me against a too-convenient parked car. Damn. Hadn't thought of *that*. He shoved a thick, hard thigh between my legs. His hands snaked under my top.

I suppressed a groan as his palms found the cotton-covered peaks, abrading them stiff. "Tell me, Bo. Tell me the truth. Confess."

"Why? Because it's the law?" His fingers rubbed and played over my nipples. "I'm sorry, Detective, but I'm not a rules-and-regs kind of man."

How had he figured that out about me? "Not because it's the law." I gasped as he tweaked. "Not even because you'll feel better if you confess...although you will."

"Why then?" His blue eyes lit with amused interest.

"You *need* to tell me—because it's *right*."

"Ah. Well, *right* now, Detective, I have other *needs*." His mouth fell onto mine and I found out what it felt like to be plundered by a Viking.

His tongue thrust hotly into my mouth. Both hands shoved under my bra. He pinched my already-sensitive nipples, not gently. My shriek went into the dark cave of his mouth.

I grabbed his shoulders to push him away. He tweaked until I clutched instead. Rock-hard muscles were firm under my fingers. I couldn't help the groan that escaped.

His thigh flexed between my legs. Bearing down on my pubic bone, he rubbed against the seam of my jeans. Heat seared me. I grabbed his thick thigh with both of mine. To stop him, but my hips began to rock. My fingers dug harder into heavy, knotted muscle.

Bo whispered my name. Trailed hot, possessive kisses down my neck. I throbbed under his lips. He nipped, sharp little bites that ravaged me.

His fingers twitched on my nipples. Pleasure shot through me, so hot it was almost pain. His enormous bulge pulsed against my leg, branding me.

I pressed my hips into him. His fingers plunged down into my panties, plundered me to within an inch of climax.

"Elena." He nipped my neck. Tweaked my clit. "Let me...let me take you home." His breathing wasn't too steady. "Let me make love to you. Civilized...in a bed. My control...shit."

Viking-style rape and pillage was doing fine by me. I grabbed his head in both hands, insanely pressed his mouth to my pounding pulse.

In return Bo released a sound almost like a whimper. "Sweetheart...oh, fuck."

Hot breath fanned over my skin. Something sharp pressed against my neck. I jerked in reaction. Knocked into the car.

The car alarm started whooping at a zillion decibels.

I shrieked. For me, Cupid's quiver was loaded with prank arrows.

Bo reacted swiftly, throwing open the hood and yanking wires or something. The noise blissfully stopped.

He grabbed me again. "Now. Where were we?"

But I'd had time to recover. To remember the phone call from Eastern European Guy. "Bo, I can't. I have work to do."

His hands tightened almost painfully. "Damn it, Elena! I want *in*. Now!"

I narrowed my eyes at him. "Don't threaten me."

"Not threat. Hunger." He ground his hips against me. "You have no idea how much I want you."

Mr. Big Horn was painfully large, so I had *some* idea. But...dead body. Vital evidence. I pushed him until he gave me some space. "I want it every bit as much as you do, Strongwell. More." Five years, three months and six days more.

"I doubt that." He crossed his arms. His eyes were so bright they were almost red. His jaw worked hard. The enormous bulge in his pants was straining so fiercely it made *me* ache.

"It's not a contest, Bo. And it's not forever. Just a few more hours."

"*I can't wait a few hours.*" His lips were so tight they barely moved.

My body iced over. "Meaning what?"

But I knew. Meaning he was giving up on me. Meaning he'd find another woman, maybe his ex-playmate Drusilla. Meaning my personal countdown would never end.

I'd waited five years to find Bo. And even if I waited five dozen, I guessed I'd never find another man like him. Never find someone I responded to like him.

Bo Strongwell was a once-in-a-lifetime kind of guy.

I had a horrible choice. I could go home with him, have what promised to be pleasure and fulfillment beyond my wildest dreams.

Or I could do my job. And lose him.

Bo. The best thing that ever happened to me. In a weird, bitey sort of way.

I tried to convince myself. I wouldn't jeopardize my job if I went with Bo. In fact, regs said I shouldn't follow up without EE's name.

Seemed like a no-brainer, right? But while Bo might be the fuck of a lifetime, my job was my *life.*

I turned from him and headed for Nieman's parking lot.

There was no body.

I stared at the spot where Napoleon Schrimpf had lain. I could have looked anywhere—the lot was tumbleweed empty. But I couldn't see it so well. My vision was unaccountably blurry. Still, a body would have been obvious, if it was here to be found.

Unless it had been dragged away. I wiped my wet cheek before digging through my pockets for my flashlight. Wiped the other cheek while I shone the light on the blacktop. The pavement was clean. No skid marks or smears. Nothing.

I'd given up Bo for nothing. *Nothing.*

Staring at the circle of light, my insides crumpled, chilled, like I'd swallowed an ice pack. Like I'd never be warm and happy again.

That was my first clue. Not about the case. About how I felt about Bo.

Somehow, when I wasn't looking, it'd come to mean more than just getting laid. Somehow a simple attraction had mushroomed into…more.

And now "more" would die before it even had a name.

"Did you expect to find something in an empty parking lot, Detective?" The black satin voice was distinctly grouchy.

I jerked around, too surprised to hide the tears on my face. Bo took one look at me and his gaze softened. He hooked my chin with gentle fingers. "I'm not quite such a jerk, Elena."

"You said…" The words were sobbed, embarrassing me.

"I shouldn't have said." His thumb caressed my cheek. "That was my frustration talking. Every time I get near you…" He blew out a breath and stood. "It's like a compulsion. I know better."

I gave a watery laugh. "You make me sound like a drug addiction."

Bo's eyes darkened and he almost growled. "You *are.*"

"Don't look at me like that." My cheeks warmed. "Like I'm supper."

"You *are,*" he repeated, even darker.

I leaped to my feet. "Supper? Come on. Something sweeter, please." I attempted to make a joke of it. "Dessert maybe. Or at least an after-dinner mint."

"You're more than that, Elena." Bo's eyes flashed before he turned from me. "Much more."

"Cocktails?" I willed him to lighten up. "Get it? Cock? Tail?"

He groaned. "That's horrible." But when he turned back the corner of his mouth curved. And his eyes were their normal sea blue.

We stared at each other for the longest time. I nearly fell in and drowned.

"Elena," he said slowly. "I have something to confess. I think..."

I watched his beautiful lips move. "Yes?"

"I think I'm falling..."

His lips stopped short. His eyebrows snapped into a frown. His nostrils flared as if he smelled something *bad.*

And his eyes turned red. Not tired red or flash-picture red but glow-in-the-dark red. Hard, ruby red.

Blood red.

Shadows congealed around us, condensed rapidly into the solid bodies of three men. Two had spiked hair and wore long leather coats open over muscle shirts and jeans.

The third wore a flowing silk shirt and tight pants, like an eighteenth-century poet or a pirate. He had long walnut hair and distinctly Eastern European features—high cheekbones, deep, pale eyes. A Mikhail, or a Boris.

Bo spun toward the trio. Snarled at them like an *animal.*

"Strongwell." Boris's voice had a Eastern European flavor, too. Baritone, but light. It sounded like..."Lord Ruthven sends his regards. And a message."

Lord Ruthven? No, must have heard it wrong. He said *Lorne* Ruthven, that weird tin-can voiced guy on the phone. And this guy sounded like EE, the *other* voice, the anonymous tip that led me... Damn. He'd lured me here. Should have followed regs. "Bo? You know these people?"

"I know their boss." Bo's eyes never left Boris. Underneath his words was a low, warning growl. "What's the message?"

Boris polished nails against his shirt. "You are to give us what we want. This town will soon be ours, anyway. Give up gracefully and we will not harm you." His eyes wandered over me, insultingly. "Or yours."

I eased a hand toward my gun. "This is a joke. It has to be."

"No joke, I'm afraid." Boris smiled at me, slowly. His eyeteeth were disturbingly long. "Well? Your answer, Strongwell?"

"This." With a *ka-click,* Bo whipped out a really big switchblade. I wondered if it was regulation-length or if I'd have to arrest him. (Ooh, there was the cuffs idea again.)

Then I had no more time to wonder about anything.

The two long-coats jumped Bo, unnaturally fast, even faster than John Smith. And unnaturally fluid, practically flowing. It was creepy, how inhumanly they moved.

Just as fast and fluid, Bo met them with knife and fist.

Before I could aid Bo, Boris lunged toward me. I drew my XD. "Stop! Police!"

He kept coming. Maybe English wasn't his primary language. Still, showing the gun should have translated. I flicked off the safety, chambered a round.

Still coming.

As he barreled toward me, my vision narrowed. Everything went black, except for Boris. His claw-like hands reaching for me, his sneering face.

His glowing, blood-red eyes.

Deep breath, I told myself. Aim. Smooth trigger press.

I fired.

I intended to wound, and his shoulder jerked. It was enough to stop most crooks. But it didn't stop Boris—it didn't even *slow* him. He grabbed me by the throat and hoisted me like a flag. I choked.

Bo whirled, *roared.* Leaped toward us, baring teeth sharp as a saw. His hard red eyes became laser-deadly. His face was so contorted it looked—armored.

The parking lot was unevenly lit. There was dust blowing in my eyes. I *had* to have been seeing things. Bo's red eyes, the plated face...and please tell me I was only imagining the tusk-like canines I saw splitting his chiseled lips.

But I didn't imagine Bo chopping off Boris's head.

With a dazzling-fast slash of long silver blade, Bo sliced through meat and skin. Boris staggered, dropped me. I stumbled back. A second slash hacked bone. A third severed the man's neck. Blood spurted, barely missing me.

Boris's head toppled.

All movement ceased, except for that head. It tumbled down the collapsing body, winding itself in its own long hair. As fast as the attack had happened, the head seemed to roll forever.

The skull hit pavement with a clunking thud. The body fell with a wet splat beside it.

Bo was revealed, hands clenched, chest heaving. His neck was bowed. Beyond him were the white, horrified faces of the other two assailants.

He straightened. Turned with that terrible, inhuman fluidity toward the spiked-haired attackers. They melted away.

"Elena." Bo's broad shoulders were set. "Go back to the police station. I do not wish you to see this."

"See what? What's going on?" My gun was still in my hand. I stared at the headless corpse. "Why didn't my bullet even slow him?"

"*Elena,*" he repeated. "*Go.*" It rang through me with the force of imperative.

I turned and was halfway down the block before I even realized I'd moved.

As soon as I did realize it, I spun. "Hey!"

Bo was gone. Like a ghost.

I crept back to the corpse. Not only was Bo missing, so were Boris's head and heart.

Chapter Eighteen

I should have reported the incident. I should have cordoned off the scene and started the paperwork.

Instead I ran all the way to Gretchen's. Not exactly regs, but neither was what the hell had just happened. Regs, right. If what I was beginning to believe was true, the corpse would be only a charred streak by the time officialdom got there. If Tight-ass thought I was bonkers before, that would make him rocket me to Nurse Mildred Ratched (Meiers Corners' psychiatric nurse...don't ask).

I pounded on the cedar-and-crystal door until the windows rattled. The door cracked open to a sleepy, lined face and tousled silver hair. Jeeves Butler, complete with blue tartan dressing gown. "Detective O'Rourke?"

Any other time I would have made some smartass comment about how Queen Victoria would be proud of him. "I need to see my sister. Let me in."

"Of course." The door closed and I could hear the rattle of chain. The instant the door opened again I pressed past him. Leaped up the elegant stairs two at a time.

"Gretchen!" I knocked sharply. "Wake up. I need to talk to you."

"Elena?" My sister opened her door. Despite the early hour she was wide awake and dressed. "What is it?"

I pushed inside. Tonight the apartment seemed straightjacket small. "I want to know how much you trust him. How much you trust Strongwell."

She blinked. "With my life. Elena what is this all about?"

"Then how much do you trust me?"

She looked taken aback by that. "You're my sister. You know I trust you."

"Yeah, well, something happened tonight. Something impossible."

"You're upset." My sister put a hand on my shoulder. "Come sit down. I'll get you some tea, you'll feel better."

"No." I broke away from her to pace. "Gretchen...you're going to think I'm nuts. But tonight..." I reached the far end of her living room and stopped.

In the dark of the bedroom hallway, two red eyes glowed.

I pulled my gun. I'd drawn my gun more in the last few days than I had my whole career. Such unnatural shit going down. "Who's there?"

The eyes blinked. Approached. As they neared, they cooled to a soft brown. Raised hands emerged from the darkness. Steve.

His pleasant face was arranged in a carefully neutral expression. "What's wrong, Elena?"

I didn't say another word. If tonight was what I thought, Steve's uncanceled death certificate made a whole lot more sense.

Because he wasn't really alive.

A world lurked beneath my nice safe one. A shadow world, an underdark. Bo was a denizen, and Steve. Thor, and Mancuso...hell, maybe even Dracula.

Nah, probably not him.

But certainly Boris was one. It was why Bo cut off his head.

Creatures out of legends and nightmares *were real.* I stared into Steve's seemingly friendly eyes. What would he do to me if he realized I knew his secret, *their* secret? What would Bo do if I told?

I wanted to scream it to the universe. I even had evidence, but who would believe me? Blatzky? Ruffles? *Tight-ass*? Evidence, hell. Even Charlie Ignatek would laugh if I told him what the evidence meant.

My sister needed to know, though. I had to tell Gretchen and somehow make her believe. Only knowing about this darkness would keep her safe.

And then I had to find a way to destroy it.

"Elena, calm down." Gretchen spoke slowly and carefully from behind me.

Except...what if she already knew? What if she was already in too deep? If she did know, was somehow *connected*...fuck, of course. It was the only explanation that made sense. It was why she'd lied to me, made up that whopper story about Steve.

"It's okay, Elena," Gretchen said.

I reminded myself she'd been devastated when she lost her husband, her soul-mate. Emotionally shattered. Now he was back and she was deliriously happy. Stella had a daddy again who loved her. Who was I to interfere? How could I justify wrecking their little family?

How could I *not*? My job was to keep law and order in Meiers Corners. That included cleaning up whatever grimy shadows lurked beneath. And though Steve had been the other half of Gretch's soul, I had no idea who—or what—he was now.

No idea, except what I saw in front of me. Red-eyed Steve,

frowning at me. Dead Steve, reanimated and starring in the Hallway Version of *Dracula*. I backed slowly away.

Steve's eyes lifted over my head. My spine tingled. Damn, now what?

"Detective." A black satin voice, *right behind me.*

I spun.

Bo stood there, axe-sized fists planted on hips, muscles pumped. My back was open to Steve but I couldn't turn back. I couldn't *move*, arrested by the sight of Bo in the center of Gretchen's small living room, dominating it.

His eyes were the blue of a stormy sea, his beautiful lips were set with grim determination. Because he was going to kill me? Despite being a kick-ass cop I had the ghastly realization that, preternaturally strong as he was, it would be pathetically easy for him.

Two inhumanly fast strides brought him to me. He grabbed the back of my neck with one hand. Immobilized my head.

Kissed me, hard.

All fear of being killed fled. Hell, all thought fled, period.

Hot, questing lips. A thrusting, conquering tongue. A powerful, masterful hand. My lust, simmering all night, *boiled.*

Gretchen gasped. Steve made a primitive sound in the back of his throat. Bo ignored them. He wrapped his arm around my waist and yanked me hard against his ripped torso.

"I'm done fighting it, Elena. This attraction...this raw need... If you learn everything, so be it. But I'm not holding back anymore."

Fuck me. He'd been *holding back*?

I could practically smell the adrenalin shooting through his system, recognized it because it was the twin to mine. The attack must have fired him up too. Fired him up until *something* had to burn.

I wanted it to be me.

Insane. I had to be. Bo Strongwell was a vampire. The red eyes, the plated face...the orgasmic biting...and all I wanted was to lie under him and have him turn me into a pincushion. So unregulated, so out of the box, so not me.

And yet *exactly* me. Something deep inside needed Bo, craved him. Something profound. I didn't recognize it, but, like Bo, I was tired of fighting it. I made a decision. Not forever, but for now. "Take me somewhere private."

"You read my mind," he growled, and swept me up.

He moved so fast the wind tangled my hair. In the time it took him to lay another potent kiss on my mouth, we were in his bed. Cool sheets were beneath me, heavy warmth on top of me. A scalding mouth sealed mine.

He did his clothes-melting thing again. Mine he simply slashed. With what, I didn't know and didn't care. Because his hands were on my breasts and his mouth was on mine. His hard prow rocked against my pubic bone with a delicious pressure.

I ran my palms over the sleek muscles of his back. Stroked the roped power of taut hips and buttocks. Delighted in the rippling strength.

He pressed me into the bed with his nude, pumped body. His tongue invaded my mouth. Something big and smooth slid between my damp thighs, nudged my pussy lips. Three straight days of foreplay insured I was dripping wet and ready.

Oh boy. This was *it*.

I squirmed under Bo, trying to seat him. Big and smooth rubbed me in all sorts of luscious ways. But not the one way I needed—in.

He reached down. I shifted so he could guide himself home.

He only pressed open my cleft with his fingers and rubbed. I arched at the lovely cascading pleasure. He purred at my response and rubbed harder. The harder he rubbed the more I arched and moaned. The more I responded the harder he rubbed, until he was abrading my clitoral hood like a match to a strike strip.

And the more aroused I got, the bigger his erection pumped. I felt every hot, teasing twitch, its head caught in the vestibule of my pussy. Every pulse stroked my tender inner flesh. It was the most exciting, erotic torture ever.

"Bo, please!" Five years, three months and who the hell knew was eating me alive. "In!" I wrenched my hips up, splitting my labia on his prodding erection.

The head sank deeper.

And that was all. Just the glans, pulsing gently. Stretching me with engorged expectancy.

His eyes squeezed shut. "You're so hot, Elena."

Definitely hot. I was burning up, on fire with anticipation. "Inside!"

"Not...not yet." A deep purr rumbled from his chest. Bo rotated his hips, his cock slipping in my entry like a ball-in-socket. "I want you...hungry."

I felt every swivel like a hammer. I jerked my pelvis, trying to drive him deeper. Getting not one millimeter. Pleasure pulsed in shallow waves. "I'm beyond hungry. I'm so beyond hungry my vagina's eating my brain. In, damn you!"

"Not...yet." His mouth clamped on my nipple. Hot tugs shot me like electric arrows.

I howled. "You're evil. I knew it, but this proves it."

His only reply was to grab my clit hood between two fingers and pump.

I shrieked. Fisted my hands and beat on his heavily muscled back. Solid thuds sounded good but did little damage. He was just too blasted strong. "Dammit, Bo! If you don't finish this fucking *now*, I'm going to pull my gun and shoot you."

He raised his head, panting through distended nostrils. His eyes blazed down on me. He looked ready to rupture. "That's...hungry."

I was barely breathing, fertile with need. He began to push forward. *Finally.* I could feel my body begin to stretch to fit him. And then...and then...

My cell phone rang.

I shrieked. "Not now!"

Bo *roared.* He vaulted off the bed. Snatched my jeans from the floor. Tore the phone out.

Hurled it into the wall with such force that it shattered.

Silence fell, punctuated only by my rasping breath. Bo turned to me, nostrils flared, eyes liquid fire. He breathed deep, his massive chest inflating.

"Elena. Are you...ready?" As he spoke, his rippling abs bunched. His fists clenched and released. His Viking prow stood out, thick and proud, straining for me.

I knew why he was asking. He wanted more than sex. If I said yes, he'd invade my body. He'd penetrate my sex with his luscious cock. He'd pierce my neck with his elegant fangs.

And would he invade my heart?

I'd worry about that later. I opened my arms to him.

Bo leaped back onto the bed. He split my legs with a muscled thigh. Seized my butt with one hand. Thrust the other into my hair.

Pulling my head ferociously to the side, he exposed my neck. I pressed my mons wantonly into him, too far gone with need to care.

His hips reared back. His cock stroked down my labia. Slipped between. Locked into place.

Every single muscle in my body clenched. I was a mass of constricted need, a black hole of desire.

My glazed eyes found Bo. Pleading. Now. Take me now.

"Mine," he growled, and slammed home.

He impaled my tight vagina with shocking power. *Filled* me. He slammed hard and deep enough to kiss my cervix.

I arched against him with a long moan.

"Fuck, Elena. You're tight as a virgin." He actually swelled *bigger* inside me. "I can't stand it, sweetheart. I'm losing it." He held himself over me, chest muscles clenched hard as boulders. His head was bowed, and he was breathing like a locomotive.

I rolled my hips under him. His thick manhood grew even fatter. I purred. "Then lose it."

"Elena, sweetheart, stop. You're killing me." He shuddered, trying to get his breathing under control.

I grabbed his tight ass and pulled.

With a hoarse cry he fell on me. A tremendous surge of hips drove him into me, to the hilt.

My eyes flew open. He was thrust so deep I thought he was screwing my throat.

Whatever I'd done finally broke his control. He beat into me, hard and fast. My entire body tightened, wound up like a spring. I arched against him, clutching his brawny biceps.

"Elena." His voice was a pain-filled rasp. "I want... I need..." His mouth opened on my neck. His breath burned the tender flesh of my throat.

"Yes, Bo. Oh, *yes*."

He bit me. My blood ignited, became a flaming river. I screamed. Bo pummeled me with his huge cock, a pounding force that fanned the flames even hotter. His tongue swirled where he bit, licking like an animal, rough on my sensitive skin. I trembled helplessly between the two assaults, his driving cock and burning tongue.

I started to come.

His thrusts slowed, deepened. I teetered on the edge, his cock ripening inside me. He stroked, one last time, thickening and lengthening until it was almost too much to bear.

Then he roared and erupted into me in a great oceanic tide. Fierce contractions blasted wave after wave, powerfully deep. His intense climax rushed around me, where I clung to a last tattered shred of sanity.

The heat, the force, pushed me over. I sailed off the precipice and burst.

I ruptured like a blown volcano. Like a tree hit by lightning, exploding into splinters. I was the Big Bang, catapulting plasma through the universe.

And then I was fairy dust, floating down onto the huge bed. I cooled, gradually forming back into Elena.

Bo lay heavy on me, his mouth open on my neck. His lips suckled now and then like a sleeping baby.

I felt sleepy and sore and wonderful. With Bo, five-plus years had been more than worth it.

Until I thought to wonder who had phoned me.

☙❧

"Captain Titus, I can explain." I adjusted my borrowed shirt, wishing Bo weren't quite so large, wishing it weren't quite so obvious the shirt wasn't mine. Wishing Tight-ass weren't between me and the safety of my desk.

It was five thirty and I was back at the station, attempting to come out of this with my skin whole. Bo may not have left me bloody. But Tight-ass certainly would.

"I don't want to hear a single word other than *the name.*" A vein pumped angrily in Tight-ass's temple. His pumpkin head looked about to explode. The smashed pumpkin image distracted me for a moment.

I opened my mouth to admit it. To admit I'd had sex during duty hours. To name Bo Strongwell as co-conspirator. "B—"

"No buts!" Titus shouted. "I want the name of the person who killed Napoleon Schrimpf!"

He could have knocked me over with a donut. I was thinking about Viking sex. He was thinking about the *job.* Which only proved how far in over my head I was with Bo.

"Well..." I gathered my thoughts. "Cause of death is loss of blood. The mechanism is uncertain."

Tight-ass started chafing his arm. "Come on, O'Rourke. The wounds were pretty distinctive. Some sort of knife."

He was calling the stabs to Schrimpf's 'nads "distinctive" wounds. Was Tight-ass hinting he knew how "distinctive"? Maybe he wouldn't think I was a complete nutcase if I told him what I was really thinking.

Well, not exactly what I was thinking, because that was too unbelievable. But maybe I could get close. "Yes, sir. I think they may be, um, bite wounds."

He stopped chafing. "Bite wounds? From what?"

The incredulity in his voice should have warned me. I was being cautious but not cautious enough. Maybe I was high—too little sleep and too much great sex. "From the prostitute Drusilla, sir. I think she bit Schrimpf during sex and he bled—"

"Are you *insane*?" Tight-ass's face mottled. His voice went castrato-high. "What are you implying, O'Rourke? That this hooker is some sort of monster? A bloodsucking v-v-v—"

"A vampire? No! Well, not exactly." I shrugged, hunching a bit.

"This is unbelievable!" He was beyond jet-engine and heading for a range only dogs could hear.

I winced. "Captain Titus, please. I'm not saying it was a vampire."

He must only have heard "vampire". His voice revved like a turbo. "Do you think this is the *National Exploiter*? 'Police Reveal Killer is Vampire Vamp.' Fuck, O'Rourke! What do you think this would do to our department's reputation? To *my* reputation?"

"Sir, once again. I'm not saying Drusilla *is* a vampire—"

"You're off the case! And if I have anything to say about it, *off the force*!"

Tight-ass whirled and stalked out.

Shocked, I could only stare after him. Off the case. And off the force?

I made my way slowly to the desk, slumped behind it. My father stared out of my family photo in condemnation, and Chief Dirkson's painted eyes were very disappointed. "That could have gone better." My eyes stung. I fisted them, was chagrined to feel hot trickles thread down my cheeks.

All my life, I wanted to be a cop. A detective, yes. But even more basic, to right wrongs, to protect the innocent, to serve the public. To fight for justice.

A fighter for justice. Alice was right, much as I hated to admit it. It was who I was. I knew that now. Because if that were taken away...I'd be nobody.

The wall clock said five fifty-five when the scrape of feet brought me out of it. "Ma'am?" A muddy rasp. "Detective Ma'am?"

As if my night couldn't get any better. I wiped my eyes. "What is it, Ruffles?"

"I saw Captain Titus. He was pretty angry."

"Yes, Ruffles." My voice sounded as listless as I felt.

"He says you're off the Schrimpf case."

Hearing it from Ruffles made it real. "Yes."

"Isn't this kinda sudden?" He sidled up to the desk, his muddy eyes tinged with compassion.

Compassion, coming from the Dirkenator. Somehow that made it even more awful. "Yes, Ruffles." I couldn't seem to say anything else. Now how would I get to be a full detective?

"But why?"

I didn't want to talk about it. "You find out anything about Josephine Schrimpf? Where she was the night of the murder?"

"Well, yes. But I don't know...if you're off the case...maybe I shouldn't tell you."

"Oh, for pity's sake." I clasped my head with both hands. "Well, make sure you *do* tell whoever takes over." My big chance. Gone.

There was no response from Dirkenstein. The silence was so unusual that I found the energy to look up. His face was a study in sheepish pride.

"Oh, no. Who'd Titus assign? Who took over the Schrimpf case?"

Dirk thumped his skinny chest. "That would be me."

ʚɞ

So what did I do now? With all that had happened, maybe I should stop and think. Reflect. Try to make sense of my life.

Or maybe I should stuff myself with chocolate.

As if that was really a decision.

I went to the Caffeine Café, where I ordered a double mocha latte with whipped cream and chocolate shavings. Carting the mug to my favorite back corner table, I sat and dipped my spoon into the whipped cream. Licking the soft sugary goodness was an awful lot like licking Bo's smooth goodness.

I tossed the spoon. *Not thinking about Bo.* Or the Case of the Poked Penis. Not Bo, not v-creatures, and especially not the Case of the Bit Balls. I drank chocolate coffee. Let it soothe me. I was *not* thinking about Bo, or Ruffles, or Tight-ass, or Gnawed Gonads.

It wasn't working. Pricked Privates. Even drowning my confusion and sorrow in chocolate wasn't working. Punctured Prick.

Yeesh. I needed to *talk* to someone. Preferably someone a) human and b) who wouldn't shriek when I said the v-word. Someone who could walk with me through all the weird.

At that point I was not entirely surprised to see my sister Gretchen come in. When you'd been through that much alien landscape, even impossible coincidence began to look normal.

"Hey," I said as Gretch sat.

"Hey, yourself." My sister waved at the Princess. Ha. Gretch might as well have been waving to a wall. The owner—a regal blonde who looked like an older version of Princess Diana, had she lived—sat behind the bar like her stool was a throne. The Princess *never* waited on tables.

Her Highness called, "Your usual, Gretchen?"

Well, shit. Alien coincidence was one thing. Then there was plain impossible.

"Sounds good, Diana." To me, Gretch said, "Diana owes Bo. She repays him by feeding his people."

"Diana?"

"Diana Simone Prince. The coffee shop owner."

Huh. She really was Prince-S Di. "And she gives you great service because Bo gives her great sex?" My throat seized. I couldn't believe I'd said that.

But my own words accused me, made it pathetically obvious that I was jealous. Jealous of my man...who wasn't mine, and wasn't even a man. Oh, goody. Even deliberately *not* reflecting on life (and Bo), I was finding out all sorts of things about myself (and Bo). And I didn't like it.

Gretchen said, "Not sex. Diana owes Bo her life. As do I."

I grabbed two packs of sugar. Tore them into my latte. This was going to be a long morning. "And Steve. Steve owes Bo his life."

Gretchen sighed. "Not exactly. That's what I came to talk to you about."

Not unexpected, but it was still a bit freaky. "How did you know where to find me?"

Before Gretch could reply, the Princess brought her drink, a frappe. "Anything else?"

Gretch nodded. "Another mocha for Elena. And could I have one of those raspberry scones, please? With extra frosting?"

"Coming right up. On the house." The Princess swayed away.

Wow. I never got service like that, not even with my gun. I covered my amazement with a big swig of mocha latte. "How did you know I was here?"

"Bo told me. I would have arranged to meet you somewhere more private, but your cell phone...er, Bo told me about that too." Gretchen colored. "Not everything."

But enough that she would blush. I was going to have a talk with Mr. Mouth. Which made me think about Bo's mouth, how he used it on me...which made me hot, which made me blush too.

Except that was all a ruse, right? If Bo was what I thought, he was sex personified. And I wasn't his girlfriend, I was dinner. Anger flared, fueled by pain. "Enough stalling. How did Bo know where I was? I didn't tell him. I didn't even know I was going to the Caffeine Café until I got here. Did he know because of *what he is*?"

Gretchen jerked. Bull's-eye. "He said it was time to tell you. I didn't believe him. Elena, please understand. I didn't keep *this* from you because I wanted to."

This being the dark underbelly yawing below Meiers Corners. Imaginary creatures made real. And naturally, because it was me, it couldn't be leprechauns or the Easter Bunny. My imaginary creatures had to be bloodsucking monsters.

A clunk caught my attention. The Princess slid a thick plate in front of Gretchen, a raspberry scone dwarfing it. Icing flowed like a glacier over the scone and onto the plate. Another whipped-cream-topped mug appeared at my elbow.

Food and drink. Homey warmth. It made the creepy recede a bit.

As the Princess moved off, Gretchen cut into her scone. The fork's tines sank through gooey frosting and soft dough. Steam rose, smelling of butter and sugar.

"C'mon, Gretch. How'd Bo know where I was?"

She slid scone into her mouth, but it didn't seem like she tasted it. Reluctantly, she put her fork down. "Master Bo knows where all his donors are."

"*What?*"

"It's some sort of internal sense he has. They all have it. Even Steve." Gretchen raised blue eyes to mine. Pleading. Pleading for understanding...for sympathy.

But she'd confirmed my fears. "*They.*" I spat the word. Monsters. Soulless creatures of the night.

Vampires.

"Tell me about *them*," I said. "What are donors? What happened to Steve? Why do you call Bo 'master'? And *are they hurting you*?"

"No!" Then more softly, "No, of course not. Steve is my husband, Elena. And Bo saved my life."

"But he's your master."

She picked up her fork. Toyed with the scone. Pulled off little moist flakes. "Bo is master of our household. He runs things. Makes sure there are enough of um, *them*, to protect all of um, *us*."

Um-*us*, I translated, were humans. Um-*them* were vampires. *Evil, dead, soulless killers.* Except Gretchen was alive. And so was I, despite Bo holding me helpless in his evil clutches (sexy, strong evil clutches...*yeesh*) several times. It didn't square. "How many of *them* are there?"

"Three. In our household." She muttered the last.

Three—but "some restrictions apply". A qualified answer, suspicious enough in a witness. Coming from my sister it screamed evasion. "And outside of your 'household'? How many in Meiers Corners?"

Her fork stopped. "A couple. I'm not sure."

"A couple, I see." I killed my first mocha...er, drank it off, and set it down with an irritated thud. I decided to change my attack.

Attack? I was treating her like a hostile witness. I would have been ashamed, except my own sister was protecting fanged *evil soulless* monsters from me. True, one was her husband. But one had *me* in his sexy, strong...*evil* clutches. I had to get to the bottom of this. "Fine. What and where is this 'household'?"

She heard my tone and started tearing scone again. "The apartment building is the household. We all live together. It's easier to protect us that way. We try to make it as easy as possible for Master Bo."

"Him being overworked, and all."

"Well, he is." She flashed me a resentful glare.

"If he's so overworked, why not just get some help? Or is he just into the drama?"

To my surprise, she blushed. "He has Thorvald. And Steve."

"Who, by your own admission, aren't enough."

"Well, yes, but...I don't know. Maybe it's hard to find that kind of help. Or maybe Bo doesn't trust anybody else to protect us well enough."

The whole mistrusted-partner thing again. "Right. Protect you against what, for pity's sake? The worst crime we have in Meiers Corners is kids stealing smokes." Well, usually. And I was frustrated enough to ignore the evil undead underbelly.

Her head shot up. "We just had a *murder*, remember?"

"Oh, I see. It's Bo who protects you from murderers. Not the cops. But Bo Strongwell, ninja apartment manager."

She dropped her fork with a clatter. "Bo protects us from being slaughtered in the most horrible way imaginable. And he protects *every single soul* in this city. He works like a dog, risking his life every night for people who never know it. You should be grateful, not insulting him!"

"Okay, okay. Calm down. You have to admit this is all pretty hard to swallow." I waited for her color to subside. "So Bo doesn't manage an apartment. He 'runs a household'. And he runs things because...?"

"He's oldest. And strongest."

"Oldest? At thirty?"

Gretch pushed her plate away. "He's not thirty."

"Right. He's fifty but he's been drinking formaldehyde."

"Elena, he helped Reenie with a history assignment. On the American Revolution." At my questioning look she added, "One of the kids in the building."

Bo helped a kid with homework? *Father material,* I thought, then slapped myself. Was I Rita on *Dexter*? Soulless monsters were not father material. "Big deal. He helped a kid. That shows maturity, not age."

"Bo knew things no book has. And...he had a letter signed by General Washington. Addressed to a Sergeant Bo Strongwell."

Which might be an ancestor with the same name. Or might make Bo *hundreds* of years...no. That was impossible.

But so were vampires. "All right. Say I believe all that. Why are you living in the Cullen Apartments instead of the home you love?"

"Cullen...? Oh, *Twilight*. You and your taste in reading." She almost smiled. "I'm living there because of Steve. Because of...the attack." The smile disappeared. "Elena...there's something I've never told anyone. Never been able to tell anyone." Her eyes got suspiciously glossy and she blinked rapidly.

Oh, snap. She was going to cry. Yeah, Gretch had been wandering in the land of weird long before me, alone. And she was even more scared than I was.

Time to put aside the cop. Gretchen needed her big sister. I covered her hand with mine. "You can tell me." She didn't answer, still fighting tears. "Pretty please with puke on top?"

That earned me a watery smile. "Thanks." She took a deep breath, let it out slowly. "The mugging. It wasn't just a mugging."

Chapter Nineteen

Gretch took another deep breath. "There were two of them. One attacked me, one attacked Steve. The one attacking me also wanted to...he tried to..."

Her face was so twisted in horror, I knew what she couldn't say. Rape. "I'll kill the fucker."

"Oh, Elena, I love you." Gretchen gave a little laugh. "My protector."

"Your big sis."

"Same thing. You don't have to kill him. Master Bo already did." Her smile faded. "Stella was screaming. I was on the ground. The monster was on top of me, pawing at my skirt. His strength... It was inhuman, Elena. I couldn't do anything. My little girl was scared and I couldn't do a *thing*."

"Shh." I scooted my chair next to hers and wrapped an arm around her shoulders. "It's over. It's over and you're safe. Drink some of your frappe, you'll feel better."

I held the cup for her. Gretch took a sip. Her shoulders loosened under my arm. She drew a breath. Closed her eyes. "Suddenly the man's weight was gone. I got to my hands and knees...and there were...bodies. Three bodies. One was Steve's. He had a huge wound in his throat. I looked around for Stella. She was gone. I got hysterical." Gretchen trembled violently.

"It's okay." I held her with both arms, hugged her tight. Good God, what had I unleashed? She was hurting worse than I could believe, had faced horrors I never would have wished for her. "We can stop."

"But I...I want to tell you. I need to." Gretchen turned in my arms to look me in the eye. "I crawled over to Steve. He was so still. His throat was torn open. He was...even I could tell...oh, God. I burrowed into his arms as if he could still hold me. Still protect me." She was trembling again so I picked up my hot mocha latte and made her drink some.

"The other two bodies were our attackers. They weren't breathing.

But suddenly—oh, Elena. *Their eyes snapped open.* And they were *red.* Bo had only knocked them out so he could get Stella somewhere safe. He didn't want her to see when he...when he..."

"When he killed them?"

My sister looked surprised. The question seemed to bring her back from someplace dark and scary. "Oh, no, Elena. You don't kill them. You have to *destroy* them."

"Destroy." I thought back to the strange attacks, John Smith and Boris. "Cut off their heads?"

"And remove the heart." Gretchen's tone was so matter-of-fact I nearly smiled. But she was serious.

"And burn them?" I was thinking about the black charred streaks.

"That's best. Although if you leave them out, the sun does the trick."

The sun. *Buffy* and *Dracula.* And my comfort read, *Sunshine.* "Then the stories are true? Blood drinking, silver allergy, flying bats? All of it?" *Evil, bloodsucking creatures.* It appalled me. I had sex with a soulless monster. Oh hell—what did that make *me*?

I wished the legends were wrong. That the books were wrong. That some vampires were not beyond redemption.

And that I was therefore not beyond redemption.

"Most of the legends are true." When Gretchen saw my face she added quickly, "The physical ones, Elena. Like the sun and the dirt. Not the religious ones."

Wondering what that meant, I remembered the time I'd had coffee with Bo. "What about mind reading?"

"Not that, either. Or, not exactly. They read scent and expression so well, it seems like mind reading sometimes."

Okay. Not mind reading, or religious legends. Just sun, and...what about the dirt? Something to do with the dirt-floor den...dirt floor...*sleeping in a shallow grave*?

No! Bo said he relaxed there, not slept. He had a bedroom. He slept *there.* I hoped. Because if his bed was a shallow grave how could I cuddle up after really great sex...dammit! What was I thinking of? I had no future with a monster, especially not one who drank people smoothies. "Bo got back in time to save you. And then what?"

"I didn't feel safe any more, knowing there are inhuman monsters out there. I asked if I could move into Bo's household. He'd already taken Stella home, left her with Drusilla while he rescued me. Dru's one of them, you know."

Double-D Dru. I was righter than I knew when I called her a fanged little whore. "The hooker with the heart of gold."

"She is." Gretch spoke sharply. "She can't help the way she looks. Or her libido. It's natural for their kind...from what I understand...oh hell." Her face collapsed to a helpless red. "Steve's the same way, now.

Inhumanly handsome. Supernaturally virile."

"Lucky you."

"Lucky you," Gretchen retorted, and I was the one blushing.

Then she paused, put one hand briefly over mine. "But thanks, Elena. I haven't been able to talk about that day with anyone. Well, with anyone human. I feel better."

"Oh. Well. You're welcome." I'd been driven to learn her secrets out of loyalty and love. And though it had cost us both, in the long run maybe it had been worth it.

She smiled at me, shaky but real. "A while back I said that you had changed. That you were always on the job. I guess I was wrong. You're still my big sister."

"You weren't completely wrong. But Gretch, I'll *always* be your big sis." I returned her smile, and all was right in my world. "So the v-guy attacking Steve turned him? I thought there had to be an exchange of blood for that to happen."

Gretchen snorted. "No. That part's hogwash. Humans can't replace blood by drinking it. That's just stupid."

"What do you mean?" Some of my favorite stories featured a blood exchange.

"If a person drinks blood, it goes into the *stomach.* Not the circulatory system. The stomach *digests* blood. Just like food. It's broken down before it ever gets into your bloodstream. And blood is an emetic."

"A what?"

"It makes you throw up." Gretch lifted her fork. "Speaking of throwing up—I'm pregnant."

"You're what—? Gretch, congrats! Wow, you don't look six months along. Why didn't you tell me?"

"Because it's only three months." She cut into her scone, letting me absorb the implications.

"But Steve...he isn't the father?"

"Of course he's the father, Elena. And the baby is perfectly normal." She emphasized the word normal in such a way that I understood *human.* "But that's one of the reasons I've been so emotional lately. Why we fight so easily."

"I really feel bad about that now."

"Don't. You were trying to protect me from what you thought were monsters." A large moist square of scone, dripping frosting, went into her mouth. Her eyes closed and her face transformed. Tasting it for the first time. "Now you know they're not."

"So they don't drink blood?" Maybe vampires just bit people without tasting. Maybe they weren't *complete* monsters. I remembered Bo's hot tongue swirling over my neck and I shivered. It wasn't with fear.

"They drink it, but not like you're thinking. It's not for food. Not like drinking three squares a day. In fact, that's another job for the master." Now that we were on the ghastliest part of the conversation, Gretchen ate scone and sipped frappe like this was all situation normal to her. "Balancing donors to need."

"Need. Uh-huh. And if they don't need three, er, squares a day, how much do they drink?"

"About three pints a month. Naturally, if they've been fighting, or if they're young, they take more."

"Oh, naturally." My hand trembled a bit as I lifted my mocha and took a deep draft. Beings who were supernaturally strong and handsome and fried in the sun. Incredible, but if anything made it real for me, it was the businesslike way Gretchen rattled off obscure blood information. She was Suzie Homemaker. This stuff she was telling me was way more than casual knowledge.

How would she know it—*why* would she know it, unless she really lived with them? With v-v-v...bloodsuckers? With v-v-v...fanged monsters. *Oh, just say it, Elena.* With..."Vampires!"

The whole café stared at me. I'd said it, all right. Out loud. Very out loud. "Uh...yes, who knew. Meiers Corners has trouble with...uh...LAMPREYS. Lamprey eels, yes. The Meiers River is just full of *lampreys*."

Heads turned back to their coffees and pastries. Some were shaking in disapproval.

"Nice save," my sister said.

"Yeah." I took a deep breath. "So, if it wasn't a blood exchange, how did Steve, you know, change?"

"He was bitten several times during the attack." She shrugged and finished off her drink. "Apparently no one knows the exact mechanism of it, not even the, um, 'lampreys' themselves."

"But that much is right? One bite, and *bang*? Why isn't everyone a v-guy or gal, then?"

"Because it isn't *bang*. The person has to die, or be dead." She stole my mocha latte and sipped. "Unfortunately, if they're bitten *after* they're dead, well, the brain deteriorates pretty quickly. They're no longer themselves. Probably gave rise to the whole 'evil creature of the night' thing. Decayed minds, overwhelming need for blood."

I stole my mocha back. "So it's bite, die...and then bang?"

"No." Gretchen tried to slide the mug back, but I hung on tight. She tugged harder. I pulled my badge and stuck it under her nose. She smiled and signaled Diana Prince before letting go. "Very few of those bitten turn, dead or not. Could I have something hot, tea, maybe?" The last was to Diana.

"Coming right up."

As the Princessy Proprietor sauntered away, Gretch took another bite of scone. "There don't seem to be any constants as to who turns and who doesn't. Being killed in a gang attack seems to increase the chances. Maybe it's the multiple bites. Can I have just a sip of your latte, Elena? To wash this down?"

"Just a sip." I passed over my mocha. "How do you know this stuff?"

She took a huge swig. Passed my mug back nearly empty. "Master Bo belongs to a group of v-guys who believe humans are equal. They keep their existence secret. But for the humans who know, they share what information they have." She snorted. "In fact, the training is quite rigorous. That first month I felt like I was back in school, between the lectures and practicums. Of course, Steve's patrol training is even harder."

Diana brought Gretchen's tea and caught sight of me draining the few drops my dear younger sister left me. "Anything else for you, Elena?"

"Me?" I blinked. She knew my name? And was now offering me the same service my sister got because of Bo? "Um, no. Thanks."

"Okay. Call if you need anything." She sauntered away.

"Whoa. That was just strange." As if this whole day hadn't been Whedonesque. "So, what lectures? And practicums on what?"

"Oh, you know. How not to act like prey. Attack drills. That sort of thing."

Of course. That sort of thing. "Well, thanks for being honest with me, Gretch. I know it can't've been easy."

"Actually, it's a relief." Gretchen smiled, full and easy for the first time in months. "Now you won't think I'm messing up Stella's head with a fake Daddy."

"And I know why her bedtime's skewed. You were acting so odd I was going to haul you down to the cop shop for a serious grilling."

Her face turned sober. "I know you're a cop, that it's your job, your instinct—but you can't say anything, Elena. About Steve, about Master Bo. V-guys have been underground for centuries. Please, you can't expose them."

"Pretty please with pus?" I raised a hand. "My job, as both a cop and a big sister, is to protect and to serve. To keep you and Stella happy and safe. As long as Steve makes you happy, and you feel safe at Bo's, I won't rat. But—" and here I tapped the table for emphasis, "—if they *ever* do anything to harm or scare you, deal's off."

"I understand. Thanks, Elena."

I left her to finish breakfast. When I hit the sunlight, I squinted a little. I wasn't sure I believed everything Gretchen told me. But if true, it cleared up quite a few things.

Like where all Schrimpf's blood had gone. Drusilla's flat tummy. Unless female vampires were like camels. Maybe they stored the blood they drank in their boobs. It would explain her foot-long cleavage.

Then I remembered I was off the case, and it made my thoughts feel petty and cheap. I dug my hands into my pockets, bowed my head, and started toward home.

Only to reverse when I remembered stiletto knives.

Stilettos, according to Officer Mancuso, had killed John Smith. At the time I thought fangs, and maybe it was. But I hadn't ruled out actual knives.

By the book. Check it out.

My destination was Meiers Corners' premier survivalist shop, Armageddon Three. I really didn't want to know where One and Two were.

Armageddon Three was run by a big guy dripping hair and conspiracy theories. His name was Bruno Braun and he looked like a shaggy brown bear. He was ex-SEAL, had tattoos braided in with all the hair, and was the sweetest guy you'd ever want to meet. It was seven thirty Friday morning but I wasn't worried about the store being closed. Bruno opens at eight p.m. and doesn't lock the doors until the last diehard scoots for the bunker. For Bruno, it was still Thursday night.

I cracked the door. A cheery tinkle welcomed me—and ten zooming surveillance cameras. "Hey, Bruno." My eyes passed over aisles of desert cammie and racks of guns, rifles and grenades. Everything you'd need in the event of the country completely disintegrating. "What's new?"

"M16 fire sale." His voice was deep and growly, as bear-like as his appearance. "Good as new."

"Sweet. What do you have in the way of stilettos?"

He lumbered out from behind the counter. "Heels?"

"No, knives."

"Knives? Oh. Oh!" Bruno flushed red. "Of course. Stiletto *knives*. They're in back."

I followed him. "What did you think I meant?"

"What did I...oh, I just got confused, that's all. Thinking of something else, you know how that is." He laughed, self-consciously. Bruno was *never* self-conscious. "Yeah. Well. Here we are." He patted a couple display cases. "We have all sorts of knives, but the stiletto is best for stealth. Slim, easy to carry, useful for all sorts of puncturing."

Puncturing. Schrimpf's wounds could have been made by knives, not teeth. Maybe I was off base about DD-Drusilla.

Bruno pulled a long wicked blade out of the display case, handed it to me. "Isn't she a beauty? I call her Charletto."

"Um, okay." I respected my deadly tools, but I didn't *name* them.

Sticking his face next to mine, Bruno pointed. "Note the blade. Hollow grind."

His whiskers tickled. I stifled a sneeze. “Hollow grind?”

“As opposed to flat, or chiseled. Gives a nice, sharp edge. Like a cutthroat razor, you know?” He made a slashing motion across his throat, accompanied by an *ack*.

Ew. “Sure.” Such a blade could easily have caused puncture wounds, not only with John Smith, but with Schrimpf. I was almost relieved. The Case of the Punctured Prick didn’t have to mean the v-word.

“Not as good as a meat cleaver, but what is? Now look here.” Bruno turned the stiletto until I was looking point-on. Sharp, wicked. Definitely puncture-material. “See this?” He pointed at the blade. “Triangular cross-section. Hallmark of the stiletto.”

“Triangular?” I looked closer. The blade was not round, as I had first thought. Not like a skewer or a knitting needle.

Nothing like a fang.

“Do you have anything I could try, er, Charletto on?”

“Sure.” He rummaged behind the display case. Pulled up a two-by-four, plunked it on the glass. “Go ahead.”

Carefully, I stuck the end of the stiletto into the board. Just the tip went in. When I pulled it out, I’d only made a little dot.

“You gotta whack it.” Bruno pulled something red and shiny from under the case, raised it over his head. Whammed it into the board. It sank in a half inch and stuck.

It was a lady’s spangled spike heel, scarlet, size thirteen and a half.

Bruno flushed just as red.

Huh. Apparently small towns still had secrets. “Friend’s shoe?”

“Yeah.” Bruno flushed brighter.

“Why don’t you show me with Charletto?” I handed him the knife. Red-faced, he wiggled out the pump and stowed it.

Bruno switched the knife to his right hand with an expert flick. Stabbed the board, almost too fast to follow. He might have been a closet cross-dresser, but it didn’t mean he wasn’t dangerous.

He pulled out the blade, slid the board over to me.

I stared at the hole. Triangular. Subtle, but definitely not round.

Napoleon Schrimpf’s puncture wounds had *not* been made by a stiletto blade.

ఆఙ

On the way home I stopped to replace my cell phone, then I dragged myself to bed. I had no sooner dropped into a fitful doze than my new cell went off. Slapping a hand on it, I cracked an eye to check the number. Blocked.

I stifled the urge to shoot someone, anyone. *Not professional.* And when I flipped the phone open, it was *not* like how I pulled my gun. "What?"

"Elena O'Rourke." The hollow voice from hell.

"What do you want, Ruthven?"

"You ignored my warnings, Elena O'Rourke. I was forced to take direct action. So I phoned my old friend Ernest Titus."

"What? Why?" I was suddenly, unpleasantly awake. "Why's CIC Insurance so interested in this case, anyway?"

The pause let me know he hadn't expected that. "I am calling you, Elena O'Rourke, because it was your idea."

"What was my idea?" His constant use of my name was hitting me between the shoulder blades. Maybe I could shoot him just a little.

"How creative of you, Elena O'Rourke, to tell Titus the corpse's holes were made by a vampire."

"What? I said no such thing!"

"Since dear Ernest is already thinking vampire, the rest was pathetically easy. I simply pointed out that Bo Strongwell is suspiciously absent during the day. That a search of his so-called apartment building—especially the basement—might yield surprising results. And it's all thanks to you, Elena O'Rourke."

I gritted my teeth. If he pounded me with my name one more time I was going to arrest him for assaulting an officer, throw him in our three-cell jail (a converted greenhouse, but still) and throw away the key. "Titus is a seasoned police captain. He wouldn't take action based on unproven suspicion."

"No? Then perhaps I mistook his urgency to have the case solved, Elena O'Rourke. Perhaps it was eagerness, rather than *desperation*."

"Dammit, Ruthven!" If I could have climbed through the phone I *would* have shot him. So much for last month's sensitivity and communication skills refresher. "Titus doesn't believe in vampires."

"Are you sure of that, Elena O'Rourke? Sure enough to *stake* your lover's life on it?"

"My lover—how did you know—" I was talking to a dial tone.

It took me a long time to get back to sleep after that.

ଔଔ

I woke that night to a warm weight on my body and a very clever mouth nuzzling my neck. "Bo?"

"Elena." More nuzzling. "Why aren't you getting ready for work?"

I should have freaked, gone for my gun. Instead I turned my head to look at the clock, giving him better access to my throat. Donate my brain to science, I was done using it. Evil creature of the night, vampire—and I was throwing open the door to Six Flags Over Jugularland.

But his lips only warmed and stroked skin. The eight-oh-one on the clock blurred to pleasure. "I'm off the case."

The lips stopped. Bo raised his head. My throat felt unaccountably lonely.

He rolled off me and raised himself on one arm. Concern etched his face. "Why?"

I grimaced. "Why do you think? I told Titus my theory that Schrimpf's puncture wounds were really bites. Don't worry, I didn't mention the v-word. I just said Dru's love-bite turned a little deadly. But Tight-ass shot into space anyway."

I didn't say anything about the call from Ruthven. No need to worry Bo with vague threats, even when they weren't so vague. Captain Titus was an ass, but he was a good cop. Too good to haul Bo in only on Ruthven's say-so. I hoped.

I realized then that I was afraid for Bo. Surprise made me blink. I was *never* afraid for people. Well, except Gretchen, but she was my sister and I loved her...oh no. Couldn't be that.

"Elena. You can't think Drusilla had anything to do with Schrimpf's death."

Resolutely I turned my mind to work. "Hello? Holes in balls? Fangs? How can I *not* think that?" I remembered Widow Schrimpf's dress-up routine and groaned. "It was there in front of me all the time."

"Drusilla didn't kill Napoleon Schrimpf." Bo said it with the calm authority of a man used to being obeyed. Of a male capable of *making* others obey.

"And I'm just supposed to trust you on that." I shook my head, smiling reluctantly. He was all earnest blue eyes and honest, chiseled features. Spank me with a puppet, the man was gorgeous. "For heaven's sake, Strongwell. You're a soulless creature of the night. Why should I believe *you*?"

He rolled on top of me with that supernatural speed and agility. Caressed his lips over mine. "Are you so sure that I'm soulless, Detective? Have you proof? Ever actually seen a soul to know I'm without one?"

My skin sparked pleasure where he kissed. Excitement fizzed along my nerves, buzzed into my brain. "Bloodsucking killers...don't have...souls." Or beds, maybe. I opened my mouth to ask but he short-circuited my brain by nibbling down my jaw.

"Didn't Gretchen explain it to you? We don't suck people dead. We take transfusions. Think hemophiliacs."

His mouth moved past my neck, surprising me. He crawled down my body until he landed on the small strip of exposed skin between my sleep shorts and tee. Somehow my shorts loosened and lowered on my hips. His tongue found my navel, licked it delicately.

"Someone sucked Schrimpf dry," I gasped.

"Rogues." His breath heated my belly. "The bad guys. I'm one of the good guys."

I pushed against his head. My fingers threaded through his thick blond hair. His neck was incredibly strong. I couldn't budge him. "Oh, for heaven's sake. Good guys, bad guys. You're all vampires!" I couldn't believe I said the v-word.

Something sharp ran lightly across my belly. "And you and Jeffrey Dahmer are both humans. Does that make you a serial killer?" Fingers gently tugged off my shorts.

The sense of his words came through a haze of delight. His lips pressed warm kisses against my mound. I moaned. "But humans are not soulless...soulless..."

"What makes a monster, Detective?" His tongue dipped into the crevice of my pussy, tangled in pubic hair. Dug around, trying to get past the mass of curls. I pushed my hips into his face, made a frantic note to myself to shave down there.

Bo raised his head and grinned at me. Two long, elegant fangs glinted between the curve of lips.

A scream rose in my throat.

Before it emerged, he used one fang to untangle my curls. That sharp canine parted hair as easily as a comb. Bo's tongue dipped back into my crevice, quickly finding the hood of my clit.

My scream melted into a warm sigh. "Monster...bad."

"Really?" he said between licks. "Like this?" With incredible agility, he kept his tongue moving and shifted his hips up to my face. I was confronted with his Viking Horn of Plenty. And oh, boy, it was a quadruple-scoop.

"Monster...good." I took that long, smooth cock into my mouth.

"Let me show you how good."

Chapter Twenty

After two hard orgasms took the edge off, Bo got creative. Foreplay squared, and squared again. Sixty-fourplay. He started by tongue-fucking every hole I had and it just got steamier from there.

"You know, tonight's Friday." He somehow managed to speak from the depths of my thighs.

"Uh," I said eloquently.

"Isn't that your free night?"

"Uh," I agreed.

"So you're not really playing hooky." He shifted up my body. His Viking flagship trailed along my thigh.

"Uh."

"I am. Playing hooky, that is." He nibbled the outside of my breast while fitting himself to my vulva. "I should be patrolling tonight." His fangs scraped the skin of my breast, making me shudder. "Hell, the way rogues have been attacking this week, all of us should patrol every night."

"Nuh. Uh." That wasn't fair. Even a rookie detective got one night off a week.

"Maybe it's not fair," he said, as if he'd understood me. "But it's needed. Now more than ever." He paused, his throbbing erection inside me.

"Huhhhh." Which, roughly translated, meant enough talk. Soul-baring later. Pummeling now. I arched under him.

"I tried to patrol. I've been responsible for this city for decades. And up until tonight, I've done my job, no matter how, no matter what."

Overly responsible was my gig. I arched more desperately. It levered his cock against my slit, felt like getting whacked in the crotch with a hot teeter-totter. "*Oooh.*"

"I should be out there." How could he still speak? "But your smell, Elena. It haunts me." He looked down at me, his eyes the blue of a stormy northern sea. "Your taste. Your *feel.*" He rotated his hips. "You fit me like you were made for me. I want to thrust into you and never stop. I want to spend the rest of eternity inside you."

Well, *finally*. I clutched his shoulders and jacked up my hips.

"I take it that's a yes?" He drove into me.

"Uhhhh." My eyes rolled back in my head.

"Even now, I worry." Sweet mother, he was still talking. "There's something going on. Too many rogues lately. I should be out there. Protecting people." He began to thrust, regular, strong.

He needed to protect. To protect and serve, just like me.

"You understand, don't you? Ah, Elena. I've been dying to talk but who else would understand? You're so perfect."

If I were perfect, wouldn't I have bigger tits? Would I have this awful hair? *Just love me,* I said, only it came out "Grizzle vemmy." English was apparently no longer my native language.

"It's getting hard." *It sure is,* I thought. He drove into me, over and over. "It's getting hard to fight the rogues, but still keep our nature hidden. Sweetheart. You're a refuge, you know that? With you, I feel capable. Powerful."

"Yuhshur!" *You sure are.* Two orgasms already and past the white flag to a third.

He began thrusting double-time and I turned the corner for the finish line. Oh, damn. I could see the tape. I stretched for it—

The bedside phone rang. Bo's head turned.

Not now! He couldn't stop now. "Noo! Dnn *stipp*!"

"I thought it was your night off." Thankfully, Bo didn't *stipp*. He didn't even miss a beat. "Who would be calling you?"

"*Grnng zzz*!" I replied. I was sooooo close to the big O.

No problem. Bo did translations. "Yes, Bo, it is my night off," he said through steady thrusting. "But I, Detective Elena O'Rourke, am a consummate professional. I need to answer the phone anyway."

"Fffk nnnooo."

"Fffk? That's a new one." Hips still grinding firmly, Bo leaned over and picked up the handset, glanced at the caller ID display. "Expecting a Dirk Ruffles?"

"Shfhft," I complained, grabbing onto his buttocks with both hands. The man—er, vampire—had an incredible ass. I felt myself coming just from touching gluteus heaven.

"Uh-uh, not yet." Bo altered his rhythm, just enough to keep my oh-oh-O out of reach. He shifted his angle, thrusting *down.* I actually started building higher.

Bo pressed "on" with his thumb. "Hello? Yes, this is Detective O'Rourke's home. May I say who's calling?" Still thrusting, he held the phone to his chest. It nearly disappeared between the two huge slabs of pectoral. "It's 'Detective Dirk'."

I concentrated on speaking as clearly as I was able. "I'm—ohh...*not*—ohh...home—*ohh*." Each word was punctuated by a powerful thrust which sent spasms flitting through my groin and accounted for the ohhs.

"Sure you're home. I know you now, sweetheart. You'd blame yourself if you missed something important." Bo put one hand flat on the mattress next to my head, used the other to prop the phone next to my ear. He began riding me with a wave-like motion, swiping my clit with the whole length of his cock on each stroke.

I yodeled into the phone.

"Detective Ma'am?" Dirk's muddy rasp was tentative. "Are you...okay?"

"Fi-*eye*-ne," I bleated on an especially potent downstroke. Bo grinned. "Fine," I panted. "I'm fine. A-number-one fucking fine."

"Oh, good. Because I have a question about the case."

"Ruffles, I'm *off* the *case*—hey!" Bo's tongue was now flicking my erect nipple in time to his thrusts. I turned my head from the phone. *Stop that,* I mouthed at him.

No, he mouthed back, lips reattaching quickly to my nipple.

I shrieked.

"Detective Ma'am? Is there a problem?"

Hell, yes, there was a problem. But not one that I cared to explain over the phone. Even if I could. "Look, *Dirk*...could *you* call *back* la*ter*?" I can say this for Strongwell—he had great rhythm.

"It's something quick, Detective Ma'am. And I really feel your input is important. It's about Josephine Schrimpf."

"*What* a*bout* her?"

"It's about the plane reservations."

"Ohhh, I'm com...shit..." Bo the mad drummer changed rhythm again. Now he was banging on my cymbal at the same time that he was paradiddling my tom-tom, if you know what I mean. "Was*n't* she *on* the *plane*?"

"No, Detective Ma'am. I mean yes. She was on the plane, along with a Maria Martinez."

"The *maid*? Oh, *shit*..."

"Exactly," Dirk said, as if I'd made some brilliant comment. In actuality, Bo had just latched onto my other nipple. "I knew you were really smart, Detective Ma'am, even though you're a girl. You knew all along, didn't you?"

"I *knew* what *all* a*lonngghh*!"

"That Maria Martinez is Josephine Schrimpf's lover. That the maid bit is just a pose. That they both went to the conference to carry on their affair."

"And *alibi* each *oth*er," I wept.

"Yes, ma'am. I have return flights for Maria on the afternoon of the eighteenth and Josephine on evening of the nineteenth, both well after the murder. It looks like our best lead is out."

"Oh...oh...oh shit!" Bo thrust cock and fangs into me. Caught like a butterfly between two electric cattle prods, I zapped into cinders.

I came to with Dirkenstein's voice in my ear. "Exactly, Detective Ma'am. Shitake mushrooms."

ঔ

Bo disappeared to patrol at nine. Just as well, because after two monster sex sessions in less than twenty-four hours, I was a little sore.

And stiff. I stumbled into the shower. My brain suggested all sorts of cute analogies with vampires and stiffs—or just stiffies—but I ducked my head under the hot water and ignored it.

Finally I felt alive enough to turn off the shower and towel dry. My hair and I fought for half an hour before it won. I settled for pulling it back and twisting it into a claw-of-death clip. "Here's a good omen for the night," I said to my mirror twin. She didn't look any better than I felt.

In my bedroom I pulled open my underwear drawer. It went flying across the room.

Oh, yeah. I'd forgotten to do laundry. But there were a lot of layers to go through before I was absolutely out. Level one was good underwear. Level two was stuff with a little wear. Level three was emergency underwear. Level four was really-emergency underwear.

Level five was Stuff I Wouldn't Be Caught Dead In.

A lot of layers. I usually did my laundry well before I got to the emergency stage. But my life had been frenetic of late. The drawer was almost empty.

Completely empty would have been better.

I pulled out my only remaining bra and panties. Stared at them like you did an accident—both horrified and fascinated.

One bra, so stretched and ratty my left tit fell out. One pair of bikini briefs that my sister gave me as a gag. The crotch was emblazoned with the picture of a billy club. A pair of handcuffs balanced on the ass, one cuff on each cheek. Front and back were emblazoned with the words "Cop a Feel". Cop, get it? Yeah, Stuff I Wouldn't Be Caught Dead In.

Which only meant I would have to make sure I didn't die.

Day-old jeans went on over the panties. Whew. One disaster covered. I paired the jeans with a shirt I'd been meaning to give to charity for ten years. It was a scoop neck knit in an appalling shade of pink that was way too small.

My left tit fell out. The shirt's low-cut neck made it easy to put back. Lord save me from advantages like that.

In this ego-building ensemble I hit the street. People stared as I passed. Goofy grins popped onto their faces. I growled at them, but the little pink girly top ensured no one took me seriously. I would have killed for a really sexy black leather coat that swirled threateningly around my ankles. *That* would have gotten respect. Trinity got respect.

Making do, I pumped confidence into my stride—and turned my gun belt, pulling the gun right over my belly button. It didn't stop the staring, but it did go a long way to suppressing the goofy grins.

I was headed for Nieman's Bar, following up on a hunch. My night off, and not my case, but I needed to solve the murder. Even if my pride weren't involved, there was my sense of justice. And I had a feeling Dirk would need my help. Sweet guy, but a bullet or two shy of a clip. A detective only if you subbed an *f* for the first *t*.

As I waited at Fifth and Main to cross the street, a shadow swooped out of nowhere, wearing a sexy black leather coat that swirled threateningly around his ankles.

"Aw, I'd kill for one of those coats." I holstered my XD.

Bo's delicious lips turned up. "Would you like to earn it, Detective?" The twinkle in his eye left no doubt in my mind how he wanted me to do the earning.

"I don't want the pressure to perform." The light turned and I stepped into the crosswalk.

"Ten at night and you obey traffic laws? Nice top, by the way. I think one of your breasts is waving at me."

"Oops." Left one had come loose again. I stopped mid-crosswalk, tucked it into place. "I obey all the laws. Have to set a good example."

"But there's no one around to set an example for."

"There's you." I arched a brow at him. "Evil creatures of the night can always use a role model."

Bo looked interested. "A good role model, or a *bad* one? Are you offering to lead me astray, Detective?"

I pulled him to the opposite side. "Nice try, Viking."

That made him laugh. "Viking. How fitting."

"Hopefully not in the ugly evil-rape-and-pillage sense."

"Vikings were family men too."

Well, wasn't that an opening? At Nieman's door I turned. "Did you really help a kid with her history homework?"

"Reenie? How did you hear about that?"

"You should know. You're the one who sent Gretchen to me."

He smiled. The dimple winked. Ow. "Reenie hates history. Poor kid needed an A+ on her final project just to pass the class. I simply helped the subject come alive for her."

"That was nice. They're just people in your building. Just, um, donors."

Bo cupped my chin in one hand, raised my face to his. His eyes were serious. "Those people are not just donors, Elena. They're my *family*. I do everything in my power to make their lives better, happier."

Father material? How about husband materi...no. Not going there. Not going... Bo's smiled widened. I drowned between the Dimple and the Deep Blue Sea.

I was going under for the third time when his smile darkened to a frown. Whew. He seemed to notice for the first time where we were. "What are we doing at Nieman's?"

"Following up on a hunch. I'll explain inside." I pushed the door open, let my eyes adjust to the dim lighting. "Drusilla was in Nieman's parking lot that night."

Bo was right behind me, scanning the place. Apparently his eyes didn't need adjusting. Which I suppose made sense for a possibly evil but definitely hunky creature of the night. "Dru didn't do it."

"The problem is, if *she* didn't do it—and I'm not writing her off just because you, my sister, and my supervisor say so—but if Dru didn't do it, there aren't a lot of suspects left. Maybe an opportunistic killer."

"Opportunistic?"

"Yeah. Cop lingo for the killer was nearby and saw his opening and went for it."

"Someone in the parking lot."

"Or someone in the bar who just left at the right time. That's why I want to find out who was here the night Schrimpf was killed."

Bo took my elbow, guided me over to the rail. "You say 'he'. Wouldn't bites on the testicles indicate female?"

"The biter and killer aren't necessarily the same person." My vision finally cleared to Granny Butt's scrawny semi-naked ass wiggling on top of the bar. I dug fists into my eyes. Nope. Still able to see, in excruciating, living color. "And we know at least one male bit Schrimpf."

"Really? How?"

I focused on Bo, and only on him. "The ME tested the wound area. Found saliva residue."

"Ah. Spit." His eyes were also locked on mine. Which meant one of three things. He found me fascinating. He found what I was saying was fascinating.

Or he was just as scared by the half-naked old ass on the bar. "How does spit indicate a male?"

"DNA. But the results are confusing." A silver orthopedic loafer planted next to my elbow. I shuddered, eeled away, but not far enough. A thigh-high landed on my shoulder. Oh, fuck me. Though I wasn't on duty, I was a cop and I was carrying and regulations said nothing stronger than soda. But when the bartender came, I laid a five on the bar. "MGD. With a shot of tequila."

The bartender was a silver-haired gent who reminded me strikingly of Jeeves Butler. While I ordered he pitched a couple glasses down the bar, hitting open hands like sinking billiard balls. "One boilermaker, right. I have a party of ten, it'll take just a bit. Anything for you, Mast...Mister Strongwell?"

"A Red Special, Buddy." Bo slid another bill under my five.

I turned on Bo in surprise. "Buddy? You know the bartender?"

"Yes. Buddy Butler." Bo flashed me a short twinkle of dimple. "Daniel Butler's twin brother. Apartment Three-B."

"Both of them live with you?"

"Yes. I was instrumental in rescuing the whole Butler family a few years back."

"The whole family like Mom, Dad, Buddy, Jeeves and the Beaver? That would be more than a few years back."

"Whole family as in colonial ancestors Nathaniel and Martha Butler. And a few years back as in three hundred." At my wince Bo patted my cheek. "You'll get used to it. But back to what you were saying. Why are the DNA results confusing?"

I shook my head. I'd get used to it? Bo saved a family centuries ago and their *descendants* were living with him. He was *old*. He could have known my parents. Could have known my grandparents. Shit, my boyfriend could have known my *great*-grandparents...my mind boggled. Not at the age, so much as the *boyfriend*. Lover, maybe. But boyfriend? What would that article be? "When Vamping Your Vampire's Not Enough: Make Bo Your Beau"? Leaping Luminol, maybe *I* was the one a few bullets shy of a clip.

So I went back to thinking about the case, much more solid mental ground. "There's at least two sets of DNA. One matches our favorite hooker." Drusilla's hair, the one I recovered after our last chat, didn't have a root tab. But the hair itself was enough for mitochondrial testing.

That got his attention. "My kind has DNA?"

"Yes. Remember those two guys who attacked us?" I explained about the char marks. It was a relief to be able to be completely honest about it, although I still avoided the v-word in public. "'Your kind' not only has DNA. The DNA's completely human."

"Incredible." Bo gazed at me with respect. "Brava, Detective. That's quite brilliant."

I blushed, glad he couldn't see it in the dark. I hated anyone knowing I was such a pushover for compliments. Especially my *boyfriend*.

Then he grazed my cheek with one finger, a gently amused look on his face. Busted. I forgot he could apparently see in the dark. "Yeah, well it doesn't really tell us anything. Drusilla's saliva is consistent with her story. And we still can't identify who else had their mouth down there. Only that it's male."

"Thus the 'he'."

"Yeah. Since Nieman's is right next door to the crime scene, and since most of the bar's clientele is male—" A yellowed bra, its straps let out to the knees, hit me in the cheek. I winced at the sting, then checked quickly to make sure my own aged tit-trap was holding up. Left One was slipping loose, so I surreptitiously stuffed her back. "I thought the bar the logical place to start looking."

Buddy the bartender returned. "Your special, Mr. Strongwell. Your boilermaker, lady." He handed Bo a glass, and me a glass and a shot. Mine were amber and clear. Bo's was dull red.

Bo arched one blond brow. "Should you be drinking on the job, Detective?"

A thong came zinging through the air, hit a bowl of bar peanuts. Peanuts flew everywhere, little legumey pellets spitting into patrons, mirror, and floor like machine gun bullets.

I craned my neck to see behind the bar. The thong lay amid scattered peanuts like a dead snake.

I had decided never to break the rules again, but if I didn't blind myself pronto, I was going to run out the door. Screaming. And if I ran out (screaming), I'd never get the names. Without the names, we'd never crack the case.

So, break the rules and drink. Or not break the rules and fail justice. 'Cause Dirklet was never solving this case on his own.

Pulling my gun, I ejected the clip. Brass-checked the chamber, empty. After handing Bo the ammo, I dropped the shot glass into the beer. "Hazard pay. Cheers."

I slung back enough to make my eyes water. This was as close to blindness as I was going to get.

Tomorrow, I promised myself. Tomorrow, I could go back to being by-the-book O'Rourke. I could quit any time. As the alcoholic glow threaded my veins, it occurred to me that's what all the addicts said.

Bo smiled. "I understand. *Skål.*" He sipped his own drink. The liquid in his glass moved sluggishly, like tomato juice.

"What's that?"

"A Red Special."

Maybe he thought he could put me off with that lame excuse for an answer. He'd forgotten I had a younger, pestier sister. "Uh-huh. Which contains...?"

The lip-curve thing. "If *you* asked for a Red Special, it would be cranberry juice and brandy."

I *tinked* a finger against his glass. The liquid shivered like setting gelatin. "That's too thick for cranberry juice."

"Is it?"

He wasn't going to tell me. I decided to play big-sister hardball. "Okay, buster. How about you give me the glass and I try some?"

"Buster. I like the way you say that. Sounds almost like lover."

"Does not."

"Does too." The curve deepened.

"Does...fuck. What is that?" I emphasized each word with a poke to his iron-hard stomach.

"So persistent. All right, Detective, What do you think it is?"

I stared at the drink in his hand. "Red, viscous, smells like pennies...oh no. That's just...ew!" Blood, here? A bar wouldn't have donors, would it? And if the bar didn't have donors... "Where does that stuff come from?"

He shrugged. "The mortuary, most likely."

I should just learn to keep my mouth shut. "Oh, yuck."

"Or the hospital. Don't worry. My kind pays top dollar, and we never take rare blood types."

"Great. A conscientious bloodsucker." I slugged back the rest of my drink. A nice buzz hit my brain, dulling the horror of sluggish red drinks and yellowed thongs.

Buddy unfortunately thought my empty meant I wanted another. Within moments he plopped a refill at my elbow. Without a word, Bo paid.

Well, I just had to drink it then, didn't I? I didn't want to let Bo's money go to waste.

I drained it. Plop, plop, fizz, fizz, oh what a relief. It *did* make me feel better, and warmer. I set my empty down. Buddy swooped in with a third boilermaker. Bo paid for this one too. I knocked back half and felt even better. And much, much warmer.

"Detective O'Rourke?" A finger tapped my shoulder.

I swiveled to see the horse face of Dieter Donner. I blinked. This was good for some reason. Oh yeah. I was here to get the names of Nieman's customers on the night Schrimpf was killed. Donner had been here, and he might know who else was. I should intrrograte...intrro...grill him. "Just the guy I wanted to see."

Beyond Donner, the refined, polite Franz Blitz bowed. "Not here for the floorshow, Detective O'Rourke? Brunhilde is in rare form tonight."

I slewed a one-eyed glance at the bar. Wrinkles undulated way too close. Ow. My eye throbbed like I'd been clocked in the face.

I set my half-empty glass down. Picked it up again when the silver loafer threatened to send it flying. Yikes. Better, but not better enough. I slapped the glass to my mouth and drank more.

An aged ass wiggled in front of my eyes. It was now totally naked.

I spazzed. The rest of my drink poured into my nose and gaping mouth. I snorted, choked, and coughed. My eyes watered uncontrollably but some demon of black karmic hell was at work because I could *still* see.

Bo pried the glass gently from my hand. Replaced it with another, straight beer this time. I drank. For an evil creature of darkness, he was pretty considerate. "So, Bzziz. *Blitz*. Who wus...I mean *was*—here? Then. That night. When youze guys found Chimpf...Shim...yeah."

Donner exchanged a look with Blitz. "That night? Here?"

I nodded. Strangely, the room wobbled.

"At Nieman's?"

I nodded again. The room started spinning. Like a merry-go-round. It was kind of fun. I nodded some more.

"You want to know who was in the bar that night?"

I nodded until I thought my head would pop off. The room twirled like a kaleidoscope. Whee!

"I'm not sure..." Blitz cut a troubled glance at Donner.

Bo put a hand on my rattling head. Slowly, the room stopped spinning. Bo said for me, "Surely you remember who was here, Mr. Blitz. Since I know you have a photographic memory."

He did?

Donner looked worried. "This is a neighborhood bar, Mr. Strongwell."

Somehow I'd lost control of the intrrogra...inerroga...fuck. I broke in with a clever, witty comment. "Yes." I looked from Donner to Blitz to Donner again, waiting for an answer. They really did look like a horse and carriage. Or carriage and horse. Horse, carriage. Carriage, horse. Which came first? No, that was chickens and eggs.

Neither horse nor carriage answered so I prompted, "That's why I thought you'd know who was here. In the bar. That night." The words were clear in my head. They didn't make as much sense when I said them out loud.

Donner picked up an unlit bar candle. Examined it. "We know who was here."

"So whazz the problem?" As I lifted my glass a breeze wafted over the skin of my tit. I looked down. Sure enough, Left One was peeking out. She obviously wanted to hear the problem too. But Left One wasn't the cop, *I* was. I tucked her back in. She didn't fit as neatly as she had before. I spent a couple moments trying to stuff her in right.

Bo's purr sounded right in my ear. "Allow me, Detective?"

"Sure." That was nice of him. Now I could get back to my hard-boiled interrogation without Left One poking her nose in. So to speak.

Bo's warm hand slipped over my breast. Cupped it gently. Kneaded it a few times before sliding it home.

I gulped down the rest of my beer before I choked on it. "So, Blitz. Donner. Uh, Blitz. Tell me who wuz...was here."

"We can't." Donner tipped the candle at the other customers. "These are our friends, Detective O'Rourke."

"Good friends." Blitz pulled out a matchbook. "Like family. We can't betray them."

"Befray...betray? I'm a *cop*. It's not like you're befray...*tray*ing them if it's legal. Wait. That didn't come out right."

"Drink this." Blitz slid another glass into my hand. "It will help."

"Okay." How nice they were. How helpful. Except for telling me who had been here that night. I smiled amiably around me.

"Perhaps a compromise," Bo said.

I turned my smile on him. Everyone was helpful. Especially Bo. Left One nodded her agreement. I shushed her.

"A compromise." Donner set down the candle and tore out a match, carefully closing the matchbook cover. "Well...it would be different if you were one of *us*, Detective O'Rourke."

Who was us? Fuck, *us*. Was *everyone* in Meiers Corners a vampire?

"A regular customer," Blitz clarified.

"Oh." I giggled with relief. Immediately I stifled myself. I *never* giggle. What was wrong with me?

Nothing another drink wouldn't fix. I drank. "My parns...parets...dad and step-mom were born here. Does that count?"

Match poised to strike, Donner paused. "In Nieman's Bar?"

"Not in the bar. In Meiers Corners."

"Has to be Nieman's if you want to be—a *Niemanner*." Blitz emphasized the word with a heartfelt thump on his chest, a *whump* loud enough to make me jump.

Donner lit the match. His tongue stuck out as he concentrated on extending the flame into the candle vase. The dancing flame caught, lighting a corresponding bright look on Donner's horsy face. "She's not a *Niemanner*." He set down the candle and thumped, not quite as chest-resonant as Blitz. Too stringy, I guess. "But she could be."

"I could be." I nodded eagerly, like a boingy-toy.

Bo put his hand on my head. He had a nice, warm hand. I nodded into it, feeling his palm rub against my hair. But when he spoke, he was growly Bo. "How, exactly, would Detective O'Rourke become a Niemanner?"

Donner thumped.

"It's simple, Mr. Strongwell," Blitz said. "All the detective has to do is prove herself."

"Like Brunhilde," Donner agreed.

I kept nodding like a fool. "Yeah, like Brun—Granny Butt?"

"Exactly." Blitz was beaming. "Bar dancers are automatically granted *Niemanner*—" whump, "—status."

"And if you're a *Niemanner—*" Donner thumped, "—we have to 'fess all."

"It's required," Blitz agreed.

"So up you go." Donner grabbed my hands and yanked me off my stool.

Chapter Twenty-One

"One moment." Bo flashed his teeth. No fangs, but Bo's knife-sharp pearlies were enough. Donner released me like I was the burning match.

I reeled, the whole room spinning.

Bo caught me. "Elena. You don't have to do this."

"Izz'ere any other way to be a—*Niemanner*?" I thumped my chest like Blitz and Donner had.

Lefty popped out.

Bo's hand flashed. Lefty was back snug in her nest before anyone but me knew.

"There's no other way," Donner said.

"There's one other way," Blitz said.

Bo and I leaned forward.

"Attend five consecutive dart tournaments. Or sheepshead. The next tourney is in two weeks."

"Yeah." I deflated. I sucked at darts and was what Gretch kindly referred to as a chronic underachiever at sheepshead. So... "Gotta dance." I maneuvered one foot onto a stool and hoisted.

"Elena," Bo said.

Wavering on the stool, I looked down. Bo's attitude was a peculiar mixture of protective, outraged and—wow, was that a hopeful little testosterone monster I saw? *Without* Hulk It?

The protective wouldn't have stopped me. The outrage certainly wouldn't have.

But it was kind of cute to see Mr. Loch Ness poking his head up for a looky-see. "Iz my job." I clambered onto the bar and stood. And swayed.

Whoa. The bar looked much narrower from here. And there were road hazards. Bowls of peanuts, beer spills, and...ew. Granny's yellow bra. Apparently when she threw it into the peanuts, the peanuts had thrown it back.

"Woo-*wee*!" A gravelly voice bellowed from the back. Louder than Niagara Falls, it cut through talk and music like a foghorn. "New blood! Dance, girly!"

I tried a few experimental jumps. My shoes hit a wet spot and *bang,* my legs went out from under me. I nearly swan-dived into the floor.

A strong hand instantly steadied me so I only landed on my butt on the bar. "Elena." Growly again. I guessed Bo was upset.

"I'm fine, I'm fine." I leaped to my feet to prove it, instantly skidded. Caught myself, barely. I saw my arms flail in the mirror to my right.

"Elena!" Bo leaped onto the bar in front of me. Seized me by the arms. "Don't do this. Please." His face was absolutely serious.

He was so cute, worried. I grinned up at him. "Have to." I shimmed around in his arms, turning my back on him.

"I guess you'll do anything to get your clue," he muttered.

"Not anythin'." I wouldn't be doing this if I weren't desperate for those names. Well, I was pretty sure I wouldn't.

He sighed loud enough for me to hear before his heat disappeared.

When he was back on his stool, I started again, a little more cautiously. I worked myself from shimmy up to gyrate.

A chant came from all around me. "Do it, do it!" Foghorn Bullhorn led the pack.

So I tipped the sleeve of my pink shirt off my shoulder. Glanced down. Donner and Blitz were all appreciative grins. Bo's face was thunderous.

But his testosterone love bat was hitting random fly balls.

Bat. Like baseball bat, get it? The wooden kind. No, *not* like the squeaky flappy kind. I know, I know, a vampire lover *implies* the flappy kind. But a girl has to have some standards.

I twisted the other way. Several patrons were watching. The jukebox started pumping out DragonForce. Their great driving rhythm loosened me up.

"Take it off!" Bullhorn-man yelled. Several voices joined in.

I twirled back to see Donner and Blitz nodding in agreement. And to see Bo, steaming, both mad and aroused. So I smiled and raised my arms over my head as I danced. It lifted my breasts. And incidentally blocked his red face from my sight.

In films, the stripper turns, unzips her gown, and it falls away. I turned, but my pink shirt was a pull-on. I groped along the back for several seconds before I remembered. Turning back, I took the hem with both hands. Pulled up. It was stubbornly tight. I pulled harder.

The shirt peeled away like stuck wallpaper. I had to practically mud-wrestle it.

But finally, I got it off. A huge cheer greeted my small contribution to stripper history. I twirled my shirt triumphantly over my head a few times before throwing it behind the bar.

I mean, I was drunk but not stupid, right? I wanted to put the shirt back on. If I threw it into the crowd, it was gone forever.

A breeze tightened my nipples. I glanced down. Stared, caught by the horror. Not stupid? Then how about *stoo*pid?

Because my bra, my good old baggy bra, had come off with the shirt.

I crossed my hands over my naked tits. Got *booed.*

That hurt. I mean, this was free, right? They should be grateful for what they got. And they got a whole hell of a lot more than I had meant to give them.

Though to be fair, with my near-B's they only got about a tenth of what Double-D Drusilla would have given them.

Still, free was free, true? So I booed back. And anyway, only Bo fully appreciated small and mine over big and hers. So only Bo should get to see my good buds Left One and Right One in their full nipply glory.

And speaking of Bo... "Dance," he murmured in my ear.

I looked back in surprise. "How'd you geddup here?"

"A better question would be why."

"Oh...'kay. Why'd you geddup here?"

That got a small lip-curl out of him. "To return this." He held out my traitorous bra. "Keep moving. They'll think it's part of the show."

"Puddin...puttin' *on* clothes?"

"Dance," he murmured, so I did.

The man had magic fingers. He got the bra back in place under my tightly clenched hands while I was dancing like a pogo stick.

"Take it off," Bullhorn-man shouted.

"I jus' did!" I shouted back.

"The jeans," Bo said.

"Oh." I unsnapped my jeans, forgetting all about Level Five.

Brita had taught me to always wear clean underwear. Now I know why. It was for accidents, all right.

Like train wrecks.

As Bo stepped back, I pulled down the zipper. Peeled my pants down my hips to my ankles. I was careful this time that the underwear didn't go along. When I bent over to pull my jeans off around my shoes, a roaring cheer broke out. The bar filled with raucous applause. Hooting.

A choked profanity came from behind me. Two very large, very warm hands plastered themselves to my ass cheeks. They burned through combed cotton.

"What?" I twisted to look at Bo.

In front of me, the bar was going wild. People were jumping up and down like giddy school boys.

One man reached for my crotch. I jumped back, into the Norman Rock-wall chest. The man made another grab.

"Hey!" I said. "Thaz private!"

"You're inviting them." Bo towed me away from the hand.

"Am not."

"*Cop* a feel?"

I grinned. "Yeah, cop. Like p'lice, get it? 'Cop' a..." My grin faded. Shit. I got it.

"Show's over, folks." Bo hustled me off the bar, stuffed shirt and jeans into my arms.

I found the darkest corner in the whole bar. Bo stood in front of me, legs braced, arms folded. He looked like a prison guard. I certainly felt like a criminal.

But as I pulled on my clothes, the most amazing thing happened. Donner and Blitz came over with the candle, held it up to me. I took it, confused.

"Niemanner!" Bullhorn-man shouted.

"Niemanner!" Donner and Blitz joined in with a *whump-thump*.

In two seconds everyone in that bar was thumping on their chest, shouting, "Niemanner!"

I let the resounding *whumps* wash over me. Fill me. "Whadja know?" I said to Bo. "I did it. I'za Niemanner."

"I guess you are." He took the candle and blew it out.

ଔଓ

Seven hours later I plodded along, one hand holding my head so it didn't just split and fall off. We had tramped over the entire city of Meiers Corners since leaving the bar, interviewing the people from Donner and Blitz's list.

My head hurt like hell. "This is unfair. You're not supposed to have to suffer a morning hangover until *morning*."

"It is morning, Detective. Almost six a.m." Bo glided next to me, ultra-smooth, beyond graceful. I guessed he wasn't trying to hide his true nature from me anymore. I almost wished he was. His supernatural glide made me feel five times as hung-over.

"Then why's it still dark?"

"Sunrise isn't until six ten."

"I find it slightly creepy that you know that so exactly." As I plodded, I ran over the list one more time. "Was the entire city at Nieman's that night?"

"Want to stop? We've interviewed about half the people Blitz gave you. Well, the half that's awake."

Seven hours of tromping, hell yes I wanted to stop. But... "Just one more." I held up the list. Snapped fingers against one name. Winced at the sharp sound. "This one." I remembered the slightly frightened look on Blitz's benign face when he came to that name. Donner whispered, *We don't know what his real name is. We just call him—Vlad.*

"He'll be hard to find, if Vlad is who I suspect he is."

"And who's that?" Working my brain boosted the volume on my headache another notch. "Wait. Not my-name-is-Dracula."

"Exactly."

"Why would he be hard to find? Aren't you the master vampire? Don't you know where everyone is in your nest or pod or iPod or whatever it is?"

A small smile played over Bo's lips. The man had a finger-licking good smile. Or Elena-licking good. I thought of that smile between my thighs, and my stride hitched.

That made him smirk. Of course Bo had to smirk like sex. His lips not only curved, they undulated when he smirked. Rippled like my hips did when he played tongue-hockey on my clit.

A bolt of sheer lust incinerated me at the thought of tongue-hockey. Ow. Forget love hurting. *Lust* really hurt.

Except...Rocket Five Years Three Months had already launched. Why was I as horny as a teenager from watching *lips*? I narrowed my eyes at him. "Did you hypnotize me into being your sex-slave or something?"

Which only made the lips play more. Ow, ow, ow. "Which question do you want answered first, Detective? Vlad's location, or sex?"

The job comes first, I told my throbbing, beleaguered...er, brain. "Fakeula. Can you find him?"

"Not the question I would have chosen." Bo's smile edged from smirk into *wicked.* Owie ow. "I can find Dracula, but not easily. Now, if I had tasted his blood, I could track him anywhere in the city. Unfortunately, I haven't."

"Tasted his blood? Yuck."

Bo bent to me, his breath warm on my neck. Fingers skated along my skin like feathers. The sharp point of a fang traced behind them, making me tremble. "Tasting the right blood isn't yuck, Detective."

My headache drained away. "Yeah, okay. Convinced." I jammed the list into the first pocket I could find and leaned into him.

His arms went around me, his hand sliding easily into my stretched-out bra. Fingers caressed a nipple. My breath exploded in an "*Uhh.*"

He plastered my back against his hard chest. My butt moored on his Viking ship, anchoring on the big sea serpent rearing up its bow.

Fingers unsnapped my jeans. Pulled down my zipper.

My pleasant arousal turned to panic. "Stop! What is it with you and sex in public?"

"It can add to the thrill." Bo's hand traced the tops of my Level Fives.

I shivered with response. Ground out, "I got enough added thrill throwing my bra away in front of a couple dozen people."

Bo sighed, straightened away from me. "Such self-control, Detective."

"Right. That's me. Hard-nosed cop." I surreptitiously adjusted my panties. The sodden crotch had welded itself into my slit.

"Shall I help you, Detective?" A warm hand slid in.

I yelped. "Don't...ah." Fingers found the bunched up cloth, straightened and smoothed it. Gave my clit hood a stroke. I gritted my teeth. "I *have* to interview one *more*."

"Are you sure, Detective? Wouldn't you like to take a small break?" The finger stroked hypnotically.

We were outside the empty Roller-Blayd factory. Nobody was around. It was dark. Who would know?

A second finger increased the friction. I forgot about interviews. I forgot about my hangover. I forgot about us being in public. "Oh...oh..."

I forgot to turn off my damned cell phone.

Tweedle-deedle-dee! "...oh, shit!" So freaking cheerful. So stupidly oblivious. A bolt of renewed headache skewered my brain as I yanked the monstrosity out, flipped it open without checking the caller ID. "O'Rourke."

"Detective Ma'am! Am I calling at a bad time?"

"As the matter of fact..." The two fingers stroked deeper. Sliding forward, back, forward...and in. Even with my hangover I arched. "Bad," I gasped. "Very bad!"

"Because I have some *news*." Dirklet was as perceptive as my cell phone. "You're not going to believe this. Maria Martinez and Josephine Schrimpf are lovers! And they alibi each other for the night of the murder."

"You *told* me that."

"I did? Oh."

But did that stop the Dirk-o-matic? Noooo. "Did you know the medical report says there's spit on the victim's testicular sac?"

"Dirk. I'm not..." Bo's two fingers split, one on each side of my clitoral hood. Long, strong fingers grabbed me and milked me. I was throbbing at both ends. "*Not* on the case anymore. So if there's nothing else..."

"Well, what about Captain Titus making me a detective?" The

Dirk-man wouldn't know a social cue if it smacked him in his own dangly little eight-balls.

"Yes, Dirk." Bo added another finger. I was getting close to critical mass. "I'm going to blow...I mean I have to *go*! Go, not...er."

"Then what about the blood?"

"Yes, yes! No blood at the scene or anywhere around." Bo cupped me. His palm ground into my mound while his fingers stabbed. My hips rocked in time to his thrusts. My butt thwacked into his thick erection with every stroke. His fangs touched my skin.

"I mean the black-market blood."

"Ohhhh!" As Bo penetrated me, teeth and fingers, I arched back. He ground me between cock and hand. I came in a blaze of heat and light. Somehow the pain in my head only augmented the sweet pain of my climax.

"Yes, oh!" Dirkenstein said. "That's what I thought. Oh! The killer drained the body to sell the blood on the black market."

"That," I panted, "is an awful lot of trouble for a few pints of blood." I panted some more, trying to slow my heart. It was difficult because Bo was still stroking into me, though gently now. "Why wouldn't the killer just get a couple donors?"

"At a thousand dollars a pint?"

I stopped panting. In fact, I stopped breathing. "Who's paying that much for blood? And why?"

"Dunno," Dirk said. "That's why I called you. Where are you, by the way?"

"Uh..." I straightened away from Bo. "Fifth and Grant. You know, the Roller-Blayd warehouse." Where I'd first met Flakeula.

"Oh, goody! I'm on Fifth and Jefferson. Just a couple blocks away. Oh, there you are, Detective Ma'am! I see you. Yoo-hoo!"

Something crawled up my spine. Slowly I turned my head.

Waving like a maniac was a rumpled, potbellied beanpole wearing a yellow hat. From here Dirklet looked like an overused yellow Q-Tip.

Speaking of Q... "This is your cue to exit," I said to Bo. "Unless you want to find out what's worse than a bloodsucker."

Interest lit his face. Either he was a glutton for punishment or he'd lived so long even a cruel novelty was welcome. "What's worse than a bloodsucker?"

"A person that vacuums all the life, energy and soul from you."

"Oh. A psychic vampire." He looked disappointed. "Met a few during the Victorian era. Will I see you later?"

The Victorian era? As in Queen Victoria? Sweet Madonna on a trampoline. "I'll try. If I can drag myself to your place after my soul is sucked dry."

He wiggled his eyebrows at me. "I'll suck something else wet,

Detective."

Hellooo, nurse! My Bo-holster clenched. Bo-*holster*? I couldn't believe I just thought that. I really needed to lose the horny. Or stop drinking. Or even just get out of the cop shop more. If I started calling my pussy a furry donut I'd shoot myself. "Yeah. Okay. It's a date."

"Indeed it is." With a smile, Bo disappeared.

Literally. Poof. Cloud of dust. Gone.

For once, it was useful to be an orphan. How do you bring a dissolving boyfriend home to meet your parents?

"Detective O'Rourke. How nice to see you again, *bleh.*"

I spun. Held my head. Well, looky here. Just the fake vampire I wanted to see, the mysterious Vlad.

Fakeula solidified from the Roller-Blayd building's shadows. He kept casting anxious glances in the direction Bo had disappeared. Apparently satisfied the coast was clear, he approached, walking with some of Bo's eerie grace. I frowned. Could he really be...?

Then his cheap plastic cape crackled like cereal. Nah.

"Elena O'Rourke." Fakeula's eyes darkened. "You are under my spell."

His burning eyes must have hit the hangover in my brain. The toxic fumes released left me confused and a bit dazed. I opened my mouth but nothing came out.

Vlad flowed closer, his fangs gleaming. They didn't look so fake any more. "You are in my power."

For a frightening second, I thought he might be right.

"Uh, actually Detective O'Rourke is in Meiers Corners."

I jerked at the muddy rasp. For the first time, I was actually glad for Ruffle's social cluelessness, breaking in—and breaking the trance.

Dirk trotted up. "Did I do good, Detective Ma'am? Figuring out where the blood went?"

Fakeula floated around, apparently trying to get the measure of this new creature.

"Well, not where the blood went, because I didn't. Figure that part out, I mean."

"*Bleh.*" Chocula curled back his upper lip to show thumbnail-long fangs. "You there. You are under my spell."

Dirk ignored him. "But *why* it went. I mean why they took it."

Freakula planted himself in front of Dirk and aimed a menacing eye stare straight at him. "You are in my power—"

Dirk rattled on. "The blood, that is. Why they took the blood. Whoever they are—"

Creepula jumped up and down, his cape flapping like plastic bat wings. "Stop that bleating. *Bleh!*"

Both Dirk and I stared. Dorkula's eyes ping-ponged between us.

He must have realized he looked like a toy bouncy bat because he stuttered to a stop.

With a swirl of cape he struck a sinister pose. Classic Bela Lugosi, arm masking his lower face. Only his burning red eyes showed. The red *wasn't* the gleam of reflected light.

Vlad, I realized, was a real vampire.

Then the fangs were real too. I tapped Ruffles on the shoulder. "Um, Dirk? Maybe we'd better go."

The clueless wonder ignored me. Dirk stared intently into Freakula's glowing red eyes. "Uh-oh." He cocked his head and, insanely, shuffled closer. "Somebody has pinkeye. Tsk-tsk. You can get drops for that, you know. My mother got drops when I had pinkeye. It's been years since I had it but I bet you can still get them. The drops, that is, not my pinkeye. Which you don't need because you have your own pinkeye. We can ask my mother where to buy drops, if you'd like. I'll just call."

"*Bleh*!" Fangula fell back a step. "I don't have pinkeye! My eyes *glow* red. Like *bloood*." He swept his cape out with both arms. "For I am—Vampyre!"

"Vam-*pier*?" Dirk's face blanked. Not blank like impassive, or even wooden. Blank like a sheet of paper and an essay deadline. "Vamp-pier. Is that like a place you dock a vamp-boat? Or is that one of those things in England?"

"England, yes yes! *Vampyre*."

"Oh. Vamp-*peer*." Dirk lit up. "Like a vamp-earl, or a vamp-duke?"

"No, no. You are an imbecile. I *was* going to drink the blood of the lovely young woman. But not now. Now I open your imbecilic throat and drink *your* blood! For I am *Vampyre*." Fangula's *r*'s rolled like thunder. "Undead Creature of the Night."

"Really? That's so cool." Dirk clapped his hands together in delight. "Creature of the Night. Fight, fight, fight!"

I slapped myself discreetly on the forehead. Ouch. I was going to have to have a talk with that boy. If he lived.

"No. You do not understand." Fangula tapped his toe impatiently. "I am a killer. I drink mortal blood." He resumed his eerie ghost walk toward Dirk, fingers extended and alarmingly pointy. "I will drink *your* blood, *bleh*."

Dirk looked offended. "*My* blood is not bleh! I know for a fact *my* blood is very sweet. Mosquitoes love my blood. Just ask my mother, if you don't believe me."

Fakeula faltered.

"Or ask my uncle. He was my summer camp counselor. There wasn't a single trip he didn't have to drive hordes of mosquitoes out of my tent. Called me a bloodsucker's paradise. So there. I have sweet blood, not bleh blood!"

Flakeula came to a stop. His cape drooped and his arms hung limply at his sides. His fangs were gone. His eyes had cooled to a light brown. “Bleh,” he said, kind of weak. “Bleh?”

“And if *mosquitoes* don’t know blood, I don’t know who does. So insult my intelligence all you want. But don’t insult my blood!”

Flakeula’s eyes glazed over. “Bleh,” he said. “Bleh. Bleh. Bleh.”

I suppressed a smile. A horrible vampire had tried to hypnotized Dirk and me. To paralyze us so he could drink our blood. But Dirk with his endless, pointless chatter had numbed the vampire senseless instead.

The sun’s rays peeked over the horizon. Fangula’s head jerked up in horror. “I must...retire...” He fled. Not dissolving like Bo, but supernaturally fast all the same.

He left a streak of smoke behind. I thought of the charred remnants of the mugger vampires, and my smile broke free.

“Detective Ma’am!” Dirk pointed at the trail of haze. “Look!”

My amusement turned to wariness. How would I explain this?

Dirk hit his yellow fedora to tilt it at a rakish angle. He struck a pose, finger pointed up, feet spread. He smiled broadly. In a sassy voice, he said, “Sah-mokin’!”

I grabbed Dirk by the wrist. “Come on, Jim Carrey. We have work to do.”

“Where’re we going, Detective Ma’am?”

“To track down your black-market blood, Detective Dirk.”

“Um, okay. Uh, did you know your pants are unzipped? And what does ‘Cop a feel’ mean?”

Chapter Twenty-Two

After zipping away my Level Fives, I dragged Dirk to the local funeral home. Bo said they sold blood to vampires. Maybe they sold it to other customers as well.

Like black-market customers.

With the promise of a new lead (and after dry-swallowing a couple aspirin), my hangover receded enough that I could ignore it.

A nondescript man, mid-thirties, greeted Dirk and me at the door. He wore a neat suit, an indeterminate shade of blue-brown-black-green. Subdued gray tie. Pewter shirt buttoned down at the collar. Maybe not nondescript so much as gray as an overcast day.

The man's face was as somber as his clothes. Not his expression, his face. His skin was taupe, his eyes almost the same color. His hair was medium brown. If he were a designer collection, he would have been Deeply Sombre Neutrals.

He gestured solemnly for us to enter. In a sonorous voice he intoned, "Welcome to Stark and Moss Mortuary. I'm Josiah Moss. This way, please." Moss led us down a set of carpeted stairs. The sepulchral hush of the place was overpowering. I felt like weeping for no apparent reason.

Downstairs was more thick carpet. We *shushed* into a large room. In one corner was a desk with chairs where grieving survivors could order their urns and headstones and thank-you cards. To the left were caskets, set in rows. From plain metal to polished wood, each sat on its own casket-sized luggage rack. They were side by side in rows four deep, like seven-foot dominoes.

At the back was a set of double doors marked "Do Not Enter". Huh. Must be where they prepared the bodies for...ew.

Moss turned to us. His expression was Sober Sympathy Number Eight. He stood with his hands clasped neatly in front of him, cupped right over his groin. Maybe he was posing for *The National Embalmer* or *Cosmortician.* Or maybe Mr. Stiffy Jr. was too much of a party boy to be even hinted at in such a solemn place.

Moss's taupe eyes moved from Dirk to me. "I'm sorry for your loss. Was the loved one your parent?"

That snapped me out of my musings. He thought Dirk was my *brother*? Dirk shared more DNA with a chimp. Okay, that wasn't nice. But I was beginning to think of Ruffles as Dirkus-Interruptus. And too much Interruptus made Elena a crabby girl.

I drew myself up to my full five-nine. Flashed my badge. "Detective Elena O'Rourke. This is Detective Ruffles. We're not here because of a dead body."

Dirk nudged me. "Uh, Detective Ma'am? Technically, we *are* here because of a dead body. Schrimpf—"

"Yes, yes, all right." I faced Moss. "I have a few questions. You drain corpses of blood before you embalm them, right?"

Moss nodded. He even did that somberly. "It's actually more of a displacement. A disinfectant/preservative is injected into the arterial system. The blood comes out through a vein."

Okay. There's too much information and then there's Too Much Info. This lopped over into Don't Even Go There. "Once it's out—however it gets that way—what do you do with the blood?"

"Government guidelines regulate the disposal of human fluids, Detective O'Rourke. We follow them most stringently."

"And what are those guidelines, exactly?"

"Better you don't know."

"Uh-huh." I grabbed Moss's arm, pulled him toward the desk and chairs. Keeping my voice low, I said, "Look. A friend of mine says you sell it to Nieman's Bar for...special customers."

Moss blanched, then reddened. Ruddy cheeks clashed with his muted suit and tie. "Who told you that?"

"I'm sorry, it's confidential. But this person's authority is unassailable, if you know what I mean." I smiled, showing my eye teeth.

Moss glanced at Dirk, who was admiring the caskets. "Yes, all right, it's true." He kept his voice down too. "Although strictly speaking, I don't sell the blood. Mr. Stark does."

"Let me speak to Stark, then."

"Mr. Stark is unavailable during the day."

"I don't care if he's sleeping."

Another glance at Dirk. "Mr. Stark is a very *sound* sleeper...if you know what I mean." He showed his eye teeth.

I got the message. Stark was a vampire.

Still, he might be my only connection to the black market, if there was one. I didn't want to leave without answers. Maybe Stark could be wakened. After all, Bo was active during the day. Very, very active. "I happen to know that's not completely true, either."

Moss looked disgusted. "The unassailable friend, I presume?"

"Yes."

"Well, not everyone is as powerful as Strongwell. Mr. Stark must sleep while the sun is up." He glanced again toward the coffins. "Hey. You!" Moss's somber manner cracked with a bang. "Get out of there!" He ran toward the showroom.

At the far end of the coffin dominos was a row of one wood and three metal caskets. Ruffles was apparently taking a metal one for a test drive.

His butt and one skinny leg were inside the casket. The other foot was on the handle, like some morbid running board. One hand clasped the open lid, the other braced against the edge.

Seeing Moss charging like a Bears offensive tackle, Dirk gave a whoop. He tried to scramble out, overbalanced. Caught himself on the hinged lid.

The lid snapped shut with a crack—with Dirk's foot still inside. Dirk howled. He wrenched the lid open and pushed the casket away so hard it tottered on its stand.

Moss sprang forward. "No!"

Too late. Dirk's good foot landed on the floor. He launched himself away.

Isaac Newton and his apple would have had a field day. Dirkenstein rocketed one way. The casket tipped the other. Toppled ever-so-slowly from its stand.

I would have stepped in but it didn't seem like such a disaster. A single metal coffin, a few thousand dollars. Moss could still have sold it at a scratch-and-dent sale.

But the coffins were stacked too close. Dirk's coffin crashed into the one next to it. The second coffin tottered.

Moss dashed past Dirk. Poor Dirk was rolling on the floor, moaning and hugging his injured leg. Moss ignored him, darting around, hands shooting out to steady the second coffin.

An instant too late. The second coffin bashed into the third.

Moss reversed, almost wheelie-ing in his haste. He skipped toward the teetering third coffin. It looked like he was going to make it. He actually got a hand on the thing. Pushed with all his strength.

But the coffin kept coming. Moss spun his back into it. He braced like he was holding back a train. Like a gray-suited Spider-Man without the really cool special effects.

And without Spidey's super-strength. The casket rolled onto Moss, crushingly heavy and inexorable, like April fifteenth. Both man and box took a nose-dive toward coffin number four.

With one last, desperate shove Moss managed to skew the coffin. Instead of rolling into coffin number four, it pitched into it, end-first.

Metal hit wood with a loud *crack*. Moss barely caught himself, jumped back, his mouth an *O* of horror.

The wood coffin *burst.* Splinters and pieces flew everywhere. Little flying needles and puffs of liner stuffing. Fragments of panel and stand.

When the dust settled, three bashed caskets lay amid the splintered remains of the fourth. Thousands of dollars of expensive mahogany were now just kindling.

Moss stood in the middle of the carnage, stiff as a...well, stiff. His hands were folded over his groin. His color scheme hadn't changed all that much. His somber shirt was dusty gray. So was his somber tie. Even his suit was now a somber, dusty gray.

Slowly, Moss dropped his hands. Huh. Not everything was dusty. A clean spot covered his fly, the shape of clasped hands.

But the hands themselves...the backs bristled with splinters. They looked like two porcupines.

And now that I looked, his face wasn't totally gray either. No, under the dust his face was livid red. And his eyes just might have been burning with the open fires of hell.

Oops.

I smiled, extracted Dirk from the rubble. "Well. We'll just come back later." I pulled Ruffles toward the stairs. "When Mr. Stark is available."

Moss *growled.* Bared his teeth, which might or might not have included fangs.

Dirk and I lit out of there. At this point, the vampire was a safer bet.

ઇ૪ઈ

At home I got rid of my Level Five disaster team. I had just slid between the covers for some well-deserved shut-eye when my cell phone rang yet again.

"Aw, crap." I pried an eye open. Who...? Double crap with a side of fried phooey. Captain Titus. I flipped the phone open. "Yes, sir?"

"O'Rourke!" He did not sound happy. But at least he wasn't singing soprano. Yet.

"Um, yes, sir?"

"What the hell were you doing *stripping* at a sleazy bar?"

Uh-oh. "Getting information, sir. It was my night off, sir. And I was, er, undercover."

"The significant thing about *undercover* police, detective, is that they *aren't recognized.* Half the city stopped by to tell me about you!"

"Sir, I can explain—"

"This is an incredible embarrassment. How could you do that to the department? How the hell could you do that to *me*?" His voice climbed up the scale as he spoke. Ho-boy. Now he was singing soprano.

"It was for a case—"

"A case? At *Nieman's* Bar?" Not just soprano. Sopranino. Headed for ball-twisting falsetto. "What the *hell* case is that?"

"Um...Napoleon Schrimpf, sir."

Titus exploded. "You're *off* that case!"

Oh, fuck. The second time I hadn't done things by the book. And look what it got me. "I'm only assisting Detective Ruffles—"

"I don't want you anywhere *near* that case, do you hear me? You're on probation, *Officer* O'Rourke." His voice drilled my ear like a piccolo. "As of now."

"But sir—"

"And if I catch you in *one* more compromising position, *officer*, you're fired!" He slammed the phone.

I collapsed on the bed. Stunned. Busted back to officer.

My dream of being a detective. *Gone.* I took a deep, shuddering breath.

Worse yet...if Titus fired me...God. I'd have to leave Meiers Corners to find another job. Leave my sister, my best friend, everyone and everything I knew.

It was so painful I couldn't even cry. *Officer.* I creaked up, towed on my jeans. I couldn't face the bra and disgusting pink top, so I dug in my dresser. Uncovered an ancient fleece sweatshirt. Loose, unflattering, but soft against my naked skin. Comfort clothes.

Then I headed to Bo's.

I don't know what I expected from Bo. Maybe I thought sex would cheer me up.

Or maybe I had already come to rely on him for some of the basics, like my sanity.

He appeared the moment I stumbled into his spacious mahogany foyer. He took one look at me and folded me in his arms, carried me someplace warm. Lay with me on a big soft russet-and-indigo comforter. Petted me while I cried.

When I wound down, he asked me what had happened. That was good for another round of bawling.

"Shh, Elena." He stroked my head, smoothing back my unruly hair. "I know. It looks bad now. But that's because you had such high expectations."

"I didn't have high expectations." But I had.

"You're tired and hungry. Go downstairs. Mrs. Cook is fixing lunch, and she'll feed you. That will make you feel better."

"I was hoping for some sex to make me feel better," I said in a small voice.

He chuckled. "After. Go on, now." He nudged me off the bed.

"What about you?"

"I'll be in the basement. Gathering energy for a bout of mind-blowing sex."

"Oh." I shivered with pleasure. "I'll go eat then."

Mrs. Cook was a rotund, bustling woman with white hair and snapping black eyes. She reminded me of my Grandma Sanchez. I felt immediately at ease with her. She sat me down and gave me cookies and milk while she made lunch. The cookies were fresh-from-the-oven chocolate chip and the milk was frosty cold. I fell in love.

"These are great," I said through a mouthful of gooey cookie.

"Save room for lunch. I'm making cheese-and-onion enchiladas."

I moaned. I was in heaven. Grandma Sanchez used to make those, and *chiles rellenos* that would set your eyelids on fire. Gretchen was a great cook, but she'd never gotten the hang of Grandma Sanchez's recipes. Though early for lunch, I hadn't had a decent cheese-and-onion enchilada in forever.

Bo was right. After finishing my third enchilada and polishing off the rest of my cookies and milk, I was a new woman.

When I ascended the stairs, I found him waiting for me in his bedroom.

"I have a surprise for you."

"A surprise? Good surprise or a bad surprise?"

"Good." He felt under the pillow. "Ta-da!"

Dangling from his big hands were two skimpy pieces of lace. Intrigued, I floated closer to see. He held a lavender thong and a matching smooth-cup bra. I took the bra and found the tag. Size Near-B.

"Oh, Bo." I flung myself into his arms. "I love you!"

Chapter Twenty-Three

Immediately I pulled back. I hadn't meant to say that.

His smile softened. He drew me into his arms and caressed my hair. "Like you love enchiladas, Detective?"

"Uh, yeah. Sort of like."

Only it wasn't like that. Not love like I loved enchiladas, or lattes, or even chocolate. Something deeper. More profound.

What I felt for Bo might be the real deal.

But if it was love, it wasn't anything I ever read in a magazine. "He'll Adore You in Your New 'Do"? Bo could touch my impossible hair without puking. "Guys Want 'Em Big, How to Buy 'Em"? He *liked* my near-Bs. "Daytime Boss, Nighttime Vixen"? He even fit in with my graveyard career (if you'll pardon the pun). And the biggie. "Poles Apart: Three Steps to Becoming His Opposite Attraction"? Bo was a fighter for justice, just like I was.

If this was love, it wasn't anything that followed the rules.

But it felt good. No, more. Right. *Me.* Not by the book, maybe. But by Elena.

I smiled into Bo's warm blue eyes and planted a kiss on his lips. Working open the top few buttons of his shirt, I slipped my hand inside. Hot, hard muscle flexed under my palm. "I want to show you my thanks."

"For the underwear?"

"That too." I pushed him toward the bed. He went willingly.

There was an instant when I had mist under my palms. And then I was pushing smooth, naked male flesh onto the mattress.

I could get used to this vampire thing. I crawled on top.

His hands slipped under my sweatshirt. Warm fingers met naked breasts. His eyes widened, then deepened to sapphire blue. "No bra, Detective?"

"Level Six." I didn't bother to explain.

Little explosions of desire lit as his fingers played with my nipples.

His thumbs rasped over the sensitive skin, sending tiny shocks through the mounds. Heat from his palms highlighted the lightning bug sensations.

I leaned into his hands. He captured nipples between thumb and forefinger, milked me with small rhythmic pinches. Bright sparks lit desire though my entire body.

But this wasn't for me, much as I loved it. I put my hands over his, stopping him. "Hey, buster. I'm showing *my* thanks." I pulled his clever fingers from under my shirt.

Lacing my fingers through his, I planted our joined hands next to his head. Then I lowered my mouth until it was a breath from his. "This is for you."

The tips of his fangs peeked out. "For me. Oh, yeah."

I kissed him, taking my time. Tasted the full curve of his lower lip. Savored the chiseled perfection of the upper. I tongued each corner of his mouth, slowly. Licked the seam between. His lips parted and I slipped in, explored his masculine heat.

My tongue brushed against his teeth. It startled a groan out of him. So I did it again. He rolled under me, abs rippling.

So of course I did it again. In passing, I licked one elegant fang.

His whole body jerked.

Well, well, I thought. *What have we here*? Deliberately, I flicked my tongue against the other canine.

He bellowed and arched, hard. His body undulated between my legs. The sensation of hot movement against my bottom was a sweet shock.

I licked again. He gasped and arched harder. His powerful belly hit like a hot iron against my crotch. Desire rushed to dew my labia. I wondered how that surge of muscles would feel without clothes. Just his silky skin against my pussy.

Yeah. Pure electricity.

I jumped from the bed and started stripping off my shirt.

Bo's eyes riveted on me, started glowing red. So I slowed, took my time raising the sweatshirt's hem, put a little wow-chicka-wow-wow into it. Gave my breasts a shake while I slipped off my gun, set it aside. Turned with a smile, and bent over and wiggled as I peeled down my jeans.

His Viking horn jacked up another size.

Everything felt different with a sexy guy watching. My breasts felt fuller, heavier. My clothes rubbed coming off, rasping against my skin.

Even the air felt different. Hot, moving. Currents ran along the curves of my breasts and belly, streamed between my thighs.

I dropped the last stitch on the floor. Naked, my body felt strange. Nymph-lithe, yet swollen. Bo's hot regard sparked tingles in my lips, nipples, pussy—everywhere I was pink. Glancing at myself, I amended that. Everywhere I was ruby red.

I crawled back onto the bed, directly onto Bo. Retaking his hands, I lowered myself onto his hard, hot washboard of a tummy. Bump, bump, bump. Oh, yeah. The friction of his rumblestrip belly burned into fire. Flames licked my soft slit.

Urgently now, I kissed Bo's gorgeous lips. Thrust my tongue into his mouth. Swiped the entire length of a fang.

He reacted like a bronco. His muscles clenched, his body arched up off the mattress, wrenched so hard he nearly threw me. I seized his torso with my thighs to keep from being unseated. He bucked at the tight pressure, his belly rasping hot against me.

"Mmm. More." I licked fang again.

He nearly bent in two. And again. He arched like a wild stallion. "Elena," he gasped. "You're killing me, sweetheart."

"That's the idea." I squirmed on his stomach, slipping in the moisture between us.

"You're going to fall off." He was panting.

"I'll just have to find something to grab onto, won't I?"

"*Please.*" His fully erect cock nudged my back.

"After this."

"Elena...!"

Releasing him, I crawled backwards until I knelt next to his hips. I was face to face—er, head...with his huge erection. And I do mean huge. Chin to hairline, it was satin fire licking my face.

I nuzzled his sleek Viking longboat. He groaned. He groaned as I placed warm little kisses on his testicles. He groaned as I nibbled along the base of his erection.

He shouted when I licked his cock like a lollipop.

"Do you think they're connected?" I licked again, a broad swipe. "Your fangs and your cock, I mean? They're both long and hard. They're both sleek and gorgeous." I opened my mouth over the head. Sucked him in.

He yodeled.

"They both make you yell."

He watched me from eyes fevered with arousal, breath rasping.

I released him. "Actually, I don't know if they both make you yell. I've never sucked on a fang."

"That *would* kill me." Bo threw back his head, revealing his broad, strong throat. Swallowed hard. "Want to try?"

"Well, since you're dead already." I skimmed back up his body. Straddling him, I lowered my mouth to his.

"Maybe you should anchor yourself first," he suggested hoarsely.

"What a great idea." I reached behind and pulled up his hot anchor. Raised my hips.

Planted myself on his long, hard shaft.

He sucked in a lungful of air. Swallowed several more times. Let his breath out slowly, a long, hissing groan.

"Ready?" I asked sweetly.

"Stars above, Elena. I wasn't ready for *that.* You're *burning.*"

I flexed my pussy. He shrieked. I smiled. Though I'd been functionally celibate for five years, I hadn't neglected those all-important pubococcygeus muscles. *That* article had been well worth it. Kegels did wonders for the woman on top.

Slowly, I took the tip of a long, luscious fang into my mouth. Sucked lightly.

Bo *roared.* His hips drove up, hard enough to impale me to my eyeballs. He nearly bucked me off.

At the last second his arm wrapped around my waist, seating me. His chest was mottled red. His cock throbbed heavily inside me. His eyes were clamped shut, his nostrils flared. His mouth was wide open in a silent shout of agony—or ecstasy.

He was ready to come. But I wanted *more.* I grabbed his ears, bent and licked both fangs. He made a throttled noise, like he was dying. His control, I could tell, was almost gone.

Almost wasn't good enough.

I pulled the whole length of fang into my mouth and suckled.

Bo screamed. Both thick arms shot around me. With great, muscular strokes, he began to beat up into me, hard.

I could only hang on for the ride. Clutching at his mighty pectorals, I closed my eyes, loving the feel of his strong hot body undulating between my thighs. "More. Oh, *more.*"

With a strangled cry he seized my hips, pulled me down as hard as he was pounding up, doubling the impact, my near-B's joggling with each thrust. I started to come. He yanked my head down and bit me.

We came together in a flood of heat and stars. His cock, tugging my sex with each spurt, extended my orgasm until I was dizzy. After, I could only brace myself against his chest, trying not to pass out.

"More," he rasped, eyes burning.

"No," I mumbled. "No more."

"That wasn't a choice." He pulled me flush with his hot, sweating body. Curled forward. Flipped.

I gasped, suddenly on my back.

Bo's hands landed next to my head. He started pumping, savagely. Pounding into me like a freight train. Wild, uncontrolled, driving himself into me, over and over. He was frenzied, almost wheezing in his need.

His muscles clenched violently, released, clenched again. Biceps, triceps, pecs were pumped huge. His skin gleamed with extreme exertion.

I had done this to him. Me, Elena. I had set this wildfire, had started this conflagration. It was *sweet.* And suddenly I did want *more.*

I seized his head, latched onto a fang and suckled.

He shouted. His cock swelled up inside me. I tugged on the fang, sucking deep, flicking the tip with my tongue. Nicked myself, releasing a tiny drop of salty blood.

"Elena, your taste…sweet heavens." He *exploded.*

I rotated against him, working his fang with my mouth. He came buckets but kept chugging. He was still hard and showing no sign of flagging. I whimpered, the constant, rhythmic pounding driving *me* wild.

He grabbed my hips, raised them so he could pound *deeper.* I gasped. His fang came out of my mouth.

Went into my neck.

My blood sang like current. Bo's hot breath scorched the skin of my throat. He lapped as he rode me, beating me toward the edge. I grabbed his heavily muscled arms, tilted my hips so that his thick, driving cock skewered every inch of my spasming canal. I was at the top of a rollercoaster, staring at a climax so sweet I'd never be the same.

Bo's pummeling slowed. He thrust once, deep. Again. All my muscles contracted into one tight, electrifying knot. I trembled on the precipice of a gigantic climax. Then he drove himself in past my tonsils and burst like a hand grenade.

I detonated in chain reaction. We came in wave after wave of contraction and release. His, mine, yeah ours. It went on and on.

Gradually I eased. Little fireflies danced around me as awareness came back. Occasionally my body would go *bzzt,* as if one had hit a zapper. Bo lay on me, his weight a solid comfort. My sweat cooled except where our bodies pressed warmly together. I was at peace.

So this was togetherness. This was what my sister had found, why she'd married her high school sweetheart, why she hung onto him even after he was dead.

This peace. This togetherness that made any trouble insignificant. This knowing that, while all might not be right in the outside world, all was right *inside.* I smiled to myself. "You know, I thought guys only liked big boobs and well-trained tongues."

"I only like you." He slurred it, half-asleep.

The words rang in my ears. *I only like you.* I didn't have to change to be what he wanted? I was good enough as I was? Damn, was I dreaming?

At least part of me was. "My leg is asleep." I nudged Mr. Viking Anvil with my hips.

"Oh. Sorry." Bo tried to roll off. He grunted, tried again. Nothing.

He finally managed to ooze off.

"Haven't had sex like that in a few hundred years?" I teased.

Bo turned his head, looked me in the face, abruptly awake and very serious. "Elena, I haven't had sex like that—ever."

"Wha…?" Hit me with a howitzer. "Not ever?"

"Never." He raised himself just enough to kiss me tenderly on the lips. "In fact, I wouldn't call what we did sex. I'd call it making love."

Love? Face-smack me. Use a broad shovel, ka-*whang*. Laugh and point as I reel around with a halo of twittering birdies.

It was okay for me to think about assigning an officer to investigate the alleged crime of me possibly using the word *love*. But for him? For Mr. Barbarian Conqueror, Mr. Master Vampire?

And *love* in combination with me, undiluted Elena? "Are you sure you're awake? Maybe you're dreaming I'm Drusilla or something."

"Drusilla?" A frown creased his forehead. "I know things have changed in a few hundred years, but is there something you're not telling me?"

"Something…no! *I'm* not interested in her."

"And why would you think I'd be, when I have you?"

Was he blind? "Well…I haven't had a boob job, and my hair is impossible, and I never finished reading 'Eight Steps to Blow Him Right'. And don't get me started on how I have to 'Change My Personality to Be His Dream Gal', and—"

His finger, warm on my lips, cut me off. "*Elena.* You don't have to change to be what I want. And you shouldn't change to be what other people want."

"Oh…well, I…that is…" He was so serious. So passionate. Like he cared, a lot. Like he really did lov…shit.

Flustered, I rubbed my neck. The skin where he'd bitten me was smooth and whole. "Hey. Why don't I feel bite marks?" I was seriously shaken by the whole L-word thing, so I grabbed the first topic I could.

He must have sensed it, because he backed off. "I licked you. Our saliva heals." He touched my neck with a gentle fingertip. "With small punctures, almost instantly."

And because work was the antidote for just about any awkward stupidity (like feelings), I connected the dots with the Schrimpf case. "There were unhealed holes in Napoleon Schrimpf's balls. Does that prove it wasn't a vampire bite?"

"Not necessarily." Curling his arm around me, Bo lay back. "The holes don't close automatically."

"No?" I snuggled into him. Great sex, then a cozy chat after, nice. As long as it wasn't about lov…yeah. "Why not?"

"Maybe not enough saliva on the teeth. You have to coat the skin. Or maybe the blood running out washes the healing away. Come to think of it, that's probably it. Wounds heal best if you apply a little pressure with the lick."

A cozy chat about bloody wounds. Definitely not normal bedroom banter, but Bo didn't seem to mind. Was he perfect for me, or what? "Bo, if I gave you the list of people at Nieman's Bar the night Schrimpf died, could you tell me which ones are vampires?"

"I can tell you without the list. I know every vampire living within ten miles of Meiers Corners. But Elena..." Bo raised himself on one elbow and looked down at me. "You're not still working on that, are you?"

I wasn't officially on the Schrimpf case anymore. I wasn't even a detective anymore. But the death was unsolved. If I could figure it out, wouldn't that look good on the department record? Wouldn't that make Tight-ass want to reinstate me? "Well..."

"Sweetheart, I have to go out of town tonight. It can't be put off. That worries me."

"I can understand why, with only Thor and baby vamp Steve to back you up."

"No, that's not it. Well, yes, it bothers me that they have to handle the whole city, especially with the increase in rogues. But I feel worse that I'm leaving *you* unprotected."

"*What*?" I raised myself on my elbow too, mirroring him. "I'm a trained police officer, Bo. I can handle myself."

"Against humans. But vampires...well. Even the newest fledgling is stronger and faster than you can believe. I don't want you going after one, Elena. Not alone."

"The killer might not be a vampire."

"Then why are you asking about bite wounds?"

I squirmed. "You've got to admit the evidence points to someone long in the tooth, as it were."

He shook his head. "Sometimes you're too damned smart for my peace of mind. Yes, it looks like one of my kind did it. Which is why you should stay out of harm's way and let *me* handle it."

He had a point. Even a year-old vampire like John Smith had unbelievable strength and speed. Bo, when he wasn't trying to hide it, could do things that seemed supernatural. I should let him take care of it.

On the other hand, ordinary humans like Willow, Giles and even Xander had poofed vamps in *Buffy*. How hard could it be? "Schrimpf was murdered. Crime's *my* job. Look, I agree I shouldn't go it alone, but you're overworked. Why not at least let me help out?"

His eyes went ice blue. "Elena, I'm not going to argue with you. If a vampire's involved, it's my business, not yours."

I shrugged. "Okay. You don't need help. You were just jawing air the other night when you said you should have been patrolling instead of having sex."

He didn't respond, which was reply enough.

"Let me ask you this. If I were a vampire, would you let me help?"

"That's moot. You're not, I am. This is my city. I'll handle it."

He was getting awfully defensive. Looked like Thor was right. "Someone who was supposed to help you let you down, didn't they? And not just *someone*. A partner."

He jerked. "Do you read minds?"

"I wondered the same thing about you, buster." I blushed, remembering what 'buster' meant to him. "I mean, Bo. Tell me about it?"

That got him to smile and relax some. "I like 'buster', rather. You're right. I had a lieutenant years ago who was eager and clever. And ruthless, though I didn't see it at the time. I relied on him more and more, finally made him my equal. My partner. Turned out he was using me and my training to gain power in the Chicago Coterie."

"The what?"

"A group of vampires, head of several gangs of rogues. Neither here nor there, except after my ex-lieutenant joined, the Coterie developed an unhealthy interest in the Meiers Corners' Blood Center."

"Our blood center? Why? Don't they have blood centers in Chicago?"

"Yes," Bo said. "But they also have a lot of vampires needing blood. The Coterie wants ours because, frankly, blood is power in our world. He who controls the blood controls all."

"But Meiers Corners is so tiny. How can a few pints matter?"

"We're the Hemoglobin Society's new regional distributor. Thousands of units will pass through."

"Shit," I said.

"Agreed. One of my jobs is to protect the people of the city. The other is to protect the Blood Center. We're already spread thin. I don't want to also have to worry about *you* going after vampires alone."

"But you need my help, Bo, at least with the murder. And it's probably a local vampire that did it, not one of those Coterie creeps. You say vamps are stronger and faster than I can believe, but how strong is someone like Vlad? Or Drusilla?"

"Can't you leave that damned murder alone?" Bo's eyes went violet with temper. "Drusilla didn't kill Schrimpf."

"Fine. Besides Drusilla, what other vampires were even there that night?"

His jaw worked. Finally, with obvious reluctance, he said, "Only Vlad."

"Who, as an older vampire, would know how to close holes."

Bo blew out a breath, flopped back on the bed. "You're like a terrier, aren't you? Vlad isn't old. Though he pretends otherwise."

"He isn't?" I could just see the tips of Bo's fangs. Damn.

"No. Vlad rose two years ago. Chicago. But even the youngest vampire—"

"—is stronger and faster than I can believe. I heard." Vampires were his job. He was warning me off. But murder was *my* job. "Why is Vlad here in Meiers Corners, then?"

"I suppose he thought he'd stand a better chance of finding a place in a household. The bigger Chicago houses don't take fledglings. Damn it, Elena, I don't like where this conversation is going. Enough."

He was getting angry because I was pushing. This was the reason I was alone. Only my dad ever understood that driving need for justice. And even he had left me.

But I wasn't going to stop, not even for Bo, who I might actually l...l...oh, just say it. Love. I loved Bo Strongwell. Fuck me, but I did.

But police work wasn't just my job. It was *who I was*. "Why didn't Vlad find a household?"

I braced myself for the backlash. I'd already felt the anger. Now I'd get the condemnation.

Now Bo would dump me. Like countless before him.

Fangs extending, eyes darkening to red, he leaned up on one muscled arm and glared at me. Opened his mouth to deliver his blistering rejection.

He blinked. His eyes traveled over my face, softening to a puzzled blue. "Elena...?"

I sat perfectly still. Bracing myself for the unthinkable. Thanks to Murphyous Interruptus I'd been dumped before, plenty of times.

This was the first time it would hurt.

A lot.

Chapter Twenty-Four

Bo stared at me for the longest time. Slowly, his lips curved in a rueful smile. “Ah, Detective. Don’t worry. I know you can’t help yourself.” He lay back down. “When Vlad came, I didn’t have any openings. And Stark is very choosy.”

A great weight lifted from the neighborhood of my chest. I could hardly believe...he meant it. I didn’t have to change for him. Well, damn. “Makes sense, considering Stark and Moss are sitting on the Fort Knox of blood.”

“Something like that. You know, Elena, at first I tried to keep this secret from you because I was afraid for me. Then I tried because I was afraid for you. Sweetheart, don’t go looking for trouble, please? At least not before I get back.”

“Looking for trouble is against regulations.” He wasn’t angry. He was concerned. Oh, I so *could* love him, if I didn’t already. I crawled on top of him and gave him a big kiss (albeit a cop-mode kiss). “If vampires are so strong, why would Vlad want to be in a household? Couldn’t he just, um, forage?”

“A household guarantees a constant supply of blood. The youngling is trained under an older, more experienced vampire. And—I destroy rogues.” Bo’s eyes momentarily flashed ruby red.

Destroy. As in cut off the head and dig out the heart. I shivered. “Why haven’t you destroyed Vlad?”

Bo must have felt the shiver because he started stroking my back. “Vlad isn’t a rogue. He doesn’t have a household, but he doesn’t kill for his blood, either.”

“How does he get it?”

“Buys most of it. Steals some, I suspect.”

“Why don’t you stop that?”

He thought a moment. “I guess I feel somewhat responsible for his condition. I didn’t have room two years ago. When Drusilla left, I took Steve in instead of Vlad. My household, my decision. But I feel badly about it. So I leave him be.” He took me by the shoulders. Looked deeply into my eyes. “Elena. My point is, no matter how young, a vampire is still dangerous to you. To any human. Please, wait to pursue this case. At least until I return.”

“You don’t think I’m going after a vampire by myself, do you?” I injected as much sincerity as I could.

With another sigh, Bo shifted me off. Sat up. “Sometimes I wish I could compel you. Elena, it’s almost impossible for a human to destroy a vampire. But there are ways you can immobilize one.”

“Really?” This was important information, since Dru was my prime suspect. Especially if I was going after her alone. Which, of course, I was not. Honest. Swear on a stack of cream Danish.

Bo took my face between his warm hands. “Listen to me carefully, Elena. You need to drive a stake through the heart.”

“I know.” Pointy stick, grab and stab. Easy.

“You *don’t* know. The stake has to be *big*. About this thick.” He seized my forearm. “Thick enough to punch out the heart.”

“Okay.” Still seemed easy enough. Sharpen a baseball bat and stick it through the vampire. Poof, dust.

“You can’t just pop the chest. Bones are in the way, the breastbone and the ribs, even harder than a human’s. Go up, through the belly.” He grabbed my hand and demonstrated, driving two of my fingers into his amazing abs.

“Through the belly, uh-huh.” My fingers started petting.

“Elena. Pay attention.”

“I am.” So was his auxiliary Mr. Stakey, rising thick and pointy from its nest of pubic hair.

“You have to thrust hard, Elena. The diaphragm is also in the way.”

“Thrust hard, uh-huh...diaphragm?” Like something that covered a cervix? A barrier, with something hot banging it, something hard and hot banging and banging until it burst, blasting eager little swimmers?

“The breathing muscle. Think of an inch-thick sheet of rubber. Imagine driving the stake through that. You have to thrust *hard*. Elena, concentrate.”

I was trying. But all this talk of thrusting and driving—

“And this only works if the vampire is asleep. Or on a youngling who doesn’t know enough to pull the stake out.”

That got my attention. “They can pull it out? They don’t just...poof?”

“No. And if the stake isn’t thick enough, the heart heals around it and goes on pumping.”

“Sweet exploding Cracker Jacks.”

“Yes. Remember, the stake doesn’t destroy the vampire. It only immobilizes it.”

"Run me over with a Humvee."

"One more thing. Even an immobilized vampire will go for your throat if you get too close. It's reflex. So jump back after you stake it."

Sometimes there was only one word to use. "*Shit.*" Staking a vampire was way harder than it looked on TV. "So, um. Where are you going, and when will you be back?"

Bo fell back on the bed. "Thank goodness. She *may* be sensible." He rolled up on one elbow and smiled at me, taking the sting out of his words. "I've reached an age where I'm going through certain changes. There's someone in Iowa who can help me through them."

"Age changes? Like puberty?" A horrible thought hit me. "*Menopause*?"

He laughed. "More like graduation. It's a good thing, reaching a thousand. I'm going to learn some new things. But I don't know how long that will take. Maybe a night, maybe a week."

"A thousand?" I repeated blankly. "A thousand what?"

Bo took one of my hands, his thumb playing gently over the skin. "Years, Elena."

My eyes widened. Ah-*oo*-ga. Wild take number thirty-three. "You're kidding."

"No. I've been a vampire for a thousand years."

"You really were a Viking." Another thought struck me. "And you haven't had better sex *in all that time*? Wow. I must be pretty special."

A smile lit Bo's eyes. "Very special, Detective. Very special indeed."

ଓଃ

That night I sat in my living room, two lists on the table in front of me. One was the short list of vampires Bo produced before he left. Thorvald and Steve in Bo's house, Solomon Stark at the funeral home, Drusilla and Vlad on the streets.

Only two names overlapped the Nieman's list. Vlad. And Drusilla.

I was considering my next move when the doorbell rang. Either the UPS man was working late, or I had a visitor. Not Bo, he was on his way to Iowa (and he'd show up in my bed, not on my doorstep). I opened the door.

Ah yes, Duck Tracy. "Hello, Detective Ma'am!"

Detective. A pang went through me. "It's not detective any more, Dirk. Titus...demoted me."

Dirk shook his head. "Being a detective isn't a title, Detective Ma'am. It's who you are."

I blinked. Dirk—cluelessness personified—had actually said something nice. "Why Detective Ruffles, that's almost philosophical."

"My uncle told me it."

"Still nice." I invited him in. Like adopting a cat named Trouble, but after that, how could I not?

He saw my lists on the coffee table. "What's this?" Before I could stop him, he picked one up. Did I say Trouble? I meant Disaster. He got my list of *vampire* suspects. Dirk was clueless, but even a blind chicken gets a piece of corn occasionally.

I snatched the list out of his hand, folded it and slid it into my back pocket. Skimming my butt I was electrifyingly aware of the new lacy lavender thong underneath, and my mood improved dramatically. "We need to follow up on the black-market blood angle. Let's go check on Stark."

"That's it, Detective Ma'am. Get back on the horse. Down, but not conquered. Stay in the race!"

"Um, yeah." Dirklet was either more philosophical than I knew, or... "Did your uncle tell you those too?"

"Uh, no. Ms. Barton." Dirk removed his yellow fedora and brushed a hand through artistically tousled hair. He gave me a goofy smile.

Dolly Barton, head of gossip central, knew. Which meant the whole damn town knew. I felt like crying.

No, I didn't. I had sexy new underwear, a gift from a hot man, which added to the empowerment. Nothing like a present of lace to keep a girl's spirits up. "Come on, Detective Dirk. Let's head out."

At Stark and Moss, our old friend Somber Graysuit Man opened the door. One look at Dirk, and Moss's face turned as gray as his suit. "What do *you* want?"

I said, "We're here to see Mr. Stark."

Moss eyed me. "O'Rourke? You're off the case."

Janet Jackson's tits. Did *everyone* know? "I'm not here in an official capacity. Look, can we just see Stark?"

From behind Moss, a voice dark as bittersweet chocolate said, "Let them in, Josiah."

"But, sir...!" His reluctance plain, Moss stepped aside. "As you wish, sir."

A tall, angular man was revealed. Somber, but not gray like Moss. No, Solomon Stark was somber like a bayonet. Heavy cheekbones, heavy eyebrows. Deep-set, brilliant dark eyes. He wore a black suit and tie, and black wingtip shoes. He looked like every scary undertaker ever imagined. The only thing missing was the tall black hat. "Please come in, Detective O'Rourke."

"It's not detective." I couldn't quite keep the sourness out of my voice.

"Ernest Titus is not the only authority in Meiers Corners. And he certainly is not the most influential. We'll use Detective, Detective O'Rourke. Hello, Detective Ruffles."

To my delight, Stark pronounced the name Tight-ass. It occurred to me Stark might be the one person (besides Bo) who could have said Tight-ass to the captain's face and gotten away with it. There was a height and presence to Solomon Stark.

Dirk poked me in the ribs. "Ask about the black-market blood."

"Er, yes. Mr. Stark, we have a few questions. Specifically, about the blood you drain from corpses. What happens to it?"

One thick eyebrow went up. "We follow government guidelines, Detective O'Rourke. All the proper handling and disposal procedures."

"Off the record?"

"Ah. That's different." He turned to his associate. "Moss, perhaps Detective Ruffles would like to see the new casket display. Would you show him?"

The look on Moss's face—white shriek with a dollop of barf—said that was the last thing he wanted to do. But it wasn't a request. Moss turned reluctantly downstairs. Dirklet traipsed after, babbling on about cable TV, cheap restaurants and Oprah.

"This way, Detective O'Rourke." Stark led me upstairs to a hushed, old-fashioned office. The funeral home had been here since the founding of Meiers Corners. They were on their fourth Moss. This Stark might be the original. His office certainly looked like something from the eighteen hundreds.

Stark might be hundreds of years old. It was daunting. Except...my boyfriend was a thousand. A few hundred years was practically nothing. With greater confidence I said, "We're investigating the death of Napoleon Schrimpf. You've probably heard he was drained of blood."

"Yes. The amusing Dolly Barton. Curl Up and Dye." He chuckled.

Obviously some sort of undead joke. "Uh, yeah. We're following up on a lead. I know you sell blood to Nieman's Bar. Pretty high-priced stuff, from what I've heard. I want to know if you sell it to anyone else."

Stark steepled his long, slender fingers. "You think someone who buys blood at a high price will sell it even higher? Perhaps black-market high? A good conjecture, but I am sorry to have to disappoint you, Detective O'Rourke."

"You don't sell blood?"

"No, we sell it. Off the record. And we make a good profit too."

Blood money. "I bet you do."

Stark only looked amused. "Before you scorn us, let me assure you we don't keep the profits."

"Goes to the orphanage, does it?"

"I admit our largesse isn't totally selfless." Stark smiled, revealing large, even white teeth. "We donate equally to the American Red Cross and the local blood bank."

"Then who buys your blood, besides Nieman's? And how do you know they aren't turning around and selling it at a huge profit?"

"Because I know who's buying it and why. Vampires purchase most of our blood. Besides the bar, we supply many of the larger households in Chicago. Occasionally we sell to the passing unhouseholded one."

Which I translated to homeless vamps. "Drusilla?"

Stark laughed outright. "With her trade? Drusilla has more blood than she can handle. Men beg her to bite them. Women too."

"She's never bought blood?"

"Once. When a fledgling needed a complete infusion. A Steve Johnson. Perhaps you've heard of him?"

The hooker with the heart of gold. "Yeah. So you're saying there's no black market on blood in Meiers Corners?"

"There was." Stark folded his hands on his desk. His long, elegant fingers made the gesture quite pleasant to watch.

Like Bo's fingers folding over my naked breast...whoops. Apparently the lust itch was something that actually got worse after getting scratched.

"You said 'was'. There *was* a black market."

"People were killed, their blood sold. Not by my kind, I might mention."

"Let me guess. Nineteen twenties?"

"You're very well informed. Yes."

"But there's no black market any more. What happened?"

"Bo Strongwell happened, Detective O'Rourke. He started personally patrolling the streets. Waiting. Watching. Though the killer was cautious, Strongwell caught him."

"And?"

Stark shrugged. "Let me put it this way. A crematorium was not needed to finish the job."

Meaning the pieces were too small to burn. That sounded like Bo, all right. Thorough and conscientious.

But it killed the black-market theory for Schrimpf's murder. The only reasonable alternative meant vampire, which narrowed down the suspects but meant the case could never be officially closed. Not an option I liked. "Are you sure? I mean, couldn't the black market have started up again? With new people?"

"Not without Strongwell knowing. There's a network of our kind. We keep very close watch on the goings-on of our world."

"Then why doesn't Bo know who killed Napoleon Schrimpf? Because if it wasn't some black-market ring, it has to be one of your kind."

"I suspect he does know."

Bo knew? That rattled me. He hadn't said a thing.

"Do not upset yourself, my dear. He will no doubt do something about it as his schedule permits. He is rather overburdened, you know."

"So I keep hearing. Why don't you help out?"

"I do as much as I can. Protecting the blood here is already a fulltime job, not to mention the additional chores of my chosen profession."

Bo'd get around to it when he could. Stark helped out when he could. Neither was good enough for me. I had to solve this case and figure some way of bringing the perp to justice, vampire or not.

And that meant another very hard look at the only two suspects left—Vlad Dracula and Drusilla Strongwell.

I stood. "Well, thanks for your time."

Stark rose too. "I wish you luck, Detective O'Rourke."

The door banged open. "Detective Ma'am!" Dirk rushed into the room. "Mr. Moss showed me the crematorium, and I accidentally started it, and do you want to guess how fast a solid walnut coffin burns...?"

I sighed. Interview Dru, yes. But first, I would have to get rid of Mr. Bigears-Littlebrain.

ଔଓ

Dirk was like those last five pounds. Ungainly, uncomfortable and impossible to lose. I tried everything I could think of. I even went back to the cop shop and pulled the bathroom trick again. He scrambled through the window and followed. With his lumbering gait, he looked like The Mummy shambling after me.

And like The Mummy, he just kept coming.

It was impossible to take him along. I had to ask Drusilla some very pointed questions. Pointed tooth questions so direct even Dirk wouldn't believe we were discussing a root canal. But how to grill her alone? A mental perusal of both *Elena's Book of Rules* and *Midwest Police Monthly* articles came up empty.

A thought hit me. Desperate, but it just might work.

I lured Dirk to Nieman's Bar. Customers thumped their chests and saluted me as I came in. I smiled and nodded and cast around frantically for Buddy.

The bartender was swabbing glasses with a crisp white towel. I sidled up to the bar, put my head close to his. "Is there a back way out of here?"

Buddy glanced at Dirk. "Past the end of the bar there's a doorway to the back corridor. First door's the gent's, second is the ladies'. Third goes out."

I thanked him. He quirked a finger at me, to lean back in. "Don't go east," he said. "Straight or left once you're out the door. If you want to lose someone."

"Why?"

"There's a window. Big picture window, has a perfect view of the east parking lot."

I snapped a frown. A view of the lot where Schrimpf was killed? Then not only Dru or someone randomly stumbling outside had opportunity. Someone stumbling to go to the bathroom would as well. "North or west. Got it."

After that, I only needed a diversion.

I'm not proud of what I did. In fact, I still feel a little guilty. I was hoping Granny Butt would be dancing, and that would be diversion enough. But the Butt was missing and the bar was unusually quiet. Not even any music playing. So I had to. Really, I did.

I bought a couple sodas and led Dirk to the end of the bar. Sipping, I waited until there was a knot of customers between us and the front door.

"Omigod!" I stood up. "I can't believe it."

"What? What is it, Detective Ma'am?"

"Look, Dirk. Look!" I pointed at the knot.

Still seated, Dirk craned his neck. "What? Detective Ma'am! What do you see?"

"I don't believe it. It's...it's *Oprah*!"

"Oprah? *Where*?" Dirk shot to his feet. His muddy brown eyes were actually *glowing*.

"There! The front door."

"Really?" He did his kangaroo impression, bouncing around, trying to see over the clump of people in the narrow bar.

"Straight from Chicago. Go catch her before she leaves." I gave him a little push. "Maybe you can get her autograph."

"Oh boy, oh boy!" Dirk bounded toward the front door, to catch sight of his hero.

Like I said, I felt guilty. But it didn't stop me from dashing into the back corridor and heading out the door.

I hoofed west a block before circling back around. Drusilla would be in or near the Nieman's parking lot. The east end of the alley was decently dark. I prowled it, hand on my gun, my Spidey-sense tingling. She was near.

"Detective O'Rourke, how nice to see you."

I jumped. Apparently "near" meant "right on top of". Damn. I was going to have to schedule a Spidey-sense tune-up, right after I got my lie meter fixed.

Unless the problem wasn't me. Maybe vampires were just white noise on the Psychic Network. Huh. That was a thought.

"How is your lovely sister?" Drusilla stepped from the shadows, a gorgeous vampy princess of the night, complete with cleavage-baring, pavement-sweeping gown.

Lacy violet underwear, I reminded myself, gifted by an outrageously handsome male. I did *not* have to feel inadequate. "Gretchen's good. And Steve and Stella." And then, because I did feel just a teensy bit inadequate, "Bo's great."

Dru smiled, ruby lips glossy in the moonlight. "So I heard. You wanted me?"

"I have a few more questions. Now that I know the real score."

"Yes. Welcome to our world, Detective O'Rourke."

That threw me. Was she the vampire Welcome Wagon lady? Handing out night-school tips, and coupons like two-for-one Bloody Marys? "The night Napoleon Schrimpf died, you bit his balls."

"Yes, Detective. As I explained. Nappy liked sex on the edge. And, as you have perhaps discovered, it is exceptionally pleasurable."

"Um, yeah." I shivered. "But I've also discovered biting doesn't leave marks."

"It does not have to." Casually Drusilla examined her inch-long scarlet fingernails. "*I* never do. So sloppy."

"Never? Here's my theory. You bit him for a little fun, a little profit. He got carried away, you got carried away. He died before the bite could heal. Once the body's dead, the skin can't heal."

"That's not quite true. Skin cells live after the corpus dies—"

"*And then,*" I said, overriding her because I did not want one more cherished legend torpedoed (bad enough you couldn't stake a vampire and make it poof). "*And then* you sucked out all Schrimpf's blood, because you were thirsty, or because no use letting good blood go to waste—"

"But I did not, Detective. I was not thirsty. I get plenty of blood from my johns. More than I need."

So Stark had said, but I hated to hear it.

"And I never drink more than a sip from Nappy." Dru leaned in. "In truth, I didn't really like his taste. Too many steroids and too much alcohol, you know?"

Well, hell. It was such a good theory too. But I believed her. Besides, there was that damn male DNA. Too many things argued against Dru being the killer.

Which meant I was down to one suspect, and not one I wanted to pursue alone. Because Vlad had already almost mesmerized me twice—albeit once when I didn't know any better, and once when I was reeling with a hangover. Hopefully Bo'd get back soon.

"Fine, Drusilla. You're free to go. But stay avail—"

"*Psst.* Dru!" The high, tight whine of a jet engine startled me. "Where are you?"

Jumping SWAT teams, what the hell was Tight-ass doing here?

Drusilla looked as horrified as I felt. "You must hide."

Footsteps rang, closing in. "*Where*?" I spun frantically. The area was pathologically clean and empty, nothing but pavement and back walls. Even the garbage cans were all stowed for the night.

"Here." Drusilla raised her voluminous skirts.

I choked.

Titus said he'd fire me if he caught me in one more compromising position. Hide between Dru's legs? *Majorly* compromising.

But being caught with a hooker—in any position—was a surefire end of my career. No. I could *not* let Titus see me here.

I dived under. Crinoline settled over me. "Over here, Titty," Dru called sweetly.

Titty?

"There you are." Tight-ass's voice came nearer. "Where's your one o'clock?"

I could hear in my hiding place but couldn't see worth a damn. It was dark and warm under the skirts, and mortifying. Boy, when they said undercover police work was tough, they had no idea.

"Canceled. The DA's wife came down with the flu. He needed to stay home and take care of her."

"You have nothing until two?"

"Yes, Titty. My weekly session with Diana Prince."

Diana...? Sweet cream donuts, I would never drink a latte again without thinking of Diana and Dru. But next Tight-ass would ask for a free blowjob.

"You have the money?"

Huh?

"Five hundred." I felt Dru reach in her pocket. "Mr. Moss paid by credit card."

"Idiot." A rustle announced bills being passed. "He'll get caught one day."

A shrug from Dru, rippling through the crinoline. "Not as disastrous to his business as some."

"Hearing his dick has some life after all? It might actually increase it."

"Life, yes." A purring sound started. "Quite a bit of life, actually. He paid for two sessions."

"Just make sure I get my percentage." Tight-ass was heading toward soprano again.

The purr stopped. "I would have had it ready for you, but I wasn't expecting you until tomorrow. Why tonight?"

"Lana needed a new mattress. And Luci lost another set of handcuffs. You know, Dru, running a stable of part-time whores is a costly business."

"Poor Titty."

I sat in my dark tent as the truth smacked me in the face like brass knuckles. Ernest Titus, third shift police captain, always worried about the department's reputation.

Tight-ass was a *pimp.*

No wonder he insisted Dru hadn't killed Schrimpf. He didn't want his star hooker accused of murder. Now that I thought about it, Titus had done everything he could to push me in any direction *but* Dru. Maybe he'd even hid the paperwork for the vampire dust from Charlie Ignatek, thinking it was connected with the Schrimpf case.

Titus's voice came again, high and tight. "Uh, Dru. You haven't, uh, bitten anyone lately, have you?"

"Titty. I told you I didn't kill Nappy. I told you I saw someone at the big window in the back of Nieman's Bar, watching us, who is probably the murderer. Why won't you believe me?"

"I believe you, honey." Titus's coloratura soprano told me otherwise. He thought Dru did it. That was why he had tried to blame Josephine Schrimpf for the murder. Why he assigned me Dirk. Why he took me off the case and assigned Dirk as primary.

Tight-ass didn't *want* the case to be solved. If Dru took the witness stand, her occupation would come out—and Titus's connection to it. Which would ruin his reputation, making a bid for Chief of Police impossible.

"Thanks for the cash, Dru. You'll have the rest for me before dawn?"

"Of course, Titty. Are you collecting from the others now?"

"Yes. You wouldn't believe how costly a good set of handcuffs is."

Chapter Twenty-Five

After Tight-ass left I thanked Dru for her quick thinking and headed for the cop shop. I was sort of scared that I'd run into "Titty" there (how the hell could I keep the smirk off my face?) but apparently he was still out collecting.

I sat at my desk and tried to keep busy. Only one suspect was left, Vlad, a.k.a. Dracula. He had the means, his fangs. He had the opportunity, being at the bar that night. I didn't know what his motive was, but did vampires need a motive to suck a human dry?

I wanted to make the arrest so bad I had to staple my shoes to the floor. But Vlad scared me a little, and I'd promised Bo I wouldn't go looking for trouble. So I waited, chafing all night, Saint Dirkson glaring a hole in my back. I cleaned my gun, even though Saturday wasn't my usual night any more than Wednesday was. "Detective Dirk" called, asking if I'd gotten any leads. Four times, at an hour a pop. I was actually kind of glad for the distraction.

Morning finally came. At home I stripped out of my violet lace and stuck it in the sink with delicate soap. As I was rinsing, I smiled. Bo had given me sexy underwear in my size, near B. He liked me just the way I was. It surprised me how good that felt.

All those articles. Endless reading, trying to change into the woman I thought men wanted. And I hadn't had to change at all. I laughed. All those rules, and really all I had to do was be *me.*

My cell rang. I snapped it open. "O'Rourke."

A pause was followed by that annoying hollow voice. "Elena O'Rourke. I have news for you."

"Ruthven, how's it hanging? Hey, I met up with one of your cronies. Long-haired guy, high cheekbones? Looked like a Boris? Don't bother waiting for a check-in from him. Bo took care of it."

There was a short silence, the kind that says *gotcha.*

But Ruthven bounced back with alarming speed. "I called Captain Titus, Elena O'Rourke. He seeks a murderer." His voice sharpened. "I named Strongwell."

"*What*? But you have no evidence!"

"I did not require evidence to accuse, Elena O'Rourke. The good captain is desperate. He will believe whatever I tell him."

About to yell, *You'll never get away with it, Ruthven,* I blinked. Talk about hokey. "You're an ass, Ruthven." Much better.

"And your mouth is foul, Elena O'Rourke." Ooh, hit a nerve. "But it does not matter. When Strongwell returns to town from his little jaunt, he will be arrested, tried and convicted for the murder of Napoleon Schrimpf."

"No way. Bo's not the killer. And Titus won't just take your word for it."

"Ah, but I am a respectable businessman. Ernest Titus was more than willing to believe me, Elena O'Rourke. After all, it solves so many things. For the good captain, for the people of Meiers Corners. And, oh yes, for me."

"Really. What does it solve for you?"

"Why, it leaves that nice new Midwest blood distribution center without a protector." Ruthven cackled like an evil chicken.

"Over my dead body, Ruthven."

"What a delicious thought. Adieu, Elena O'Rourke."

"Ruthven! Don't hang up...Ruthven!" I slapped the phone shut. Damn. What did I do now?

I had promised Bo I wouldn't take chances while he was gone. Promised I'd wait for him to get back to confront the killer, if the killer was a vampire.

But now Bo *couldn't* come back. Not if Tight-ass was lying in wait for him. I had to warn Bo, but he was in Iowa. So I called Gretchen, and after promising a lifetime's groveling (and two free babysitting passes), she got Thorvald on the line for me.

"One more time," Thor said, sounding like he had a very bad headache. "You want to call the Ancient One, why?"

"It's police business. Honest, Thor, I wouldn't bother you with it if it weren't vital."

"Bothering *me* is no problem. Bothering the Ancient One, though...well. I would admire your guts, but they'll be puréed."

"I won't *bother* this Ancient One, whoever he is. I just want to talk to Bo, and I need a phone number."

"Elena, the problem is the Ancient One is very strict about training. No interruptions. Zero, zilch, zip, unless it's beyond urgent."

"It *is* urgent—"

"Life or death urgent."

"It's almost that important. Please, Thor? Just the number. I won't tell this AO guy who gave it to me."

Thor gave a dry laugh. "He'll know. He always knows. But I'll give you the number."

I jotted it in my notebook. "Thanks. I owe you." I hit *off*, wondering what kind of dude got even bad-ass Thor's undies in a bundle. But no sense in taking chances, so I punched in the code to make my call come up "Private Number" before dialing the three-one-nine area code and number.

It didn't even ring. Just a single click, and I was shocked to hear, "Greetings, Detective O'Rourke."

The sub-bass voice was as dark and vast as the ocean. I floundered for a reply but he simply overrode me. "You're calling for Bo Strongwell. I will waste neither your time nor mine. He can't come to the phone. Goodbye."

"Wait!" Some guys exude power. This guy felt like a mountain dropping on me, or like I'd been nailed between the shoulder blades with a block of ice. I blurted, "Good fuck. Are you the Ancient One?" I could understand Thor's attitude a little better now.

A deep, magnetic chuckle answered that. Absolute authority, yes, but layered with a raw, potent sexuality that made me want to tear open my shirt to bare my—er, throat. "Look, I've *got* to talk to Bo. I understand his training can't be interrupted, but it's crucial. You see, there's this guy. And he—"

"Detective O'Rourke." The Ancient One's dark voice never changed, but somehow he cut me off like a knife. "Are you calling from an emergency room or morgue?"

"Well, no, but—"

"Then it's not what I would define as crucial."

I digested that. "Right. You're some hardass, aren't you, AO?"

His dark, sensual laugh caressed my ear. Damn, if he packaged that laugh it'd have women on their backs everywhere. "No more than you, Detective."

"Somehow, I doubt that," I muttered. "Just let me talk to Bo for a second. I promise not to distract him from his training."

"You're concerned enough about this 'guy' to call. That alone would distract him. The subject is closed, Detective O'Rourke. My answer is no." He put an ever-so-slight emphasis on the word no. A disproportionate chill speared me. Oh, yeah, Thor's attitude made tons of sense now. Suave as all hell, but with this guy, no meant no—with a few dollops of death.

"Could you give Bo a message, then?" Even that felt dangerous, like asking Hannibal Lecter to be an errand boy. "It's about my case. Bo will know which one. I can't go into details, but he should wait until I call before he comes home."

"Ruthven, hmm?"

I nearly dropped the phone. I suddenly, fervently wished that eerie ancient fucker were somewhere I could shoot. "How the hell did you know *that*?"

He hit me with his pornographic chuckle. "Ruthven's a bit of a boil that ought be lanced. You need to know that he's the one."

"The *one*. Ain't that all Matrixy."

"Droll, yet rude. Detective. Ruthven's the reason Strongwell won't have partners."

"He wha—how did you know I knew...fuck, never mind. Tell me."

That got a real laugh out of him. "I can see why Strongwell has fallen so quickly. What you need to know, Detective, is that Ruthven was Strongwell's lieutenant, the one who investigated the exsanguination killings in the twenties. Ruthven found the killer but, instead of stopping him, used Strongwell's name to appropriate half the stolen blood and force the killer to commit more murders."

"Extortion."

"Exactly. Strongwell trusted Ruthven, and Ruthven betrayed him. Strongwell's never been the same." A beat. "Until now."

"Really? What's changed?"

"For the first time I think he may be open to healing—by the right person. I'll speak with Strongwell, Detective O'Rourke. Goodbye."

I closed my phone slowly. Let the shivers I'd been suppressing run through my body. That man...er, vampire...seriously fried my gunpowder.

What the Ancient One told me was mind-boggling enough. Ruthven was the original cause of Bo's deep mistrust, telling lies and using Bo. And now he was up to his old tricks, getting Bo in serious trouble with Captain Titus.

My jumbled thoughts prodded me into pacing. The most pressing problem was the murder accusation. If Bo came back to Meiers Corners before the real killer was named, he would be arrested. If Mr. Scary-Ancient passed my message on, Bo would stay safe in Iowa—unless Bo got all heroic and decided to come home anyway. No, I needed a clean, simple way of protecting Bo.

Like collaring the real killer, Dracula.

Abruptly I stopped pacing. That, of all solutions, was definitely not on the table. One, I'd promised Bo I wouldn't go after a vampire myself. Two, if I didn't wait for Bo, by-the-book demanded I go into an obviously dangerous situation with backup, which meant Blatzky or Dirk. But even if they didn't freak at an honest-to-bleh vampire, as humans they were just as disadvantaged as me.

My cell rang. I slapped it to my ear. "*What*?"

A pause. I thought, *Oh no,* Ruthven, calling back. "What the hell do you want now?"

"Elena? What's wrong?"

Only Nixie. "Nothing's wrong. Exactly."

"Don't fap with me. Something's up. Something bad. Schrimpf

case?"

Friends knew you too damned well. But in this case, it was time to let off some steam. "Tight-ass has the wrong man. Someone fingered this guy but he's innocent. But Tight-ass doesn't care... Dammit, Nixie, it's all balled up!"

"Tight-ass doing a George on the Schrimpf case?"

Leave it to Nixie. Her cultural polyglot forced me to stop and think. "If you're asking is Titus bungling it, not exactly. He's trying to derail the Schrimpf investigation, but this one guy is framing this other guy, and...well, it's complicated."

"And you're upset. Hottie manager guy?"

"Nixie, how...? Oh, never mind, I don't want to know. Yes. For some reason this insurance guy—"

"Insurance! Break out the holy water. Get the priest. Out, foul demon!"

"—got involved, and he accused Bo of the murder."

"Why?"

"I don't know exactly." I hedged, forgetting who I was talking to.

"You know. You're just not telling."

"Nixie, I can't. It's privileged information."

"It don't break my crayons, Badge-Bitch. So what're you going to do?"

That made me smile, even as agitated as I was over Ruthven and Tight-ass. Nixie wasn't upset with me. Like Bo, she could live with me as I was—all tight-lipped cop—and still like me. A real friend. "I can't say a lot. But it has to do with Bo protecting the Blood Center."

"This demon wants our Blood Center? Elena, that sounds a whole lot worse than just one hottie manager's freedom. So again. What are you going to do?"

"Nothing I can do. Tight-ass is my superior. And even if he weren't, I'm off the Schrimpf case."

"Yeah, I heard. That's why I called. See if you wanted to douse yourself with me at Nieman's."

"Oh, Nixie, thanks. But—"

"But you're going to get hottie apartment manager off the hook. Have you decided how?"

"I just explained, there's nothing I can do. Regs—"

"Sure, sure. Rules and regs are the only things that matter. Justice isn't an issue. And I'm sure Mr. Hottie would shrug off a little jail time."

"Um, maybe." Actually, when I thought about it, our converted-greenhouse jail had awfully big windows. With an eastern exposure. "Look, Nixie. I promised myself never to break the rules again, no matter why, no matter for who. It just screws me up."

There was a pause. Then, in a flat tone I'd never heard before, Nixie said, "Fuck that, Elena."

I blinked. "Sorry?"

"You heard me. I sit here listening to you like I've done for years. I never understood that attitude, and I *sure* as hell don't now. Because even if the Blood Center weren't at stake? The music in your voice when you talk about Mr. Hottie says you bit the big one, bitch. You're in love. And the Elena O'Rourke I know wouldn't let anything stop her from saving the guy she loved."

She paused. Let me chew on that, then said, "But you knew that already, didn't you? You're just looking for the bathroom pass. For someone to give you permission to do what you already fucking know is *right*."

"I want to rescue Bo, but...oh, if I could only ask my dad. He'd know what to do."

"Your dad is dead, Elena. Has been for four years."

"That's a low blow."

"Sorry, but that's the way it is. *You're* the adult now. You make the choices. And it's your choice if this Bo is important to you—or not." She hung up.

Damn. So like a friend to kick you when you really needed to be petted and held and loved...oh, Bo.

Nixie was wrong. Bo *was* important. He was the most important person in my life. I didn't *want* to let him down. I wanted to save the Blood Center and its protector. But what could I do?

WWDD? What would Dad have done? Patrick O'Rourke was my role model, a fighter for justice and a hell of an attorney. But Nixie was right, Dad wasn't here.

I was.

Dad couldn't save Bo. So I had to. Somehow.

I kicked into pacing again. Not WWDD, but what would *I* do? Well, obvious. I needed to collar the real killer. Right. Easy as donuts. Just find evidence that Vlad was the killer, capture him and bring him to justice—all before Bo returned to Meiers Corners and Tight-ass arrested him.

Just rip off my shirt and tie and change into SuperElena, a kick-ass detective.

Except I hadn't *changed* anything to be a kick-ass woman—I had been one all along. Maybe I was naturally a kick-ass detective too. Maybe instead of following all those rules and books, I should have followed my own instincts. Although the last two times I'd broken the rules things hadn't gone so well.

But maybe breaking the rules had backfired not because I broke them, but *because I hadn't thrown the rule book away.*

Hell. It'd be the hardest thing I'd ever done. With Bo's freedom at stake, his life at stake...with my heart at stake...aw, fuck. Nixie was right. Somehow, in less than a week, I'd bitten the big one. I loved Bo.

I pulled my clothes back on and hit the street. The late August sun beat down on me, but I ignored it. Bo could come back as early as tonight. Tight-ass would be waiting for him. I *had* to apprehend the real killer before then.

Just catch a supernaturally strong, supernaturally fast vampire.

The biggest trick would be corralling him. If I could solve that, I'd be a huge step closer to saving Bo. Second biggest would be actually stopping him. Human backup wouldn't work. Maybe Steve or Thor, but if Bo left them instructions to keep me safe, they'd just try to stop me. Couldn't risk it.

So. I needed to box Vlad in on my own. And I'd need a stake.

Now, where would I box him? Since I had encountered Vlad lurking near the Roller-Blayd factory, I started there.

All the doors were chained and boarded. The windows weren't boarded but they were high, maybe ten feet up. I loosened a plank on the front door, spun it aside to peep in. More wood sat inside. That gave me an idea. I'd need to unchain this one door, and bring a staple gun. But it could work. I replaced the plank.

As I left I got inspired and visited Bruno Braun. Damn. The more I thought outside the box, the better it got. At this rate I was going to throw that fucking rule book off the top story of the Sears tower.

Chapter Twenty-Six

That night I dressed carefully. After all, I was going after a vampire, soulless creature of the night. I needed to be at my best.

Black T-shirt and jeans, check. Gun, check. Ankle gun, check. And violet thong and violet lace bra, double-check. If I ended up dead, I didn't want Stark and Moss seeing me at less than my best.

And, thanks to Bruno, a bazooka. Fuck the stake.

The minute the sun set I rattled my front door like I was leaving (Dirk was skulking around the apartment). When I heard the lumbering rustle of bushes I scooted for the back door and slipped out.

I made my way undetected to Fifth and Grant, slinking from shadow to shadow. Clouds veiled the full moon, so there were plenty. A block away from the abandoned Roller-Blayd warehouse a shaft of moonlight picked me out like a spotlight. I froze.

Vlad Dracula swept from the darkness. "Detective O'Rourke. At last, we are alone, *bleh*!" His black cape billowed threateningly, evil incarnate swooping down on me. His eyes were red and glowing. They burned into mine. "You are in my power." He raised clawed hands. "You are getting sleepy. Very sleepy."

Sleepy? Not *this* time. I shouldered the bazooka and let off a rocket.

"*Bleh*!" He jumped back with a shriek.

The rocket whizzed harmlessly by him. It hit the pavement, exploded with a *bang*. He threw hands in the air. "What the hell are you doing? You could have hit me!"

"That's the idea." I stuffed in another rocket. The need for stealth was gone. "You have the right to remain silent." I raised the big tube to my shoulder. "If you give up the right to remain silent, anything you say can be used against you in court." I pulled the trigger.

The payload shot forward with a *foosh*. Vlad turned and ran. The rocket flew behind, gaining on him.

He ducked at the last moment. Cape swirling, he avoided most of the blast but the cape wasn't so lucky. It burst into flames. Vlad screamed, bounced around like a monkey. His flaming cape dropped little fire spores onto the ground.

I caught him, forced him down. Rolled him until most of the fire was out. He struggled against me, the idiot. "You have the right—"

"*Bleh*!" Vlad jerked away, stumbled to his feet. I grabbed for him. His ass took off down the street.

Proper procedure meant a trail of evidence, the careful accumulation of facts, administering Miranda rights, turning it all over to the courts. "You have the right to consult with an attorney. If you are indigent—"

He bee-lined for the Roller-Blayd warehouse. Wisps of smoke followed.

"You have the right to—oh, fuck it!" My by-the-book shell exploded, revealing a naked blue-woaded warrior-queen. I set off after that little creep like Elena the Barbarian. "Vlad Dracula, I charge you with the murder of Napoleon Schrimpf. Stop, or I'll shoot."

"You're mad! *Bleh*!" Vlad slowed in front of a boarded-up door. Frantically he worked a board loose.

"Damn right I'm mad. *You* killed Napoleon Schrimpf. Bo Strongwell is not going down for *your* crime, not if I can help it." I dove for him as he wedged through. "Stop, dammit!"

His leg was the last thing to disappear. I snaked a hand after him, caught one foot and yanked, hard.

Vlad yelped, shook his foot like a rabid dog. I lost my grip. The foot was swallowed up by darkness.

Seizing the loose board, I wrenched it totally off. I wormed through, dragging my bazooka after me. Inside I stood straight and tall with my guns, my bazooka and my purple underwear. The Ter-mauve-nator.

The cavernous warehouse was dark. Stray moonlight filtered in through dirty upper windows. It picked out a few landmarks—water pipes, a packaging machine and a pallet of dusty boxes marked "Roller-Blayd". A spiral staircase led to a platform office.

A few feet away, Vlad was bent over and breathing heavily. Trapped.

My prep had paid off. I found the pile of planks and industrial staple gun, stapled the wood over the hole with two quick *ker-chunks*. Then I turned on Fakeula. My own eyes might have been glowing red. He certainly reacted like they were.

The little creep took off. I dashed after him. We ran in circles around the warehouse, first one direction, then the other.

I got smart and cut across.

He saw me at the last instant, swerved to avoid me. His unnatural speed kept him just out of reach. "*Bleh*! Why? Why do you care if Strongwell gets charged?"

Of all the insane questions... "Because I *love* him, asshole!" I tried to aim my bazooka. Vlad was flitting like a crackhead moth, too fast to get a bead. I needed something to even the score.

My eye lit on the boxes. Empty? Or old product? This part I hadn't planned out. Luckily, doing things By Elena let me improvise. I trotted over to take a look.

Vlad thought I was taking a breather. He dropped hands to knees, panting. Geez, for a supernatural being, he was way out of shape.

I found a box marked size nine, eased off the lid. Bingo. Roller-Blayds. I'd never skated as a kid, but how hard could it be? "So why'd you do it, Drac? Why'd you kill Napoleon Schrimpf?"

"*Bleh.* You don't really expect me to answer that, do you?"

"I answered your question." Keeping my eye on Fakeula, I set down the bazooka and pulled on a skate. As I started to lace it up, Vlad lunged for me.

His depth perception was as good as his stamina. He started the lunge from about halfway across the warehouse. I snatched up the bazooka, had it pointed at his chest before he was close.

"Just try it." I couldn't resist adding, "Make my night."

Vlad raised both hands and backed off.

I patted my bazooka, pleased. "Way to go, partner." That didn't sound quite right. "Way to go, bazooka." Nope. "Way to go, *Bob.*" Me and Bob, yeah. "As soon as I get skated up we'll finish this, you and me."

When I set Bob down to finish lacing the skate, Vlad took off for the single unchained door like a...well, like a bat out of hell. He grabbed the wood I'd fastened on and yanked. I heard the creak of staples giving.

I sprang up, tottering on one skate. Hell with it. I only needed one. I grabbed Bob and pushed off. It was like riding a skateboard.

I shot straight for Vlad. He saw me coming at the last instant and sprang aside. I smashed into boards, bounced off like a superball.

On the plus side, the impact nailed the staples back in place.

Vlad dashed away. I swayed to my feet and shoved off. Wavered, nearly fell, but not because I'd banged myself stupid against the door. Dammit, now I remembered why I'd never taken up skating—stupid weak ankles. Even Stella rolled circles around me.

I stiffened my resolve, if not my ankle. Wobbled after Vlad, who was dashing up the metal stairs to the office platform. At the bottom of the stairs, I stopped, suddenly in sympathy for people in wheelchairs.

Vlad peered over the railing at me. Stuck out his tongue. "Can't get me up here, copper!"

Rules said wheels and stairs didn't mix. But I wasn't going by the rules, I was going By Elena. "What do you think I am, a Dalek?" I grabbed stair rail and hauled up. Thud-*bang*, thud-*bang*. What goes ninety-nine, bang, ninety-nine, bang? A centipede with a single skate.

As I neared the top, Vlad's face poked over the edge, turned white. "*Bleh*!" He disappeared into the office.

I pushed onto the platform. The office took up the center, leaving a foot or so on each side. A low railing gave the illusion of safety.

The office door was opposite the stairs, opening out. Vlad slammed it behind him. The office itself was mostly Plexiglas, so I could see him hanging hysterically to the knob, his body cantilevered almost parallel to the floor. He was using his whole weight to keep the door shut.

No lock, then, or not enough time to engage it. Either way, my advantage. I clumped around the platform. "Come on, Vlad. Tell me why?" Gut feeling urged me to add, "Something to do with...*Ruthven*?"

I'd pulled the name out on a guess, definitely not by-the-book, but it *worked*. Vlad's eyes squeezed shut, and he started muttering. "Made me do it. 'Make trouble for Strongwell,' he said. Threatened me. Me, Dracula! I wanted revenge on Dru, but...oh, damn Ruthven. And now this."

Vlad's motive. The last piece clicked into place. I grinned like a ripsaw. Vlad opened his eyes, saw me and squeaked. "Go away!"

"In your dreams." I got a hand on the knob and pulled. "Or nightmares." The door didn't give an inch. I pulled harder.

Still nothing. So I gripped the knob like death and jerked my entire weight against that door.

I apparently had not watched enough Road Runner cartoons as a child. Vlad let go. I went ass over tea kettle over the railing, off the edge of the platform.

Not the stairs. They were around the corner. Oh, no. I went sailing off the second story grate into nothing but *air*.

I fell. Had enough time to think *shiiiit* before landing—

On a pallet stacked high with empty boxes.

The boxes crushed on impact, cushioning me. I staggered off, shaken but whole. I stood stupidly for a second, blinking at my landing site. I didn't remember that pallet being there.

A flash of wind and a *bleh*-like cackle snapped my head up. Vlad was dashing for the boarded-up door.

I lit out after him, wobbling like a Slinky. Vlad had the plank loose before I was halfway across the warehouse. Just as I skated up, panting, he hoisted the board high. "You lose again, piglet!" With a triumphant grin he ducked into the hole.

Biting back a scream of rage, I tossed myself on my ass to tear off the stupid Roller-Blayd.

"Detective Ma'am!" A muddy rasp came from outside. "I'll get him! I've got...*erk*!"

Dirkenstein's voice cut off with an ominous choke. And then—

nothing.

Horrible images plastered my brain as I practically ripped my foot off to get free. Vlad, slicing claws into Dirk's guts. Vlad, bleeding Dirk dry.

Vlad, actually getting Dirk to shut up.

No, no! I missed the big lug's nattering. I wriggled out of the hole. Thick clouds covered the moon, so dark I was almost blind. "Dirk! Dirk, are you okay?"

No answer. Ice slipped down my spine. Throwing aside caution, I ran—

Straight into Vlad's claws. Five razor-sharp shivs skewered my belly. I gasped. My body went hot, then cold.

A voice was whining in my ear. Vlad, curiously free of *blehs*. "Detective O'Rourke! I'm sorry... I didn't mean... Oh, I only wanted you to stop, I didn't mean to kill...oh, this is just like Schrimpf. Don't die, please don't die!"

A deathbed confession. Proof that Vlad was the murderer. Although I was pretty certain the deathbed was supposed to be the killer's, not the cop's.

The knives withdrew. "Oh, please, Detective O'Rourke. Don't die. But if you are dying, tell Strongwell it wasn't my fault, not really. It was Lord Ruthven's fault, he threatened me if I didn't make trouble for Strongwell. And when I saw Dru biting Schrimpf, I knew it was perfect, almost meant to be. I didn't mean to kill Schrimpf, only sip a little. They'd blame Dru, and Strongwell would have to rescue her. Why should she get all the blood and never even give me a quickie? Oh, please don't die!"

His babbling was getting dim. I put one shaky hand to my midriff. Hot trickles ran down my belly. My one regret was my beautiful violet lace thong. Blood stains were hell to get out.

But I still had a job to do. Even if I wasn't a detective any more, I was a cop. Protect and serve. Somehow, I needed to stop the vampire.

My vision was blurry. My aim wasn't so good.

But you don't miss point-blank with a bazooka named Bob. I blew half of Vlad's chest away. He gave me a look of surprise before crumpling to the sidewalk.

I crumpled after him.

ఆ

A warm, gentle tongue licked my belly. The fiery pain eased with each stroke. I opened my eyes to a head of Viking-blond hair and a set of broad, strong shoulders. My pants were around my knees, and I was wearing ultra-sexy Level Zero underwear.

This, I decided, must be heaven. "Wow. Being dead is really great."

"It is," a black satin voice agreed. "But you're not dead."

"I'm not? But Vlad...claws..."

"I got to you in time. You lost very little blood."

I raised my head. Bo's eyes were blue and twinkling. His clever tongue was still working. And since the wounds were all closed, he was working...lower.

I laid my head back down. "I thought you were out of town."

"The Ancient One in Iowa is an excellent teacher. I learned what I needed in less than an hour. I would have been back sooner but he made me practice for the rest of the night."

"A stern taskmaster."

"You can say that again. I'm sore all over."

Bo might have been sore, but I was feeling *no* pain. "How long have you been here?"

"Long enough to hear you say you love me."

Aw, shit.

"Actually, I followed you from your townhouse."

"From my..." My head shot up. "Why the hell didn't you step in earlier, buster?"

"But you were having such fun, Detective."

"It wasn't fun when I nearly died falling off the platform...oh, no. You didn't."

"Move the pallet for you to land on? Would you be mad at me if I did?" Bo's tongue snaked under the tiny lace triangle of my thong.

"Oooh...probably not. If you keep that up."

"Then I'll keep it up." He gently stroked the nose of my clit. My breathing rasped faster.

Muddy rasp. I jacked up. "Where's Dirk?"

Bo sat back on his knees. "I pulled him aside just before Vlad emerged. I suggested to the good detective that he make himself scarce."

Which was a much happier explanation for the *erk*. "And he went? Good grief, what powers of persuasion did you... No, never mind."

"I only had to bite him a little, Detective."

I winced. "Well, I got proof Vlad killed Schrimpf. He confessed." And with his confession, Bo was safe. I considered Mr. Edible Bo-dy, folded on his muscular haunches. "Did you know Vlad was the murderer?"

"You're working again, aren't you." Bo sighed and slid my violet lace back into place. "Not at first. And before you slice off my head and stuff my mouth with garlic, once I did know I couldn't have told you. Not without giving away too many secrets. You ask tough questions, Detective."

"Is that a compliment?"

His lips curved. "By the time I knew I could trust you, Vlad had disappeared. And I was rather distracted, by the rogues, and by you. Now, my turn. Why did you go after Vlad alone? Why didn't you wait for me?"

"Lorne Ruthven." I pulled up my jeans, a little disappointed, but Bo was right. I *was* working. "He tried to convince me you were the murderer. Then last night, or actually early this morning, he ratted you out to Tight-ass. I had to catch the real murderer before Tight-ass arrested you."

"Ruthven." Bo said the name with an angry growl. "I'm sorry you had to deal with him, Elena. I only found out he was behind the murder when I visited my mentor in Iowa. I suspected, but...well, he confirmed it."

"Speaking of your mentor, he was supposed to tell you to *stay* in Iowa."

"You spoke to the Ancient One?" The streetlight might have wavered, but it seemed like Bo got paler.

"Yeah. He also told me about your problems with Ruthven." I turned, checked Bob. He lay nearby, looking oddly sated. "He said Ruthven's the ex-lieutenant who used you to join that Coterie dealie. That's why Ruthven tried to implicate you. He was trying to get rid of you."

"Because hc wants the Blood Center." Bo shook his head. "I can't believe you spoke with the Ancient One."

"Well, he wouldn't let me talk to *you*. But he did say he'd pass on my message. Did he forget? Or was he *lying*?"

"He doesn't forget, and he rarely lies. He doesn't have to. What exactly did he say?"

I thought. "He said, 'I'll speak with Strongwell'...dammit! He didn't promise to pass on my message at all. Why, that sneaky bastard."

"You learn a few tricks in a couple odd millennia."

I stared. "He's that old?"

"Older."

"You v-guys are kind of scary." I glanced at Vlad's broken body. "Well, most of you." Flakeula looked like a life-sized gingerbread man with a giant Cookie Monster chomp out of his chest. "Poor Vlad. He wasn't trying to kill Schrimpf. He was just scared of Ruthven. And resentful of Dru."

"Still, he killed." Bo's gaze followed mine. "He can't be allowed to run loose. I bit him too, so I can locate him immediately. We won't have this problem ever again."

"He's dead, Bo. We won't need you to find him, period. Although I would have found some way not to put him on trial."

Bo raised one sleek brow. "Really? But what about justice, Detective?"

Justice. Patrick By-the-book O'Rourke might have prosecuted, and damned the fallout. Maybe, maybe not. Dad wasn't alive to ask. But... "Rules alone don't make real justice. What about Gretchen and Steve? Outing the bad vamps would also out you good guys. Where's the justice is that?"

"Mmm. That's sweet, Detective. But you can put Vlad on trial—as a human. I'll see that he sticks to the story."

"But he's dead." I waved at the broken corpse. "Vlad's dead."

"Yes. But he's been dead for several years. That hasn't stopped him."

"You don't mean he can recover from *that*!"

"Actually, yes. If we find him another heart, all we have to do is put him in the ground. In a few days we dig him up, pump him full of blood. He'll be as good as new."

I gaped at Bo. "You're saying your kind is indestructible!"

His eyes turned serious blue. "Not quite. But close. That's what I was trying to tell you before I left for Iowa."

"Shit." I grabbed my knees. "It's a good thing I didn't understand that before. I would have been terrified." I gazed with new respect at the slim, small vampire.

"Or a very bad thing." Bo shook one finger at me. "Elena. You are a good cop. But from now on, leave the destruction of vampires to me."

"Well, sure. If I don't have my trusty Bob-zooka, that is." I patted the tube.

"Elena." I could hear the warning growl in his voice.

"All right." I held up both hands. "You got it, Viking. No destroying vampires. Except..." I lowered my hands. Scooted over to where he sat on the sidewalk.

Bo's eyes sharpened on me as I approached. "Except...?"

Slowly I opened the buttons on his shirt. "Except...can I destroy you?" I put my palm against one of his powerful pecs. Latched onto the nipple through cotton and suckled.

He gave a satisfying jerk. Groaned. Unsteadily, he said, "You got it, Detective."

Chapter Twenty-Seven

Later that night I was sitting at my desk, typing up my notes. Bo was off burying Vlad (and I really didn't want to know where he got the heart). I had to get this down before I forgot it.

I had solved the Case of the Punctured Prick.

A warm sense of accomplishment washed over me as I typed. I had solved it, not by being a textbook cop, but by being Elena. Dirk was actually right. Being a detective wasn't a title. It was who I was.

Vlad had come to Meiers Corners as a newbie vamp. Maybe he thought that as a big-city boy he'd own the place. Instead, he found it already owned—and well-protected—by Bo. Vlad couldn't kill people without Bo knowing and he really didn't have the temperament to be a rogue, but he only had so much cash. Blood was scarce. He watched with envy as Drusilla not only got regular donations from Bo's household but from her clients.

And to top things off, she refused to give Vlad sex. Not even a quickie.

When Drusilla left Bo's household, Vlad probably thought he was heir apparent to the spot. But Steve and Gretchen moved in. Worse yet, it was with Drusilla's blessing. Vlad was likely angry with Bo but he must have been furious with Dru.

She still wouldn't give him sex.

Then Vlad got the phone call. The one from Ruthven, threatening him unless he made trouble for Bo. I didn't know what Ruthven threatened. Vlad came from Chicago, he might very well have been turned by Ruthven himself. Maybe Vlad had human relatives under Ruthven's control. Or maybe Vlad just wanted the excuse to get back at the Meiers Corners vampires. He decided to do it.

His opportunity came, possibly when he went to pee after a round of Red Specials at Nieman's Bar. The window had a perfect view of the parking lot. Vlad saw Dru join Napoleon Schrimpf in his car. Either he saw her bite Schrimpf, or knew Nappy's kink. With those domestic disturbance calls, the Schrimpfs didn't exactly keep it secret.

Vlad saw how to get a fill-up of blood while making life difficult for Dru—and her mentor, Bo. Vlad approached a sated Nappy Schrimpf (probably hypnotizing him) and bit him in the 'nads.

I thought Vlad told the truth when he said he hadn't meant to kill Schrimpf. As a young vampire, I guessed Vlad didn't know a human body goes into shock after losing only a few pints, that it dies after only losing a few quarts. So he drank Napoleon Schrimpf nearly dry. Left the wounds, because he wanted Dru and Bo to get the blame.

In writing the report, I didn't put it quite that way. Instead of "vampire", I worded around it. Dru "played the vampire" for Schrimpf. Vlad "thought he was a vampire". Bo would make sure that when Vlad took the witness stand, he'd stick to that story.

"Detective Ma'am! Thank goodness you're all right." Dirk's yellow fedora bobbed into the office, his muddy eyes almost giddy with relief.

"Ah, yes. Detective Dirk." If I were going by the book, I'd now give the report to the detective in charge of the case, who would take all the credit.

Thankfully, I was doing things By Elena. I could take this report, turn it in and get the credit I rightfully deserved. I hit print. As the pages churned out, I imagined Tight-ass's wide-eyed appreciation. "Oh, Elena," he'd say, no longer chafing his arm. "You've solved the case. Our department's reputation is saved. And you did it without implicating Drusilla, saving my reputation as well. Elena, Elena, I misjudged you so. Here's your permanent shield, the smallest token of my profound gratitude!"

"What's that?" Dirk asked.

I surfaced from my daydream. Dirk smiled at me with his eager, puppy-dog devotion. He was genuinely happy I was all right. I remembered he dreamed of being a detective too.

I pulled the report off the printer, stared at it. I'd had fun writing it. I'd had even more fun imagining Tight-ass eating humble pie.

But a while ago I'd asked Bo to tell me the truth, not because of the rules or because he would feel better confessing, but because it was right. How could I do less?

With a deep breath I held the report out. "This is for you."

Dirk took the pages, muddy eyes clouding. "But...what is it?"

"The solution to the Schrimpf murder. File it. You'll have your permanent shield in no time." I didn't do it because it was by the book. I didn't do it because it was By Elena.

I did it because it was *right*. And it was worth it (and not just because it shut Dirk up). It was worth the mixed look of shock, hope and joy on his face. But more, it was worth it because justice had been served.

Besides, *I* knew I'd solved the case, even if I didn't get the credit.

Dirk left, clutching the paper to his chest. I was sitting at my desk, feeling pretty good in general. Until Tight-ass stalked through the doorway.

"O'Rourke!" His voice was like a Cessna, his expression Scary Jack O'Lantern Number Four. "What the hell are you doing here? You're fired!"

I stood. In a quiet, firm tone I said, "I don't think so, sir."

His voice raised another notch. "What do you mean by that? Don't give me any lip, young lady!"

"You only busted me back to patrol. I'm still a cop."

"And now I'm firing you!"

"Well, sir, if I'm fired, I'll have to get a new job. And to get a new job, I'll have to get a good haircut."

"What the hell does a haircut have to do with—"

I took Titus by the arm—the one my father broke all those years ago. "While I'm sitting in the chair with *Dolly Barton*, I just might let something slip about your night-shift work. *All* your night-shift work, if you know what I mean. Sir." I released him.

Tight-ass's mouth kept flapping but nothing emerged.

"Dolly has been wondering how you afford those four-hundred-dollar haircuts in Chicago, sir. She wonders where you get the extra money. After all, a shift captain doesn't earn that much. She'll be relieved to know you're not involved in anything...too illegal."

Titus squeaked like a mouse. "All right! You're not fired." Chafing his arm, he stalked away. Spun in the doorway for a parting shot. "But you're not a detective. And if I have anything to say about it, you never will be!" He stomped out.

I expelled a breath and fell back into my chair. I wasn't fired.

But Titus would have plenty to say about me being a detective, none of it good.

Without Tight-ass's recommendation, the Chief of Police would never promote me. Blackmailing Tight-ass was fine for keeping my job, but I wanted to earn my badge, dammit. And while the mayor had promised to put in a *goot verd* if I solved the Schrimpf case, he wouldn't know I was the one who solved it.

I tried to remember that I *had* solved the case, even though no one would know but me. And as Sinatra sang, I'd done it my way.

A poor substitute when you've lost your dream.

☙❧

A couple nights later I brought an empty box to work, to pack away my things. I removed them from my desk—no, from the detectives' desk—one by one. My family picture went in last and left an empty spot on the scarred wood. My hands felt heavy cleaning out the last vestiges of hope.

But I couldn't put it off. The case was solved, the suspect arrested. At sunset Bo had dug Vlad up and fed him a half-dozen bags of blood. Sure enough Fakeula was back to *blehing* like he'd never been injured. I'd dragged him into the station where he confessed. He was sitting in a cell waiting to be questioned. Since the cell had mammoth east-facing windows, hopefully that would happen before sunrise.

I collapsed in the chair. Not my chair anymore. I rubbed the worn armrests with my thumb, trying to buck up, to get back on the horse. Down, but not conquered, stay in the r—the sharp *ahem* of a throat clearing brought my head up.

The waxed handlebar mustache and bristling sideburns were as familiar in Meiers Corners as Dolly Barton's boobs. Even more familiar to me, since it had looked over my shoulder every night for the past month.

The Chief of Police, John Dirkson himself.

Belatedly I snapped to my feet. Wiping my suddenly perspiring hand, I offered it to him. "Sir. Det—Officer Elena O'Rourke. Sir."

"At ease, O'Rourke. This isn't the damn army."

"Uh, yes, sir."

"You're as eager as my nephew. He thinks it's the military too. Actually salutes. Nearly brained himself the last time he did."

Now why did that sound familiar?

"In fact, that's why I came. To discuss *this*." The chief held out a sheaf of paper.

My report on the Schrimpf case.

I was confused. "Sir? That's...Detective Ruffles's report. Sir."

Dirkson only chuckled. "We both know Ruffles didn't write this, O'Rourke. I love my nephew dearly, my sister's boy, after all. But his brain works at the speed of drying concrete." The chief tapped the side of his nose. I never believed anyone actually did that, until Dirkson did. "No, I think we both know who solved the Schrimpf murder."

I allowed myself to hope. "Yes, sir."

"We have to let my nephew take the credit. You were officially off the case. Going against a direct order could cause more trouble for you than help."

Hope hissed flat. "Yes, sir."

"But I think I can see my way clear to crediting you with the collar. After all, that was opportunistic. You were just in the area, saw the suspect and apprehended him."

Just wandering around Meiers Corners with a bazooka. "Yes, sir."

"And you rescued my chuckle-headed nephew in the process. I think such bravery deserves a promotion, don't you? To, say...full detective?"

Full detective? Me? *Detective Elena O'Rourke.* My dream come true. On the outside I was perfectly calm, but inside I was doing the Hamster Dance. "You won't regret it, sir. I'll work so hard...I'll be the best third-shift full detective you've ever had."

Dirkson sighed. "The young. So enthusiastic. So energetic."

"Yes, sir," I said, forgetting myself and saluting. I hit myself in the forehead and nearly gave myself a concussion. That *hurt.* Whoa. Maybe that was how Dirk had lost all his brain cells. I made a stern promise to myself never to salute again.

The chief was chuckling. "Thank you again, Detective O'Rourke. And good luck."

Detective—until Tight-ass heard. My hamsters fell flat. "Uh, sir? One more thing?"

"Yes?"

"Uh, Captain Titus, sir. He's not very happy with my performance."

Dirkson nodded. "You were doing too good a job. Ernie thought you'd point a finger straight at his favorite hooker." The chief put a finger to the side of his nose again. "She's my favorite hooker too."

Did *everyone* know Drusilla? Then I realized what Dirkson's statement implied. "You know about Captain Titus's...second career?"

"What a nice way to put it. 'Course I know. Old Tight-ass has been gunning for my position since day one. I made it my job to dig up every piece of dirt I could find on him." With his finger aside his nose, Dirkson looked like a shrewd Santa Claus. "I was a pretty good detective myself, back in the day. Don't worry about Ernie. I'll handle him."

"Thank you, sir. Thank you so much."

"Well, goodbye, Detective O'Rourke. Congratulations again."

"Goodbye, sir." I sank back into my—*my*—chair.

I don't know how long I sat like that...half-stunned by all the revelations, half-basking in the glow of my permanent promotion...when a mist gathered in the office. It swirled around my feet and up my legs, forming into two clever hands opening my pants. Attached to the hands were a warrior's body and a face so handsome it could stop a woman's heart.

"There was one good thing about the old days," Bo murmured. "Lift your hips, sweetheart."

"What's that, Viking?"

"Skirts, Detective." As soon as my butt came off the chair, he peeled the pants down to my ankles. Seeing what I wore underneath his face lit like a light bulb. "But I have to admit, thong panties more than make up for it."

Bo pushed my knees apart and began his program of plundering. His tongue swept aside the lace triangle. Licked at my slit.

"Blatzky's in the can, you know." My panting made it "Blz in t'can."

As if in reply, a huge grunt came from the bathroom.

"He'll be in there for a while. In fact..." Bo grabbed the ends of my jeans and yanked them all the way off. Sliding his hands under my knees, he draped my legs over the arms of my chair and knelt before me. My vulva was fully open to his perusal. His eyes turned the clear blue of a warm sea. His expression was close to worshipful. He used one careful finger to pull aside the string of the already-damp thong.

"Fully-flowered and absolutely beautiful." His canines erupted long and sleek. He bent, rubbed one inside my crease, stroking my slit stem to stern. I shivered. When he thrust a finger into me and pumped in rhythm with fang and tongue, I shuddered. Sweet tension built deep inside, released in a rush of heat and damp. He kept thrusting and I built higher. His fingers started to make *thwucking* noises sliding in and out.

He put his mouth to my clit and sucked. I hit the ceiling. He sucked me into nirvana, into heaven. Sucked until I was a bundle of nerve endings. Until I shot to my feet because I was about to blow.

Bo rose smoothly to his feet too, grabbing my waist and turning me into my desk. I seized the edges, glad I had when a second later he rammed his thick cock into me from behind. He filled me in one powerful thrust.

His claws nailed my desk on either side of my head. He began to ride me with deep, steady strokes. My vagina heated like paper on the edge of flame.

"I love your hair," Bo said. Each word was punctuated by a stroke. "Your gorgeous mass of curls shudders every time I thrust. Pure seduction. Hell, Elena, everything about you is seduction. Your body. Your smell."

"What about you? Your clever hands. Your massive shoulders. Your sweet words." I groaned as he grew bigger inside me.

"Not nearly as exciting as *you.* Your beautifully shaped breasts. Your heat. Your pulse."

"My blood?" I turned my head, exposing my throat.

"*Elena.*" Bo bent over me, his mouth plummeting to my neck. His fangs flashed white and pierced deep.

Lightning cracked. Thunder rolled. My whole body ignited. Wave after wave of climax rolled through me. Bo swelled and burst, filling me with liquid pleasure.

After, he sat in my chair and cradled me in his arms like an infant. I smiled sleepily at him. "Sex?"

He smiled back, and I didn't imagine the tenderness there. "Love. I love you, Detective."

Happiness bloomed inside. For some reason it wasn't so

threatening now, maybe because it was *so* right. "I love you too, Bo." I snuggled a bit. The serenity fountain burbled, sounding a little giddy. "How long have you known?"

"That you were the one? First time I bit you."

"Really?" I thought back to that first stunning orgasm, pressed to the floor of the Fudgy Delight. "Wow. Lucky I had that accident."

"The fall was an accident. The kiss wasn't."

"It wasn't?"

"No. I needed to taste you."

"Why?"

"I can find anyone I've tasted. You were always out, alone, at night. With increased rogue activity. Totally clueless."

"Hey, I object."

He smiled. That sensuous curve still made me want to surf his waves. "I wanted to protect you, Elena. I maneuvered you into that kiss so I could bite you. I wasn't counting on your taste, though. Like I'd been with antimatter—instant annihilation."

"Huh. And I thought it was the perfume. Don't ask."

"I'd never smelled or tasted anything so good." His eyes lit bright red, and I was surprised to see his fangs come to full attention.

"Yeah, but after that, it seemed you were trying to, well, not avoid me, 'cause you showed up everywhere I was." I frowned. "But you weren't as enthusiastic."

"My reaction that first time scared me. My mentor explained that there's a taste that signals a perfect lover. A mental strength that makes it long term."

"Are you saying I'm your vampire love slave?"

He lifted his head to eye me strangely. "Just what have you been reading, Detective?"

"Um..."

"I was attracted to you, which frightened me. But I had to keep tabs on you. You were investigating a killing done by a vampire. Smart and determined as you are, it was only a matter of time before you figured out the truth."

"So you *did* try to throw me off."

"Only for your own good, Detective." He nipped little kisses down my neck, and I shuddered. "But I got tired of fighting both you and myself. So I decided to woo you instead."

"Woo me. That's so old fashioned."

"I'm an old-fashioned kind of guy."

"Yeah. So you said. Skirts."

"Don't give up the thongs. I can modernize."

Just before dawn, Bo carried me to my place. Drew the curtains and made love to me six or seven times before I passed out from sheer exhaustion.

He was still there when I woke up a few hours later. "Elena. I have something to ask you." His expression was very serious.

"I'm clean," I said. "No STDs." No opportunity, which for the first time looked like a good thing.

Bo laughed. "I can't get them anyway. Actually, I was going to ask two things."

"Ask, already."

"I've waited lifetimes for you, sweetheart. Would you live with me?"

Pleasure flooded me, followed by caution. "Live with you? Where? I thought the apartment building is full up."

"Yes...but I hoped you wouldn't mind sharing my room. The common areas are fairly good-sized."

"Your bedroom upstairs?"

"Um, no. Downstairs is the one I actually use."

"I remember. One to sleep, and one to make love. Although why two...?"

He flushed. "If we want a human partner...not that I've had any in the past few...we can't bring them to a room without windows. Causes too many questions."

"But you expect me to sleep with you in the basement. Where it's dark, with no windows."

His flush deepened. "It's safer for me that way."

"Uh-huh. Bed or shallow grave?"

"Elena..." His cheeks went brick red. "*Bed.* I'm not...we don't..."

I smiled. I'd made Bo Strongwell sputter. "You don't sleep in a coffin?"

"No! Or a grave, or anything but a nice warm bed."

"And the dirt floor den, what's that for? Mud wrestling?" I pretended to think on it. "That might be stimulating. Watching you and Thor mud wrestle."

"Elena!" He turned bright red. "It's where we rest up. Re-energize. But we don't sleep there."

"Where you re-energized for that bout of mind-blowing sex?"

His flush faded. "Which one?"

"Um, yeah." I relented. "As it so happens, I'm a night person anyway. And windows are overrated, especially when you're trying to sleep during the day." I thought about it. "Besides, my friend Nixie is salivating to get out of her parents' house. My place is cheap. She wouldn't have to teach those satellite classes anymore."

Bo's eyes raised, cautiously hopeful. "Is that a yes?"

"That's a yes." He whooped and reached for me, but before he could show his appreciation, I stopped him. "What's the other question?"

"The other...oh, yes." If anything, he turned redder. "I didn't use any protection. Tonight, or all the other times."

"But I thought you couldn't get STDs. And if you can't get them, you can't pass them on, right?"

"Yes, but..." Bo cleared his throat. Looked awkward. "Have you considered having children? Um, with me?"

"Oh, shit, am I pregnant?" And if I were? "You'd be on hook for half the feedings, buster."

"I could do that."

"And half the diaper changes."

He made a face, but nodded.

"Well..."

Almost wistfully he said, "Mrs. Cook has missed having babies in the house. She had six children. And twenty grandchildren."

"And they lived with you? *All* of them?"

"Yes."

"And you didn't kill them?"

Bo managed to look offended. "No, of course not. They're children, Elena. They need to be nurtured."

Wow. I was right. Primo daddy material. "Yeah. Okay."

"Okay?" he echoed, almost as if he didn't remember what he'd asked.

"If you're up for it, I am. I'd rather plan, but—"

I was cut off by him sweeping me into a tight, joyful embrace. "Elena! I'll make you happy, sweetheart. I'll be the best husband a woman ever had."

"Husband! Put me down, I didn't say I'd marry you."

He set me down. "But—"

"You didn't ask."

"Oh, Elena." Bo retrieved his pants from the floor, dug into a pocket. Going down on one knee he held up his palm to me. Something glittered in it. I peered closer.

Light flashed, so bright it blinded me. "Ow! Hey." I clamped my eyes shut.

"Sorry." Bo chuckled. Then his voice went soft and serious. "Elena O'Rourke. Detective extraordinaire. I love you to heaven and beyond. Will you marry me?"

Eyes tightly shut, I stuck out my left hand. "Well, it's about time, Viking. Yes. I'll marry you. 'Til death...do we part?"

"We'll talk about that later." Bo took my hand and slipped something on my finger. When he released my hand, unexpected weight dragged it toward the floor.

"Whoa." I opened my eyes, blinked. Rubbed them and blinked

again. "What is this, the fucking Koh-I-Noor? Can an apartment manager *afford* this?"

Bo's beautiful lips curved, his blue eyes sparkling like a sun-drenched sea. "I've spent centuries amassing a fortune. I'm more than a billionaire. I thought you knew that."

"Uh...no." I sank onto the bed. Bo Strongwell, Viking Building Manager—a billionaire? I would never, ever, *ever* look down on someone because of their profession again. "So why don't you build a mansion? Or a palace?"

"My kind is powerful, Elena, but very few in number compared to humans. And still vulnerable. To sunlight. To bazookas." He smiled.

"But rich."

He rose and sat next to me. "Even so, we must stay secret, for as long as we can. Though it's getting harder."

"Why? Is someone going to give away your secrets?"

"Not intentionally. But some of us are getting incautious. And there are so many more of us, now."

"More rogues?"

"Yes. But also more vampires, period."

"But still only a handful compared to billions of humans," I murmured. "We humans can help, you know. *I* can help."

He drew a sharp breath. "I thought we had this conversation. I don't want you policing vampires on your own, Elena. It's not safe."

"Not alone."

"Detective Ruffles isn't enough—"

"Not Dirk, you. I can patrol with you, as your backup. As your partner."

"You and me?" He blinked. "I don't know, Elena. I haven't worked with a partner in, well, decades. Generations."

I touched him gently. "I'm not Ruthven, Bo. I won't betray you."

"No." He put his hand over mine. "You're not anything like Ruthven."

"That lameass. I'll be a much better partner." I grabbed him around the neck, planted a big kiss on his lips. "Prettier too."

"Much prettier." Bo laughed.

"Besides, if there are any humans around, I can deal with them."

"I suppose it would help to have someone to get the humans out of harm's way. But partner...I don't know."

I could see he wasn't going to accept it easily. "I could at least make sure people don't see you chopping heads. And I could solve crimes like the Case of the Punctured Prick—without revealing the v-population exists."

"The Elena Strongwell Vampire Detection Agency?"

The name, "Elena Strongwell", made me shiver. Bo was such a

strong, darkly erotic male. And I was *marrying* him. "Sure, after I get in a few more years with the department."

"I could use the help," he said reluctantly. "But not a partner."

"Bo, hate to break it to you but I'm already doing the job."

"*What?*"

"Partners have an equal stake. Equal responsibility." I caressed his cheek softly. "I went after the murderer. Solved the case. When it comes to justice, I'm your equal."

Bo stared at me as if I'd nailed him with a rock. "You're already my partner. Huh." Then, slowly, he smiled. He took me in his arms, rolled me under him on the bed. Thrust into me. "Elena, you're beautiful, you're brilliant—and you're damned sneaky. My wonderful fighter for justice. Partner. And sexy as hell."

Fighting for justice. Sounded like my calling. Like *our* calling.

As I raised my hips to meet Bo's, I amended that. Not our calling. But who we were.

ঙ৪ঙ

I raised the weapon, pointed it at the headpin of the gang. "You," I said in my toughest cop voice. "You're going down."

"If you don't gutter it again," Alice said.

"A little quiet, here," I said. "This isn't easy."

"Because your fiancé keeps goosing you," Nixie said helpfully.

"He isn't goo...whoops!" The hot pinch to my behind made the ball squirt from my hand. It thudded onto the boards and rolled promptly into the gutter.

"Damn," Alice said. "Next time I get the shrimp and the Viking on my team instead of Bombs-away and Preggers."

"Hey," said Gretchen. "I heard that."

As I sat, my cell rang. I pulled it, noted the ID with resignation. The mayor's office. "Hold for the mayor," Heidi barked.

A click. "Elena, *meine Freundin,* congratulations on your arresting of the killer! The Schrimpf case is solved. The tourism is saved. I am so happy."

"Thanks, Mayor."

"The Mayors of Urban Centers United Society no longer tease me. I am so very happy. Heidi is also happy, which is making me so very, very happy. I can tell she is also happy because she is using her softest whi—"

"Good, good. I'm glad you're happy and Heidi's happy and the whi—I mean, everyone's happy. Glad to be of service."

"*Ja,* well I put in the good word with the Chief of Police for you. But surprise! He is already promoting you. So *alles ist gut, ja?*"

"Yeah, everything's good. Bye, Mayor." Chuckling, I shut the phone.

Gretchen leaned over. "You know, Elena, I said you changed, and I was right. You have changed, a lot."

I remembered when she said that. When she was angry. When our bonds of sisterhood had cracked. "Yeah?"

"For the first time, I think you're happy."

"Oh." Just like that, the crack was gone. I watched Bo gliding up to the line. Perfect form, perfect grace. He slid into the release like a pro. And all that perfect male was mine. "Yes. I think you're right. I am so very, very happy."

Just as Bo's ball cracked into the headpin, his hip started *tweedling.* While the rest of us watched the ten pins at the end of the lane practically explode, Bo turned and pulled his phone. "Strongwell. Yes, Thor. Of course. I'll be right—" He looked at me and smiled. "*We'll* be right there."

I stood. "Sorry, everyone. The neighborhood watch just called. Bo and I have to go."

We got into our street shoes, and I picked up Bob and my new backup knife from a rental locker. The knife I slid into my jeans, into a secret holster Bo had sewn inside, just like he had for his patrol blade. "Where are we headed?"

"Northwest. Two rogues were sighted near the Meiers Corners work camp."

"Is one of them Vlad?"

Bo's eyes got faraway, as if checking an internal map. "No, he's still inside."

We hit the street. "Maybe they're trying to break Vlad out."

"Hope so." Bo grinned. "I'd like a good fight."

When we passed the AllRighty-AllNighty, I said, "The night we met, I was called in on a robbery and the strangest thing happened. There was a wind...and it tied Scout knots."

Bo smiled. "Even then I couldn't resist running my hands through your hair, Detective."

"Oh." I blushed. "Are we near those rogues, yet?"

"Around the corner." Bo smiled. "Ready—partner?"

I grinned back, wide as a mile. Partner. That felt so damn right. "Oh, yeah. Let's go."

About the Author

Mary Hughes is a computer consultant, professional musician and writer. At various points in her life she has taught Taekwondo, worked in the insurance industry, and studied religion. She is intensely interested in the origins of the universe. She has a wonderful husband (though happily-ever-after takes a lot of hard work) and two great kids. But she thinks that with all the advances in modern medicine, childbirth should be a lot less messy.

To learn more about Mary Hughes, please visit www.maryhughesbooks.com.

LaVergne, TN USA
29 July 2010
191341LV00005B/9/P